California CHANCES

California CHANCES

Three Brothers Play the Role of Protector as Romance Develops

CATHY MARIE HAKE

TRACEY BATEMAN

KELLY EILEEN HAKE

BARBOUR
PUBLISHING

One Chance in a Million © 2005 by Cathy Marie Hake
Second Chance © 2005 by Tracey Bateman
Taking a Chance © 2005 by Kelly Eileen Hake

ISBN 1-59789-110-X

Cover art by Getty/Photonica

All scripture quotations are taken from the King James Version of the Bible.

Published by Barbour Publishing, Inc., P.O. Box 719, Uhrichsville, Ohio 44683
www.barbourbooks.com

Our mission is to publish and distribute inspirational products offering exceptional value and biblical encouragement to the masses.

Printed in the United States of America.
5 4 3 2 1

ONE CHANCE IN A MILLION

Chapter 1

San Francisco, 1871

"Stand back, else I'll make ye shark bait."

Miriam Hancock suppressed a shudder and shuffled backward to give the seaman space. He had plenty of room to get past her, even with his rolling gait. He and the other men sailing the vessel were more than ready to do her ill. She'd done nothing to deserve their wrath, but they'd served it up in large portions ever since the *Destiny* set sail.

Another crewman clamped his hand around her elbow. "I'll help you down the plank."

She fought the urge to yank away. Within the first days of the voyage from the islands to San Francisco, Miriam had found it necessary to push away overly familiar hands and use her hat pin to counter unwanted advances. Twice she'd been accosted by men who had gotten into her cabin. Both times, she'd managed to save her virtue; but the captain, needing to safeguard her, took to locking her in her cabin.

The *Destiny* had finally docked. Today was the first time in weeks she'd been on deck.

"Here. I'll carry that." The rough seaman grabbed the valise from Miriam's numb fingers and hauled her toward a gangplank. The splintered length of wood looked anything but safe. His steadying hold would keep her balanced if she cooperated. Truth be told, the way the gangplank seesawed between ship and dock, the most able assistance might not be sufficient.

A wry smile twisted her lips. Even now, she still might become shark bait.

Once she reached the dock, Miriam fought to stay upright.

"You've lost yer land legs," her escort chortled. He seemed oblivious to the fact that he had no business mentioning lower limbs to a woman of decency. "Stand here a bit. I heard you have a slip o' paper 'bout where to go." He leaned closer and jabbed his callused thumb at his chest. His rotten teeth made for fetid breath. "You could lose that paper an' wait fer Jake O'Leary. I'll be on shore leave in nigh unto an hour. I could show you a right fine time."

She snatched her valise from him. Before she could say anything, someone barked, "O'Leary!"

The sailor jolted to attention. "Aye, Cap'n?"

Captain Raithly stalked down the gangplank. "I'll see to the lady." He pried the valise from Miriam and braced her arm as he led her off the dock. "I did my best by you. You have to understand that."

"It was a difficult voyage."

"Aye." Within a quarter hour, he'd hired a beefy shoreman to heft her two trunks to the street. From there, she took a hansom cab to the address Captain Raithly gave the driver. Already weary, she relied upon the skill of the mercantile's owner to arrange the next leg of her journey. Miriam ardently hoped he'd suggest she spend a night at one of the local boardinghouses before he sent her along, but as luck would have it, a stage was ready to leave and there was room on it for her.

By the time the stage stopped in Reliable, Miriam was perilously close to tears. She stood in the street of the tiny town, steamer trunks at her side, as a chilly breeze swirled dirt about her and twilight warned she'd best find shelter. She looked around. Despair welled up. She saw only two women in the whole of the town. Neither could be mistaken for a lady.

Men abounded. They assessed her with more than polite glances. She'd been subjected to far too many leers to be innocent of the lurid intent behind such looks. To her mortification, Miriam knew she was a spectacle. She hurriedly searched up and down the street to spot the local boardinghouse. She desperately needed a fresh bed and a solid night's sleep.

Just as she came to the dismaying conclusion that no boardinghouse existed, a brick wall of a man burst through the place across the street. The bat-wing saloon doors banged wide open, and he held two adolescents by their ears. Both scrambled to match his stride, and from the looks on their faces, they'd do a jig to keep up so he'd not pinch any harder. The smaller one whined, "Only two beers, Gideon!"

"Neither of you has any business in there," the man growled.

"C'mon, Gideon," the older protested, "I'm fifteen!"

The brick wall hauled them to horses hitched directly to Miriam's left. "Fifteen and foolish," he said. "If you ever sneak off and try a stunt like this again, I'll tan your hides 'til you can't sit."

The younger of the two lads seemed a bit loose limbed. Gideon grabbed him and half-tossed him into his saddle. He took the fifteen-year-old by the back of his trousers and gave him a very uncomfortable-looking boost onto his mount. He unhitched all three horses, and as Gideon mounted his own gelding, the first boy mishandled his reins. His horse danced sideways until his hindquarters swung around. The youngster lost his balance and fell right out of the saddle—onto Miriam.

Miriam watched in astonishment as the horse's hindquarters came close. She'd stepped back and twisted, but her steamer trunks blocked any further escape. When the boy slumped and slid toward her, she let out a breathless yelp and tried to right him, but he didn't help in the least. He hit her with just enough force and weight to rob her of her balance.

Oomphf! Air whooshed out of her lungs as she landed flat on her back on a trunk. The considerable weight of the youth sandwiched her there.

"Whoopie!" he shouted as he clumsily wrapped his arms about her, then tried to nuzzle her neck.

Miriam kicked and shoved. Instead of dislodging him, she only managed to cause them both to roll off the trunk and onto the filthy street. He held her fast as they tumbled round one more time. Her head hit something hard. Just as nausea and panic welled up, Miriam felt the weight lifted off her. Through pain-narrowed eyes, she watched the brick wall shake the kid.

"Logan, behave yourself for a change." He flung the kid away and hunkered down. "Ma'am? Are you all right?"

She lay there, still unable to draw air back into her lungs. Her head hurt something fierce. She closed her eyes and gritted her teeth.

A rough hand cupped her jaw. "Ma'am? Logan, you brained her!"

"Schee's re–al purdy, Gideon. Kin I keep her?"

"Drunken fool," Gideon muttered as he tunneled his arms beneath her. Miriam heard him from a great distance and felt the world tumble into a cold, dizzying swirl.

The next thing she knew, Miriam roused to find herself draped across a strange man's lap. A host of tattered-looking men encircled them, and a good half-dozen lanterns illuminated her less-than-circumspect situation. Pain and mortification wrung a moan out of her, and her lashes dropped a mere second after they'd lifted.

"She's comin' round," someone observed.

The man who held her cupped her head to his shoulder and ordered in a quiet tone that carried exceptionally well, "You men mosey on back to your own business. This gal isn't going to want to be crowded. She needs breathing room."

"Whatcha gonna do if your kid brother addled her wits?"

"I doubt her wits are addled," he gritted.

Miriam dimly wondered if she ought to thank him for his faith in her or if she ought to be angry that he'd made such a pronouncement without first checking with her. She hadn't even begun to evaluate the damage done yet. Her head felt abominable, and her stomach roiled. She drew in a slow breath to steady herself and push away the pain. A rough thumb brushed lightly back and forth across her cheekbone. Oddly enough, it comforted her.

"All right, sweet pea, open your eyes again. Look at me and say your head doesn't hurt too bad."

She slowly lifted her lashes and stared up into a pair of bright blue, concerned eyes. Three lines furrowed his forehead. Clearly he was worried about her. A flicker of warmth stole across her soul. A lock of black wavy hair fell onto his forehead. He impatiently shook it back out of the way and gently combed his fingers through the loosened mess that had once been her modest, practical coiffure. His fingers hit a spot behind her ear, and she sucked in a sharp breath. The darkness started to swirl around her all over again.

He moaned. "Sorry. You've got a nasty goose egg there." His rough hand curled around the nape of her neck and gently kneaded. "Just give yourself a minute here."

A minute. Oh, it was going to take far more than a paltry minute for her to feel decent again. She shivered, partly from cold, partly from pain, and mostly because she'd never had a man hold her like this. Miriam closed her eyes and fought the urge to burrow closer to the stranger. She felt miserable, afraid, and lonely, and she never knew being held in the arms of a behemoth could be so comforting.

"Hey, now, Bryce. The little lady's starting to shiver. Get my bedroll." A second later, he lifted her and slipped her into the folds of something thick and a bit scratchy that carried the scent of wood smoke. Solicitude the likes of which he'd never known surfaced. He gallantly wrapped her, then tucked the edges of the blanket around her throat.

Was it the instant warmth of the blanket or the deft way he held and enveloped her that let her lie limp in his arms? She moved her head ever so slightly, and pain streaked from nape to temple. Pain. Definitely pain was the culprit in her unladylike place of repose.

"This'll help, ma'am." He didn't act at all as if this were an unusual circumstance or one worthy of alarm. He kept his deep voice pitched low and calming. "Why don't you tell me your name and where you're bound? I'll send for someone to come fetch you."

She wet her lips and whispered, "I'm Miriam Hancock. I'm here to help my sister."

"Your sister?" His voice sounded a bit strained. "Who is she?"

"Hannah Chance."

The arms holding her tightened.

Chapter 2

She peeled her eyes open. "Do you know her?"

"Yes."

Several of the bystanders murmured, but Miriam couldn't distinguish what they said. Her head pounded like a marching band. She slipped her hand out of the blanket and cupped it over the part of her head that felt so awful. "Perhaps, if it wouldn't be too much trouble, you could ask her husband, Daniel, to come fetch me."

"Miss Miriam, there's no need." He paused and said very quietly, "Daniel is my brother."

"Which one are you?"

"Gideon." Before she could ask about her sister, he said, "Don't say another word, Miss Miriam. Rely on me. I'll take you home."

"The Lord works in mysterious ways," she whispered.

"Shh. Best you go on and sleep through your headache."

"Hannah—what did she have?"

"A girl. She's a darlin' little thing."

She sighed, but her lips bowed upward. Just as she opened them to ask more, Gideon ordered, "No more questions, Miss Miriam. If you're fretting about your things, let me put your mind at ease. We don't have a wagon, so your trunks can stay at the livery tonight. The owner there is a friend of mine, so I can guarantee everything will be safe."

He stood and handed her off to someone. Miriam barely muffled her whimper at the loss of his comforting strength.

"Hand her back. Careful."

The man holding her lifted her high, and suddenly the world that already felt unsteady began to spin. Miriam let out a small cry.

"Here we go, sweet pea." To her relief, she ended up in Gideon's arms again. "I mean no disrespect, but I aim to hold you close."

She didn't know what the proper response to such a comment should be, and she couldn't think well enough to concoct a reply. Her head hurt too much.

"Bryce, you see to it Miss Hancock's trunks are taken care of. Then do what you need to, to make sure Logan stays on his horse and gets home. Bring Miss Hancock's valise."

It seemed as if they rode forever. Miriam's head pounded, and Gideon acted as if he understood she couldn't summon the strength to be sociable. He held her securely, and she abandoned any hope of sitting properly. He made no comment about how she draped limply across his lap like seaweed. In fact, every once in a while, he'd give her a soothing stroke as if she weren't a bother at all. The beat of his heart was the only sound between them, and for some reason, the steady rhythm lulled her just as invitingly as the constant surf she'd heard from her bedroom window back home. The drowsiness she felt was a blessing—it kept the nausea at bay.

His order for her to remain silent could be considered a veritable godsend. Miriam knew she'd embarrass herself if she had to carry on much of a conversation. Even if the queasiness waned, her thoughts scattered too hopelessly for her to stay coherent. She finally tilted her face up to his and whispered, "I don't mean to be impatient, but is it much farther?"

"We're traveling at a walk. Too many gopher holes. I can't risk having Splotch break a leg. It's a solid hour more. Need me to stop for you to, um, take care of, ah, business?"

Though chagrined, she confessed, "I'd be most appreciative."

He eased her forward, then his solid torso crowded her for a moment as he leaned with the action of swinging out of the saddle. The whole while, his hands stayed clamped securely about her waist. Once he was on the ground, he slid her off the horse.

Her first impression couldn't have been more accurate. This close, there could be no denying the fact that Gideon Chance was a brick wall. He towered over her, and her feet hadn't even touched earth yet. When he set her down, she was anything but steady. Concern colored his voice as he braced her. "I'm going to turn us back to town after you're done. This isn't right."

"Land. Not used to it. The ship. . ."

"Ahh." A wealth of understanding and relief filled that single syllable as he drew it out.

When they got under way again, he smoothed the blanket around her, dipped his head, and said in a quiet rumble, "I want you to go ahead and sleep now. No use in sitting here hurting if you can drowse through the pain."

"You're most understanding." She tried to hide her yawn, but from his smile, she knew he'd caught her at it. The way he nestled her a tad closer caused an extraordinary sense of security to wash over her. For weeks, she'd lived in dread of every man aboard the *Destiny*. Though she'd just met him, she had an innate sense she could trust Gideon Chance. Besides, Hannah said he was a fine man. Miriam let her heavy lids drift shut and left herself in capable, caring arms.

Gideon watched sleep overtake her and let out a sigh of relief. He'd managed to keep her from asking any questions yet. He tried to figure out what to do. Things were going to be a mite sticky for a while.

He'd taken the closest horse when he left the ranch in such a fit. The snappy little paint carried him well, but it was a good thing Hannah's sister was a tiny woman. Gideon didn't believe in pushing an animal too hard. If only he could train up his kid brothers as well as he'd tamed Splotch. . . .

His brothers rode up. Bryce showed the good judgment of letting their horses travel at a mere walk, too—in part to keep Logan upright but also out of caution. Still, since Gideon had stopped along the way for Miriam, they'd made up for the time spent hauling her trunks to the livery.

"Whatcha going to do with her?" Bryce asked.

"We'll see."

"Didja tell her yet?"

He glanced down to be sure she still slept. "No."

"Why not?"

Gideon glared at his brother. "Because her head hurts, you dolt." Bryce could make animals do anything he wanted with a mere look and gesture, but when it came to people, he never quite seemed to comprehend the finer points. Most of the time, it didn't much matter, but tonight, Gideon had spent his patience.

"I'm sorry, Gideon," Logan mumbled. The brisk air helped sober him up a bit.

"You'd better be sorry. If I ever catch you going into the Nugget again before you're a full-grown man, I'll make you wish you'd never been born." He then turned his attention toward his other brother. "And I hold you accountable, Bryce. What were you thinking, taking him in there?"

"Well, I was thinkin' on how pretty Lulabell—"

"Hush!" Gideon hastily assured himself the woman in his arms hadn't heard his brother's confession. Bad enough, she knew they'd been far too liberal with libations. The last thing he needed was an unmarried missionary's daughter to find out the second-to-the-youngest Chance male foolishly had just tried to visit a house of ill repute.

Hannah would have pitched a hissy fit over Bryce and Logan's trip to the Nugget. As it was, she'd made her disapproval clear on the rare occasions when the older brothers bent an elbow. They'd all tried to shield her from their forays to the saloon by chewing a few sprigs of mint on the way home to disguise the smell of the single mug of beer they'd indulged in. Inevitably, when their ploy failed,

Daniel managed to cajole her into masking her scorn for their sinful indulgence when "thirst got the better of their judgment."

Only now, Daniel wouldn't hold any sway with Miriam. No doubt, she'd be every bit as priggish as her sister. Under his breath, Gideon muttered a desperate man's prayer: "Heaven help me. I'm not up to dealing with all of this."

He studied her a bit more. Her eyes had been murky green, but he wasn't certain whether pain caused that. Then again, from the shadows beneath her eyes, it could well be from weariness, too. She'd traveled a long way. Her skin looked fair as could be, and that made no sense since she'd been living in the tropics. When Daniel brought Hannah home, her skin held a bit of sun bronzing. Her hair had been moonlight pale, but this woman's carried a warm golden cast.

He'd need to get her a new bonnet. The one she'd been wearing got knocked off in the mishap, and the gelding managed to relieve himself on the ugly creation before it could be rescued. To Gideon's way of thinking, Knothead probably judged the milliner's nightmare and did that as a declaration of his opinion. Secretly, he counted the ruination of such a homely concoction of straw and flowers no great loss. *In fact, Knothead did Miriam a favor by destroying it.*

Miriam Hancock looked much like her sister. At best, she could be considered a small dab of a gal—and Hannah's frailty proved to be problematic. Ranch life had been too harsh for her. Gideon often considered her to be an exotic orchid, but only weeds and wildflowers survived this rugged land. Hannah barely made it past the second birthing in three years and finally succumbed to what an itinerant, self-professed sawbones diagnosed as "the punies."

When Miriam woke, he was going to have to tell her she'd traveled all of this way in vain. He didn't relish the notion of breaking the news. As the eldest, the unpleasant responsibility fell on his shoulders.

They rode along in near silence. Gideon got to thinking it was a crying shame Miriam didn't feel a far sight better. She'd undoubtedly agree with him that nothing on earth could match the sheer beauty of this slice of land. The sky looked close enough to touch, and the light breeze carried a refreshing, brisk pine scent. As she slept, little Miriam missed the crickets' song, too. He might not be one of those Bible-thumping men, but moments like these let him know God was God, and man owed Him his thanks.

When they reached the ranch, Bryce reined in his gelding and shifted in his saddle. "You gonna wake up Daniel so she can go stay with him?"

Three years ago, when Daniel got back, the brothers were glad to see him, but the surprise of his having a bride—let alone a preacher's daughter he'd snagged in the islands—set things awry. They'd been without Mama almost a year before Dan originally left, and most of the civilized niceties had fallen by the wayside in the intervening months. Hannah made Daniel a happy man, so his brothers all tried their best to change things to suit her. They even pitched in together and built the newlyweds their own little place so they'd have a bit of privacy.

Gideon cast a glance at the tiny cottage off to the side of the main house. He couldn't see a flicker of a lamp, so he shook his head. "Daniel's got the girls to sleep already. Go on in and hang a blanket between my bed and the rest. She can use my bunk tonight."

Bryce tromped in. Titus came out and raised his brows at the load Gideon nestled on his lap. He shook his head in disbelief, then paced off to the stable. A moment later, he passed by with a fistful of nails and a hammer. Within a few minutes, the sound of their work ceased. Gideon waited outside until they were done. The last thing Miriam needed was to hear a bunch of hammering. Judging from the lump on her head, she'd suffer a beaut of a headache for a few days. Titus came out. "It's ready. I pulled back your blanket."

Gideon nodded acknowledgment. He walked across the plank floor and asked, "Where is her valise?"

"Next to the bed," Paul said. He plopped down on the bench and stared at Miss Hancock as if he'd never seen a woman. Sad truth was, it had been a long while since he'd set eyes on a decent one.

Once behind the makeshift partition his brothers made by hanging a moth-eaten blanket from the ceiling joist, Gideon laid his feminine burden on the bed. His nose wrinkled. Come morning, she was going to be one very unhappy lady. Logan had managed to roll her over toward the hitching post, and she'd gotten what polite women called "road apple" ground into her gown, petticoats, and stockings. She'd be mortified if she ever found out her skirts had been in a froth clear up to her knees. He made a mental note to threaten his brothers with dire punishment if they ever dared to mention that embarrassing fact.

His lips thinned. There was no way around it. She had to get out of these clothes. Feeling less than gallant, Gideon unbuckled her valise and peered inside. He fished about and found a nightdress. Now he had to get her into it.

His hands started to sweat. It nearly undid him, just handling that oh-so-white, soft-from-a-hundred-washings bed gown. She'd embroidered flowers and tatted a tiny row of lace along the neckline, making the simple piece captivatingly, impossibly feminine. If that wasn't bad enough, it smelled like sunshine and honeysuckle. He abruptly set the piece on the foot of the bed. He had no business seeing her unmentionables or touching them.

Gideon tried to pet her cheek and coax her to rouse, but she slept on. He whispered a prayer for strength. Bad enough he'd seen and touched her light-as-air nightdress. Worse, now he'd have to help her if she didn't wake up right quick.

"Come on, Miriam. Open your eyes, just for a few minutes," he said a bit more forcefully. She gave no response. He decided to take off her shoes. Maybe that would wake her up. After carefully lifting the hem of her truly ugly brown serge dress a scant few inches, he unbuttoned her tiny black leathers from ankle top to instep. With a quick twist and yank, he divested her of the footwear.

Less than eager to glide his hands up her stockinged calves, he took the toe of her left black lisle stocking and pulled. He met with some resistance, so he gingerly pinched both sides of the ankles and tugged. To his infinite relief, the garters yielded and he pulled off the stocking. By the time he got the other stocking off, he felt like he had a fever. Looking at Miss Miriam's trim, lily-white ankles was enough to make a man loco.

His voice sounded hoarse as he tried once more to summon her from her sleepy world. "Miriam, wake up."

The woman didn't even flicker an eyelash.

He couldn't very well leave her to sleep in her badly soiled day gown. Gideon gritted his teeth against a rush of sensations as he reached out and unfastened the first button at her throat. The dress had twenty-eight tiny mother-of-pearl buttons aligned in disciplined ranks, two by two down the front. He stood there and prayed if he loosened the first pair, Miriam would come awake. Undoing one practically drained him of whatever control he possessed. He certainly couldn't handle twenty-seven more.

Heaven must have heard him, because he learned in the next instant that only half of those buttons needed to be undone; the other half were decorative companions. He'd just undone the second one and grimaced. She still hadn't roused. Bad enough, he'd had to loosen her clothes—she'd be utterly scandalized if she awoke to him dragging a wet cloth over her throat to rouse her. Gideon rested his hands on her shoulders, but he didn't want to shake her or shout. Poor thing didn't deserve that. He leaned closer and opened his mouth to whisper her name.

Chapter 3

Miriam came awake with a vengeance. A cry burst from her as she catapulted into a sitting position. She windmilled her arms and whacked Gideon in the chest and jaw. For a wee bit of a thing, she sure showed spunk. Titus, Paul, Bryce, and Logan all scrambled over to see what the ruckus was about. When she spied them, Miriam let out a terrified shriek and tried to bolt from the far side of the bed.

Gideon did the most expedient thing. He grabbed the blanket and yanked it shut again, effectively containing and covering her. "Calm down." He sat down and pulled her back into his lap. "Everything is fine, sweet pea. Don't bother with them. They're leaving. You nitwits get on outta here before I knock your heads together."

"Oh, Lord, have mercy," she quavered. "Deliver me, I pray."

Gideon crooked his forefinger and used it to tilt her face up to his. Her eyes were wide with terror. "Hush, Miss Miriam. You don't have a thing in the world to fret over when it comes to me and the boys. You've got my ironclad guarantee on it. When you took your tumble in town, you got some, uh, stuff on your day gown. I tried to wake you a bit, but you're a sound sleeper."

She continued to shiver in his arms and stared at him in abject fear. White, even teeth clamped down hard on her lip, and he knew she did it to keep from screaming. Her breaths came in sharp little pants, causing her whole body to jerk.

He slowly smoothed a few errant strands of hair from her brow. "How's your head feeling?" he asked softly, trying to divert her attention and let her gather her composure.

"Please don't hurt me. Don't touch me. Just let me go." She tacked on for good measure, "It's a sin."

"Sweet pea, nobody's planning to hurt you one bit. I'm sorry you got so spooked, but you don't have a worry in the world when it comes to that sinning business. I won't abide any man accosting a woman." He trailed his fingers down her cold, pale cheek. Brave as could be, she'd not shed any of the tears glistening in her huge eyes. Her skin felt as soft as baby Virginia's. At the moment, she looked almost as young and innocent as little Ginny, too.

She managed to tear her gaze from his only long enough to hastily scan the room. The instant she refocused on him, she swallowed hard. "Where's Hannah?"

Gideon bit back a groan. He'd wanted to delay this.

"Saints have mercy," she whispered in a breathless rush. Eyes huge and swimming, she said, "You're not really Gideon, are you? If you were, Hannah would be here."

"Easy now, Miss Miriam. Easy." His arms tightened a shade. "I'm Gideon. Don't go letting your imagination lead you into unfounded fears."

"Then where is my sister?" Even though the volume had to make her head hurt, Miriam raised her shaking voice. "Hannah? Hannah!"

Gideon gently pressed a finger over her lips. "Hannah isn't coming, Miss Miriam."

"Why not?"

The whole way home, he'd tried to put together a few mild phrases that would gradually ease her into the sad truth. Maybe not something flowery, but, well. . .

For all his pondering, he'd concocted a hundred phrases, but none of them seemed right. The time had come, and he still lacked the words.

Gideon's momentary hesitation was all it took. Miriam went rigid in his arms. One of her hands snaked out from beneath the flap in the blanket and desperately clutched at his shirtfront. "No!"

He sighed and drew her closer. Gliding his palm up and down her back, Gideon confirmed her suspicion. "I'm afraid so, Miss Miriam. Hannah passed on soon after having little Virginia Mae. You must not have gotten Daniel's letter."

She burrowed her face in his neck and shook her head. Gideon wasn't sure whether she shook to deny the death or because she hadn't gotten the letter. He'd shocked her so deeply, he knew she'd not cry yet. In time, it would all register. For now, the shock protected her a bit. Gideon knew his words would echo and elicit a full reaction later.

Boots scuffled, and Paul appeared. He thrust a glass into Gideon's hand. It held water, but a telltale sweet odor clung to it. Paul mouthed, "Laudanum," and his brother gratefully accepted it.

It took some coaxing to get Miriam to drink it. She swallowed the first few sips out of shocked compliance, but when she realized the cup didn't contain plain water, she tried to refuse more. Gideon used all of his persuasive powers, and finally she finished the rest of the glass. The dull grief on her face was all too familiar. Daniel still wore it much of the time.

She eventually pushed away from him and said in a shaky voice, "I thank you for your honesty. H–Hannah mentioned you and your brothers in the most complimentary way in her missives. Now perhaps you would be so kind as to take me to her grave site."

"I'll be willing to take you there, come morning. It's real late. You need to go to bed."

"But I came to see Hannah."

The bewildered, lost look on her face tugged at his heart. "Sweet pea, you'll have to trust me. I'll take you to pay your respects tomorrow—first thing in the morning, if you like. Right now, you need to lie down." He patted her bed gown so she would focus on it. "If I leave you for a few minutes, can you change into this all by yourself?"

She nodded.

He stood and set her on her feet. After assuring himself that she could balance, he slowly let go. "About your clothes, just drop them on the blanket."

"Very well."

He moved her nightgown so she could reach it more easily. Even that fleeting contact left his fingertips burning. He cleared his throat. "Soon as you're changed, climb on into the bed."

Gideon left her and tried to ignore the sound of rustling clothes and the whisper of petticoats. He and his brothers waited in vain for the muffled crackling sound of her settling on his hay mattress. Finally, he shrugged and drew closer to the blanket curtain. He quietly murmured her name, but she didn't answer, so he stepped back onto the other side of the makeshift partition.

His heart twisted. Miriam looked like a little angel, dressed in her pure white nightgown. She'd fallen asleep while kneeling to pray. Instead of being confined in the prim bun that had been coming loose all evening, her hair now hung in a loose braid that measured the full length of her spine. Her back bowed from the way her arms winged out onto the mattress, and she rested her cheek on one small, dainty hand.

He tiptoed over and winced at the noise his boots made on the gritty plank floor. Thankfully she didn't jar awake again. The poor woman couldn't possibly withstand another shock. Gideon gently scooped her into his arms. For a moment, he held her close.

Other than Mama, he couldn't remember ever holding a woman just because she needed tenderness. Oh, he cherished his nieces, but they were tiny little scraps—not full-grown women. Miriam's head rested on his shoulder, and even in her slumber, she let out a tiny whimper.

"Shh," he murmured. "Sleep, darlin'. Just sleep." As he did when Polly or Ginny Mae was a bit fractious, he dipped one shoulder to the side, then the other to make his torso rock. For some odd reason, that swaying action always calmed them down. It worked for Miriam, too. After a minute or so, her features softened, and she let out a tiny puff of air.

"There you go," he whispered, then slipped her onto his bed and pulled up the wool blanket he normally used. Coarse. The blanket felt much too rough for a lady, but he figured she was too far gone to let a detail like that register tonight. In the morning, he'd rummage through a trunk and see if he could find one of Mama's quilts. Hannah had taken a shine to them, so her sister would probably appreciate having one to use while she visited.

Miriam turned her head to the side. The gentle curve of her jaw and the slight lift of her brow made him think an angel must have just whispered a word of comfort to her. Unable to resist, he bent down and brushed a chaste kiss on her cheek. . .just in case the angel hadn't done a good enough job.

After he straightened up, he cast a quick look over at the partition. Relief flooded him. None of his brothers was peeking around the blanket, so no one witnessed him pampering this strange woman. Even though he'd meant nothing personal or improper, he'd have to watch his ways for the time Miriam stayed here. He didn't want her—or his brothers—getting any crazy notions.

Gideon gathered the soiled blanket and clothes from the floor and noted she'd been orderly enough to fold each garment. A wry smile tilted his mouth. She'd tried to observe all propriety by placing her dress atop the pile so the men wouldn't see her unmentionables. Something was missing, though. Then he spied a white length of cording hanging below the blanket at the foot of the bed. Prissy little Miriam had hidden her corset from him.

Much as it embarrassed her, Miriam had no choice. Someone had carried away all of her proper clothes. She'd need to traipse about in her nightgown and robe until her dress or trunks reappeared. Her head ached, but the sharp pangs of grief in her heart rated more attention. She brushed and put up her hair, pulled on the jade green robe, and tiptoed past the hanging blanket.

The sight before her almost felled her. Four other beds stuck out from the wall. Clothes hung from pegs pounded into the rugged wood walls, but more littered the mud-encrusted floor. Though it wasn't exactly the height of good manners to gawk at anyone—especially someone of the opposite gender—as they slept, she couldn't help noting each bed held a strapping man and a single blanket. No sheets were in sight.

Her bare feet made no noise, but they seemed to find every dirt clod and pebble on the floor as she made her way past the beds and out the open door. She closed the door behind herself and stifled a gasp.

A big trestle table flanked by benches filled the middle portion of the house. As she got closer, Miriam quelled a shriek as a mouse skittered by. The table hadn't been scrubbed in months. A sputtering candle sat in the center of it. Any number of items littered the floor, too. A harness, work gloves, a whetstone, and two saddles all blocked her transit. The windows were dingy beyond belief, and no curtain hung there for the sake of modesty or privacy.

Worst of all, the kitchen would make any woman's heart fail. A big Acme stove promised sizable meals, but a fleeting touch confirmed it to be stone cold and in desperate need of scraping and scouring. She peered into the water reservoir and almost screamed when she found two trout there. Crates nailed to the walls held provender. The Chance men might not clean at all, but from the looks of the supplies they kept, they certainly ate. Dirty dishes lay on every available surface.

Miriam cringed, then used the edge of a dubious-looking dishcloth to wipe a tiny circle on the windowpane until she could see. It was still dark outside. She couldn't determine the time. Regardless, she couldn't go back to sleep.

She used the candle to light a kerosene lamp and set to work. It was hard to determine where to begin. A quick touch of the broom handle, and she drew back in disgust. Sticky. She wiped it clean, then brandished the business end against the cobwebs in the corners. The overhead beams and walls soon were whisked clean, too. Next, she filled a bucket with water from the pump and relocated the fish into it.

It made no sense to try to suds down the stove until she scraped off the worst of the grime with the blade of a hoe she found on a bench. Though it wasn't exactly the usual application for the tool, the inside of a house wasn't a normal storage place for it, either. The hoe also helped her shovel the mountain of ashes from the stove. She set the buckets of ashes off to the side. They might be needed to make soap.

A bottle of ammonia allowed her to scrub the top of the range and the bottom panes of the windows. She couldn't reach the higher ones until she dragged over a bench, but with all of the rubbish in the way, she simply couldn't. Miriam pretended not to notice how the bowl stuck to the tabletop as she mixed flour, salt, baking powder, water, and eggs together in it. She'd started a small fire in the stove and would make some drop biscuits as soon as she heard the men begin to stir.

The coffeepot looked battered, but that indicated these men liked the bitter brew, so she refilled it with fresh water and measured out the grounds. Miriam put the coffee on the stove, and as she turned around, she bit back a cry. A pot holder she'd quilted for her sister hung on a rusty nail. Memories flooded her. All of the grief she'd tried to hold at bay with her frantic cleaning overwhelmed her. She hugged the pot holder to her bosom, sat at the sticky table, and wept.

Chapter 4

Gideon had gone out to the stable to sleep. He woke to answer the call of nature, and on the way back to the stable from the outhouse, he noted the light from the house. That struck him as odd. The lights normally didn't show much at all. His brothers must be up trying to comfort little Miriam for the place to be ablaze like this. It was a solid half hour before they normally got up, and all of them prized their sleep. Things must be bad if they sacrificed their time in the sack. He strode over to assess the situation.

As he drew closer, Gideon realized he could see the light through the windows more clearly than usual. He opened the door and groaned. Miriam sat on a bench, her elbows propped on the table, her face buried in a pot holder, of all things. Her shoulders shuddered with her nearly silent weeping.

He went and sat beside her, his back against the table and his hip alongside her bed gown. As soon as he reached for her, she tumbled sideways into his chest. She cried brokenheartedly—just the way Mama had when Pa died. Gideon remembered it well. He felt just as helpless now as he had then. Wrapping his arms securely about Miriam and holding fast were all he could do—precious little to guard her tender heart from such terrible news.

When she finally wound down, he gave her time to let his presence sink in. Hopefully she'd find consolation in knowing she'd not be left alone in her first moments of grief. She mopped her tear-ravaged face with the pot holder, and he tenderly stroked her brow. "You're tuckered out. I want you to sleep the whole day away. We'll talk things over this evening."

He stood and thought about letting her walk back into the bedroom. Her movements as she stood and stepped around the edge of the bench were stilted, and her features looked bleakly wooden. If her appearance alone wasn't reason enough, the obstacles in her path convinced him she'd never make it. Gideon swept her into his arms. She sagged against him and whispered in a shaky voice, "What about Hannah's babies?"

"They're right as rain. God never made cuter dumplin's. You'll meet them after you've rested up. Young as they are, they'll run you ragged if you don't store up a bit of energy."

As he spoke, he plowed through everything cluttering the floor and into the room where his brothers all sat, fully dressed and waiting for a chance to escape from a woman's weeping. He didn't bother to introduce them. He simply passed by all of them and tucked her into his bed while they hastily exited the room.

He suffered an awkward moment, realizing she'd not want to shed her robe in his presence. She'd fallen fast asleep earlier; she probably didn't comprehend he'd already seen her in her bed gown.

Miriam shivered.

Relief flooded him. He considered the room much too warm from having his brothers sleeping in it all night. Obviously Miriam thought otherwise. "That one blanket won't be enough to keep you warm, Miss Miriam. You'd best keep on your robe for a bit of extra bundling." He settled her onto his mattress. The mattress smelled a mite stale. How long had it been since he replaced the cornhusks and hay inside the ticking? He couldn't rightly remember. No use fretting over anything that minor. He pulled up the cover and tucked it around her narrow shoulders. "Sweet dreams."

"I apologize for being such a bother."

"You're not a bother. Now hush and sleep." He turned, paced out of the room, and shut the door to give her privacy.

All five men sat at the breakfast table, drank Miriam's restaurant-perfect coffee, and ate her melt-in-your-mouth biscuits. Titus looked around. "This place is a pigsty."

Gideon nodded. "I don't want her waking up and coming out to this. Hannah was always finicky about cleanliness; I don't imagine Miss Miriam will be any less so. Bryce, you get all of the stuff up off the floor and carry it back out to the stable. Titus, you wash the dishes. I don't reckon we have a clean one left in the whole house."

Gideon knew his brothers didn't welcome those orders. Because they all worked from can-see-to-can't, seven days a week, those chores normally went undone. They'd shed the burden of domestic frills as soon as there wasn't a woman around to protest. The problem was, a woman occupied the house again.

He continued, "Logan, you're going to have to use sand to scrub the junk off the floor. Everyone needs to get back in the habit of scraping off their boots before they come in. For a few days here, we're gonna have to act civilized."

Bryce scowled at him. "You're mighty good at makin' us do the dirty work. What're you putting your hand to?"

Gideon wrinkled his nose. "I'm going to wash the stuff from her clothes."

Logan nodded. "I got it on mine, too. I'll toss them in the pot."

Gideon muttered as all of them volunteered him to do their laundry. He'd rather do just about anything but laundry. Since he was the eldest, he usually managed to order someone else to do the chore. The only reason he'd been ready to do it was because he didn't cotton to the notion of his brothers touching prim little Miriam's unmentionables. Frankly, he didn't want to deal with them, either. It went against all decency, but he'd left her trunks in town, and the woman needed something to wear. *Stuck between a rattler and a brushfire.* Gideon let out a gusty sigh. "Let's get to work."

Everyone set to his chores. Titus left most of the dishes to soak in three big tubs. He took the pots down to the creek for a sand scouring. Bryce hauled an armful of junk out to the stable, then milked the cow before he came back. He set down the milk pail, hauled out the harness, and came back with the eggs he'd gathered.

Logan took out the swill to slop the hogs, came back, scowled at the floor, and grumbled, "Don't know why I have to scrub it. It'll be dirty again, soon as anyone walks across it. Can't see wasting my time." His brothers all gave him nasty looks, so he grabbed the broom.

After shaving half a cake of soap into the wash kettle, Gideon set it over a fire in the yard and filled it with water. As it started to heat, he paced back into the cabin. Quietly as he could, he eased the bedroom door open and tiptoed in. He stood still for a moment, but he didn't hear a thing. Every step he took sounded clumsily loud as he walked across the planks to gather shirts and britches off the pegs and floor. Finally, he reached the far side of the room and paused outside the blanket partition.

"Miss Miriam, I aim to fetch the laundry if you don't mind."

She failed to answer, so he peered in to be sure she was okay. He strained to listen and heard soft breaths in a slow, deep cadence. *Good. She's sleeping.* Moving away, he snagged his shirts off the pegs, used the toe of his boot to hook out the blanket stacked with her soiled clothing, and finally went to the other end. He reached under the bed to get his grime-encrusted britches.

In morning light, she looked more delicate, more ethereal. The way her braid unraveled across the pillow invited a man to test each rippling, golden wave.

Hannah's kid sister—the one he'd heard her mention and somehow pictured as a schoolgirl in pigtails—was an eyeful of femininity. Gideon tamped down that line of thought and beat a hasty retreat. He left the clothes by the boiling laundry pot and headed toward Daniel's tiny cottage.

The Chance men never stood on formalities. Gideon walked in without knocking and scooped Polly from the floor. Over at the table, Daniel tried to get Virginia to take one more sip of apple cider. The two of them seemed to be wearing more of the contents of the glass than drinking it.

"I'm doing laundry," Gideon announced as he started to toss clothes into a crate.

"Great!"

After he filled the crate, he turned and looked at his brother. Daniel showed remarkable patience with his two little ones. Three-year-old Polly chattered twenty to the dozen, and Virginia had hit the walking stage a few days earlier.

After Hannah died, Daniel had advertised for a housekeeper, but the only one who responded made it clear she held far more interest in matrimony than in mending. After a short time, it became clear that for the sake of Daniel's sanity, the Chance brothers were going to have to handle matters on their own. They devised a simple solution: Each man took a day every week to watch the girls. Daniel took both Wednesday and Sunday since the girls were his, and he minded them from sundown to sunup all of the time.

"Dan, we've got a visitor."

"Oh?" Daniel wiped Ginny Mae's face. "Who?"

Gideon watched his brother intently. "Miriam Hancock came into town last night."

"Miriam?" Dan looked dazed. "What is she doing here?"

"It seems Hannah wrote her and mentioned she didn't feel well. Miriam came to help her out."

"Why'd she do a foolish thing like that? Letters take up to eight months to get there!"

"Don't ask me to figure out the mind of a woman. Fact remains, Miriam is here. I figured I'd best tell you before you ran into her in the yard. I'm sure she'll want to see her nieces today."

"How long is she planning to stay?"

"I didn't ask."

As it was Saturday, it was Gideon's day to have the girls. He popped both of them into the fenced-off play area Daniel had made to contain the girls while his brothers did yard chores. Some of the clothes were so badly soiled, Gideon couldn't even put them in the wash kettle. He toted them down to the creek, knelt, and swished the worst of the grime from them. Beating them on a rock worked, but he had neither the time nor the patience to do much of that. Instead, he hauled them all back to the fire.

Steam rose from the huge, cast-iron cauldron. The soap bubbled a bit on the surface. Yeah, that looked just like it did when Mama used to have laundry day. Satisfied with the wash water, he dumped in Miriam's white clothes and stirred them with a paddle. After he made sure they'd come clean, he double rinsed them so the lye residue wouldn't irritate her delicate skin or rot the thin cotton fabric, then wrung out each snowy garment and hung it on the clothesline. It seemed mighty strange to see a woman's things there.

He washed the baby's white things next, then did the rest of the laundry. It was a hot, miserable job, and he didn't feel guilty in the least for how he kept leaving things in the pot to boil a bit while he went off to tickle Polly or play peekaboo with Ginny Mae.

Once all the clothes fluttered in the wind, he hitched each of the girls under his arms and hiked over to the garden. They played in the dirt and mud while he staked up the tomatoes and watered the melons and beans. Polly was giggling, and Ginny Mae just about put a worm in her mouth when Gideon looked up to see Miriam standing there. He snatched the worm from Ginny Mae and stammered, "They're dirty right now, but they're good girls."

A tender smile lit her face. "They're beautiful, and they'll clean up. Little girls deserve to make mud pies." She self-consciously tugged at her robe, then stooped down. Instead of grabbing, she simply opened her arms. Polly went right to her. "Hello, poppet. You're my Polly-girl, and you are every bit as precious as your mama said."

Polly rubbed her hand up and down the soft fabric of her aunt's green dressing gown. "Pretty."

A becoming blush stained her cheeks. "Yes, well, Auntie Miriam needs her clothes."

"They're on the clothesline. It's hot today, so they'll be dry in a few hours," Gideon said.

"What about my trunks?"

"They're in town. I'll see if we can't fetch them in a day or two."

"In the meantime, I'll take the girls inside with me. There's plenty to do. I'm sure you have more than enough to accomplish."

He looked at her, then slowly said, "It's my day to have the girls."

"Your day?"

"We each take a day. Daniel takes two days since they're his daughters."

Still fussing with her dressing gown, she murmured, "Seeing as I'm able to mind the girls, I'm sure you have much to do elsewhere."

"I won't deny that, but I don't know that leaving the girls with you is such a keen plan. Polly doesn't cotton to strangers."

"Polly and I will get along famously." One of the brothers walked past. Miriam wasn't sure which one he was, but she blushed at the way he eyed her in her night wear. "So if you'll excuse us, we'll be off."

He cast a glance at his brother's back, then eyed her attire with a frown. "You can't traipse around in that all day. Borrow something from your sister's trunk."

"I don't know if I can. I—"

"I'll handle it with Daniel. Go on inside."

She took both girls back toward the cottage. The dirt felt good under her bare feet. After all of that time on a ship, she wanted solid earth beneath her for the rest of her days. The slight breeze carried the scents of pine, horses, and hay. Men's baritones mingled in the background, a deep counterpoint to the musical trills of songbirds and the scolds of jays.

This place was all that her life in the islands had not been. The air felt dry, not humid. The flowers were plentiful but tiny instead of cloying and exuberant. Browns and muted greens dominated the landscape instead of a kaleidoscope of brilliant jewel tones. These men crowded in one home, shared one bedroom. This was a far cry from the stringent rules they lived by back home to ensure privacy, modesty, and decorum. In odd juxtaposition to that, everyone here—except for her, she thought wryly—was completely dressed; whereas back home, the natives wore only the barest minimum.

Dear, sweet Hannah scribbled letters in secret, telling how she hated living here. Homesickness, she confessed, plagued her. The cold weather made her spirits plummet, and no matter how hard she worked, everything looked dismal and dusty. The brothers were all good men, but she felt sadly outnumbered and lonely for female companionship. Mama and Daddy listened with grave misgivings to Miriam's offer to go help her sister, but they'd decided it was for the best. Clearly, with six men and a second child on the way, Hannah couldn't take care of matters on her own anymore.

As Miriam left, Mama had whispered, "There are no decent, God-fearing white men here for you, darling. Surely Miriam will introduce you to a few worthy young men of good character."

Miriam looked about and cuddled the girls a bit closer. Worthy young men wouldn't be a part of her life. Moping about that wouldn't do much good. All her life, Papa taught her to deal with whatever God allowed to happen in life without complaint. Hannah heard that same speech countless times, so for her to have poured out her laments underscored the gravity of her plight.

Miriam ached to have a husband and children of her own. At twenty, she didn't exactly rate as an old maid, but she couldn't expect Daniel and his brothers to play matchmaker for her. Since she'd come and Hannah was gone, she knew her destiny lay in being a spinster aunt. Surely God had sent her here. These girls needed a woman's caring. Polly's tangled and matted hair bore mute testimony to that fact.

Miriam quietly and immediately accepted the bittersweet fact that if she couldn't have a man and babes of her own, she'd at least have dear Hannah's wee ones to cherish.

Off to the side of the main house, two big trees bracketed a tiny cottage. Hannah's letters mentioned the brothers building a "habitation" for her. Surely this was it. Miriam hitched Virginia Mae higher on her hip and stepped across the threshold. The building was a tiny box of a place—a simple, one-room affair. Once she winced at the mess, Miriam noted the room featured no kitchen. The fireplace was tiny—only enough to warm this little place but not big enough to cook over. A small cabinet on the wall and a pint-size table and chairs were the only things that defined one corner. The rest of the place held a bed, a trundle that was undoubtedly Polly's, and a crib for the baby. She deduced Hannah must've been making meals for all six of the Chance men over at the main house.

Unable to navigate the room without stepping and tripping on things, Miriam made a game of picking up Daniel's possessions. The little toddlers had fun holding items up for her reactions. She'd pinch her nose and point at one corner for laundry. Though someone had done laundry today, they'd missed half of the load from this residence.

It was more than embarrassing to stay in her night wear. She checked the clothesline and sighed. Her sodden clothes still dripped on the line. Unaccustomed to the weather here, she couldn't tell how long before her dress would be dry. Much as she didn't want to go through Hannah's things, Miriam decided to obey Gideon's instructions.

Back in the cottage, she found Hannah's trunk. As she opened the lid, Miriam cried. They'd always shared clothes, and she knew her sister wouldn't begrudge her these essentials; but the scent of Hannah's perfume brought back a flood of memories, and seeing her favorite fan, even touching her clothing, tore at Miriam. She desperately wanted to slam the lid back down. Gideon said they'd fetch her things in a few days—surely she could tolerate wearing only one set of clothing for a while.

Ginny Mae tugged on her arm. The sleeve pulled, causing the wrapped bodice of her robe to gap and expose her nightgown. Miriam pulled the baby into her lap and cradled her there. Polly tugged on the other side.

"I gotta go potty, Auntie Miri-Em."

Miriam hadn't located a chamber pot in this mess. She dried her tears. "Can you wait just a minute, Polly?"

Polly nodded.

Miriam hastily went through the trunk. The pieced skirt on the blue dress didn't conform to any style. *Feed sacks. Hannah made these out of feed sacks—and she stitched huge waists to permit her room for her family condition.* Miriam delved deeper and located a rose-colored gown she'd sewn for her sister's trousseau. That and a few other essentials would serve satisfactorily. She latched the cottage door shut and changed.

Once she'd dressed, Miriam took Polly to the outhouse and came back to the little cottage. Dressed in decent attire, she felt free to move about and do whatever she deemed fit. She opened the door wide to air out the cottage and dusted. Polly followed her like a lonely little puppy, and Virginia Mae toddled behind. Miriam gave them each a cloth, and they "helped." She shoved the trundle beneath the bed, then picked up a few more stray items that had fallen there before she swept.

Spoons and cups went onto the table, and blankets were piled onto the beds. Whimsical wooden animals kept turning up. The Chance men must enjoy whittling, because they'd turned out a plethora of miniature beasts. Miriam admired each one for her little nieces, then stored them all in a bowl. "Like Noah's ark," she said.

Polly gave her a perplexed look.

Miriam knelt and used the bowl like a boat as she tried to remind the little tyke about the Bible story. Clearly Polly hadn't heard it before. That fact alarmed Miriam. Weren't these men rearing the girls to know the Holy Scriptures?

Miriam busied the girls with the wooden creatures and set to earnest work. The clothesline had a bit more space on it, but she earmarked that for the remaining laundry. The blankets all needed airing, so she cast them over several shrubs and weighted them down with a few rocks to keep them from blowing into the dirt. Though it seemed bold, she stripped the sheets from Daniel's bed and added them to the laundry pile. Her nose wrinkled in distaste. Now that she thought about it, there hadn't been a single sheet on any of the beds back in the main house. These men were barely civilized.

Boots crunched leaves outside. Miriam turned as Gideon filled the doorway and cast a shadow across the room.

"This place hasn't looked like this since—" He stopped short, then finished diplomatically, "For a long time."

They exchanged stricken looks, then Miriam pivoted to the side and washed her hands in a bucket. She dipped in a cloth and swiped at the dust and mud on Virginia's hands and face. "I assume it's close to your luncheon hour. The girls and I will come to the big house and—"

She didn't finish. Someone else arrived. Miriam heard a shocked gasp. Though she hadn't heard it in almost five years, she recognized Daniel's voice. "Hannah!"

Chapter 5

Gideon watched Miriam go stark still. She slowly turned, and deep sadness painted her features. Tears glistened in her eyes. "Daniel. I'm so sorry—"

Sensing his brother's shock, Gideon braced his arm. This was a terrible blow. Daniel had adored his bride, and the grief still ate at him. The longing and hope on his face changed to nothing short of hatred.

"Dan, I told her to—"

"How dare you! Take that off."

Miriam's lips parted in shock.

Daniel leaned forward, and his hands knotted to fists that shook with the effort it took to keep them down at his sides. He demanded in a tone that trembled with rage, "Take it off! How dare you touch her things!"

"Dan—" Gideon tried to calm his brother but to no avail.

Daniel shook off Gideon's hand, wheeled around, and plowed out the door. Virginia Mae's voice echoed in the suddenly all-too-quiet cottage. "Daddy! Daddy!"

Gideon turned back to Miriam. She'd curled her hands around the slats of a chair as if to shore herself up after receiving a hefty blow. She kept blinking and breathed through her mouth to hold back the tears that welled up. "Miriam, I'm sorry. This was my fault."

She bit her lip, then quavered, "Please go give him my apology."

His heart went out to her. She'd just followed his instructions and hadn't knowingly done anything to upset her brother-in-law. Truth be told, she did look enough like her sister to cause a grieving man to mistake her for the woman he'd loved. He searched to find the right words to soften her hurt, but nothing came to mind.

"Please," she whispered brokenly, "go."

Gideon nodded once, then left her to whatever anguish she felt. Of all his brothers, Daniel was the most volatile. Five years ago, he'd been off drinking in San Francisco when he got shanghaied. While his ship docked in the islands, he'd met Hannah. He never said a thing about that year of his life. He'd come back a more contained, disciplined man. Gideon wasn't sure whether marriage or his time aboard ship had done that, but since Hannah died, there were days when Daniel's rage knew no bounds.

Daniel went out to the woodpile. The ring of the ax splitting wood let Gideon know where he was and to keep a wary distance. He stood and watched his brother work himself into a full lather before he finally said, "It was a shock, Dan, but she didn't mean to upset you. It's my fault—I told her to borrow something."

Daniel set the next piece on the chopping stump and split it with a single powerful blow. The storm in his eyes matched the violence of his action. He set the next log up, then gritted, "No one touches my Hannah's things. No one."

"Fair enough."

"Get rid of that woman. I don't want her here."

It was worse than he'd imagined. Gideon hitched his hip and half-sat on the fence. He moved slowly in an effort to appear casual and untroubled. "I don't reckon that's going to be possible for a few days. She came a long ways and needs to rest before—"

Daniel cut him off by repeating in an unyielding tone, "I don't want her here."

"What did she ever do to you?"

"Look at her. Just look! They could have been twins!"

The anguish behind Daniel's words let Gideon know his brother's shock was still too fresh and raw. "All right, Dan. I understand. We'll get rid of her as soon as possible." He paused, then added, "In the meantime, you're going to have to be civil to her."

"That's not a problem. I'm not going to see her."

Gideon's patience started to unravel. He'd managed precious little sleep last night and wasn't of a mind to put up with a brother having a tantrum. He fought to keep an even tone. "You're a better man than that, Dan."

Daniel hefted the ax. His knuckles were white as he gripped the handle, raised the blade, and buried it into the stump. He stared at the deeply marred place he'd wedged the blade and didn't look up as he said in a mere rasp, "You don't know what you're asking."

"Maybe not—but if you had any notion how brave that little gal tried to be after you thundered at her and left, you'd try to match her courage." He figured he'd said as much as he dared. Gideon straightened up. "We'll see you for dinner."

"Supper."

He let out a snort and walked off. Half an hour later, Gideon walked into the house. It looked miles better after all of his brothers had tended to their assigned chores. They'd all need to hustle a fair bit to get the real work done, but from the smell of things, Miriam's cooking would be ample reward for their efforts.

Miriam. Dressed in the gown he'd just washed for her, she stood over by the stove. Though not exactly wet, the garment rated as excessively damp. She made no reference to that point, even though it had to feel clammy. He hoped she wouldn't catch a chill from wearing it. Overall, the dress didn't exactly cling to her, but a man would have to be dead and buried not to notice the way every last inch of the cloth accentuated a very feminine shape. Miriam seemingly ignored her uncomfortable clothing and diligently worked over a few pots.

She lifted a lid on something, and Gideon's mouth watered. One of his brothers didn't even bother to muffle his groan. When she started to dish servings onto a plate, Gideon stated, "Don't make so much work for yourself, Miss Miriam. Just stick the pots on the table. We'll serve ourselves."

She set aside that plate. Without a word, she did as he bade. His other brothers filed in and sniffed the air apprecitively. "Whatever you whipped up, it sure does make a feller's nose take notice," Bryce said.

Miriam shot him a wobbly smile. Gideon sat and swept Polly into his lap. "Bet you're a hungry little bear today."

"Uh-huh. She maded 'tatoes."

Logan chuckled. "Now you've done it, Miss Miriam. You made a friend for life. Polly loves taters."

All of the men sat and started to fill their plates. Miriam stayed at the stove and cut the food on the plate she'd already dished up. One place at the table remained conspicuously vacant. Titus said in a slightly too jovial tone, "Come sit here with us, Miss Miriam."

Gideon's fork was halfway to Polly's mouth when Miriam shook her head. Polly grabbed for the bite. Miriam poured a bit of gravy on her plate, then set the gravy boat in the center of the table. She gently swept Virginia Mae from Bryce's hold and claimed the plate from the stove.

"Aw, I can feed her. We're all pretty fair hands at that kind of stuff," Bryce said.

"I'm sure you are." Miriam's gaze swept across the already decimated pots, bowls, and half-cleared plates. Her features went taut. A soundless sigh heaved her bosom, and she left. Gideon scowled. "Hey. Come back here."

Her voice drifted over her shoulder: "Ginny Mae's wet."

In no time at all, the brothers finished off every last speck of food. Daniel hadn't gotten to eat, but if he didn't bother to show up, he had no call to bellyache. Food this good deserved to be appreciated down to the last bite. They'd eaten real loaf bread for the first time in ages. Normally they ate either sticky or rock-hard biscuits. She must have kneaded the loaves before she came out to the garden.

"She set beans to soak," Bryce reported. "Think she'll sweeten them and add in ham or bacon?"

"I reckon whatever she does," Titus said as he sopped up the gravy with the last crust of his bread, "it'll be better than anything we've had in a coon's age."

Logan sighed appreciatively. "She sure can cook."

"Yeah, well, quit mooning over the vittles and get back to work. Logan, you take the buckboard to town and fetch Miss Miriam's trunks. If I so much as catch a whiff of beer or whiskey on you when you get home, I'll tan your hide so you can't sit 'til Christmas."

Titus pumped a bucket of water and dumped the plates into it. He took Polly and said, "I reckon it's best we keep the girls to their naps. I'll go tuck this little one in and bring back Miss Miriam's plate."

By the time Titus returned, Paul, Logan, and Bryce were long gone. Gideon moved the bucket with the trout onto the table and hoped Miriam would pan-fry them for supper. He had a hankering for a nicely turned hunk of trout. Titus interrupted his longings. "She fed Ginny and was singing her off to sleep."

"How did Polly do?"

"Much as she don't cotton to strangers, she truly does head straight to Miss Miriam for a pat or a smile. I told her they both nap a good while this time of the day."

"I hope she naps, too."

"I don't much think so. She asked me where Hannah's grave was."

Gideon grimaced.

"I think you'd best leave her alone. She didn't look none too good. Kind of reminded me of the air Mama carried when she needed us to leave her be."

"I'd better go anyway. Daniel might be there."

"Nah. I just saw him. He's taking all the logs he split to the woodpile."

Supper came, and Gideon tried not to make a spectacle of himself when Miriam set a platter of trout on the table. Every last piece was fried to crispy, golden brown perfection. She served rice and greens, too. Her day gown was dry. Polly kept a fistful of it and shadowed her every move.

"Logan, go on over to the cottage and bring back a chair," Gideon ordered under his breath. "Put it at the foot of the table so Miriam has a place."

Paul brought in the evening milking and asked, "Where do you want this, Miss Miriam?"

"What is it?"

"Milk. I already strained it for you."

"Do you men drink it or do just the girls?"

"Depends on whether you need any milk for your cooking."

"Why don't you save half of it," she said uncertainly, then turned to open the oven door. Gideon's mouth watered. The fragrance had teased him ever since he came inside, but he'd tried to deny the possibility. Cobbler. He inhaled deeply. Apple.

"Lord, have mercy," Bryce moaned.

Miriam set the cobbler on the stove top and shut the door. She moved stiffly and said with great precision, "I hope that was a prayer, because I will not have the Lord's name taken in vain."

"Sorry, ma'am. I mean, miss. You surely can take that as a prayer of thanksgiving."

Logan arrived with the chair. With supper on the table, everyone flocked to the benches. Gideon seated Miriam and tried to take Polly back with him, but she wouldn't turn loose of her aunt. "Here, poppet." Miriam gently lifted their niece onto her lap. She wrapped her arms around Polly's and folded their hands together into a steeple. "Who asks the blessing?"

The chorus of uncomfortable "uhs" left Gideon embarrassed. He took his seat as Daniel came in. Daniel answered with undisguised hostility, "Nobody prays here."

"Papa always said things can change," Miriam said. She kept hold of Polly's little hands, dipped her head, and whispered, "I'll say something, then you say it, too."

Polly nodded.

"Dear God," Miriam began.

"Dear God—"

"We give Thee thanks for our food."

"Thee thanks for food."

A few more quick lines, and they finished off with a duet of "Amen."

The whole while, the other brothers respectfully bowed their heads; but Dan had made a point of reaching across the table, noisily serving himself, and grunting a disdainful snort. Gideon resolved to string him up by his heels if he tried that stunt again.

As they filled their plates, Logan said, "Mama taught us a different grace."

"Then you may teach it to us tomorrow," Miriam said as she tied a dishcloth around Polly's neck.

Polly chattered, and Daniel's brothers tried to make conversation to cover his stony silence. Miriam spoke when directly addressed but otherwise stayed quiet. Her responses were softly spoken and brief, as if she was doing her best to be polite and invisible at the same time. He caught the way she hesitantly glanced at Dan out of the corner of her eye and winced at how her shoulders curled forward just the tiniest bit. Gideon noticed how Miriam's hands shook, and he worried over her pallor. He'd talk to her after supper and promise that, mad as Daniel might be, she had no cause to fear he'd ever raise a hand to her.

Bowls got passed around again, and his brothers scraped every last morsel of food out of the pans and onto their plates. Gideon thought to offer her more, but she didn't eat much of what was on her plate, so it seemed silly to ask if she wanted anything else. More went into Polly's mouth than her own.

The tension bugged him. He said nothing, because Miriam and Daniel would have to work things out between themselves. Surely by morning, Dan would come to terms with the situation and could be counted on to behave himself decently for a few days until Miriam went back home.

Once supper was over, Dan swiped little Polly straight off of Miriam's lap without so much as a word of warning. Only the ring of his boots on the floor planks broke the crackling silence until he reached the door. He kicked the door shut behind himself.

Every last brother watched as Miriam flinched. Bryce opened his mouth, but Gideon booted him under the table to keep him from saying something stupid.

Titus offered, "I'll wash the dishes. Paul, you dry."

"Fine." Gideon stood. "Bryce, see to the beasts and be sure to check that latch on the chicken coop."

Miriam wet her lips, then murmured, "Please excuse me." She slipped out of her chair and across the floor, her gait a soundless glide. Then she shut the door behind herself noiselessly.

"Poor thing," Titus mumbled.

"Sadder'n a hound that tangled with a porcupine," Bryce added.

Paul smacked the tabletop, and all of the dishes jumped. "Dan tries that again, and I'm gonna deck him!"

Though he privately agreed, Gideon didn't want his brothers brawling. "No one's going to do anything." He glared at his brothers. "All you'll do is pour kerosene on his temper if you stand up for her. His temper will burn hotter, and she'll get the blast. Stay out of it."

"Now wait just a minute—"

"No, you all hold your horses." Gideon folded his arms across his chest and stared them down. "Some things are best left alone. Dan's raging, but he'll run out of steam. In the meantime, just try to keep her away from him. He'll come to his senses."

"It ain't a matter of keeping her away from him," Bryce groused. "It's a matter of keeping him away from her."

"No," Gideon said heavily. "He can't bear the sight of her. She looks too much like Hannah."

"Ain't her fault, Giddy." Bryce cocked his head to the side and continued as if he'd come to a brilliant deduction. "They were sisters."

Titus ignored Bryce and stacked dishes into a bucket. "The real problem is going to be keeping her away from the kids."

"I don't give a hang if Dan doesn't want her seeing them," Gideon decided. "There's nothing wrong with her singing and playing with them."

"More likely *praying*," Logan corrected him.

"Yeah," Gideon said, "but Hannah and Mama both would've done the selfsame things. Until she leaves, let her enjoy them. We've jawed about this enough. You all pitch in and get things done."

Gideon fought the urge to dab his thumb into a little pile of sugar and cinnamon crumbs left from the cobbler. He'd love that last little taste, but he needed to look stern and in control just now. Sucking a sweet off of his thumb would spoil the effect. Instead, he picked up his plate and shoved it on the top of the teetering stack in Titus's bucket.

A few more minutes passed. Gideon figured Miriam had gone off to the privy and taken a little extra time to regain her composure, but when she didn't come back after a while, he grew concerned. He didn't want his brothers setting off like hounds after a frightened hare, so he silently went in search.

The privy was empty, the door hanging off to the side in careless disregard to privacy. They'd left it that way so Polly wouldn't be afraid of the dark when they took her there. With Miriam visiting, that needed to be fixed—at least temporarily. All day long, little details like that illustrated just how lackadaisical they'd become in regard to propriety. Having a woman around—even for a handful of days—was making his to-do list grow by leaps and bounds.

Gideon pondered where to turn next. Since his brother had told him she'd asked about the grave, he paced toward the tall pines. Wildflowers lay at the base of the wooden marker Daniel had carved as Hannah's headstone. That had to be Miriam's doing, because Dan hadn't ever once taken flowers to it.

Where was Miriam?

Chapter 6

He found her in the garden. A small basket with a trio of tomatoes and a pair of small melons lay in the soil by her skirts. At first, Gideon thought Miriam was on her knees, leaning forward to pick something. It took a second for him to realize she'd doubled over. She'd huddled down like a pitifully cold little rabbit that couldn't find its way back to the warren. The backs of her hands rested in the loam, and her fingers curled upward to cup her forehead. She looked so vulnerable and forlorn. He hunkered down beside her and tried to take stock of the situation.

Placing a tentative hand on her shoulder, he murmured, "Miss Miriam? You all right?"

"Head hurts," she whispered in a voice thick with tears.

"Aw, sweet pea, I'll bet it does." He eased his weight onto his knees and pulled her into his arms. She came unresistingly, but she didn't nestle into him for comfort, either. She was too limp to do anything.

Gideon called himself ten kinds of a fool. After the way Logan flattened her and knocked her noggin, she still had to be feeling poorly. Gideon carefully cupped her head to his chest and amended his assessment. The lump beneath his fingers made him wonder why she hadn't been cross-eyed and sick as a hound dog. Why had he let her cook and clean most of the day when he'd originally told her to sleep? He should have hauled her back to the house and tied her to the bed instead of letting her wear herself to a frazzle.

Just as bad, she still needed time after getting the awful news. One good cry didn't wash away grief. It was a marvel she hadn't dissolved into a puddle of tears over the way Daniel treated her.

Gideon's fingers slid beneath her thick golden braid and slowly kneaded her nape. Her breath hitched. Every last inch of her shuddered. "Aww," he murmured, unable to concoct anything meaningful for such a catastrophic time. Her breath hitched again, and he snuggled her closer. He'd tried hard to be strong after Pa and Mama each died, but he'd ridden Splotch off to a secluded spot and shed his fair share of bitter, aching tears, too. Folks expected a man to be strong, even in adversity, but a woman. . .

Well, a woman wasn't supposed to be this brave. She'd spent the last scraps of her composure when Daniel thundered at her, then later at supper. Clearly she was spoiling for a decent caterwaul. "Might as well let loose," he whispered into her soft hair.

"Weeping w–won't make it an–nee bet–ter," she whispered in choppy syllables that made her frame bump against him.

"Holding it all in won't lessen it," he countered. His words freed her, at least to some degree. Tears silently slipped down her cheeks and wet his shirt. He could almost taste the salt in them.

Crickets chirped and cicadas whirred. Horses whinnied and the cow lowed. One of the dogs barked a few times. Gideon knelt there and wished he were anywhere else. He wasn't cut out to comfort a grieving woman. He felt awkward and stupid. Had he thought even once, poor little Miriam wouldn't have worked herself into such a frazzled mess.

Right now the bitty, worn-out woman needed rest more than anything. His bed would have to do. It didn't quite seem fitting for her to be sleeping in a room with a bunch of men. Even Mama hadn't when they moved here.

A banker had cheated them out of their old ranch when Pa died. They'd packed up everything they owned and pretty much started fresh here. Mama was always first up and last to bed, so she'd slept in a bedstead in the main room. Since the stove sat a stone's throw away from her mattress, she'd been warm enough during the coldest winter nights.

That bed now filled a fair part of the floor space in Daniel's cabin. If Miriam were feeling any better, she ought to sleep in the cabin with the girls and have Daniel share the main house with his brothers. That wouldn't be wise tonight. She wasn't feeling up to tending the girls if they woke, and asking Daniel to give up his home and let Miriam sleep in Hannah's bed would likely set off his temper. No, tonight Miriam would have to sleep where she'd spent the previous night.

Gideon slowly rose and planned to carry her in, but she gained her feet and wrapped her arms about herself. He wondered whether she did it because she was cold or whether it was a subconscious way of comforting herself or guarding against the oppressive grief. Either way, he drew her into the lee of his body.

She fit there all too easily and molded her frame to his, making him aware again how fragile and soft women were. Somehow it felt good and right to have her in his arms, but just as quickly as that notion sneaked through his mind, he rejected it.

Bad enough they'd buried Mama and Hannah beneath the majestic pines over to the east of the house. Miriam was every bit as small as her sister had been. Two graves seemed like more than one ranch's fair share for such a short span of time. Sure as shooting, if Miriam stayed more than just a few days, she'd end up raising the count to three. This was no land for a delicate woman. Gideon resolved to hustle her out of here right quick.

"I'm s–sorry."

Her apology jarred him out of his grim decision making. "No, sweet pea. You've no call to beg my pardon," he said quietly. He hoped if he kept his tone low, he'd spare her a bit of throbbing in her head. "You have a tender heart is all." *That, and a body that's as vulnerable as your spirit.* "Let's tuck you in for the night."

He shortened his stride and led her back to the house. Only Paul was inside. He sat by the hearth, sharpening knives on a whetstone. He looked up, and his lips thinned as he took in Miriam's red eyes and nose. Gideon shook his head in a silent warning. Miriam didn't need anyone commenting on the obvious.

She eased away from his side and went to the washstand. For an instant, Gideon worried the pitcher would be empty as usual; but she lifted it, and fresh water trickled into the chipped porcelain basin. Of course. Of course Miss Miriam would have refilled it.

An odd impression struck him. She wasn't prissy about being tidy the way Hannah had been. The corners of Hannah's mouth seemed perpetually tightened, as if she disapproved of just about everything. Oh, she'd pitched in and done all the women's work. She'd been as sweet as honey to Daniel, too. No one would ever fault her on how loving she'd been to little Polly.

More than anything, Gideon came away with the feeling his brother's wife felt a tad put out with the fact of having more than just her own man to care for. He wasn't the only one who sensed her resentment, either. His brothers all yielded to Hannah's picky little preferences and allowed her some of her weepy days. After all, she'd been in a delicate condition nearly two of the three years she'd lived with them.

Then, too, a woman had a right to want a nest of her own. When Daniel appeared out of the blue with a wife, the brothers jumped in and built the cottage straightaway. Though Hannah and Daniel slept there, the fireplace was only sufficient for heat. During the winter, Hannah needed to do the laundry here in the big house, and she'd done the cooking here year-round. Mama always said cooking for two or ten didn't make much difference, but Gideon suspected Hannah would have disagreed.

So far, Miss Miriam didn't seem to mind stepping in front of a stove. Then again, it wasn't a permanent arrangement. She'd only be here a few brief days, so making fancy meals with all the fixings probably suited her. After being stuck on the sailing ship, having the freedom to decide what to eat might well be a treat to her.

Nonetheless, the first thing she'd done was set to sprucing up the place that first night. In his experience, when grief struck, folks did one of two things: They either took to their beds or lost themselves in their usual tasks. Resorting to habits and tasks helped them numb some of the impact of the sorrow. For her to have put her hand to such labor hinted that she was in the habit of keeping a tidy home. Orderliness seemed to be something that came deep from within—not the result of a rule she followed for the sake of being virtuous.

Watching her wash up felt wrong, so he turned away. When the soft splashing stopped, Gideon saw the frown on Paul's face and turned to see the cause. Miriam had folded her handkerchief, dampened it, and pressed the compress to her forehead as she braced herself against the washstand with the other hand. Her chin rested on her chest as if her head had grown too heavy to hold up.

Gideon closed the distance between them in a heartbeat. "Miss Miriam?"

She turned toward him, and he slipped his arms around her. Poor little gal had run out of steam. Even then, she didn't slump against him. Her hanky got his shirt damp as she whispered, "I know it's early yet, but would you mind too awfully much if I lie down?"

"It would bother me if you didn't." He stooped a bit, hooked an arm behind her knees, and lifted. Once he carried her behind the blanket-curtain in the back room, he set Miriam down and nudged her to sit on his bed. Taking pains to keep his voice low, he ordered, "You go on and get ready for bed. I'll see if I can rustle up some willow bark for your headache."

"That's very kind of you to offer," she half-whispered. "Truly, I believe sleep is all I need."

Later he went to peek in on her. She'd huddled into a ball and fallen asleep—but that knowledge brought him no relief, because the pillow and her cheeks were wet with more tears.

Being a man of the cloth, her father would have known the right things to say. Miriam needed flowery words of eternal peace and assurance. Gideon knew none of them. At the ripe old age of twenty-six, he reckoned he was far too old to learn them now.

In the morning, he'd check on how she felt and make plans to send her back home. To be sure, she'd need two, maybe even three days before he put her aboard a ship. It would let her come to grips with the fact that Hannah had passed on to the hereafter and also give Miriam a chance to play a bit with Polly and Ginny Mae. That way, she'd go back home with a few sweet memories to soften the blow.

He'd ask to see her ticket and make inquiries as to when that company had the next ship slated for departure. The ranch needed supplies. He'd take her back to the docks, and as soon as her ship set sail, he'd fill up the buckboard and bring back essentials. That way, he'd only miss one day's work instead of two.

Gideon came back out and took out a sheet of paper. He whittled the nib of his pen and set the inkwell on the clean tabletop. It was nice, sitting down to a clear writing surface. Fact was, the usual chaotic mess around the place didn't much register, let alone bother him, when it was there; but now that it was all cleared away, the uncluttered room felt. . .well, it felt different. Better. Homey. He shook his head. *That doesn't matter. Just make the list and go bed down in the barn.*

The next morning, Miriam had already gotten up and set coffee to perk on the stove before he even reached the house. The aroma wafting from the oven promised something delicious for breakfast, and she cracked eggs into a bowl with the efficient moves of a woman accustomed to cooking. She wore a plain slate blue day gown, and a white apron covered most of the front of it. Not a ruffle, speck of embroidery, or ribbon adorned either garment.

"Good morning," she greeted him in a subdued tone.

Gideon looked at her keenly. Was she whispering because her head hurt, or was she trying to stay quiet so his brothers could snatch a few last minutes of shut-eye? Either way, she wasn't supposed to have shown her face yet. "You're still supposed to be in bed."

She simply cocked her brow askance.

"How does your head feel?"

"Not as bad today." She set aside the eggs and ladled a little hot water from the stove's reservoir into a bowl. Soon the yeasty smell of bread dough mingled with the other aromas. Gideon felt awkward drinking coffee when she already had set herself to doing chores; still, it wasn't right to rob his brothers of the last bit of their sleep just because Miriam Hancock gave a rooster competition, racing for sunrise. He sat at the table and frowned. Someone had added several things to the bottom of his shopping list. Neatly penned as the letters were, he knew Miriam had taken it upon herself to get involved.

He squinted, then moved the paper a bit so he could read it more easily. *Tea, rolled oats, confectioners' sugar, cinnamon, nutmeg, oregano, paprika, curry, cloves, paraffin, pectin, four cards of shirt buttons, fabric—one half bolt white medium-weight cotton, one quarter bolt each of blue, brown heavyweight serge, and tan wool.*

"What's this?"

"It's a start. I'll add as I take stock of your supplies today. I can do without the curry and cloves if money is tight."

"You won't have time, Miriam."

"Time for what?" She sprinkled flour onto the far end of the table, dumped the bread onto the spot, and kneaded it with negligent ease. Dusted with flour, her hands still looked incapable of managing any but the simplest and lightest of tasks.

He cleared his throat and looked for a way to say what seemed almost cruel. "Hannah doesn't need your help anymore, Miriam. Your reason for coming no longer exists."

The heel of her hand sank into the dough and stretched it, then she pinched off a third of the big, fragrant white blob. A few deft flips of her hand shaped a portion of it into a loaf. She made the second loaf and started to form the remaining dough into a third when she said, "If anything, the reasons I came are more pressing now than when Hannah first penned them."

"You can't stay."

Chapter 7

Miriam blinked at him and thought she'd misheard. The state of affairs in this household was so appalling, the very idea of this man shoving away her help didn't make a speck of sense. Then she reasoned out what he was saying. "Of course I can't stay in the back bedchamber and occupy your bed," she agreed crisply. She hoped her cheeks didn't go pink at the fact that she'd already ousted him from his bed for two nights. "We'll have to come up with an alternative arrangement at once."

"The arrangement," he replied, glowering over the rim of his coffee mug, "is for you to romp with the girls for another day or so, then go back home."

She set her hands on her hips, not caring that she'd leave flour prints on her apron and dress. Flour would brush off easily enough, but she. . .she would not be brushed out of this home as if she were a bothersome gnat. Gideon Chance had best understand here and now that she'd not back away from duty. She locked gazes with him. "I'm not going to sail back to the islands."

"Listen, lady, I don't know what whim brought you here, but it's nothing more than that: a whim, and a plum crazy one at that."

Her jaw hardened, and she did her best to keep a civil tone as she informed him, "My sister's needs for assistance constituted a clear need, sir."

"Hannah must've written on a day she was just a tad blue. A woman in her, um. . ." He glanced down at the tabletop and mumbled, "Carrying months is entitled to a melancholy day or two."

Miriam, too, looked down and fiddled with the second loaf. Its shape was a bit off, so she evened it out as she struggled to reply. "Had only one letter been melancholy, we'd have understood; but Hannah was always a cheery soul, and though she mentioned kind things, in all but the first two letters, she couldn't hide her loneliness or the fact that help was necessary."

He folded his arms on the tabletop and leaned forward. His tone went hot. "Well get this, and get it good, Miss Miriam: We live on a ranch. It's not fancy, and we're not rich. We can't afford servants, and every last one of us sweats hard for what we have. Your sister made Daniel a happy man, and he did right by her each and every day. This is a harsh land. If it was too brutal for your sister, it's going to be just as miserable for you. You'd best go now."

"No."

His jaw jutted forward, and his eyes lit with temper. "Women don't belong here."

"Fancy that. In case you haven't reasoned it through yet, my nieces will become women."

"By then, things'll change."

Miriam barely leashed her anger. She punched the bread dough and turned her back just long enough to grab the loaf pans. She'd already greased them, so she dumped a loaf into each one and silently recited the books of the Bible to help her keep her temper. She set the loaf pans beside the stove, emphatically shook out a dishcloth to rest over them, and finally turned back toward Gideon. "I'll stay. I'll help things change."

"Now hang on here."

"That is precisely what I intend to do," she cut in with an icy smile.

"It's not fitting—"

"Oh, I agree. It's not fitting for my nieces to be reared in a pigsty. They've not been taught to say grace, their hair is uncombed, and they'll certainly learn no table manners if left to your brothers' care."

"Now you just hold it right there!"

Miriam stared at him. "Your younger brothers were imbibing devil's brew within the tainted walls of a house of ill repute when I arrived. Don't for one minute expect me to entrust the impressionable hearts and souls of my sister's daughters to men who have no morals or manners. I won't. I can't."

"No one asked your opinion."

"Mr. Chance, I'm afraid you simply don't understand." She looked at him and shook her head. "Girls need tutelage and tenderness. They need social graces and spiritual guidance."

"Every last one of us can read and cipher just fine. Those girls won't lack book learning. As for tenderness, every last one of us loves both of them to distraction, so you needn't fret over that."

"But their manners and morals?"

The muscles in his cheek started to twitch. "Lady, you've got a heap of gall, barging in here and judging us."

"I didn't barge. I was invited."

"Yeah, but Hannah did the inviting, and she isn't—" His voice came to an abrupt halt.

Miriam sucked in a sharp breath and let it out very slowly. "Here anymore," she finished. Her voice carried a taste of the woe she felt. She paused for a moment, then said, "And that is precisely why I must stay. In honor of her memory and as a tribute to the very principles she held inviolate, it falls upon me to make sure her daughters are reared in an appropriate and decent manner."

"You can't stay."

"You've already said as much, but I'm afraid you'll simply have to reconsider."

"Daniel—"

"Is grieving. I understand that. I've already promised not to wear any of my sister's clothing."

"It's not just the clothing."

She nodded. "I know Hannah and I look—" She caught herself, gulped a big breath, then forged ahead. "*Looked* quite similar. Seeing me must have been a terrible shock for him. I'll wear my hair differently, and that should help."

"Only a woman would come up with a silly plan like that." He waved his hand in a gesture of disgust. "Applying that boneheaded logic, as if slapping a different saddle on my mare would make her—"

"You're not," she interrupted, "comparing me to a horse, are you, Mr. Chance?"

"Now don't go pitching a hissy fit."

"I'm not given to having fits, sir. You're addressing that comment to the wrong person. Daniel is the one who has let his emotions sway behavior beyond reason. Nevertheless, I understand grief is to blame, and I'll manage to deal with it. By and by, he'll become accustomed to my presence."

Gideon cast a quick glance at the closed bedroom door. Miriam understood why. The last thing either of them wanted was for this to turn into a shouting match. His brothers didn't need to overhear this conversation at all. His voice lowered to a growl. "This is his home. You make him. . .uncomfortable."

Miriam stopped and looked at him. For a moment, their gazes held. "Mr. Gideon Chance, this isn't about what makes your brother comfortable. We're all bound to be uncomfortable for some time. I'm scarcely accustomed to any of this myself, but this is not about adults' feelings—it is about children's needs."

"Polly and Ginny Mae have all they need!"

She shook her head sadly. "I'm afraid that simply proves my point. They are warm and fed, but the same can be said of your horses and hounds. Why, when I took the laundry down from the line last evening, Polly claimed the smallest man's shirts as her own dresses!"

Gideon's neck and ears went ruddy.

"At first, I could scarcely credit it, but then I took stock of the clothing, and I realized my niece was wearing the only dress she owns! Pardon me if I'm drawing the wrong conclusion, but as far as I can tell, you men let that little girl run about in a man's shirt. How could you allow such a travesty?"

"Travesty? It's no travesty. Bryce and Logan outgrew those shirts. It's shameful to waste."

"Shameful! Why, you cannot mean—"

"They serve Polly just fine." He glowered at her. "Besides, who's going to see her but us, anyhow?"

His assertions left her spluttering. The matter was far from closed in her opinion. He wasn't about to have her dictate his family's ways; she refused to leave her sweet little nieces alone with a band of barely civilized men. He folded his arms akimbo.

"Best you forget these opinions and wild notions about staying, Miss Miriam. For the next few days, you'd do well to rest. You're looking peaked, and that won't make for a very good voyage."

"Voyage?"

"Home," he asserted. His head nodded, as if to paint an exclamation mark in the air to punctuate his feelings. "We'll just trade in your return ticket for an earlier departure."

"What return ticket?"

Chapter 8

"What return ticket?" Gideon echoed for the dozenth time as he went out to work with the horses. He smacked his gloves against the fence post and tamped down the urge to bellow in outrage. He wanted to shake the teeth right out of Miriam's pretty head. How could she have come halfway around the world and planned to stay? Her father must be daft, sending her to Hannah. Hannah was only a tad bit older, so expecting her to shield Miriam from the real world and shelter her from harm was utter nonsense. In essence, they expected Daniel to shoulder that burden—but Daniel was in no shape to do so, and Gideon wasn't at all eager to fill those shoes.

"How much does a trip to the islands cost?" he wondered aloud. He moaned. Money was tight. Real tight. They had enough for provisions but not enough for frills. He yanked on his right glove. Faced with being strapped for another year or getting saddled with a prissy missionary's daughter, he'd go for the lesser of the two evils. Miriam would have to go—and soon.

Real soon.

Moments after his brothers had gotten up, they started grumbling. Paul finally stuck his head around the bedroom door. "Where the. . .uh, Titus and I can't find our shirts, and Bryce's britches up and disappeared."

"I'm responsible for the missing garments," Miriam confessed. Her tone was so conciliatory, Gideon knew he'd underestimated the scope of the problem. This woman had her heart set on staying, and she'd give in, make sacrifices, and bend over backward to convince his brothers that she belonged here. A shy smile flitted across her face as she continued. "When I took the laundry off the line last evening, I kept out the articles of clothing that require mending. Could you possibly make do with what you have? I'll be sure to catch up on the mending today."

After Paul managed to shut his gaping mouth, he stammered, "That's right kind of you, ma'am. I mean, miss. We'd all be obliged. Much obliged. Truly. None of us is any good with a needle."

At breakfast, she set stuff on the table the likes of which Gideon and his brothers hadn't tasted in years. His brothers were voluble in their appreciation and approval. Mama loved to cook like this; Hannah had made fair meals but never much pushed herself past doing plain fare.

Miriam hadn't just scrambled eggs and made biscuits. She hadn't gone the extra step and whipped up a pan of white gravy. Oh, no. Miss I'm-Here-to-Stay pulled out all the stops. She'd chopped up bits of ham, onions, and tomatoes into the eggs. As if that wasn't enough to make all of their taste buds take notice, she opened the door of the oven and pulled out a pan of coffee cake. The aroma steaming off it had Gideon reaching for a piece as soon as she put it on the table.

An hour later, trying to forget about breakfast and concentrate on work, Gideon remembered the way she'd fleetingly rested her hand on his shoulder so she could refill Logan's and his coffee cups. Her touch had been innocent and brief as could be, but when she moved on toward Paul and Titus, he'd wanted to yank her back and check to see if he'd been imagining the sweet smell of flowers clinging to her.

Disgusted at himself, Gideon pulled on his left glove and muttered under his breath, "Half-wits. My own brothers are a bunch of no-good, belly-rubbin' half-wits. If she thinks she's gonna buy her way into this family on our just-mended shirtsleeves or through our stomachs, she's got another thing a-comin'!"

Dinner reinforced her good standing with his brothers. She'd made corn bread and fancied up the beans she'd been soaking with hunks of side meat. She'd picked cabbage from the garden, sliced it into thin shreds, and mixed all sorts of stuff with it. The stuff could coax every last apostle out of heaven for want of a taste.

She didn't eat with them, either. She and Polly had held a tea party a short while earlier. While the men ate, Miriam lifted Polly up on a chair. The puzzling woman pulled a measuring tape from the sewing bag she'd brought in her trunk. Tan his sorry hide, Logan had unearthed a stack of feed and flour sacks, and Miriam went so far as to promise Polly she could choose whichever she fancied for her new dress. While she and Polly chattered like magpies about a pretty new frock, Daniel's eyes shot sparks that could ignite a forest fire. All of the other brothers lapped up the food like a pack of starving wolves.

Gideon knew he had to do something—quickly.

Gideon stepped into the cabin for supper, unsure whether to anticipate or dread what was to come. Miss Miriam had missed her calling in life. The woman could plot until she had a man twisting in circles. Had she been born a man, she'd certainly have attended West Point and become a military strategist. *And that means she wouldn't be sashaying around here, wearing that flowery scent and ugly dress and driving me half daft.*

"What have you been doing today?" Logan asked their little niece as he tugged on the ribbon tying off one of her freshly washed, neatly plaited pigtails.

"Auntie Miri-Em fixed all of the shirts. She putted lotsa buttons on 'em. And she hided all of the holes so they all gone." She paused for effect, then hiked up the hem of the dress she was wearing to show off layers of white ruffles underneath. "Looky! Auntie Miri-Em maded me panty-lettes."

Logan let out a hearty laugh.

Gideon cast a glance over at Miriam. She'd turned back to the stove, but he could see the curve of her cheek. A rosy hue that hadn't been there moments before tinted it now.

Thoroughly entertained, Bryce let out a wolf whistle and waggled his brows. "Aren't you just the prettiest little fashion plate?"

"I not a plate," Polly huffed in obvious dismay. She patiently pointed at the table. "Plates is on the table. Panty-lettes is on me."

The way she hiked up her hem to display her fancy little girl drawers to illustrate the second part of her assertion was downright funny. Gideon chuckled under his breath.

Miriam cleared her throat and said in a slightly croaky tone, "Polly, you may come be my best helper now. Put the bread on the table."

"Goody!" Polly stopped making a show of her unmentionables and galloped over to her aunt. White ruffles stuck out from beneath her hem, making what had been a too-short-to-be-decent dress look acceptable. Gideon wouldn't admit he thought it looked utterly charming—even if it was kind of girly. He also didn't want to admit that once Polly was out of diapers, they hadn't bothered to put her into any undergarments. White's Mercantile sold men's long johns, but they didn't have a thing for kids. Asking Reba White to special order something for Polly was one of those awkward things that somehow managed to slip the Chance brothers' minds when they went to town.

Polly wound her arms around Miriam's skirts for a quick hug, then looked up expectantly. Miriam stooped and gave Polly a basket full of sliced bread. She murmured something softly to the girl, then asked, "Understand?"

"No," Polly retorted in her clear, high voice that carried well. She frowned at Miriam and tilted her head to the side. "How come a lady is 'posed to wear her panty-lettes, but she can't talk 'bout them? My panty-lettes is so pretty!"

That did it. Gideon succumbed to the temptation. He threw back his head and roared. Miriam looked so disconcerted, he couldn't help it.

Daniel sat off in the corner, glowering. Gideon wasn't sure whether his levity or Miriam's prissy ways caused his brother to look like he'd been sucking on lemons. Paying attention to his surly ways wouldn't change them. *It's a temporary situation,* Gideon told himself as he stopped laughing. *Miriam will be gone in no time at all.*

As if she knew what he was thinking, Miriam used all the strategy of a general and the wiles of a woman. She put supper on the table. Everything was done at the same time, and she managed to coordinate her moves so efficiently, she didn't get in a dither while juggling platters, bowls, and the like. In a matter of moments, rich, thick, my-mouth-died-and-went-to-heaven chicken stew and her light-as-clouds bread graced the supper table. A colorful dish with whacked-up tomatoes, cucumbers, onions, and bits of herbs looked like something a fancy chef would serve at an expensive San Francisco restaurant. How she managed to knock around in their kitchen and garden and concoct such mouthwatering meals was a total mystery. No matter who cooked, none of the Chance men ever managed to create anything half as appealing.

"Supper is ready, gentlemen," she announced.

Gideon wanted to wallop his brothers. She hadn't even finished the sentence, and they were falling all over each other to reach the table. He intentionally waited a minute before taking his customary place at the head of the table.

Titus sprang up, pulled out a chair, and said, "Here you go, Miss Miriam."

"Thank you," she said. . .or simpered. Gideon wasn't sure whether she was genuine in her gratitude or trying to wrap Titus around her little finger.

Miriam claimed Polly again. They folded their hands, and the brothers fell into a chagrined silence. They'd already started to dig in. Spoons froze halfway to mouths, then were lowered down to rest in the bowls as Polly's uncles heard the little tyke singsong a prayer all by herself. Good sports that they were, they all chimed in on the "Amen."

Daniel kept hold of Ginny Mae, but he had his hands full, trying to keep her from sticking her fingers into his bowl. Miriam reached over, scooted his bowl farther to the right, and grabbed a small tin plate from the center of the table. That plate had tiny bites of chicken, vegetables, and little fingers of buttered bread on it. They were all the perfect size for Ginny Mae to pinch with her chubby baby fingers and eat all by herself. Miriam set the plate down in front of the baby, but she said nothing.

"Well looky there," Bryce said. "Hannah used to do that for Polly."

Daniel's head swiveled sharply toward Bryce. His eyes burned like coals. Bryce stared at his brother for a long moment, then cleared his throat. "I do believe I need the butter for my bread." He jabbed Titus in the ribs. "Gimme the butter."

Gideon wasn't sure whom to kick under the table first: Daniel for being mean as a chained bear or Bryce for sticking his foot in his mouth yet again.

The plate was a good idea. He hadn't spied it because it was on the other side of a canning jar filled with wildflowers. The last time they'd had flowers in the house was when Hannah was still alive. She'd gotten a fistful of them and spoken wistfully about the big, fragrant blossoms back home. It hadn't occurred to him that she was homesick; but as he thought back, that would have been about the time she'd written to invite Miriam to come. Besotted as Daniel was, all of them figured he kept Hannah happy. The fact that she'd been carrying a second child so quickly certainly reinforced the notion she felt every bit as contented about her life and marriage as Daniel was.

Gideon paused, his spoon halfway up to his mouth. He'd not thought about Hannah for months. She'd been like a rainbow—pretty but fleeting. Insubstantial. Foul as Daniel's mood had grown, if he knew his brothers were thinking of his wife, he'd have spoiled for a nasty fistfight.

As for Miriam. . .well, Gideon vowed to be sure she and her trunks made it on the very next voyage back toward her parents. At the moment, her luggage occupied a chunk of the floor over by the window. She'd pulled her outfit today from the larger of the two trunks.

An uncharitable thought arced across his mind. For being a pretty gal, Miss Miriam sure worked hard at looking homely. He'd held her. He knew her shape. It had plenty to recommend it to the opposite gender. Instead of fancying up that slate job with a lacy collar, fancy buttons, or doodads, she'd left it painfully plain. She'd proven she could wield a needle with great skill, so why did her gown bag a bit on her? Had she been ailing? Had she lost weight?

He sent the bowl of the fancy salad her way after taking a generous second helping. "You'd best eat up, Miss Miriam. From the way your gown fits, I'd guess you had a bit of trouble keeping your meals down on the voyage here. We'll need to fatten you up in the next few days 'til you leave."

"Leave!" Logan half-shouted.

"You're going? Say it isn't so," Bryce said. To Gideon's disgust, his brother looked like a lovesick calf.

"I—"

"She has to go," Gideon cut in before Miriam grabbed the chance to put in her two cents' worth.

Paul scowled. "She just got here."

"Yes, I did. Since this involves me, I—"

"Ought to stay," Titus finished for her as he set down his coffee mug with a decisive *thump*. "It's downright cruel to stick her back aboard a vessel this quick. We've all heard how difficult a voyage is, and she's not even rested up and recovered."

Daniel glared at her. "She can lie in her berth day and night if she's all that worn out."

What little color Miriam's face held seeped away. "I refuse to be locked in a cabin for weeks on end again!"

"Locked in a cabin!" Logan and Paul bellowed in outrage together.

"Now, Miss Miriam," Gideon said through gritted teeth, "there's no need to stretch the truth here."

"Oh, I'm not stretching it one bit. Two days out of port, Captain Raithly locked me into the first mate's cabin. I didn't see sky again until the day we docked."

"He didn't do it unless you deserved to be punished," Daniel snapped.

Miriam recoiled as if his words packed a physical blow. Her eyes and voice radiated hurt. "Daniel, what did I ever do to deserve your judgment and condemnation?"

Daniel glared at Gideon and slammed his fist down on the table. "I told you to get rid of her."

Polly climbed into her aunt's lap. She managed to smear food across the slate bodice, and she clung to Miriam's sleeve. Tears slipped down her cheeks. "Please don't go, Auntie Miri-Em."

Miriam kissed Polly's forehead, then gave Gideon a pleading look.

The sight of her cuddling Polly close, the way she naturally smoothed and fingered her niece's little curls, the spill of dainty white ruffles on a child who had never owned anything frilly—they tugged at his heart. He and his brothers had somehow slipped up and not tended to some of the finer points of rearing a girl. *But now that we know, we can do it.*

"Auntie Miri-Em, I need you!"

"I'll stay just as long as you need me," she pledged.

"You're going," Gideon asserted. *How dare she invite herself, then announce she is going to move in and take over matters and make decisions?* That proved the point: Miriam Hancock had to leave before she tried to change and rule their comfortable world. "I said we'd buy the stupid ticket!"

"Gideon Chance, you'll watch your attitude and language!"

He glowered at her. "The last thing I need is some prissy, holier-than-thou, missionary girl telling me what to do at my own table."

Miriam let out a long sigh. "Very well. I'll give you options to fulfill that requirement. Either I'll take possession of the cottage and take my meals there—"

"Don't you step foot in my home again." Daniel's voice rivaled a thunderclap.

She lifted her chin. Her eyes didn't snap with temper, and her jaw didn't jut forward with stubbornness, either. Gideon had to give her credit, because her eyes didn't even well up with tears. For being a woman, she had remarkable self-control. "Since that choice does not suit, I'll simply take the girls back on the ship with me."

Daniel lurched to his feet with a loud roar. "No!" He kept hold of Ginny Mae in one arm and whisked Polly out of Miriam's hold with the other. "We don't want you, and we don't need you. Get out of here. Get out of our home and lives."

Bryce hopped up. "Don't you talk that way to her! If you wasn't holding the girls right now, I'd bust your chops."

Gideon had been on his feet and about to say something similar. He caught himself before he made a buffoon of himself. *Here I am, about to be her champion, yet I want her gone.* The sight of his smallest brother, a mere teen, standing up to a full-grown man angered him. "Enough of this. We're not coming to blows or having a brawl. I made a decision. It stands."

Awkward silence filled the room. Ginny Mae smacked her little hand over Daniel's chest. "Daddy, Daddy, Daddy."

Daniel's expression qualified as purely malevolent as he spoke to Miriam. "She knows whom she belongs to, and it isn't you." He turned to Gideon. "Get rid of her. Today."

They watched Daniel as he stomped to the door, went out, and kicked it shut with a vengeance. Gideon managed not to wince.

"Gideon," Paul said.

"What now?"

Paul folded his arms across his chest. That move always warned Gideon his brother was about to render an unwanted opinion.

"You're not going to drain our savings to buy Miriam's ticket on a ship. You have no right to make that kind of financial commitment without consulting us."

"Yeah," Titus agreed. "We all do a fair share of the work. This is a voting issue."

"Excuse me, please. If you'll allow me a moment, I should absent myself from the table until this is settled." Miriam slipped from the table, took something from the oven, and set it on the table, then went out the door.

Gideon looked at the table and groaned.

Chapter 9

Gingerbread. Miriam had made gingerbread. Gideon's mouth watered as he said, "You're Daniel's brothers and owe him your support and allegiance. He loved the daylights out of Hannah. He doesn't want to be saddled with her kid sister. It's a big responsibility, and we're all doing far too much already."

"She helps, Gideon," Bryce said in a wheedling tone. "She cooks and cleans and watches the girls. She's not a burden."

"The girls need a woman's touch," Paul said thoughtfully. "Dan's not making any bones about how upset he is, but Dan is. . .Dan. He'll get over it."

"You're not sure of that at all," Gideon countered. "He carries a grudge worse than a gypped cardsharp."

Logan shrugged. "Tough luck. You got a good gander at Polly. We love her and Ginny Mae to pieces, but Miriam's already doin' things for her we can't. Seems to me, as time passes, it's going to be more important to have a woman around to tend to female-type matters."

"That's years down the road," Gideon countered. He tried like anything to ignore the aroma of the gingerbread. "By then, one of us will probably have married."

"And is Dan going to buck like a bronc then, too?" Bryce asked. "It's been ten months since Hannah passed over. I'm not saying that's all that long, but I do think he'd better learn he has to go on living. He's not thinking of his girls—he's thinking of hisself."

Titus cleared his throat. "You asked us to think of Daniel, Gideon. Well, I am. I think we have to save him from himself. All of us already stepped in and helped with those girls because he can't do it all on his own. This is another one of those times when we're going to have to intervene."

"Think this through. Where in the world does she sleep? What in thunder are we going to do with a single woman underfoot?" Gideon realized it sounded like he was weakening. He immediately tacked on, "No, it's all wrong. She has to go."

"That's your vote," Titus said. "We all know where Daniel stands on this. I say she stays."

"She stays," Bryce and Logan said in unison.

Gideon turned to Paul. "Don't vote until you think this through. I didn't make a snap decision. I've been thinking it over from the very start."

Rare were the times things came up for a vote. Gideon usually made the decisions. Because he shouldered that responsibility, they'd agreed if a vote ever came to a tie, he'd make a final determination. If Paul voted for Miriam to go, it would be a tie, so Gideon's decision would stand. If Paul sided with the others, they'd be saddled with a fussy little snip of a woman until she, too, sickened and died.

Paul was the quiet brother. Thoughtful. Did more reading. His cautious nature had stood them in good stead more than once. He ambled to the windows—the windows Miriam had cleaned—and looked out. "Have you ever wondered what it would have been like if Mama died instead of Dad? We'd have kept the old ranch, but that old ranch house would have felt so empty. Mama made the house a home. Even here, rough as this was, she set out her quilts and stuck wildflowers on the table. Hannah did that, too, and it did us all good."

And Miriam's already started nesting like a sparrow, too. Gideon glanced at the colorful bouquet on the table.

Paul turned back around. "Polly and Ginny won't remember their mama. There aren't three decent women within a day's ride. Someone's got to teach them to pick posies, cook, and quilt."

"If we couldn't keep Polly in drawers and a dress," Logan said, "we sure won't train her or Ginny Mae up so they'll be good women."

Gideon groaned. *This is a nightmare!*

"Gideon's right," Logan said. "There's gonna be plenty of trouble, keeping her here. Dan's likely to splavocate. Furthermore, we're not gonna be able to shower in the rain or talk without censoring our words."

For a second, Gideon perked up. *The tide might turn. Logan's changing his mind.*

A breath later, Logan dashed his hopes by finishing his thought: "Then again, with the girls gettin' older, those things would have to come about sooner or later, anyhow."

"Let me grab the bull by the horns," Gideon said. "If you're worried about the money—"

"Yeah, money is another consideration," Paul admitted. "We've got enough to see us through. We've already lost one ranch 'cause Dad borrowed on it. We know he paid back the money, but bankers are good about losing vital papers, and I don't trust Pete Rovel over at the bank."

"Nuh-unh," Titus chimed in. "Not any more than I'd trust a riled polecat not to spray. We empty out the account to buy a ticket and have even one disaster, and Pete's going to own this ranch."

"You're not saying anything I haven't already thought."

"Let me give you one more thing to consider." Paul looked back out the window. "Miriam doesn't want to go back. I doubt it's because life with her parents kept her miserable. Hannah constantly reminisced about how perfect everything was back on the islands."

He swung back around and stared at Gideon. "Miriam was locked in her cabin the whole voyage here. Think about how plum-outta-her-mind scared she was of us at first. How she fought and reminded us it was a sin. Locking her up was cruel as could be, but it was the only way the captain could protect her. She doesn't realize just how lucky she was that he kept her imprisoned. It's been years, but Dan still won't say a word about what went on aboard the ship when he was shanghaied. It was a harsh life for him, and he's a strapping man. What kind of men would we be to put her—a lone, pretty, tenderhearted woman—back aboard a ship full of the dregs of mankind?"

Logan gloated, "The vote stands four to two. Miss Miriam's stayin' put."

Gideon accepted the vote. Though he didn't want the responsibility of having a woman around, his brothers were more than right—the babies needed a woman's touch, and sticking Miriam back on a ship would be a low-down move.

He left the house but wasn't sure where to look for her. The woman didn't have a place to go. He craned his neck to see the graves, but she wasn't there. Since he'd found her in the garden once before, he headed back there. Though the garden lay empty, Gideon spied her sitting on a corral fence. He strode over to her.

Miriam didn't bother to turn around. She hunched forward and had her arms wrapped around herself. The evening air felt a trifle chilly. Gideon scowled. "You left without your shawl."

She nodded in acknowledgment.

"We'll see how things work out, but for now, we'll let you stay."

Slowly she turned to look over her shoulder at him. Even in the meager moonlight, he expected to see her gloating smile. Instead, she looked as somber as a priest. "I'll do my best to help the girls and stay out of your way."

That was what he wanted her to say. Why didn't it make him happy to hear it?

"Could you please tell Daniel I'll try hard to avoid him?"

He nodded. "We'll knock together a cottage for you. It'll be about a week before we can get to it, though. Someone's tacking blankets to make a space for you so you can sleep closer to the stove and be warm enough in the meantime."

"Gideon?"

"Yeah?"

"I'm sorry I chided you about your language in front of the others. In the future, if I have a problem, I'll try to speak to you privately."

"Fine. It's too chilly out here for you. Go on inside."

The next morning, Miriam hastily put her hair up into a respectable bun. After tying the blanket-curtain out of the way with a bit of twine, she set to work. She stoked the fire, had coffee going, and fried her own ham and egg. She'd finished her meal and had the rest of the eggs all scrambled and ready to cook before any of the men came out of the bedroom.

They sat on the benches around the table and yanked on their boots. Miriam had already filled both pitchers with hot water.

Logan started to take the pitcher back to the bedroom.

"Logan," Miriam called softly, "in the islands, the men almost never wear shirts. The bedroom is already crowded, else you wouldn't have had the washstand out here. I'm not offended if you men shave here."

She turned her back on them and finished cooking breakfast. Two at a time, the brothers washed and shaved. Boot scuffle, razor scrape, a chuckle, a splash, and a mixture of Bryce's silliness and Titus's early morning grumpy responses filled the cabin.

Miriam caught sight of Gideon's black eye and gasped. The set of his jaw and the way he stared at her dared her to comment. She bit her lip and turned away. *I came to help my sister, but I'm turning brother against brother.* She swallowed hard, then took her lead from him. If he wanted to pretend nothing had happened, she could play that game. . .up to a point.

Miriam set the meal on the table, then took the egg basket and left. She hoped Daniel and the girls would slip in during her absence. She also prayed the other brothers landed on Daniel so he'd behave. Bad enough he was nasty to her; he had no call to take his temper out on Gideon.

After all, Gideon didn't want her here any more than Daniel did.

Waking up to the smell of coffee and sizzling ham posed no hardship. Walking out to see a comely woman at the stove struck Gideon as pleasant enough. The matter-of-fact tone she used in commenting on shirtless men astonished him, seeing as she acted downright shy with his brothers most of the time. Come to think of it, he was the only one she ever looked in the eye. Miriam Hancock seemed more puzzling each day.

The sick look on her face when she saw his black eye let him know she was a sympathetic woman. Intuitive, too, since she'd not breathed a word about it. He hoped she wouldn't say a thing to Daniel.

Daniel didn't show up for breakfast at all. Polly skipped in all by herself. "Daddy said we get a picnic. Somebody's 'posed to put breakfas' in a basket."

Gideon turned to the side so the little one wouldn't see his shiner. Paul stepped up to block the view. "You skip right back and tell your daddy someone will bring the picnic in just a jiffy."

Bryce stuck food in a crate and carried it to the door. Gideon ordered, "Tell Dan he shows up and sits at the table, or he doesn't eat. He'll act civil, too."

A rascal's smile lit Bryce's face. "I don't expect that's going to be much of a problem for very long. Cold eggs and a jar of colder coffee won't suit him one bit."

"What about the coffee cake and ham?"

"I reckon the rest of us forgot Dan hadn't gotten his portion yet. It's all gone."

"I see."

"Yeah. Does Dan's face match yours?"

Gideon shook his head once, decisively. "Not with the babies around. One of us had to be smart enough to stay in control."

It was Daniel's day to watch the girls. The rest of the brothers got to work. Gideon rode out and inspected fences. No need to keep an eye out for trees they could fell to use for Miriam's cottage—Dan's way of handling his anger and grief had been to chop down trees and keep them in firewood. An enormous pile of logs was stacked behind the barn—more than enough for Miriam's cabin and to expand the barn to twice its width.

Thinking of a cabin for Miriam tightened Gideon's jaw. He'd been outvoted, and he'd live with the decision. But he didn't have to like it. Being responsible for a woman—and a bitty one at that—didn't set well. He'd been careful to make sure that though they didn't eat fancy foods, the girls always had plenty of good, healthy meals, sunshine, and thick blankets. They were hearty little snippets, but accustomed to tropical weather and an exotic diet, Miriam didn't have the same physical reserve. Maybe he ought to put a little potbelly in her cabin. That way, she could make some tea during the winter to warm up from the inside out, too. Besides, a little stove would save them the time of collecting stones and building a fireplace.

By chance, he spied Todd Dorsey. Though neighbors, they often didn't see each other until they went to town. Todd tipped back his hat. "Heard tell you've got Hannah's sister visitin' and she's quite a looker."

"Miss Hancock is spending time with her nieces."

"You could be sociable and give me an invite for supper. A woman's cooking and company would be welcome." The whole time he spoke, he studied Gideon's shiner. "Must be a real pretty sight if you men are coming to blows over her."

Gideon hitched a shoulder.

"She visitin', or is she stayin'?"

"For the time being, she's staying. You can pass the word that we'll be raising a cabin for her come Friday."

"Friday, huh? That's quick."

"Chances were never men to jaw around when work needed doing." Gideon jerked the front of his hat brim lower on his forehead and rode off.

Todd Dorsey's interest served as fair warning. Men in Reliable were woman-hungry. The storekeeper and his wife had a daughter of marriageable age, but they were the only decent women in the whole of the township. The rest of the place consisted of men struggling to tame enough land to finally bring families out or to start a family, but the greatest number of men fell into the latter category. They'd gotten squared away enough, and they were itching to have a decent meal and a dainty missus.

"I'll get Paul to put a steer on the spit. Barbecue's decent enough meal," Gideon muttered to himself as he squinted toward the house. "As for a decent missus, the men are going to have to search elsewhere. I'm going to have to watch out for that obstinate woman until she finally sees reason and decides to go back where she came from."

"Men coming Friday." Gideon bit into a rib and tore off a big hunk of meat with his teeth yet still managed to add, "Building a cabin—a little one."

Miriam barely kept from dropping the bowl of mashed potatoes on the table.

"No need to." Daniel glowered at Gideon. "This is a very temporary situation."

"You never could tell time." Gideon shot him a smile, then took another bite.

I've managed to set brother against brother. That fact made Miriam seek a way to make peace between them, but she knew she was the worst person to intervene. Gideon wouldn't appreciate her meddling, and Daniel wanted nothing to do with her, let alone her opinion.

Bryce stuck his elbow on the table and rested his sand-papery chin in a sauce-splotched hand. "If you two was dogs, I'd knock your heads together and dunk you in the trough to cool you off."

Logan grabbed a rib from Daniel's plate and bit into it. "I'd help him. I'd hold you under longest, Dan. You got some nerve, coming to the supper table and eatin' a woman's good cookin' when you're speaking ill of her."

"I didn't say anything about her at all." Daniel reached over and swiped back the rib. He scowled at the missing chunk.

"She has a name, and you'll use it." Gideon's voice rivaled a thunderclap. "You'll help build Miriam's cabin, too."

"Daddy, Auntie Miri-Em maded me pretty panty-lettes. Are you going to make her a pretty house?"

"Eat your supper, Polly."

It didn't escape Miriam's notice that Daniel avoided answering the question. She served herself a small dollop of potatoes and passed them on.

"Daddy says we don't get taters very much 'cause they used them all to make our fireplace." Polly smiled at Miriam. The rib the little girl had been nibbling from the center had hit both sides of her cherubic cheeks, painting her face with clownlike charm.

"Your fireplace?"

Polly nodded. "Daddy picked them out of the ground and piled them. Up, up, up!" She raised her messy little hands high. "Mama made gravy and poured it over the taters, then Daddy builded a great big fire."

"Imagine!" Miriam could scarcely fathom Daniel concocting such a tale.

"Turned those potatoes rock hard," Bryce chimed in.

"So no one can take a nibble out of them." Gideon gave Polly a pointed look and shook his head from side to side.

Her little head wagged in agreement. "We gots to leave the 'tato stones all alone."

Miriam looked from brother to brother. Daniel glowered at her, the rest looked rather sheepish, but Gideon—he simply gazed into her eyes. She said, "A grand fireplace like that would warm hands and hearts."

Gideon's lips relaxed into a heart-melting smile.

"Unca Gideon, how come you didn't wash your face? Auntie Miri-Em says we gotta wash 'fore we eat."

"It's an ouchie."

He told the truth, but he didn't implicate Daniel. Gideon's an honorable man.

"Auntie Miri-Em kissed my ouchie finger today and maded it all better." Polly licked her finger and held it up to prove her point.

Bryce and Logan started to snicker.

Polly pointed at Gideon's eye. "Ask Auntie Miri-Em to kiss your eye all better."

Gideon's brows rose. He turned toward Miriam.

He wouldn't. He couldn't.

The corner of his mouth took on an impish slant. "Well, Miss Miriam?"

Chapter 10

The man is a rascal. Miriam handed her napkin to her little niece. "Polly, you should kiss your uncle better. Here. Wipe your face first."

"Why? You're closer." Polly gave her a puzzled look.

Gideon's brothers all started to chuckle—well, all except for Daniel. Daniel finished ripping the last bite of the rib from the bone and concentrated on his plate.

Mortified, Miriam stammered.

"It's not going to hurt anything," Paul said in a stage whisper.

Miriam rose from the table. "Does anyone else want more coffee?" Just as she turned away, she brushed a fleeting kiss on Gideon's temple and scampered to the stove, sure her face was hotter than the coffeepot.

Mirth filled Logan's voice. "Gideon'll take a refill, but he's had all the sugar he needs now."

Gideon cleared his throat. "Sugar's on the list of supplies we need. I'll go to town tomorrow. Anything anyone needs?"

"Whaddya doin', Giddy?" Bryce flopped down on the back porch. Within seconds, two dogs and the barn cat all vied for his attention.

Gideon surveyed the yard and continued to stare at it. "I'm making plans."

"Plans for what?" Bryce scratched Nip between his ears.

"A cabin."

Bryce's face lit up. "You weren't kidding. I hoped not. Tell me—you gonna marry Miss Miriam?"

"Whatever put that foolish notion in your head?" Gideon glowered at him.

"Well, we built a cabin for Daniel when he married up with Hannah. I just thought you were lookin' to have a place to share with your missus, too."

"I'm not marrying her." Gideon fought the urge to add on to that assertion.

"If you ask me, that's a crying shame."

"I didn't ask you."

Bryce proceeded to check the hounds' ears for ticks. As he tilted his head to do the job, he drawled, "Miss Miriam's a fine cook and does a right nice job with the girls. Seems to me, somebody ought to marry up with her so's she doesn't get stars in her eyes for some other fellow and leave us."

The notion of not having to worry about Miriam appealed to Gideon, but the notion of her falling in love with anyone gave him indigestion. "None of the men hereabouts would be suitable for a lady like Miss Miriam."

"You tryin' to convince me or yourself?" Bryce got up and dusted off the seat of his britches.

Gideon ignored the question. "While I go to town today, I want the area between Daniel's and the house leveled. It needs to be ready for Friday."

"Fair enough."

After Bryce sauntered off, Gideon recalled last night's supper. His brothers were big teases, and Hannah never appreciated their rowdy ways at the table, but Miriam didn't seem upset in the least by chuckles and jibes. . .except when it came to the kiss. The gal's face went redder than a cardinal when Polly asked her about the kiss. *I don't know what came over me, letting the joke go on.* But Miriam didn't get snippy. Light and quick as a butterfly, her lips grazed his temple, and she'd flitted off. *The gal has gumption.*

Titus's early morning growl of a yawn and Paul's deep chuckle came from inside the house. Threaded among those was a foreign sound. Gideon strained for a moment, then closed his eyes as the hymn Miriam sang so quietly reached him.

"When darkness seems to hide His face, I rest on His unchanging grace. In every high and stormy gale, my anchor holds within the veil."

Paul joined in, "On Christ the solid rock I stand. . . ."

Gideon couldn't recall the last time anyone sang. Well, yes, he could. Titus had a habit of humming and whistling—but not singing. Hannah used to hum to Polly every now and again. Before that, Mama sang. In fact, she had a special fondness for this particular hymn. Mama couldn't sing worth two hoots. Miriam actually made listening a pleasure. Come to think of it, Paul had a decent voice, too.

Funny how even after not having heard this hymn for years, Gideon still recalled the lyrics. He had plenty to do, but he just stayed put and let the song play out.

The door to Daniel's cottage opened. Polly scampered across the yard, her hair a tangled mess. *I wouldn't have noticed that fact before Miriam came.*

Daniel held Ginny Mae and strode over. She seemed a mite unhappy, and he kept patting her on the back. "If you're going to town, get some paregoric. I can't tell whether she's teething or colicky, but she was up half the night."

"Breakfast is ready," Miriam said from the kitchen door. Polly already clung to her skirts, and Miriam tentatively reached for Ginny. "Food's on the table. Why don't you go ahead and enjoy a hot meal?"

Shifting Ginny to his other side, Daniel clipped, "Only takes one hand to eat." He shoved past Miriam and went inside.

"Daddy gots two hands," Polly said as if it were an important fact.

"Yes, he does." Miriam playfully tapped her on the nose. "So do you, and yours need washing before you eat."

Gideon went to the table and gave Daniel a dark look. This situation was going to come to a head sooner or later, but now wasn't the time. Paul bowed his head and said grace. It was short and to the point, but it was the first time any of the brothers had communed openly with the Almighty in well over a year.

Forking four thick slices of French toast onto his plate, Gideon declared, "This smells terrific."

"Do we got bacon today?" Polly climbed onto her chair. She poked at the bacon on her plate. "Daddy, see? It's not burned."

Daniel's face remained impassive.

A few minutes later, Polly shoved her plate away. "I don't like it. It's yucky."

Everyone looked to Daniel to handle his daughter's rudeness. He simply picked up his coffee and took a long swig.

"I like it just fine." Gideon reached over, speared a bite from her plate with his fork, and ate it.

"Me, too." Titus and Paul did likewise.

"I want sumpin' else."

"What you're going to get," Gideon said very quietly, "is time in the corner. Naughty little girls aren't allowed to sit at the table."

"Auntie Miri-Em sits at the table. Daddy said she's bad."

Abruptly all movement and noise ceased at the table.

"We're all bad sometimes," Miriam said tentatively. She took a shallow breath, then continued. "Jesus understands. We tell Him we're sorry, and He forgives us."

"That's enough." Daniel bolted to his feet. The brusque action set Ginny to wailing again. He glared at Miriam. "Now look what you've done."

Miriam stood and walked around the table. She barely came to Dan's shoulder, and Gideon stood behind her, ready to intervene.

"You're tired, Dan. I overheard you tell Gideon she kept you up much of the night. Polly probably didn't sleep all that well, either. I'll take them for the day. Why don't you go nap?"

Nonplussed at her gentle offer, Daniel stared at Miriam. He'd been spoiling for a fight, and she'd just knocked the wind right out of his sails.

"You don't know a thing about babies." His hands closed more tightly around Ginny Mae, and her squall made it clear she didn't like it one bit.

"I helped Mama with sick calls, and a doctor came about the time Hannah left. I often assisted him. I daresay I can handle a fussy tot." She reached up and took possession of Ginny. Dan didn't look all too certain about turning loose, but he did so.

Miriam smoothly pivoted and slipped away. She crooked her forefinger. Ginny gnawed on it and hushed. "There we are," Miriam murmured as she carried the baby toward her own bed and laid her down. Nothing short of admiration flooded Gideon as Miriam continued to let little Ginny Mae chomp on her finger as she used the other hand to lift the baby's gown.

"Your daddy thinks it's your teeth or your belly. Let's find out."

The moment she alluded to Daniel, Gideon turned toward his brother. A series of emotions flashed across Dan's face—anger, grief, worry, resignation. Miriam hadn't challenged his authority or faulted him in any manner. She'd simply offered to lighten his burden, and in moments like this, Gideon realized how deeply burdened and troubled his brother had become. *As long as she can deal with him, I need to keep my mouth shut. I won't have him hurting her, but she's got a backbone of steel and a heart bigger than the ocean she crossed to get here.*

"Daniel, some babies get diaper rashes when they teethe." Miriam reclaimed her finger and deftly unpinned the diaper. "Has Ginny Mae gotten one when she got any of her other teeth?"

Miriam acted as if she'd had a dozen of her own young'uns. She knotted the corner of a dishcloth, dipped it in syrup, and let Ginny gum on it. That seemed to help some. By the time Miriam scorched flour and used it on Ginny Mae's rash, the baby hadn't quite regained her usual sweet disposition, but she'd sure enough stopped sounding like someone was trying to murder her.

Daniel groused around the table for a few more minutes, then took his leave.

"Gid said we're to level the land for Miriam's cabin," Bryce announced.

Miriam's head shot up. She gave Gideon a startled look that slowly changed into a grateful smile. Not that a missionary's daughter ought to know how to play poker, but Miriam best not ever try. Her face tattled on every emotion she had. Endearing, that quality.

His brothers all vacated the house and set to doing their chores, leaving behind a table stacked with dirty dishes. Soapsuds, splashes, and wadded towels festooned the washstand. Polly squirmed worse than a calf getting branded as Miriam plaited her flyaway hair. Saddling Miriam with this mess didn't seem quite fair. Come to think of it, Hannah used to try her best to wrangle a ride to town whenever one of the brothers went.

Gideon cleared his throat. If ever there was a time they needed Miriam to help with the girls, surely this was it. A fretful teether wouldn't allow more than a few moments' peace all day. Polly didn't often become peevish, but when she did, she could try the patience of a saint. Both girls would be at their worst.

"You don't have to mind the girls. It's Paul's day. If you wanted, you could ride into town with me. Reliable's not fancy, but—"

Miriam started laughing as she tied a scrap of twine around the end of the braid. "Go, Gideon. I'll make the trip some other time. I'd like you to post a letter for me, though."

"To your folks?"

She shook her head. "It's too costly to do that just yet. I'll wait a few months until we settle in. I'm sending a letter to my grandmother. It's a bit heavy, but she'll be able to forward an enclosed note to my cousin, Delilah, since I'm not sure where she's living now."

"I'm more than happy to post whatever you write. Are you sure you're not coming to town? It might be a long while before you have a chance again."

She looked up at him and shrugged. "You have the list, don't you?"

"Yeah." He shifted uncomfortably. "Your sis—she always hankered to go along."

A bittersweet smile crossed Miriam's face. "I can imagine. Hannah loved adventure. Me? I'm content to stay wherever I settle."

Late in the afternoon, Miriam heard footsteps on the porch. "Wipe your feet!"

"Yes'm."

She didn't bother to turn toward the door. In fact, she didn't want to. Her face must be red as a hibiscus. Instead, she toed the runner on the cradle to keep Ginny Mae from yowling and continued to sew.

"Done?" Polly asked for the hundredth time.

"In just a minute."

"I reckon you'd like the provender on the table so you can squirrel it away wherever you want." Gideon plopped a heavy crate on the table.

"Unca Giddy, did you bring me candy?"

"Just a minute, Polly. I need to bring in more stuff."

Miriam took advantage of the seconds when he'd be outside to push in her escaping hairpins and tuck straggling strands of hair behind her ears. Her apron bore splotches of syrup, coffee, and smashed yams. It hadn't bothered her for the other Chance men to see her in such disarray. *But they want me here; Gideon doesn't.*

Yes, they wanted her here. That fact came through clear enough. Loud and clear—as they all argued on where to level the ground for her cabin. Each had given thought to the location.

Paul and Titus said it ought to be close to Daniel's cottage since she'd be minding the girls. Daniel woke up to the noise and bellowed that they were to build it next to the main house. Logan figured halfway between might be smart so she could go either way in bad weather. Bryce wasn't sure whom to listen to, so he'd just hitched up horses and started dragging a huge log from one building toward the next. They'd leveled the whole area and come inside for lunch—every last one of them filthier than any man Miriam had ever seen. It took her a full hour just to scrub the grime from the house.

Scraping sounded. "I'm wiping my feet again." Gideon's voice held more than a hint of teasing.

"Do I get my candy now, Unca Giddy?"

"In a minute, tidbit. Mind if I set the material on your bed, Miriam? I don't know where you plan to store the bolts."

"Go ahead. Thank you for getting them." She started to tie a knot in the thread.

Polly danced from one foot to the other. "You done now?"

Miriam got ready to clip the thread. "Your dolly will be ready in just a minute."

Shoulders drooping with an exaggerated sigh, Polly whined, "How many minutes do you got?"

Gideon started to chuckle.

Miriam snipped the thread and quelled the smile that fought to break free. It would be easy to indulge Polly, but part of the reason she was staying was to teach her niece basic manners. "Remember how we talked about turns today?"

"But I don't wanna wait. Can't I pick when it's my turn?"

"Nope." Gideon grabbed Polly, lifted her high above his head, and jostled her. "Everyone waits for things—even you."

"Why?"

Miriam knew she'd remember the startled look on Gideon's face for the rest of her life. He didn't have a single notion how to answer that question.

"Because you're a big girl," Miriam said. "Big girls can learn things because they are smart. You're smart enough now to learn how to wait for your turn."

"She's not just big. She's huge. I can barely hold her up anymore." Gideon pretended to drop her. Polly shrieked in delight as he caught her in midair.

"Auntie Miri-Em is making me a dolly. It's a toy, and she'll be my very own little baby. Wanna see?"

Miriam gave the doll to Polly. Gideon hunkered down and volubly admired it. "Now will you look at that? Isn't she a beaut?" When Polly wandered into the other room to tuck Dolly into one of her uncle's beds, Gideon straightened to his full height. His features went somber. "I never thought about a little girl needing a doll. I don't think she's ever seen one."

"It's just an old shirt sleeve I salvaged. I'm sure when she's a bit older, Daniel will be sure she has a nice one."

"Don't sell yourself short. That rag doll is all a little girl could ever want."

His words warmed her heart.

"Perhaps I'll sew some clothes for her doll. Daniel could give them to her for Christmas."

"You'll give them to her yourself."

He really does plan on me staying here. Christmas is six months from now.

Gideon gave her a wry smile. "Yes, I understand what I just said. I reckon you're here for keeps."

Miriam reached around to retie her apron strings. She barely held back her laughter. "It took you long enough."

"Now wait a minute. You're the one who thought you wouldn't be here for Christmas!"

"I thought nothing of the kind." She flashed a smile at him. "I already planned to make Polly a new outfit as my gift."

Chapter 11

Thursday at lunch, Miriam set a basket of rolls on the table and smiled her thanks as Gideon pulled out her chair. "How many men do you expect to come help build the cabin tomorrow?"

"Can't say for certain."

Paul crowded into his place. "Us, maybe eight more. I'd venture probably a dozen or so all together."

Titus nodded. "Sounds about right to me."

Gideon took his place and folded his hands. He gave Miriam a nod, and she said grace. The Chance brothers didn't do a whole lot of talking at the table during the midday meal. They tended to shovel in as much food as they could in the least amount of time possible. Miriam had learned that sketchy plans for the day comprised any breakfast discussion and all conversation usually took place at supper.

Still, Miriam needed to ascertain a few basic facts. "Will those eight men eat as much as you all do?"

Gideon gave her an amused look. "Stop fretting. We're putting a steer in the fire pit."

"Bunch of nonsense," Daniel groused. "Practically reenacting the Prodigal Son, killing the fatted calf." For all of his bluster, he still gently spooned a bite into Ginny Mae's mouth. "Built my cabin without anyone else coming by."

"This way, it'll only take one day," Logan reasoned.

"Paul and I'll saw the floor planks this afternoon." Gideon sopped the last of the stew from his bowl and popped the roll into his mouth. "Bryce, make sure the troughs are full for everyone's horses tomorrow."

Titus rested his elbows on the table. "You haven't said anything about the plans yet."

"No need. Same as Daniel's." Gideon rose.

"Auntie Miri-Em, you better start making gravy for the chimney!"

Miriam started to wipe Polly's hands.

Gideon cleared his throat. "No need. I have White bringing a little potbelly stove from his mercantile."

"Great galloping hop toads!" Bryce blurted out. "Really?"

"Yep." Gideon strode toward the door as if he couldn't escape fast enough. His voice went gruff. "You all get to work."

Titus was the last to leave. He tarried by the door a moment.

"Did you need something?" Miriam asked.

He gave her a lopsided smile. "I'd be happy to pick a couple of heads of cabbage so you could make that fancy cabbage salad." Once he'd built up the nerve to make that request, he added on, "You'll have to hide it from Gideon, though. He'd eat the whole bowl of it before anyone got a chance at getting a mouthful tomorrow."

"It needs to stay cool, Titus. I'll make it tomorrow."

"Make it today. I'll put it in a bucket and lower in into the well. Hovering stuff above the water keeps it chilly as can be. Ma used to do that to keep food."

"Wonderful! Thank you."

"Every last man in Reliable township is here," Paul marveled the next morning.

Gideon growled and called himself twelve kinds of an idiot. Of course the men came. Miriam was single. Pretty. Could cook. He'd hoped a few men who could spare a day's labor would get a quick peek at her today, then leave her be. He'd planned on their spreading the word that Miriam belonged to the Chance family and wasn't looking for a husband.

So much for my grand plan.

White's wagon rolled into the yard. Gideon let out a grateful sigh. Reba had come along. She'd help Miriam in the kitchen and keep any of the fellows from getting too friendly. As he helped Reba down from the wagon, she gawked about. "Looks like half the world came."

Bryce counted aloud. "Thirty-seven, Giddy." His eyes went wide. "That's more than three dozen!"

And every last one of them is hovering near Miriam, trying his best to capture her attention. I've got to do something.

Reba tugged on his sleeve. "I'm going to borrow Logan and Titus to help carry those crates inside. I figured Miriam would need some help feeding the hordes."

Gideon cast a quick glance at the crates and gave Reba a relieved smile. "You're a peach."

Daniel had a daughter in each arm and stomped up as his other brothers emptied the wagon. "I'm taking the girls to my cabin and shutting the door. This is a circus, and I'll be lucky if they don't get trampled. I hold you accountable for the whole mess. You've got enough men here to build a dozen houses!"

Gideon watched his brother slam the door to his cottage, and a slow smile lit his face. *Maybe not a dozen, but. . .*

He cleared his throat. "Men!"

They stopped palavering and turned toward him.

"Thanks for coming out. Fact is, a whole lot more of you showed up than I planned."

"Folks ain't gonna think you're so smart anymore, Chance," Chris Roland hollered. "Everybody knows you got a pretty gal up here. 'Course every man jack in the county came!"

The men hooted with laughter.

Gideon hooked his thumbs in his belt. "Well, they're gonna think I'm right smart all over again, then, because I'm going to take advantage of your strength. Daniel's been chopping down trees for months now. I figure we can organize into groups and put up *three* cabins today!"

"You ain't smart. You're plumb crazy!"

"Then, Chris," Gideon said, pointing his forefinger at the man who called out that insult, "it seems to me that your team ought to be able to beat mine."

"You're on! I'm calling Rusty on my team."

"Wait—" Rusty yelled. "What does the first team done win?"

Gideon paused a moment. He turned when he felt Miriam's light touch on his arm. She stood on her toes and whispered in his ear. He nodded and announced, "Sunday supper. Miss Hancock will cook Sunday supper for the winning team."

The men all shouted with glee and quickly organized themselves into three teams. Gideon turned to Miriam and gave her a stern look. "You stay right by Reba White. I don't want these men troubling you, and she knows how to handle them."

"You don't have to worry about me, Gideon. I had to deal with all of the sailors back on the islands."

Her innocence made his blood run cold. "Those sailors wanted sinful union and likely found it in any number of brothels; these men want a wife. You're the only prospect around."

"Then you'll simply have to tell them I'm unavailable. I'm committed to rearing my nieces."

Reasoning with Miriam was as preposterous as saddling a squirrel. Gideon hollered, "Reba? Will you come here?" Reba marched on over. "Do me a favor. Keep the men away from Miriam."

Spurred on by the prospect of eating Miriam's Sunday supper, the men worked with zeal. The simple square floor plan with a door in the front and a window in the back made for rapid construction. All of the men had built their own cabins and worked together to raise barns. When they set to business, they knew what they were doing.

Then again, each team seemed to have notions as to what would improve the basic plan. Gideon's team built on the foundation that had the floorboards in place. Clearly that would become Miriam's. They wanted to put an additional window by the door, so they set the door one-third of the way across the front instead of dead center.

The middle team, under Chris Roland's lead, determined they had a better plan. Their cabin featured a front and a back door—and Rusty was busy making Dutch doors so each one could become a window if the occupant so chose.

The cabin closest to Dan's started out exactly like the plan. Paul was leading that team. He and Titus kept quiet, but Gideon could tell they were up to something by the way the men would huddle every now and again to discuss something. Sure enough, they kept on building the walls higher while men braced the first two cottages' roofs.

No one wanted to stop, since Miriam's Sunday meal hung in the balance, but she banged a spoon on the bottom of a pot. "Gentlemen, I'm calling a break. It's only fair everyone cease laboring for the same length of time."

They grumbled good-naturedly and headed for the food. Daniel came out of his cabin, and Polly ran toward Miriam. "Auntie Miri-Em, I get to eat first! It's my turn because I already washed my hands and face. All the men gots dirty hands. See?" She held up her little pink scrubbed hands.

Gideon sat on a stump and watched as big, burly men all backtracked and waited by the pump so they could sluice off. He suspected this was the cleanest some of the men had been in ages. *Miriam probably thought the same thing of us when she arrived.*

Bryce stood over by the pit with Logan. They started slicing off slabs of meat. Men piled it high on pie tins, then went toward the table. Miriam and Reba had cooked up a storm. Good thing, too. He'd thought Miriam overdid it when she made eight loaves of bread and four pies last night. With twoscore men, that wouldn't be sufficient. Truth be told, men would be satisfied to load up on the barbecue, but they'd feel cheated if they didn't get their fill of sweets. *Thank the Lord, Reba brought pie, too!*

Gideon caught himself. He'd been thanking the Almighty quite a bit lately. In truth, ever since Miriam showed up and just lived her faith in the simple, straightforward way that she did, he'd been reexamining his own ways. He'd found a whale of a lot to be grateful for and had become a whole lot less irritable.

Society matrons would swoon, but practical Miriam did what needed to be done with what she had on hand. Two two-gallon wooden buckets held potato salad and the cabbage slaw salad he liked so much. Deviled eggs, pickles, and tomato slices made the table look restaurant-fancy. Not only were there baskets of sliced bread, but there were also plenty of drop biscuits. Best of all, eight pies lined a board the women laid over two barrels.

"Whaddya have there?" Todd Dorsey called.

Reba rested her hands on her hips. "Two dried apple pies, two peach, a custard, two chocolate pudding, and a shoofly."

A masculine chorus of groans and satisfied grunts filled the air.

"That isn't all. Miriam made oatmeal cookies."

Marv Wall elbowed his way toward Miriam. "That does it. I'm not doing another lick of work. I'm proposing marriage so Miss Miriam won't need a cabin here."

Gideon was ready to wring Marv's neck, but Miriam clapped her hands and laughed. "Oh, that was the best joke I've heard yet today, sir. You simply must have the first choice of pie for having such a charming sense of humor."

Marv got a bewildered look on his face. Gideon took pity and bellowed, "The ladies better cut the pie, else he'll take a whole one to himself!"

"I'm not averse to having a pie of my own, but I'd rather have the cook," Marv said mournfully.

"The cook," Miriam singsonged, "is here to take care of her nieces. I'm sure you gentlemen understand, and I'm thankful that you're here to help me settle in with my family."

"Guess that says it all, men." Gideon took a stance by Miriam and stepped out in faith. "I aim to ask a blessing on the food." The yard went quiet. Gideon's pulse thundered in his ears as he bowed his head. "Almighty God, we give Thee thanks for the fine things in our lives—for land and livestock, family and food. Draw us close to Thee, we pray, and bless the hands that prepared the meal. Amen."

"Amen," the men said in unison.

He gestured toward the food. "Dig in." Miriam said nothing, but she'd slipped her hand in his as he prayed. It felt. . .right. Like it belonged. His heart felt right, too. Like he'd come home—not just because they were of one accord, but because he'd been keeping the Lord at a distance, and that had changed.

The men made utter pigs of themselves. It wasn't until every last speck of food was gone that they decided it was time to start up on the challenge again. "Paul and Titus are going to take forever to get that third cabin done."

"We'll see about that!"

Axes rang out and saws grated. Men counted as they worked in accord to heave logs into place. Gideon's men went back to the far pasture to fetch more logs for the roof. He dusted off his hands and stood back to survey the progress.

His cabin for Miriam would be sound. It still needed chinking and a window set into it, but those things didn't take much time or effort. It would be a fine little place, and he'd even kept some of the scraps from the floor planks and hammered them together to make a drop leaf to serve as a writing desk that folded against the wall.

The center cabin sat square as could be, and it got a mighty fine breeze going through with both doors wide open.

Gideon surmised what Titus and Paul were doing and gave them a nod of approval. Instead of making a peaked roof, they'd built up the front and left the roof as a simple downward slant to the back. The extra height bore support trusses for a loft.

Paul sauntered over and swiped his sleeve across his damp brow. "Dan and the girls'll outgrow their little cottage in a few years. Titus and I decided we might as well bump it up a bit."

"Good thinking." Gideon looked at the three new buildings with a growing sense of satisfaction and slapped him on the back.

Bryce mopped at his neck with a bandanna. "This is the workin'est day ever." His sunburned face split into a smile, and he elbowed Paul. "Couldn't have done it if Dan hadn't been in such a foul mood and hacked down so many trees."

Paul and Bryce started laughing.

"Men," Miriam said as she daintily picked her way across chips of wood and bark. She smiled at them. "I'd like a word, if you will."

"Better make it quick," Gideon warned. "Don't want to slow down our teams."

Miriam's eyes sparkled. She reached them and looked from Gideon to Paul and Bryce, then back at Gideon again. "The men have all worked so hard. Would you mind terribly if all of them came for supper after church?"

Gideon toed the dirt and shook his head. "Miriam, there's a problem."

She turned a becoming shade of pink. "Oh dear. I'm sorry. I didn't think about how much food—"

"That's not the problem." He sighed. "Sweet pea, other than an occasional itinerant Bible-thumper who happens through, Reliable doesn't have a church."

She looked utterly flabbergasted.

"Maybe it's not quite that heathen," Paul added hastily. "The last one said he's riding circuit and will be back through every other month or so."

Her mouth opened and shut a few times. Then she smoothed her skirts. "Well, we'll just have to remedy that. It's summer, and the weather is lovely as can be. We'll have worship right here in the yard."

She turned around and sashayed back into the house.

Bryce looked stricken. "Giddy, do something!"

Gideon shrugged. "You did this. You voted for her to stay, and now she's changing everything. Live with it."

Chapter 12

"Everything's changing," Miriam murmured to herself with delight. Over the last few weeks, she'd settled into her new cottage, tacked up cheery yellow feed sacks as curtains, and braided a small rug to go by her bed.

She'd taken shameless advantage of the big move. When Paul and Titus moved into the loft cabin, she washed their tickings and had the men stuff them with fresh hay. Gideon now occupied the middle cabin. He'd seen to his own bedding, and instead of leaving his doors open all day long as did his brothers, he kept his shut. Logan and Bryce now shared the big bedroom in the main house. Miriam suspected Bryce smuggled one or more of the dogs in there each night, but she said nothing.

As soon as she'd arrived, she'd expanded the garden. Polly loved to "help," and Ginny Mae relished crawling in the dirt. The biggest challenge was keeping her from eating bugs, worms, and rocks. Polly wore pantalets and simple smocks made from feed sacks instead of hand-me-down shirts. Sweetest of all, she now said prayers.

"Breakfast about ready?" Paul called to her as she stepped out onto the porch. He'd been heading toward the chicken house.

"I need the eggs!"

"Come help."

She lifted her skirts a bit and skipped across the yard. Back home, there was more sand than dirt, and it took considerable effort to get anywhere. Here, the packed earth made for ease of travel. These men had no concept how fortunate they were to live without the ever-present irritation of sand. Grit from the beach got into every nook and cranny. Dust could be wiped clean; sand never departed.

Paul slid a bolt free and looked down at her. "Might want to stand back a shade. The hens can be pecky after being shut in all night." He swung two six-foot-high doors open, revealing dozens of boxes full of nesting hens.

"This is like a kitchen cupboard!"

"Yup." Gideon rested his hands on her shoulders. Miriam had heard him coming. She knew the assured sound of his no-nonsense stride. She fought the urge to lean back into his strength as he explained, "Mama designed it. None of us liked stooping to fit into the crowded, dirty coop. Paul, Speck is off her feed.

Bryce is having a look at her."

Paul hastened toward the stable. Miriam started gathering eggs, and Gideon reached the nests that were up high. Quickly they filled the basket. "I didn't mean to have him strand you with his chore."

"I kept chickens on the islands. I don't mind."

"You already do plenty around here."

Miriam slipped her hand beneath a pullet and admitted, "Life here isn't easy, but it's good. You men work hard."

He snorted. "We get filthy and eat like ravenous beasts. I still don't understand why you'd choose to live here and deal with us."

Miriam hitched her right shoulder. "It seems to me, no matter where they live, men lose buttons, tear shirts, rip knees, and bleed. Back home, Mama told me a woman's mending basket and laundry are bottomless. I'm not complaining."

"Miriam!" Logan called from the house. "Todd Dorsey came to see about a horse trade. Mind if he stays to breakfast?"

Neighbors stopped by with astonishing frequency—and always at mealtime. Gideon never seemed very pleased about those social calls. He bristled. "Yahoos and clods. Ever notice these mooches just so happen to turn up at mealtime?"

Miriam laughed. "I think it does them some good, seeing little Ginny Mae and Polly with all of you big, strapping Chance men. Plain as can be, those little girls need a woman's touch, and I'm the only woman around."

The muscle in his jaw twitched. "That's all they notice, Miriam—you being a woman." He stomped toward the house, and Miriam mentally dismissed Todd from the breakfast table. No one ever managed to get something past Gideon. *Except me. I'm the exception that proves the rule, because I'm staying here.*

Gideon. Once he'd accepted that she was here to stay, he'd stopped acting as if he'd been invited to his own execution. Responsibility rested heavily on his shoulders, and he took it seriously. But she wanted to be sure Gideon understood she wasn't another responsibility—she was. . . *What am I?*

Helpmeet was the first word that came to mind, but that was all wrong. It meant she was his wedded wife. She wasn't a partner. Neither was she a maidservant nor a relative. Miriam resolved not to label what she was but instead to concentrate on how she would lighten his load and ensure her nieces' ultimate welfare.

Led by Gideon's example, most of the other Chance brothers embraced her presence with ease. Some days, it seemed as if she'd been here forever.

Miriam carried the egg basket into the house. Daniel sat on the floor, struggling with a knot in the lace of his boot. Miriam set down the egg basket and handed him a fork. "Try this. The tine can help you tease it loose."

He nodded and kept his head bowed over the stubborn tangle.

Daniel seemed to be changing, too—but slowly. Instead of being surly or belligerent most of the time, he now stayed silent. Miriam removed a stove lid and shoved in another log as she mentally gave Hannah's husband credit for the love he gave his children. He cherished both daughters to distraction and showed them great tenderness. Because their welfare was his first concern, he'd grudgingly accepted the fact that Miriam would now play a role in their upbringing.

"Oh!" Miriam jerked away from the stove and started beating at the flames on her left sleeve.

"Here." *Whoosh.* Something wrapped around her, and Gideon was part of it. He held her in tight confines and rubbed her arm. "I've got it. You're okay. Titus, get the water pitcher."

Miriam rested against Gideon's chest and stared off to the side. Plates, mugs, and silverware dappled the just-swept floor. *But I set the table.*

"Quick thinking," Titus said as he hastened up with the water pitcher from the washstand.

"Here. Let me take a look." Gideon stopped rubbing and tried to twist her.

Miriam couldn't help herself. She burrowed closer.

"It's all right, sweet pea."

"Of course it is," she said. "I'm just cold."

"How can you be cold?" Logan slanted her an odd look. "You were on fire."

While Logan reminded her of that dreadful fact, Gideon managed to tug on her. Miriam wiggled, then looked down. "That's our only tablecloth! It better not—"

"Hush." Gideon finished unwinding her and proceeded to yank what was left of her sleeve clean off her dress. "Pour the water on her."

"At least let me put my arm over the sink."

Gideon made an impatient sound and glowered at Titus. Titus immediately emptied the entire gallon of water over her arm. As the last few ounces slid over her, Gideon ordered, "Now let me see how you look."

"It's just a little burn."

He looked at her arm and carefully turned her hand so he could see more of her forearm. Miriam reached over to cover the center of the sizable pink splotch with her other hand, but Gideon smoothly manacled that wrist and turned his attention toward her injured palm. "We'll wait to see if you blister. Hopefully we caught it before the heat went that deep."

"Truly it's nothing much. My dress took the brunt of it."

"Not much of a loss, if you ask me." Logan picked up the charred remains of the sleeve. "I don't mean you any insult, but that dress is ugly as a mud-stuck fence."

"It was serviceable." *Serviceable*—a word she'd learned in her youth.

"Came out of a missionary barrel, didn't it?" Gideon's voice carried a healthy dose of disgust.

"Well, I—how did you know about missionary barrels?" As soon as the words left her mouth, Miriam regretted asking. "My arm's fine. You men must be starving."

"You sit down. We'll keep a cold compress on your arm. Dan, scramble some eggs. Logan, pick up the dishes."

Miriam watched in dismay as Logan took the plates and shoved them back onto the table. "I need to wash those!"

He used his sleeve to wipe away a speck. "No need. You just swept this morning. Fact is, afore you came, lots of the time, we didn't wash the dishes."

Gideon hovered during breakfast, changing the cool compress on her arm and buttering her bread. "I'm taking Miriam into town."

"I need to change."

"No, you're not." Gideon made the pronouncement as if it were chiseled in stone.

"I can't very well saunter about in polite company in a shredded gown!"

"Town isn't polite company."

Fifteen minutes later, Gideon tucked the shawl around her shoulders as the buckboard jounced toward town. "Listen here, Miriam. You're not a missionary's daughter anymore."

"Of course I am. Just because Daddy and Mama are overseas doesn't change the fact—"

"You're Ginny Mae and Polly's aunt. Ugly day gowns like this don't teach them to be ladies. Part of the reason you're here is to teach them the feminine side of things, and you're traipsing around like a penniless waif in a servant's castoffs."

She smoothed her brown skirts. "Serge is durable and—"

"Homely as mud. Tell me, why did Hannah show up with feminine colors? I remember her dresses being pink, and they had doodads."

Miriam smiled. "The rose-colored fabric came in a barrel. I made that as her honeymoon dress. Papa couldn't very well insist that her gowns be somber when she was celebrating her marriage."

"Well, we're getting you material in town. You're gonna sew yourself a fancy pink dress."

"Gideon, I can't. I promised I'd make myself look different from my sister."

"Dan can go fly a kite. You already pile your hair up on your head so you don't wear a bun at your nape like Hannah did. Besides, your hair's warm like the sun, and hers was pale. I don't want you thinking I'm being too personal or being harsh, but Hannah—well, she had two babes in three years. Betwixt them, she never did trim down. Dan must've been sun-blinded when he first mistook you for your sis. It's high time you stopped trying to waltz on eggshells to please him and did what you want to make yourself happy."

Miriam smiled at him. "But, Gideon, I am happy."

"No, you're not. You're just accustomed to being content with settling for scraps."

Sunday arrived. Men came and sang hymns as best they could remember, though the lyrics took on more creativity than Miriam had imagined possible. Titus scrounged up a guitar Miriam hadn't yet seen and proved to be quite talented. Gideon read from the Bible about letting your light shine, and Chris Roland stood up and spoke from his heart about living a "God-fearin', devil-forsakin' life." Paul rose to say a closing prayer, and Rusty hollered, "Tack on thanks for the grub. We're hungry and want to belly up to the table straightaway."

Miriam didn't look, but she suspected Gideon fought to keep from chuckling. As soon as Paul finished the prayer, she hastened into the kitchen. Gideon hadn't let her near the stove to cook anything earlier this morning. She'd prepared each pot on the table. Then a Chance brother had transferred it to the stove. Now Gideon carried every last pot back to the table.

Soon she was dishing up meals and handing a filled plate to each man as he walked in from the back door and left through the front. Succotash, rice, roast, and gravy. The banker, Pete Rovel, came through for thirds.

"That Sunday supper did it," Logan moaned five days later. Each and every meal, they had callers. The men avidly listened to the Bible stories Miriam told the girls. They seemed even more interested in what Miriam planned to put on the table.

By Friday, Gideon glowered at three visitors and sent them packing. When he turned to the table, his eyes narrowed. Miriam kept posies on the table all the time, but they were always wildflowers from a patch here or there around the property. Three yellow roses filled the jar today.

"Marv Wall brung them for Miriam," Bryce tattled.

Gideon looked at his brothers and drummed his fingers on the table. "Miriam, you need to put the girls to bed tonight."

She gave him a baffled look. Daniel insisted on tucking his daughters into bed each night. *What is Gideon up to?*

"We've got to do something. I don't want these men to keep calling on Miriam." Gideon paced in the barn.

Logan beat the heels of his scuffed boots on the bale of hay he sat upon. "She's workin' herself silly, cookin' for them."

"She's cooking anyway," Paul pointed out. "To my mind, it's more a matter that we can't afford to feed all of Reliable."

"Rusty had her writing a letter for him yesterday, and Dorsey talked her into mending his stinkin' socks," Gideon rasped. "She's not their wife. They have no call, counting on her to do those things."

"She does it for us," Titus said quietly.

"I can write my own letters!" Bryce objected. He then muttered, "Just don't have a body to mail stuff to."

"I told you letting her stay here was a mistake." Daniel glowered at them all. "You didn't listen. Now you have a peck of trouble, and I want no part of it." He turned and walked out of the barn. The door shut with great finality.

"If that don't beat all." Logan scowled. "Betcha he's going straight back into his cottage and sending Miriam scurrying away."

"The last thing she needs to know is that we're talking about her." Hay shifted and whispered under Gideon's boots as he continued to restlessly measure the length of the barn. "Roses. Marv had to go clear into San Francisco to bring those to her. It's serious."

"I told you, you ought to marry up with her, Giddy." Bryce folded his arms across his chest. "Seems that one of the Chance men ought to."

"Dan's excluded," Paul said at once. "He's hurting too bad, and it's not fair to Miriam."

"And," Titus continued in the same vein, "we have to rule out Logan and Bryce because they're just plain too young. That leaves you, me, and Gideon."

"I reckon it's necessary." Paul cracked his knuckles. "Not my first choice, but definitely doable. I'm willing to draw straws for her."

Titus started to chuckle as he took three strands of straw and handed them to Logan. "Seems pretty hilarious to me. After all, our name is Chance. I've got a one-in-three chance of snagging a bride—and a pretty one at that—without having to fuss with getting all duded up and making a fool of myself, going courting."

Gideon gritted his teeth as Logan lined up the straws and broke one far shorter than the others with a flourish. Anger coursed through him that his brothers would concoct such a "solution" to this problem. "You're all out of line."

Logan shrugged. "You're the one who always tells us to think things through.

Someone's gotta marry up with her. Why not one of us?"

"Because she's family, not a brood mare." Gideon stared at them. "You don't treat a woman like this!"

"Nothing much is changing. She's already willing to stay and work," Logan reasoned. "And we all like her just fine—well, all of us but Daniel."

"Daniel doesn't like anybody," Bryce tacked on.

"If anything, we're truly making her family instead of a free maid." Paul nodded at Logan. "Let's get on with it."

Logan positioned the straws in his fist and held them aloft. "Who's first?"

Gideon swiped all three straws from his brother's hand, cast them down, and ground them beneath his boot. "I won't have it. No one's drawing straws for Miriam's hand. A woman deserves to be courted and cared about."

Titus leaned back against a post and shoved his hands into his pockets. A lazy smile tilted his face. "So. . .you volunteering, Gideon?"

Chapter 13

Here. I've got it." Gideon nudged Miriam to the side and hefted the kettle of oatmeal. He thumped it onto the center of the table.

"I'm fine, Gideon. Truly." Ever since she'd burned her arm, he'd hovered over her. That day when they went to town, he'd bought material for two dresses for her—two! As if that wasn't enough, he'd gotten the one and only bit of lace Mrs. White had in the store. Each time he was in the house and Miriam got near the stove, he acted antsy. "Gideon, that little burn is long since healed."

"Nonsense." He swiped the coffeepot from the stove and headed back to the table. "You got singed from your wrist to your. . ." He made a slashing mark across his own upper arm.

Miriam let out a silent sigh of relief. It wouldn't have been proper for him to mention her elbow or upper arm. He and the older brothers seemed a bit better about such matters. Bryce and Logan often said things that weren't suitable for mixed company.

"She's kept it hidden 'neath her sleeves. Even if it was hurting, I doubt she'd tell us." Titus sat down at the table.

"You can show me, Auntie Miri-Em."

"It's fine, Polly. Now would you like butter and sweetening in your porridge or cream and cinnamon?" Miriam thought she'd successfully steered the conversation in a different direction until breakfast was over and the men headed out to work.

Gideon alone remained. He waited until she'd wiped Ginny Mae's sticky face and put her down to crawl, then he towered over her.

"Did you need something?"

He gave no warning. With surprisingly nimble fingers, he unbuttoned her cuff and started to carefully roll up her sleeve.

"Gideon!"

"Don't get all prissy on me. You roll up your sleeves to wash dishes and do laundry." He ruched the sleeve higher and made an exasperated sound. "It's still red."

"Auntie Miri-Em's arm isn't all better?"

"Not yet, dumplin'."

"I know why."

Oh boy. She's going to blab about what I've been doing.

"Why?" Gideon didn't look at his niece. His blue eyes narrowed and grew icy as he stared at Miriam.

" 'Cause nobody kissed her better."

"I'm a big girl. I don't need—"

"Of course you do. You kissed me all better when my eye was hurt." Gideon took hold of her hand and lifted it. Instead of planting a quick peck on her hand, he slowly turned her hand over and brushed his lips on the inside of her wrist.

Miriam gasped and tried to pull away.

Gideon kept hold. "Still tender, sweet pea?" Instead of letting go, he pursed his lips and blew across her wrist. "There. That'll make the sting go away."

"Unca Giddy? That maded Auntie Miri-Em's face get all burny-red."

"Tell you what, half-pint. I'll lift you up. You kiss one cheek, and I'll kiss the other. Think that'll make Miriam all better?"

"Oh, I'm fine. Just fine." Desperately Miriam tried to make her voice sound breezy, but it came out in nothing more than a croak.

Gideon ignored her protest. He scooped up Polly and held her out to give Miriam a kiss. Miriam leaned forward, figuring she could play along this far. Polly gave her a sloppy peck and giggled.

Though Gideon put their niece down, Miriam was stuck because Ginny Mae was clinging to her skirts. "Virginia," Miriam said, stooping at once to lift the unsteady toddler. "Come on up here."

Gideon crooked a brow at her, then glanced at Ginny Mae. "You've got things topsy-turvy, Miss Miriam. Usually kids hide behind a woman's skirts."

His words echoed in her mind as he walked out the door. Miriam wasn't sure whether to be relieved or disappointed.

By suppertime Miriam still hadn't managed to think through the situation. She'd pulled weeds in the garden with a vengeance, hoping that might relieve the tension. Ginny Mae and Polly got so filthy "helping" her, she had to bathe them both. Grinding meat and then squishing it to make meatloaf only managed to weary her body. Her mind still returned to how Gideon kissed her wrist after breakfast.

It was the oddest thing. Gideon had acted. . .well, different. Attentive. Since the day she arrived, Miriam had appreciated what a stalwart man he proved to be. Dependable. Good-hearted. Rough around the edges but hardworking. Then, too, after she scratched the surface, she'd come to understand he feared the Lord and did his best to live an upright life. *Is he paying more mind to me, or is it just my imagination?*

The Lord knew the desires of her heart—a husband and a family of her own—but the way things had worked out, those didn't seem to be in His will. She figured she would become a spinster aunt to little Polly and Ginny Mae. *I'm doubtlessly making a fool of myself. Gideon was just being kind, and I could ruin what's turned out to be a pleasant arrangement. I won't get to wed anyone, but at least I can count myself blessed to have a man like Gideon to champion me and to have these darling little girls to rear.*

All during supper, she tried to act normally, but sitting next to Gideon made her nervous. Finally, he wrapped his arm around her shoulders and held her still. "Stop popping up and down like a jack-in-a-box. If someone wants something, he can just go fetch it for himself."

"But I'm in a chair; everyone else is on a bench."

"Forget it," Gideon ordered.

"Yeah, Auntie Miri-Em. It's your turn to forget. Unca Gideon had his turn to forget already today."

"What did I forget?" Gideon gave Polly a look of mock outrage.

"You was 'posed to give Auntie Miri-Em a kiss. Look—see? Her face is all burny-red again. Hurry up and kiss it all gone."

Mortified, Miriam couldn't imagine a more awkward situation. Every last Chance at the table stared at her—not that she could see anything more than the napkin she crushed in her lap, but she felt their stares all the same. Bryce and Logan were hooting. Titus snickered, and Paul seemed to be choking back laughter. Daniel—he huffed like a ready-to-charge bull. Worst of all, Gideon. He dared to crook his forefinger and hook it beneath her chin.

I'm not going to look at him. I can't. I won't.

His nearness enveloped her, and warm lips brushed not her cheek, but the arch of her cheekbone. Miriam forgot how to breathe.

"Stop messing around," Daniel growled.

How she made it through the rest of the meal, Miriam didn't know. Rattled, she managed to put applesauce on her mashed potatoes instead of gravy—not that it mattered much. She couldn't seem to eat more than a few bites. Daniel took the girls off to their cottage as soon as he gulped down his last bite, and Miriam practically raced out to her little cabin on his heels.

She lay in bed and stared at her cabin. The fancy, scrolled, wrought-iron bedstead creaked as she rolled to her side. All three dresses hung neatly on pegs Bryce had whittled for her. The washstand held her toiletries and a water pitcher and bowl. The little drop-leaf desk lay open, its support chains gleaming dully in the beams of moonlight that sneaked through the gap between the top of her window and the top of the feed-sack curtain.

Beside her Bible on the desk lay a handkerchief—a used one. She'd come to her room, seeking solitude and solace. Confused by her response to Gideon's really-nothing-to-it kiss, she sought wisdom from the Word of God, only to end up in the last chapter of Proverbs.

Why, God? Why did I have to read about the qualities of a good wife? I thought I'd accepted my spinsterhood. You know how much I adore Ginny Mae and Polly. I even have this sweet little home of my own. Instead of feeling grateful, I feel empty. Lonely. How can I feel so alone when I'm surrounded by these rowdy men? How could I possibly sense such a lack when I have Gideon's friendship? Was this how Hannah felt? She had a husband, but she was so unhappy and restless. Help me, heavenly Father. Help me accept what I do have, to praise Thee for the life Thou hast set before me, and to exercise gratitude instead of this sadness. Amen.

"Something wrong?" Gideon stepped closer to Miriam at the sink as they did the breakfast dishes. She'd been subdued today.

She shook her head.

"If you're mad about that little kiss at the table last night—"

"You never told me how my sister died."

Gideon set down the plate he'd dried and draped the dishcloth over his shoulder. *So that's what's troubling her.* He leaned against the cupboard and hooked his thumbs in his belt. "I didn't realize that I hadn't given you the details. Sorry if it's been bothering you."

"I've wondered."

Her confession sounded almost tentative, and Gideon decided he'd give her the truth as simply and gently as he could. "We don't have a doctor here. Reba came to help Hannah with the first birthing; she was back east, putting her daughter in a fancy finishing school, when Ginny Mae was born. Dan—well, he did his best. Hannah pulled through, but she never perked up afterward. Fact is, she stayed abed for almost three months. A doc came through and said she had the 'punies.' He prescribed a tablespoon of blackstrap molasses followed by a belt of rum twice a day, but Hannah wouldn't do it. She didn't suffer, Miriam; Hannah just faded away in her sleep."

Tears streaked Miriam's face. Hands wet with dishwater, she tried turning her face to the side and brushing her cheeks against her shoulder to dry them.

"Feelin' blue, sweet pea?" He dried her tears with the corner of the dishcloth. A thought shot through him and made him look at her more closely. "Are you ailing? Is that why you asked—"

"No. I–I just needed to know."

"Well, I think you ought to have a few days to ease off on work." She opened her mouth, but he pressed his fingers to her lips. "We already laid Mama and Hannah to rest, Miriam. Women aren't fashioned for this life. Remember me warning you of that?"

She spread out her arms, shook her head, and spun around. "Do I look feeble to you, Gideon?"

He looked at her shimmering green eyes. Miriam was the picture of good health. In fact, she looked better each day—far better than when she'd first come. The sun had kissed her cheeks, making them a fetching rose color. Never had he seen such a vibrant woman. Contentment and energy radiated from her.

"We're not taking any chances." He'd do everything in his power to be sure she stayed this bright and healthy. "You'll just have to rely on my judgment here. Today you just nap and stitch some fancywork—nothing essential. Maybe tat yourself some lace or something."

Gideon knew the minute he turned his back, she'd do a chore. He inspected a knife she'd just washed. "I'll get a whetstone and sharpen this while you tat." Pleased with himself for coming up with a way to keep her company and have her relax, Gideon nodded. It didn't take much to concoct a plan to court her.

Once he got going, he liked the opportunities that slipped into his mind. He didn't want to woo her with his brothers hovering around. Having them watch each step he took and judge every last word out of his mouth just plain didn't settle well. He could swipe her away and start to sweeten things up a mite so she'd start warming up to the idea of marriage. Pleased with his decision, Gideon announced, "Tomorrow, I'll take you into town so's you can have a visit with Reba."

"I just—"

"Tell you what. I'll teach you how to drive the buckboard tomorrow. That'd be grand, don't you think?"

Grand doesn't begin to describe this. Gideon smiled to himself the next day as he sat so close to Miriam on the buckboard seat that a blade of grass wouldn't fit between them. He had his arms about her in order to guide her hands on the traces. She'd washed her hair last night, and the little wisps of windblown hair teasing his cheeks were soft as could be.

"I think I can do it." Miriam fidgeted.

"I'll let you drive on your own after we make it around this next curve." Gideon wasn't in any hurry to stop holding her close. Still, he needed to mind propriety. If they pulled up to the mercantile with her tucked this closely to him, Miriam's reputation would be ruined. He cleared his throat and braced her left hand. "There's a nasty rut just at the bend."

"Oh. Thank you."

She's a sweet armful of woman. Tenderhearted, hardworking, and sweet-spirited. Marrying up with her won't be a hardship at all.

"You'll have to show me how to hitch the horses next time, Gideon."

He looked down at her. "Not that you couldn't, sweet pea, but there's no need. One of us will see to that task."

"The horses are beautifully trained. I imagine it wouldn't be very difficult."

"Bryce need only work with a horse a day or two, and it's a dream. He's hopeless with people, but with beasts, he's a wonder."

"God gives us all different gifts."

Her smile could make the sun look dim. "You always look on the good side of things?"

"Most of the time." She shrugged, and the action only served to remind him of his hold about her. "Bryce has a heart of gold, and he's never shy about volunteering to help out. He needs some direction, but that's just because he's yet a boy. He'll grow out of his awkwardness and into his manhood."

"He's halfway between grass and hay." Gideon sighed. "Some days, I wonder if he'll ever mature." The wagon rounded the bend, and Gideon slowly let go of Miriam. He didn't want to, though.

"He will. So will Logan."

"From your lips to God's ears."

Matter-of-fact as could be, she nodded. "I do pray for each of you every night. I trust in the Lord, Gideon—but I also trust you. Believe me. They'll become remarkable men. You're a fine example."

Boom! The rifle kicked so hard, it threw Miriam back into Gideon's vast chest. Had he not been bracing her, she would have ended up in the dirt.

"Well," he drawled from over her shoulder as he continued to hold her, "you just drilled some gopher a nice new hole."

"You saw where it went?"

"Yeah. I keep my eyes open. It's a helpful trick you might want to try."

The rifle grew far too heavy to hold, so she lowered it.

"Hey, now." Gideon stepped around and frowned as he watched her rub her shoulder. "That recoil can be nasty. Why don't we change over to something lighter? Pistols, maybe."

"Pistols?" she squeaked. "Gideon, those are for killing people."

"We already talked this to death, Miriam. My brothers and I have been working farther from home, and if a snake slithers into the yard, you'll need to protect the girls."

"I could just take them inside."

"Sweet pea, you scare the ever-lovin' daylights outta me. What did you do back home with snakes?"

Though she wanted to continue rubbing her sore shoulder, she stopped. "There weren't any snakes on the islands."

"Oh, so it was paradise before the fall, huh?"

Miriam shook her head. "Not at all. Between the natives and the sailors, it was like Sodom and Gomorrah. That's why God placed us there—so we could let our light shine."

"Your light?"

"From Matthew 5:16. 'Let your light so shine before men, that they may see your good works, and glorify your Father which is in heaven.' The islands are full of darkness, Gideon. They need the light."

"But you came here."

"I did. The day I left, Daddy told me that my light would shine wherever God placed me. He and Mama are where the Lord intends for them to serve, but they'd prayed and felt God had someplace else for me to be." She looked around them, then back into his deep blue eyes. "I feel as if I've been sent to paradise."

"That's a tough one to swallow. Hannah always spoke of how beautiful the islands were."

"They are—in their own way. Here, the colors are more subtle and muted. The scents aren't cloying; they're earthy. Instead of the beat of the ocean, you have the soughing of the wind. The islands are a testament to God's imagination. Your land is a show of His majesty. Being there was like. . . holding a fistful of jewels. Here is like. . .kneeling in God's presence."

Gideon's intense gaze made her laugh uncomfortably. "Oh dear. I've dithered on, haven't I?"

"Not at all." He slipped his arm about her and took away the rifle. Toting it over his shoulder with ease, he still kept his other arm about her waist and headed toward the house. "Those are some of the nicest words I've ever heard."

Being sheltered in his arms is the nicest feeling I've ever had. Miriam fought the urge to snuggle closer and tried to lighten the conversation. "Speaking of words, can you believe little Ginny Mae? All of a sudden, she's started babbling. She's growing up so fast, Gideon! When I got here, she could barely take a few steps, but now she's toddling everywhere and getting into everything."

"She's a handful, all right. I don't know how you understand her, though.

Other than Daddy and 'Pieee' for Polly, I can't make sense of anything she says."

"She calls you 'Geee.'"

Gideon snorted. "She's also called every one of my brothers and the barn cat that."

"She spends most of her waking hours with me. Of course I understand what she means."

He halted at once and gave her a piercing look. "I thought you wanted to mind the girls. We men can start—"

"Gideon Chance, don't you dare tromp down that path! My only regret is that I wasn't here to help with Polly when she was younger."

"You sure?"

"You know I adore those little girls! I know you all did your best for them, but they need a woman's touch. It tears me apart, knowing Hannah isn't here to mother them. But you have to know I'll love them with every fiber of my being, and I'll care for them as if they were my very own."

"They're a handful."

"They're a heartful," she countered.

"So you still want to stick around here?"

"I've never been more certain of anything in my life. I wrote a letter to my parents last night, telling them all about Polly and Ginny Mae and what it's like here."

"Did you tell them what you said earlier—about it being majestic?"

She nodded. "I told them when I wake up in the morning, this place often makes me think of the verse, 'Be still, and know that I am God.'" She laughed a bit. "Then I told them the day is so full, I don't do much more thinking until I climb back in bed."

"We can still buy your passage back to the islands."

"And cheat me out of the happiness I've found here? Gideon, you couldn't get me to budge from Reliable if you used a crowbar. I love this place, and I love the people even more. Hannah's daughters are delights."

They rounded the garden and headed toward the main house. Daniel was kneeling in the dirt, brushing off Ginny's dress and face. Polly turned and ran toward Miriam. "Ginny fell, Auntie Miri-Em!"

Ginny wiggled away from Daniel and headed for Miriam, too. Tears streaked her grubby little cheeks as she raised her arms to be lifted. "M'um! M'um!"

"Mom!" Accusation thundered in Dan's voice.

Chapter 14

Gideon tightened his hold around Miriam as his brother stormed toward her. "Daniel—"

"You stay out of this." Daniel jabbed his forefinger at Miriam. "You taught her that. You had no right. She's not yours."

"Paul. Titus." Gideon did his best to keep his voice level and calm as he summoned his brothers. The last thing he wanted was to have the babies witness this confrontation. Polly's eyes were huge, and Ginny tugged at Miriam's skirts and continued to cry, "M'um! Up!"

Both brothers had been nearby. They closed ranks on either side of him and Miriam.

"The girls." The words barely made it out of his mouth before Paul stooped to sweep the baby and Polly into his arms. "C'mon, girls. Uncle Paul wants to show you a big, fat worm." He strode away.

Titus paused a moment. His chin tilted upward, and he looked from Dan to Miriam, then looked at Gideon and raised his brow. "Do you want me to take Miriam inside, or do you need me to knock some sense into Dan?"

"It's none of your affair—neither of you." Dan bristled. "This is betwixt me and Miriam."

Titus whistled under his breath, accepted the rifle from Gideon, and headed into his cabin.

The air crackled with tension.

God, give me wisdom. It's a hard truth I have to tell. "Daniel," Gideon started.

"I told you to stay out of this," Daniel roared. "It's none of your business."

"I never meant to cause discord." Miriam reached out to him. "Daniel, please understand—"

"No, you understand, Miriam. You are not their mother. You'll never be their mother. Hannah was." He thumped his chest. "*My* Hannah. She bore and suckled them. You're their aunt, and that's all you'll ever be."

"That's more than enough for me," she replied with quiet dignity.

For weeks, Gideon had prayed and kept quiet. He knew he had to speak now. "Your girls are lucky to have their auntie M'um. That's right, Dan—*M'um.* It's a baby's way of saying Miriam. If you weren't so busy wallowing in your self-pity, you would have realized it. We've all let you have your temper fits and tried to understand your grief, but you've gone far over the line."

"Fine. Then I'll take my daughters and leave."

As quickly as her hand flew to cover her mouth, Miriam still didn't quite manage to muffle her cry.

"Go? Okay, Dan." Gideon looked his brother in the eyes and called his bluff, not at all sure it was a bluff. "Let's think it through: Just where would you go? Who's going to look after the girls while you work to earn a living?"

"I'd manage."

"You're kidding no one but yourself. You resent Miriam lavishing her love on the girls, but who else would ever treat them with such care?"

"They have my love."

"That they do. They have mine, too, just as they have Paul, Titus, Logan, and Bryce's love. Taking them away from all of us would be cruel to them, and you know it."

"You've given me no choice. It's either me or her." He gave Miriam a malevolent glare.

Gideon rested his hands on Miriam's shoulders in a silent show of support. "Her name is Miriam, and you'll use it. Polly and Ginny Mae need Miriam. She's become part of this family—an important part, and it's high time you accept that fact."

"I don't expect you to understand."

"All I know is, you're suffering from grief now, but how much more are your daughters going to suffer if they don't grow up with a woman's love? It's not about you. It's about Polly and Virginia." Something flared in Daniel's eyes, and Gideon paused a moment to let his words sink in. *Lord, please help him understand. Don't let this tear our family apart.* Gideon squeezed Miriam, then moved to the side and clamped his hand on Daniel's shoulder. Quietly he said, "It's bad enough that you sorrow. How could you deny your daughters what they need?"

A wounded sound rumbled deep in Daniel's chest. His face contorted with grief as he turned and shuffled away. Minutes later, the sound of an ax rang over and over and over again.

Tears rained down Miriam's wan cheeks. "What should I do?"

Gideon gathered her to his chest. He bowed his head and whispered into her hair, "Keep doing what you've been doing—love the girls and pray, Miriam. Pray a lot."

When they'd all been together in the one dwelling, the brothers often urged Miriam to read aloud from her Bible as they wound up an evening. Since the day they'd built all of the cottages, it would have been easy for everyone to just drift off, but they hadn't. Gideon picked up the Bible one night and started reading it aloud. Thereafter, whoever so chose took the honor. By late summer, they'd often go out into the yard, sit together, and hold end-of-the-day devotions.

The resonance in Gideon's voice made the verses seem more special and personal. Miriam didn't want to think about that fact, but as she lay in bed one night, she closed her eyes and heard the middle verses of the first chapter of 2 Timothy as he'd read it that night: *"Nevertheless I am not ashamed: for I know whom I have believed, and am persuaded that he is able to keep that which I have committed unto him against that day. Hold fast the form of sound words, which thou hast heard of me, in faith and love which is in Christ Jesus. That good thing which was committed unto thee keep by the Holy Ghost which dwelleth in us."*

Though she'd memorized that passage as a little girl, it felt as if the Lord had wanted her to hear those words again. *I've committed myself to Thee, Lord. Help me to hold fast to the tasks Thou art entrusting to me. Grant me a loving spirit and a vibrant faith so I can let my light shine in this home. Amen.*

Even after she prayed, Miriam felt restless. It would be so nice to simply dump everything into God's hands and sleep with the innocent trust of a baby. Life wasn't that easy. Especially since Daniel's outburst, she'd felt unsettled. Gideon made it clear he felt she belonged here. Titus, Paul, Logan, and Bryce did, too. Polly and Ginny Mae cuddled with her at every opportunity. Her heart told her this was where she wanted and needed to stay, but Daniel's simmering hostility had turned into a painful, purposeful indifference.

Gideon told Daniel he was acting in his own interest instead of what was best for the girls. Am I fooling myself? Am I staying here not just because I love my nieces but because I've let my heart race ahead of my head and ended up falling in love with Gideon?

"Peekyboo!" Ginny Mae went into gales of giggles as Miriam fluffed a shirt from the laundry line over the child, who sat in the big wicker basket.

Gideon leaned against the clothesline and chuckled. "She's liable to chew on that, you know."

Miriam plucked the next shirt off the line. "It's still damp, anyway."

"Why don't you leave it up awhile, then?"

"I have the irons heating. It'll steam dry."

"The whole time we didn't have a woman here, we never once ironed a work shirt. You could skip that chore, and it wouldn't matter one whit."

Miriam shot him a grin. "Strangers knew you were ranchers because your shirts all looked liked cows chewed on them, huh?"

"The finest cows in the state." He puffed out his chest. "We took it as a mark of honor."

He watched as she took a scrap of fabric down from the line and knelt with Polly. Carefully she taught Polly how to wrap up her dolly. Polly's face lit with delight. "Looky, Unca Giddy—looky at my dolly!"

"That's just how your mama used to wrap you." He'd spoken without thinking, but judging from their glowing smiles, Gideon reckoned he'd managed to say the right thing.

Miriam rose and shoved back a damp curl. "Reba said there's a circuit rider coming through, so we'll have a real preacher this week."

"Oh, so we're going to all have to be in our best Sunday-go-to-meeting duds?" He took one end of the sheet off the line and helped her match the corners and fold it. When they met in the middle, he added, "Folks have been right happy with how we've been holding worship on our own."

She tilted her head to the side. "Do you think it's the worship or that we have a meal afterward?"

"Does it matter? Whether they come for the sake of their souls or their bellies, the men are being fed. We're shining light, Miriam."

Her face brightened. "Yes, we are, aren't we?"

"Absolutely." He lifted the laundry basket—Ginny Mae included—and carried it to the main house. "Got word from Chris Roland that he'll be slaughtering a steer tomorrow. He'll bring over a hindquarter so the boys can barbecue it for Sunday."

"That's a blessing." Preceding him into the house, she motioned toward the table.

He set down the laundry and watched as she took two loaves of bread from the oven and slipped in another pair. The yeasty fragrance never ceased to please him. "Mmm-mmm. Think heaven smells that good?"

Miriam laughed. "Oh, I think heaven smells like the cedar trees past the garden—probably because of the verses about the cedars of Lebanon for the temple." She lifted Ginny Mae from the depths of the laundry basket. "Polly, honey, it's nap time."

"I'm not tired." Polly's jaw jutted out.

Gideon knew the look well, and he opened his mouth to scold her, but Miriam's reaction stopped him short. She simply plucked the rag doll from Polly's arms and walked away. Her words drifted over her shoulder. "Well, that's a sad thing. Dolly and sister are going to be lonely, napping without you."

Polly scrambled into the big, old bedroom. A corner of it now held a little trundle bed and a crib where the girls took their naps. "I want my dolly!"

"Then you need to take off your shoes and get in bed." Miriam kept the doll out of reach and started changing Ginny's diaper.

"Unca Giddy, Auntie Miri-Em is mean. Tell her not to be bad to me."

"Polly, you're being a naughty girl." He wagged his finger at her. "A very naughty girl. You're to mind what Aunt Miriam tells you to do. She loves you and would never be mean to you."

"But she gots Dolly!"

"She's being nice. She said if you take off your shoes and get in bed, you may have Dolly back. Sassy as you've been, I would have swatted your backside and kept Dolly."

"But you're a big growed-up man." Her lower lip started to quiver. "You don't need Dolly to cuddle."

"Miriam made Dolly. That makes Dolly very special, and I'd be happy to mind such a fine toy. Even grown-ups like cuddling."

Little braids swinging from the vehemence with which she shook her head, Polly said, "Nuh-unh. Hugs and cuddles is for babies and little girls."

"Snippy little girls get swats, not hugs." He folded his arms across his chest. "Now get those shoes off and climb into bed."

Miriam kissed Ginny Mae's cheek, laid her in the crib, and covered her. "Night-night."

"Nigh-nigh."

Polly yanked off her shoes, scrambled onto her bed, and thrust out her hands. "Dolly!" She hurriedly tacked on, "Please!"

Miriam knelt by the bed and carefully tucked Dolly in next to Polly. She dallied for a moment, then cupped Polly's cheek. "Grown-ups who love each other and get married hug, sweetheart."

"Did my daddy and mama hug?"

"Yes. They loved each other very, very much. Now you have a nice nap and hold Dolly tight."

With the girls situated, Miriam and Gideon went back to the main room. Miriam let out a sigh as she checked the sadirons on the stove.

"You're tired. Why don't you rest while the girls nap?"

"It's not that." Tears filled her pretty green eyes. "Polly's never going to have the security of seeing Hannah and Daniel embracing."

"Shh." He tugged her away from the stove. "Remember? That's one of the reasons you need to be here for them—to teach them those little things. You're not just shining God's light, sweet pea; you're shining light to keep the girls from growing up ignorant and backward."

The rest of the day passed, and they all gathered outside for Bible reading. Miriam caught Gideon giving her a baffled look, and her cheeks went hot with guilt. She hadn't been paying much attention to what Titus read because Gideon's words kept humming through her mind. He'd not just come to accept her here—he'd admitted she belonged and was fulfilling a special calling.

As they broke up after Paul said a prayer, Bryce said, "Betcha we have us a nice, short, misty rain tonight."

Miriam headed toward her cottage, but Gideon stopped her short. "You all that tired?"

"Not really. I was going to crochet or sew a bit."

The left side of his mouth canted upward. "You've been sticking close to home. Why don't we just walk a bit?"

Surprised, she allowed him to lead her along the property toward a stand of cedars. "Smells like heaven to me."

"Looks like heaven, too."

Something about his tone made Miriam glance up. Gideon was looking at her—not at the path. *I have to stop this. He's just being a friend. I can't twist his agreement into a compliment. I can't moon over him or make a fool of myself and ruin what we've started.*

"Look to your left," he murmured.

A doe and fawn ventured from behind a tree.

"Polly would enjoy this. If it weren't her bedtime, we could have brought her along." She hoped bringing up the girls would get her mind back where it belonged.

"She'd scare 'em away. She's so noisy, there isn't a creature God made that'll come close to her. Even the dogs keep their distance."

"And I thought Logan wouldn't take her fishing because he was afraid she'd drown!"

"There is that," Gideon agreed. Even in the failing light, she could see the twinkle in his eyes. "Then, too, wherever Polly goes, her baby sister toddles right after. In case it escaped your notice, Ginny Mae seems to enjoy eating the worms instead of leaving them for bait."

Laughter bubbled out of Miriam. For being such a big, brick wall of a man, Gideon Chance hid a well-honed sense of humor and a wellspring of tenderness.

Their conversation and her laughter sent the deer scampering. Miriam let out a sigh. "I didn't stay any quieter than Polly would have."

"I've been seeing deer day in and day out for years; 'til you came, I hadn't heard a woman's laughter in ages."

He led her along a bit farther and paused here and there for her to step over a root or to lift her over a stump. His hands were sure and strong, and when he finally left her at the door to her cabin, Miriam felt bereft as she slid from the shelter of his hold.

"Good night, Gideon. Thank you for the stroll."

"We'll have to do it more often."

"I'd like that." She slipped into her cabin and latched the door. Leaning against the closed door, she listened to him walk off. *Oh, Gideon, I'd really like that.* She thought about getting ready for bed, but the joy of that evening stroll had her wide awake. Sitting on her bed, crocheting, held absolutely no appeal. Miriam decided to slip over into the main house so she could fetch the *Farmer's Almanac.* With the climate here so different, she wanted to study when the best planting time was for various garden crops.

As she headed toward the house, Miriam noted lights still shone in the main room, so she blew out her own candle. No use wasting it. The door stood ajar, and Bryce's hearty chuckle came through. Miriam reached out to push open the door, but she froze when he said, "So she's takin' the bait, huh, Gideon? Imagine that. Drawing straws might not have been the best way to figure out who ought to marry up with her—"

Chapter 15

Miriam didn't wait to overhear another word. Hand pressed to her mouth, she fled back to her cabin.

Eavesdroppers never hear well of themselves. Mama's oft-times spoken homily taunted Miriam. She hadn't intended to eavesdrop, but she'd definitely gotten an earful. Even in those few seconds, she'd heard more than enough to keep her miserable for the remainder of her days. These barbaric brothers had drawn straws to see who had to wed her? Who were they, to treat her like chattel? Then again, what was so very wrong with her—what did she lack—that not one of them felt she'd make a suitable mate? They drew straws for her hand—an unwanted bride.

So that's why Gideon's been hanging around the house so much more. Well, no one's going to get stuck with me. I'll refuse his proposal. I won't make a fool of myself, mooning over a man who gets saddled with me because he happened to—

She yanked the pins from her hair and cast them onto the washstand. None of them truly wanted her—not even Gideon. Especially not Gideon.

She grabbed her hairbrush as her hair tumbled in disarray about her shoulders. *He participated in the travesty of drawing straws for my hand?*

Ruthlessly pulling the brush through her hair, Miriam looked at her reflection in the small mirror. *I'm not about to make a fool of myself, mooning over a man who figured he had to be honorable but doesn't really want me. It's better to discover Gideon's obligation now rather than to continue to believe a fairy tale I spun for myself.* Her hair crackled as the boar bristles raked the full length over and over again.

God, I don't understand why they'd do this. Thou knowest the desires of my heart. Please, Lord, change my heart. Don't let me have feelings for a man who doesn't hold true regard for me.

"What happened to Miriam?" Paul whispered the words to Gideon as Miriam took Ginny Mae into the other room for a diaper change.

Gideon winced and shrugged.

"I told you she'd get on our nerves," Daniel rumbled as he shoved away from the table. He cast a look at the doorway and slapped his hat on his head. Ginny Mae was in the middle of a stream of happy-sounding baby babble, and Miriam seemed to be understanding a good portion of it. Daniel turned back for a quick moment, gave Gideon a dark look, then left.

"'Member when Mama used to get a bee in her bonnet?" Titus leaned forward and swiped the last biscuit. "She'd get this same way."

"What's she got to be riled over?" Logan said. "Gideon's been a regular swain round her."

Paul snorted. "That's the problem." Titus and Logan snickered.

"She's not riled." Bryce splashed coffee from the pot over his cup and onto the table. "Why, Miriam is just bein' her usual sweet self." He tossed a dishcloth onto the table and did a slapdash mop-up job.

"Hush." Gideon hoped Miriam wouldn't wonder what all the whispering was about. He raised his voice a bit. "Any more eggs left?"

"Nope. Dan ate the last spoonful." Titus tilted the bowl to prove his point.

Miriam came back into the room with Ginny Mae in her arms. "I'll be happy to scramble more."

"No need." Gideon stood. "Bryce, Roland is bringing part of a steer today. I want you to fix up the barbecue pit. Daniel will bring wood over to you."

Miriam wouldn't look him in the eye, and Gideon couldn't figure out why she acted so. . .different this morning. She'd twisted her hair up same as always and wore one of her old, ugly dresses, so she ought to look the same, but her smile seemed forced as she started to clear the table. "Anyone have something special they'd like me to fix for Sunday supper?"

"Chocolate cake," Bryce voted.

"Pudding, please," Polly requested.

"Since you're asking—" Titus began.

"Hold your horses." Gideon glowered at them. "Miriam's going to fix whatever suits her fancy. She's not here to dance a jig to your tunes."

Miriam turned to carry the dishes to the sink. "It's no problem for me to make what someone might want."

"I do have a hankering for—"

Gideon silenced Titus with a look. "I'm sure whatever Miriam makes will be delicious. We need to get to work."

"Paul? Could you please bring me your blue shirt? I noticed it needs to be mended." Miriam dipped hot water from the stove reservoir to use for dish washing.

By supper, a platter heaped with steaming chicken-fried steaks drew the men to the table. Gideon frowned at the empty place beside him. "Come eat, Miriam."

"Oh, I already ate an early supper with the girls." She busied herself, pumping water into a pail.

"What are you doing?"

"Saturday bathwater, right?" Paul guessed.

"Yes." She flashed a smile over her shoulder.

Gideon pushed away from the table and stalked across the kitchen. He hefted the bucket of water and thumped it onto the stove, then filled another pail and placed it on the stove, as well. "Ask for help with that, Miriam. It's too heavy for you."

"Nonsense." She dried her hands off on the hem of her apron and headed toward the other room. "Come along, my little poppets." Polly scampered in her wake, and Ginny followed with the eager, flat-footed patter only a baby in a full diaper could manage.

Splashes and giggles from the bedroom made it clear the girls enjoyed bath time. Gideon still scowled at his full plate. Somehow, with Miriam absent, the meal didn't appeal to him half as much. When the splashing ended, he fully expected Miriam to reappear.

He was wrong.

"Hey." Logan elbowed him. "I asked for the applesauce."

"Oh. Here." Gideon shoved the bowl into his brother's hands. The meal was over before Miriam and the girls reappeared. Both girls wore nightgowns Miriam had made from feed sacks that bore little bitty chickens all over them. Ginny Mae's baby curls fluffed out like duck down.

"Lookit me!" Polly twirled around.

"What happened to your head?" Bryce squinted at her.

"Auntie Miri-Em sticked rags in my hair. I'm going to have pretty curls."

"I'll tuck them in bed if you'd like to take your bath now, Daniel." Miriam stooped down to fuss with Ginny's sleeve.

"No. I tuck my girls in." Daniel cast a glance at his brothers. "They can keep an eye on my daughters for me."

"Not 'til after you do supper dishes." Titus plopped down on the floor and tickled under Polly's chin. "It's your turn to dry the dishes, Dan. I'm washin' tonight."

"Dishes are a woman's job," Dan gritted.

"You didn't say that when Hannah was here." Paul's words made everything in the room go still. "We all pitched in and did dishes back then."

"Miriam's done plenty enough already." Gideon stared at Daniel. "She's washed and ironed everyone's clothes for church tomorrow. She's cooked and cleaned, gardened, and minded your children."

"Mended my shirt, too," Paul added.

The door clicked shut. Gideon wheeled around and discovered Miriam had slipped out.

"Miriam, this is Dr. Pendergast." Reba White fluttered her fan with skill any Southern belle would admire. "Dr. Pendergast, may I present you to Miss Miriam Hancock."

The doctor swept off his gray bowler and bowed quite elegantly. "A pleasure, Miss Hancock."

Miriam watched him straighten up and wondered why a man of such noble and lucrative profession would be attired in such ill-fitting clothes. She'd been reared not to judge a man by his appearance, but something struck her as being wrong.

"I'm pleased to have an opportunity to speak with a physician. With the girls so small, and—"

"Oh no. That's not it at all." Reba giggled. "He's a phrenologist, dear. I told him he simply must examine your head to be sure that bump you received upon your arrival didn't cause you any harm."

"I've worried 'bout that," Logan confessed. "I didn't mean to brain you, Miriam. You know I didn't."

"I'm fine. Truly I am."

"It would be wise to have a professional ascertain that." Dr. Pendergast started to remove his dove gray gloves.

"I don't—"

"It won't take much time, and it won't hurt at all."

"How much does it cost?" Bryce stuck his hand into his pocket. To Miriam's consternation, he pulled out half a dozen screws and nails. He pursed his lips and shook his head. "Heard the jingle. Forgot it wasn't cash money."

"Bryce, please don't put those back into your Sunday-best pants. They'll ruin the pocket."

He'd already started. As a nail hit the earth by his boot, a sheepish look crossed his face. "Oops. Too late."

"It's not a problem, young man. I can tell from here. See?" The phrenologist ran his fingers over the back of her head. "This is the area denoting domesticity. Miss Hancock is endowed with a veritable ridge in this location."

"Uh-oh." Logan's face turned an odd combination of green and purple. "Does that mean when I brained her, it broke her head?"

"That has yet to be ascertained. Come now, Miss Hancock. It's far better if you sit for your reading."

"Yes, Miriam. You must!" Reba half-dragged her to a chair.

Before she knew what happened, Miriam was sitting on a bench and had her hair streaming down her shoulders and back. Dr. Pendergast's fingers skated over her scalp. She shivered and tried to pull away. "I must insist you cease this." Miriam wiggled. "Logan, I don't believe in this. It's a dark art, and I won't be a part of it."

"Young lady, this is medical science." Dr. Pendergast kept his palm atop her head and continued to slip the fingertips of his other hand along her head. "The apostle Luke was a physician."

"A physician, not a phrenologist!"

"Ah, you're displaying remarkable stubbornness—which is confirmed here, by this region of the brow."

"She can be a mite stubborn," Bryce allowed.

"I'm going to be more than a little stubborn if you don't turn loose of me."

"Women are wont to be emotional. Here, the prominence over the seat of emotions tells me she's often overwrought. My, my. Here, over the area of spiritual enlightenment—an area of concavity."

"That's about where she got the lump when Logan brained her." Bryce leaned forward.

"Concavity means it dips in, not lumps out." Miriam wrenched loose. "Sir, to pretend education, discipline, and salvation cannot overcome natural formations of the skull is heresy. I—"

"What is going on here?" Gideon shoved through the knot of men who had congregated and pressed in around her. His eyes widened as he caught sight of her with her hair in disarray.

"We was just trying to be sure the doc got a chance to make sure Miriam's in her right mind." Three more screws clinked on the ground by Bryce's foot.

"A doctor? Good. It would be better if you did this inside."

"He's a quack, Gideon." Miriam tried to twist her hair back into a decent arrangement but had no way of making it stay since the doctor had done something with her hairpins.

"She's overwrought and stubborn, just as I determined," Pendergast pronounced in a stentorian voice. The men around them nodded and murmured agreement.

Gideon tucked her by his side. Miriam dared hope he'd see reason, but her hopes disappeared the moment he started walking her toward the house. "It'll only take a few minutes, and it'll make me feel better to know you're all right."

Pendergast trotted on their heels. Gideon didn't just seat her. He kept hold and sat on a bench, dragging her along without any hope of escape. Pendergast kept his opinions to himself and made important-sounding *hmm* and *aah* sounds as he wiggled his fingers across her head.

Miriam shuddered. "Gideon—"

"It's okay, sweet pea. He'll be done soon. You don't have to be scared." Gideon looked up. "Well, Doc? What do you think?"

"For being a woman, she has reasonable intellect and strong domestic swayings. Science never lies, and it's plain as can be she's spiritually lacking and a woman of dubious virtue. I—"

Gideon let out a roar and bolted to his feet. "You ought to get your head examined if you think that opinion holds any weight here. You're no doctor; you're a charlatan."

"You owe me fifteen cents for my services."

Gideon tucked Miriam behind himself. "You're conducting business on the Lord's Day?"

"Well, sir, the laborer is worthy of his hire."

Paul stood in the open doorway. "Gideon, the men are hungry. When's Miriam going to serve up lunch?"

"As soon as this charlatan stops insulting and swindling her."

Miriam watched as half a dozen men stormed through the house and carried Mr. Pendergast away. Gideon tilted her face up to his. "Well," she said brightly, hoping to evade more than just a second of eye contact, "that's over now."

"He needed to get his own head examined, Miriam. You're the sweetest, most special woman any fellow could ever meet."

She forced a laugh and pulled free. "That settles that. If ever a real doctor comes by, he'll need to check you, because you're definitely not in your right mind!"

Nothing is going right. Nothing. Miriam let out a sigh and decided to take a walk as the girls napped.

Since she'd learned about the brothers drawing straws, everything had seemed to fall apart. Sunday, the so-called doctor declared her to be a woman of no virtue. Monday, she'd burned what should have been a tender roast. Yesterday, the ammonia she wanted to use to wash windows spilled and left the main house reeking. Today, Ginny Mae bit Polly's arm, and Polly whacked her little sister back hard enough to leave a mark on her cheek. Getting both of them settled down for a nap drained the last drop of Miriam's patience.

The cedars beckoned her. Their scent would be a treat, and Miriam needed to indulge herself. She grabbed a pail and walked along the same path Gideon had led her along when they took that stroll—just before she'd learned the truth. Unhappy with that realization, Miriam sidestepped and wandered off a few yards and sauntered along a route of her own choosing.

Sunlight slashed in dusty beams from the treetops. The scent of cedar and pine filled the air. Beneath her feet, pine needles crunched and twigs snapped. Miriam's steps lagged. She occasionally picked up a pinecone to use as a fire starter for her cottage's potbelly stove.

It felt good to have a few minutes to herself. What once had been a comfortable, happy arrangement now felt strained. Monitoring each word she spoke, each casual touch or glance so it wouldn't carry a hint of interest or flirtation—that drained her.

Miriam knelt to harvest dandelion leaves—one of the few things around the ranch she knew were edible. *I'm like these. I'm hearty. I can thrive here.* She plucked a top that had gone to seed and upended it to reseed the patch. *I'm not going to blow away. I'm setting down new roots here.*

As she walked, she kept the cabins in sight. She couldn't be gone for long. Again, she crossed the path she and Gideon walked. Her heart twisted. A noble man, he was willing to marry though he felt no *tendresse* for her. *Why, God? Why would these feelings for a man fill my heart when all he feels toward me is fraternal concern and obligation? How am I to deal with this?*

After picking more dandelion greens, Miriam headed back toward the house. As she passed the spot under a cedar where she and Gideon had paused to talk on their stroll, she couldn't resist. Miriam picked some wildflowers and an armful of pretty leaves to put in her cottage. They would be a reminder to herself that she could find beauty and pleasure here—even as a spinster.

Miriam left the bucket by the pump in the yard and peeked in to make sure the girls were still napping. Peacefully slumbering as they were, she decided to prop open the door so she could hear them, then went to the garden to do some work.

Awhile later, Daniel startled her out of her musings by striding through the rows of vegetables. "How dim-witted can you be?"

She blinked up at him. "I beg your pardon?"

"The bucket by the pump is your doing, right?"

"Yes. Why?"

"It's full of poison oak." He jabbed a finger toward the bucket. "Go get rid of it and change before you get near my daughters. If your clothes brush them, they'll get the rash. I won't have you harming them."

"Daniel, I'd never knowingly hurt Polly or Virginia." She headed toward the pump to dispose of the leaves.

"Dump it far away," he called. "The last thing we need is you planting that stuff close by."

By the time she got back, Miriam knew she'd gotten herself into a peck of trouble. Her hands, wrists, and face all started to itch and tingle. At first, she told herself it was just her imagination, but the feeling grew worse.

Daniel sat in the doorway to the main house, using a whetstone to sharpen knives. He didn't even bother to glance up. "Go change your gown. It has to be boiled, else it'll make my girls get the rash."

She got into her cabin, shed her dress, and looked at herself with dismay. Hairline to throat, wrists to fingertips, she was covered in a fine red rash that felt fiery as could be. The cool water from her pitcher didn't help—if anything, it made the itch intensify. Afraid her stockings or petticoat might also carry the rash, she changed every last garment before going back to care for the girls.

Polly hunkered down beside Daniel on the porch, chattering like a magpie. She looked up, and her eyes widened. "Auntie Miri-Em, you is funny!"

A lady does not scratch. Miriam clasped her hands in front of herself to resist the nearly overwhelming urge to abandon her manners. "Yes. I do look odd."

"Go back to your cabin." Daniel concentrated on the edge of the knife he continued to slide along the whetstone. "We can manage just fine without you."

She didn't want to admit defeat, but Miriam couldn't stand the horrid itch much longer. She slipped back into her cottage and cried.

Hours passed, and she thought about making supper. Standing by the hot stove would amount to pure torture. Nonetheless, the girls and men would need to eat. Perhaps she could make sandwiches just this once. . . .

A single, solid *thump* on her door sounded. "Miriam. Open up."

Gideon. *Of all the people in the world, he's the one I least want to see.* She cleared her throat. "No."

"Dan's minding the girls. Something's up."

"It's nothing."

"If it's nothing, then come on out here." She could hear his boots scuffle in the dirt. "I want to show you something."

"It'll have to wait."

"I'm not going to shout through this door anymore. Now get yourself out here."

"I'm not one of your kid brothers, Gideon. You cannot order me around."

"Hey, Gid!" Logan's voice interrupted their odd disagreement. She ardently hoped Logan would draw him away.

"What?" Already irked, Gideon's voice carried a distinct edge.

"Is Miriam gonna be okay? Dan said she got it bad."

"Got what?"

"Oh. I thought you knew. Dan said—"

Unwilling to be spoken about and well aware the secret was out, she yanked open the door and snapped, "I was an idiot. There. Now leave me alone."

Chapter 16

Gideon whistled under his breath. Red blazed across Miriam's face, but it owed more to rash than embarrassment. He studied her face, her throat, and looked down at her hands. She'd kept them clasped behind her back, and he suspected she wanted to hide the full extent of her exposure.

"Aw, sweet pea. You tangled with poison oak, didn't you?"

"So Daniel said. I had no notion what it was."

He heaved a sigh. "It's wild. Grows all over."

"And you never mentioned it to me?"

If glares could kill, Gideon reckoned he'd be pushing up daisies about now. "I'll go fetch some milk and churn it. Mama used buttermilk on us whenever we—"

"I'll churn my own buttermilk."

"No." He pointed at the bed. "You go have a rest. The salt from sweat only makes the rash itch worse."

She gave him a horrified look. "Are you implying I sweat, Gideon Chance?"

He had the sinking feeling whatever he said, it would only make matters worse. He opted for escape. "I'll be back. Leave your door open so your cottage has lots of fresh air—"

"So I won't sweat?"

Figuring he'd be signing his own death warrant no matter what he said, Gideon left. Her door was shut when he returned, and he couldn't help chuckling. Feisty as could be, Miriam wasn't about to show any weakness, and this wasn't really anything more than a bout of misery. He drummed his fingers on her windowpane.

The yellow curtain swished to the side, and a slate appeared. "Leave me be," he read aloud.

The slate disappeared as the curtain swished back down.

"All right, Miriam. I'll leave you be. . ." He paused, then tacked on, "u-t-t-e-r-m-i-l—"

The door opened. "You are a nuisance, Gideon." The fire in her green eyes turned into a twinkle. "And a terrible guide. I'm holding you responsible for this tragedy."

"You couldn't have gotten this from where we went on our stroll. I know for a fact that path's clear as can be."

"You should have made sure nothing poisonous was around the property, and you certainly could have warned me about it."

"We try to keep it hacked back, but you must have gone off the path." Her mouth opened in a perfect O that could have denoted either shock or guilt, but Gideon didn't want either, so he hastily added, "Truth is, no one's sure exactly how many variations there are of the pesky stuff."

Her speckled brow creased. "Then how do you avoid it?"

He stuck his bandanna into the gloppy buttermilk and dabbed it on her cheek. "You do your best. Other than staying where things are cleared, just remember a saying: 'Leaves of three, let them be.' It seems many of the varieties of poison oak bear three leaves to the stem."

"Now you tell me," she muttered. He nudged her chin with his thumb so he could get to her throat, but she resisted and claimed, "I can take care of myself. Just tell me how long I'm going to itch."

"Can't say." He refused to stop. Dipping the bandanna back into the buttermilk, he recalled, "My last episode lasted about six days. I have water in the wash kettle comin' to a boil so we can dunk your dress."

"If that works with the clothes, why wouldn't a hot bath take away my rash?"

"Because that would make life too easy." He daubed her nose. "Life out here is never easy."

Miriam had been trying to find things to occupy her time since Gideon decreed she wasn't allowed to do anything for the next week. As dreadfully as she itched and as horrid as the rash looked, she didn't exactly mind that order the first two days. In fact, adding a cup of baking soda to the big galvanized tub was the only time she got any respite.

Gideon brought over the green paisley material and the lace he'd bought in town for her. Her hands hurt, but she stitched on the dress so she wouldn't be tempted to scratch.

"Miriam?" Paul leaned against her doorjamb. "Got any good ideas on what to make for supper?"

"What about some corn chowder?" She gave him explicit instructions and fully expected to have him return to review them a time or two. Judging from the food the men had been fixing the last few days, Miriam decided their survival bordered on the miraculous. No matter what the dish, they managed to botch it somehow or another.

She sat at the little drop-leaf desk in her cottage and finished writing another letter to her cousin. Delilah had managed to send her a note last week, and Miriam invited her to come for a visit whenever she'd like to. *It shouldn't cause a problem if she accepts. Delilah can stay here in my cottage with me.*

After she pasted shut the envelope, Miriam looked out her open door and waited until she spied the next Chance to pass by. "Titus?"

"Yep?"

"I'd like to post a letter. Could you please help me hitch up the buckboard? I'll take the girls to town with me."

He shook his head. "Nope. Gideon said you're off work detail until Monday. 'Sides, I just got back from town. Brought back more baking soda for you to soak in."

"How thoughtful. That terrible itch is almost gone now, but it's good to have a supply on hand, just in case."

Titus scuffed his boot in the dirt. "Truth is, I was hoping maybe I could talk with you a minute or so."

"Sure." She left her cottage and sat out on a bench. Titus ambled alongside her, but he didn't take a seat. Instead, he planted one boot on the bench beside her and leaned forward so he could lean on that knee.

"Something's on your mind, Titus?"

He nodded. "A gal."

"Hmm."

"She's as purty as a speckled pup, Miriam—only she'd have a hissy fit if she heard me say such a thing. She's cultured and classy—went to a finishing school."

"Oh, the Whites' daughter is back?"

"That's the one." A slow smile lit his face. The expression made him look even more like Gideon than usual. "She came in on the stage today. You've never seen such a day gown. I venture she has more rows of ribbons and lace on it than—" He stopped abruptly and went ruddy.

"So she has lovely clothes." Miriam ignored whatever avenue his mind might have been traveling and pulled him back to the subject. "Did you invite her to attend church?"

"Her mama already said they were a-comin'."

"Then you'll have to maneuver so as to be seated next to the lovely lady."

"Now that's a dandy plan." Titus leaned closer and lowered his voice. "Priscilla just got back, but a fellow can't wait—not around here. I'm figuring maybe I ought to pop the question straightaway, before some other buck does, so I have dibs on her."

"Titus! Were you and Miss White courting before she left, or did you have an understanding?"

"No." His expression turned guarded.

"How can you know if she's the right one, then? She may be a vision of beauty, but that doesn't mean the Lord intends your souls to be forged into one. It's not the outward appearance that should count. You're worth more than having a china doll on your arm, Titus. You deserve a woman who will be your helpmeet and share her heart with you."

"I could ask Paul to move in with Gideon so I'd be able to offer her a place of our own. I'd even be willing to go into town to help her pa at the store if he needs me."

"You're willing to offer your goods and your muscles, Titus. That's a start. But are you willing to share your heart? Do you even know if Priscilla has any feelings for you? Working hard and being attracted are fine, but they aren't enough to make a marriage work."

"I just don't want someone else to beat me to the punch and snap her up. We don't get many womenfolk up here."

"You asked my opinion, and from a woman's perspective, I have to tell you that a man who wants a bride based only on her availability or appearance isn't the kind of man a worthy woman would wed." She reached over and touched his arm. "Pray before you act."

"Can't say I'm surprised you said that, but ever notice that fellas move a lot faster than God lots of the time?"

"You're right. Maybe that's why the world is in such a state."

Titus wandered off to do some praying and thinking. Miriam sat on the bench and closed her eyes. She needed to listen to her own advice. A man who wanted a woman just because she was available ought never propose. She wouldn't put up with such a sham marriage. *Gideon might have drawn the short straw, but that doesn't mean I have to accept if he proposes. He can just go search for a bride elsewhere.*

"Now that was a fine meal. Don't know how you do it, but every last thing you make is a treat." Gideon smiled at Miriam as he pulled her chair back from the supper table. She'd made a zesty chili and corn bread and topped off the meal with a fine-tasting berry pie. As far as he was concerned, life didn't get better than that.

"Thank you. I'm glad you liked it." She rose and began stacking dishes.

He reached over and took the plates from her and set them back down on the table. "How about going for a stroll?"

"I'd rather not."

Her refusal surprised him. He steered her out to the porch as his brothers started to clear the table and squabble over who was supposed to wash dishes. Gideon turned her and held both arms above the elbows to be sure he wasn't bothering any last splotches of her poison oak rash. Studying her eyes, he wondered aloud, "You're not still sore at me about forgetting to tell you about the poison oak, are you?"

"I've forgiven you."

He couldn't resist smiling back at her. Sweetness radiated from the woman. Trailing his fingers down her soft cheek, he rumbled, "If you're afraid I'll walk you through a patch, I'll carry a lantern."

Miriam shied away from his touch. "There are better ways to shine your light."

He chuckled at her cleverness, but he still hadn't succeeded in his goal. He wanted to be alone with her. "Tell you what. Come with me to shut the chickens back into the coop."

"Okay. Did you know two of the eggs this morning were double yolked?"

Most of the hens were content to get back to their nests as twilight fell. A few stubborn ones scattered and needed to be chased down. Once done with that task, Gideon shut one large door of the chicken "cabinet" as Miriam shut the other. He met her in the middle and latched it closed.

"We make a good team." He silently congratulated himself on that segue. Surely it counted as a slick way to ease into an opportunity to pop the question.

"I've been impressed by the way you and your brothers work together to keep this place going."

"That's a mighty fine compliment." He smiled at her. "Your opinion holds a lot of sway with me, so that makes your words count for even more."

Miriam looked as if she were ready to head toward her cottage, and Gideon slipped a hand around her wrist to hold her back. Now that he'd worked up the courage, he wanted to get this over with.

"Miriam, you're already part of the family, but I'd like to make it formal. Will you do me the honor of becoming my wife?"

Chapter 17

"Your offer is generous, but I'm afraid I'll have to decline."

Gideon stared at Miriam in disbelief. He'd never imagined she'd refuse his proposal. It was all supposed to be so easy, so practical. Miriam never stirred up problems; she solved them. What had gotten into her, to wreck his carefully laid plans?

"Why not?" He blurted out the question.

Even in the evening light, he could see the color drain from her face. "It's not right," she stammered. "It just won't work."

"But—"

"Please excuse me. . . ." She dashed back to her cottage and shut the door so fast, a stranger would have thought the hounds of Hades were on her heels.

Gideon beat his hat against his thigh and headed toward the barn. He needed time alone. Never had it occurred to him that Miriam wouldn't consider the two of them to be a suitable match. At the moment, he had to figure out what to do next.

Unfortunately, Paul was in the barn. He folded his arms on the top of a stall door. "Well, when's the big day?"

"It isn't."

"Oh. You sure are takin' your time at all of this courtin' business. I thought for sure you were trying to get Miriam to go for a walk so's you could propose."

"I asked; she refused." The admission stung his pride, but the hurt went far deeper than that. Gideon couldn't figure out why.

"What did you do wrong?"

What did I do wrong? The question kept running through Gideon's mind. A proposal in front of a chicken coop wasn't exactly romantic enough to make a girl swoon with delight, but Miriam wasn't like other gals. Besides, he'd tried to get her to take a walk. She just didn't cooperate.

"Did you think to show her Ma's ring so she knew you weren't funnin' her?"

"I'm not bribing a woman to be my bride!"

Paul heaved a sigh. "I didn't say you were. I reckoned since she turned you down, maybe she took it for a joke—like she did the day we built the cabins. She didn't realize Marv was making a serious offer. Could be the gal just didn't understand you meant business."

"Mind your own business, Paul." *She had to know I was serious. Maybe I just shocked her. She might need time getting used to the notion.*

"Fine. She's your problem."

"She's not a problem; she's just confused. Women sometimes need to let an idea take root."

"Yeah. Ma was like that. Said she liked to sleep on things." Paul shrugged. "If it doesn't work out, Titus and I'll go ahead and draw straws."

Gideon glowered, and Paul left the barn. Gideon paced back and forth, trying to determine what had made calm, meek Miriam run off. *Maybe she thinks it's wrong to have a wedding since Hannah died. But Hannah died nearly a year ago. Silly woman scampered off too fast. I need to reason with her.*

Heart breaking asunder, Miriam curled up on her bed. Gideon had offered her what she most wanted, but it would be an empty marriage because he felt no love for her. *God, please help me. Strengthen me. Make this terrible situation go away. I can't bear to see Gideon again tomorrow. I don't know what to do.*

She'd come to her cabin because she couldn't bear to have Gideon offer matrimony when his heart wasn't in it. Her refusal was supposed to free him of any obligation.

A man who loves a woman pursues her, courts her, woos her. I won't bind him to me because he has misguided loyalties to his brothers and nieces. Someday, when he meets the woman of his dreams, he'll thank me for letting him off the hook. The idea of Gideon falling in love and marrying someone else made her bury her face in the pillow and start crying again.

Papa always spoke the message, but Mama had a knack for speaking words of wisdom at the right time. Miriam wished Mama were here to share this burden. "*I rely on God's Word and prayer, but when I flounder, God sometimes speaks to me in a song.*" Mama's words sifted through Miriam's aching heart. She huddled on the bed and waited. Soon a hymn threaded through her mind.

"When darkness seems to hide His face, I rest on His unchanging grace." The lyrics pulled at her. She started to hum but gave up. All she managed was a broken, off-key croak—a pathetic sound that matched the shattered feeling in her heart. "*When all around my soul gives way, He then is all my Hope and Stay.*"

Miriam wiped tears from her face. *Lord, be my Hope and Stay. Everything around me is giving way, but Thou changest not.*

In the midst of her prayer, a solid, single *thump* rattled her door. Gideon. No one else "knocked" like that.

"Miriam!"

No one else bellowed like that, either.

"We need to talk."

She sat on the edge of her bed. "You're not talking; you're hollering like a madman."

"If I'm insane, it's your fault." He lowered his voice. "Take pity on me and get out here."

"Why don't you take pity on me and leave me alone?"

He groaned. "You've been crying, haven't you?"

She didn't answer. Lying was a sin, but she figured keeping her mouth shut wasn't exactly the same thing. He didn't have a right to know how she felt, anyway.

"We can work this out. I know we can," he cajoled.

Waiting wasn't going to make the problem go away. If anything, the longer Gideon stood out there, talking at her door, the greater the chances were that all of his brothers would get involved in this travesty. Miriam crossed the floor.

"Any problem can be worked out if folks are reasonable."

"And," she said as she opened the door and stared up into his face, "they have a handful of straws."

Gideon gave her a baffled look.

Mortified to the core, Miriam admitted, "I know about what happened. You're supposed to be stuck with me, but I'm not going to be a part of it. So now can we stop all of this embarrassing nonsense and get back to being normal?"

"If you knew, why are you mad?"

"You mean, you're supposed to have that right because you're the one who lost and drew the short straw?" Her jaw jutted out. "You can be a happy man again. Go back and tell your brothers I let you off the hook."

"Have you taken leave of your senses? Why would I do an idiotic thing like that?"

Miriam let out a choppy sigh. "I'm not going to run away with some other rancher or cowboy. I'm committed to staying here."

"That's all well and good, but—"

"So you didn't have to draw straws. It was unnecessary."

"Sweet pea, I don't get it at all. If anything, I'd think you'd feel better, knowing how that all worked out."

She stared at him in utter amazement.

Gideon's expression shifted. "Bryce is the only one who would have blabbed. What did he tell you?"

"I refuse to discuss this."

"Tough. I want you for my bride. I refused to take a chance at not having you. My mama and daddy were a love match, and I wouldn't settle for anything less. You're my one-in-a-million chance to truly be happy, and I want to make you happy, too. I couldn't risk Paul or Titus getting the straw, so I took 'em all."

"What?"

"Right out there in the barn in front of my brothers, I grabbed those straws and ground them into the dust." He let out a rueful chuckle at the memory. "Titus teased me about volunteering, and I shocked him out of his socks when I said I couldn't stand to let you go to anyone else—that you were mine." He spread his hands. "If you're wanting fancy courtin', I'll do my dead-level best, but I'm warning you here and now, I'm liable to make a mess of it."

"Yup, he is," Bryce called.

"Hush and get in the house." Gideon didn't even bother to look over his shoulder. He continued to look her in the eyes. "I've got me five pesky brothers and a busy ranch, but that's just the world God set me in. It wasn't 'til the day you arrived that I came to life. You challenged me to be the man God wants me to be. You brightened each day."

"You feel that way about me?"

"Sweet pea, you marched in here and stole my heart before I knew what happened. I love you. Now I was hopin' to take you on a nice stroll under the moon and declare my undying love, but you're skittish of poison oak. Where's a fellow to take his gal so's he can propose?"

She stood on tiptoe and whispered in his ear, "You can take me in your arms, Gideon. That's where I'd really love to be."

Two weeks later, Gideon and Paul rode out to check on fencing. Titus went to town, and Gideon suspected he'd be there awhile. He'd nicked himself shaving, borrowed Paul's bay rum, and gladly accepted Miriam's offer to iron his shirt.

"Titus is sweet on Priscilla White," Paul said.

"I figured as much. A man's got a right to pick his mate. Can't say I'd be thrilled if he marries her, though." Gideon eased back in the saddle. "Her pa calls her 'Prissy' for good cause."

"Her mama wants her to catch the banker. Rovel has more money than anyone else hereabouts. Expensive as all of Priscilla's dresses are, I reckon she'll want a man with wads of money."

"Don't tell Titus that. He'll figure it out soon enough."

Not long thereafter, Titus rode up. He took off his hat and wiped the sweat from his brow with his sleeve. "You're never gonna believe this."

"What I believe is, you'd best better use your bandanna instead of your sleeve." Gideon scowled at him. "Miriam's already busy enough without having to do extra laundry."

"That's what I'm talking about."

"Laundry?"

"No. Miriam being busy. She's not going to be in the least bit happy, Gideon. It's going to upset her."

"What's going to upset her?"

"I saw the circuit rider."

Gideon's eyes narrowed. "Where? When?"

"He stopped through here to announce he's takin' on a regular pastorate and won't be coming through anymore."

"Not yet, he can't! The wedding's in two weeks."

Titus slapped his hat back on his head. "Well, that's why I'm here—to tell you that he'll come out to the house at breakfast tomorrow to do the wedding. It's either that, or you and Miriam will have to go into San Francisco alone to get hitched properlike."

Gideon turned his horse toward the house. During the half hour it took to ride there, he tried to figure out how to break the news to Miriam. From the evening she'd accepted his proposal, she'd been working on plans for a storybook wedding. Every evening, she'd chatter on about what she'd done that day. A whole hive of bees couldn't come close to matching such industry. Their honey wouldn't be half as sweet, either.

A newly made wedding shirt awaited Gideon. Miriam had sent all of the brothers out with fancy handwritten invitations. She'd gotten Paul to build an altar and Bryce to polish Mama's silver candlesticks. By transplanting clumps of wildflowers, she had the yard looking downright fancy. Come winter, those flowers would die out, but he didn't have the heart to tell her so. As long as she was happy and they'd make for her fairy-tale-perfect wedding, everything suited him just fine.

The problem was, if they got married tomorrow, she wouldn't have the fancy cake all baked or her dress finished. She thought she had fourteen days; she had fourteen hours.

Chapter 18

Hitching Splotch outside the house, Gideon rehearsed what he'd say. Reba White stood in the door like an avenging angel and made him lose his lines when she dramatically struck a pose very much like a starfish holding fast to the doorjamb and squawked, "Get back on your horse this very minute! You're not allowed here."

"I need to see Miriam."

"Absolutely not!"

Gideon headed for the door, fully expecting Reba to calm down and yield. "Reba, this is important."

She looked as belligerent as a just-saddled feral mustang. "Nothing is more important than your future."

"Yup. That's why I need to see Miriam." He stepped forward, figuring Reba would cave in and back up so he'd get by her. He was wrong. Toe-to-toe with her, he glared down. "I don't have time to waste here."

"You've got a lifetime, cowboy. Whatever you have to say can just wait 'til supper." She whispered, "We're working on Miriam's dress. You can't see it."

"I don't care about the dress; it's Miriam I need to see."

"She's in it—or what we have started of it. I have her pinned into the bodice, and it's taken us all morning to get it just right."

"Good. So it's done." That boded well. Relief flooded him.

"Done?" Reba laughed. "Gideon, it's just pinned. We have to sew it together and—"

"Miriam." He raised the volume slightly without letting the dread show. His bride set lots of store in having this pretty dress, and he was going to have to tell her—

"Yes?"

"Come here, sweet pea." Rustling told him she'd be there in a minute.

Wrapped in the tablecloth, she appeared just behind Reba. An area about the size of his fist got singed on the tablecloth when he'd wrapped her in it to extinguish the fire. He didn't tell Miriam he could see airy white material through the hole. She'd already listed crocheting a tablecloth as something she needed to do before the wedding. *One more reason for her to get in a dither.*

Reba waggled her finger under his nose. "No peeking." She scuttled into the other room to give them some privacy.

"You're beautiful." The words slipped out of his mouth, and Miriam's smile was ample reward. *Lord, let it all go this well.*

"It's taken hours, but we have the design all set, Gideon. I want my gown to be beautiful for you—and for our daughter to wear on her wedding day."

"That's what I have to tell you—our wedding day. It's tomorrow."

Merry laughter bubbled out of her. When he didn't join in, her laughter died out. Her eyes grew huge.

"The circuit rider will be here in the morning. He's taken a regular pastorate, so he's not available for our original date." There. He'd said the lines he'd planned, and he'd gotten them out quite smoothly.

"We'll just have to wait for the next circuit rider, then."

"We are not waiting." He gave her the glower that always made his kid brothers toe the mark. "It took us two years before we got that parson. There's no telling how long it'll take before we'll have another man of the cloth to officiate. We're getting married tomorrow."

"But that was before this area became civilized and so well populated, Gideon." Completely unaffected by his glower, she gave him her I'm-being-practical smile. "We're bound to have a parson arrive in a matter of months."

"Months!"

She bobbed her head, and her eyes brightened. "Why, it's actually a blessing, Gideon. It'll give me more time on my gown, and—"

"We're getting married in the morning, Miriam. I don't care if you're in your nightdress or Bryce's britches. You'll be my bride tomorrow." Her face went pale as he thundered those words, and Gideon wished he'd been more diplomatic. "Swathed in a tablecloth, you're beautiful, Miriam. I couldn't care less about what you're wearing. I just want you to be mine."

She held the tablecloth tightly about herself and squared her shoulders. Moments passed, and several expressions flitted across her face. Her voice quavered. "You're marrying me, not my dress. I understand. A sound marriage is more important than an elaborate wedding."

"We can still celebrate in two weeks—make that date a fancy reception." There. That qualified as a good compromise.

Miriam nodded slowly.

He trailed his fingers down her cheek. She'd lost her sparkle, and he knew he'd just destroyed her plans for a dreams-come-true wedding. "I'm sorry it worked out this way. You had it all planned out. Our only other choice would be to go to San

Francisco and get married there."

"Would everybody come with us?" Hope flickered in her eyes.

"No. Too much to be done around here."

"I don't want to go off and get married among strangers. A wedding is all about love and family."

Reba called out softly, "I don't mean to be rude, but time's a-wasting, and these girls are going to wake up from their nap soon."

"Come on out," Gideon said. "Maybe you and Miriam can fix something she can wear. Things got moved up. The wedding's in the morning."

Reba gave a yelp. "Tomorrow!" She gave Gideon an outraged look. "Impossible. She doesn't have a dress. The netting I ordered for her veil isn't even here yet!"

Why do women put store by such silly fripperies? But Gideon saw the wince Miriam hadn't managed to hide at the mention of a veil. He could solve that problem. "Veils are wretched things. A man ought to have the pleasure of seeing his bride's radiance. Given my druthers, I want flowers in her hair."

"Well now, there's a fine plan." Reba perked up.

Miriam managed a wobbly smile. "I used up all the eggs this morning. Could you go rustle up a few more? I'll need them for the cake."

"Cake?"

Her brow arched. "You don't think we're getting married without a wedding cake, do you?"

Laughter bellowed out of him. She'd do without a gown and veil, but she was still going to make this an event. Miriam always made the best of things, and he prized that trait in her. "Woman, I'm so glad you're mine."

Admitting defeat didn't come easily. Miriam rolled over in her bed and stared at the white heap on the floor. She'd tried her best to stitch together the bodice while Reba whipped together the skirt. Even then, they'd come to the disappointing realization that if they had four other women here to spend all night sewing with them, the wedding gown wouldn't be finished.

Lord, You've blessed me with such a fine man. Help me to let go of little-girl dreams and be a woman who appreciates what she has instead of mourning the inconsequential things that might be missing.

She rolled out of bed and stoked the fire in her potbelly stove. Wedging the sadiron next to her teapot, she mentally listed what she'd need to get done in the next two hours. The men were supposed to have ham and a coffee cake she made last night—she didn't want to risk having Gideon catch a glimpse of her this morning. She'd iron her green paisley dress, then do Polly's hair. . . .

"Hey, Miriam! You awake?"

"Yes."

"Open up! I'm hauling over the tub."

She scrambled into her robe and eagerly opened the door so Paul could deliver that luxury. "Oh, thank you!"

Water splashed as he thumped the big galvanized tub down. "Glad to. Hang on. Titus is bringing a couple buckets of hot water to add." He grinned at her.

Self-consciously, she reached up and touched one of the rags in her hair. "It's a good thing the groom can't see the bride before the ceremony. Gideon would run for the hills if he saw me like this."

"He was teasing Polly about her rag curls just a few minutes ago."

Miriam gave him a startled look. "I didn't put her hair up."

"Dan did," Titus said as he arrived with the hot water. Laughter filled his voice. "If he weren't so grouchy this morning, we'd tease him unmercifully."

"Don't you dare. He was being a good daddy. I'm proud of him, and I'm going to tell him so just as soon as I see him."

Paul chortled. "You might want to wait until you see how Polly's hair turns out."

The brothers left, and Miriam gratefully slipped into the tub. She wished she had time to soak, but she still needed to iron her dress. Dried, powdered, and wearing everything except her dress, she laid the ironing board across her bed and draped the green paisley on it. Fingering the lace, she smiled. Gideon bought that lace for her. In fact, he bought the material, too, saying it would match her pretty eyes. It was the first compliment he'd paid her. The memory made the dress seem dearer.

Heavy footsteps sounded outside her doorstep. After a prolonged hesitation, someone knocked. Miriam slipped back into her robe and opened the door. "Daniel!"

He stood there, his face gaunt and eyes glinting with tears. "Hannah would have wanted you to have this." He shoved a bundle into her arms.

Miriam looked down. *Mama's wedding gown.* "Oh, Daniel—"

He cleared his throat. "I'm happy for Gideon. You'll make him a fine bride."

"You don't know how much it means to hear you say that."

"I can't be at the wedding. I can't see—"

Miriam pushed the dress back into his arms. "I'd rather have you there than wear the dress. You matter far more—"

"Don't ask that of me, Miriam. It's not just Hannah's gown. I can't listen to the vows." He shook his head as he rasped, "I just can't."

The anguish in his voice tore at her. Tears spilled from her eyes.

Daniel rasped, "Don't. Gideon's already furious that I'm not attending. If he knows I made you cry. . ." He hitched a shoulder.

"I understand. I'll make things right with Gideon, Daniel."

"I'll be at the reception when you have it." He shoved the dress into her arms again and wheeled around.

Miriam couldn't believe he'd opened Hannah's chest and suffered all of this pain to give her the wedding gown with his blessing. She whispered tearfully, "Thank you, Daniel."

He nodded and trudged away.

Lord, he hurts so badly. Ease his sorrow and show us how to help him through his grief. The Whites' buggy rolled up, drawing Miriam back to the fact that she needed to get ready. She shut the door and turned to iron the wedding gown.

Minutes later, Reba rapped on the door and let herself in. "Wonder of wonders, will you look at that! That bridal gown is exquisite."

"It was Mama's. Hannah wore it. Daniel is loaning it to me."

"That's a fine thing, indeed. Here. I'll set myself to doing the ironing. You fix your hair."

Miriam unwound the rags from her hair and started styling it. "I appreciate your help so much."

"Honey, that's what friends are for. My, this gown is lovely. The men are going to be pea green with envy that Gideon swept you off your feet."

Miriam smiled. "We get along well enough. They're all happy I'm marrying their brother."

"Dear, I know that. I mean all of the other men. Logan and Bryce rode out yesterday and spread the word. Everyone's still coming today for the nuptials."

"But I only made one little cake!"

Reba started laughing. "Wait 'til you see what Gideon did last night." Miriam gave her a questioning look, but Reba swished her hand in the air. "Don't ask me. You'll have to wait and find out for yourself."

Logan brought Polly over. Polly's hair resembled a jumble of giant watch springs, and the sash on her dress looked just as hopelessly twisted. Logan stuck a basket of flowers into Polly's hands. "Gideon picked these with her. He said they're for your hair."

Polly wiggled like an eager puppy. "I want some in my hair, too."

"We've got to do something about it," Reba murmured.

"Anything," Logan agreed, "would be an improvement."

"That's what Unca Titus said 'bout Unca Giddy's cupcakes." Polly stood on tiptoe and reached over her head. "He gots a big pile all stacked up this high."

Logan spluttered, spun away, and shut the door. His howling laughter still filtered into the cottage.

Reba got the giggles. "I guess the surprise is out. Maybe it's best you know before you see it, Miriam. It's the sorriest sight I've ever seen. That man and his brothers desperately need you."

"Gideon was trying to make today perfect." Miriam started combing Polly's hair into some semblance of order. Her heart overflowed. He was doing everything he could to turn this hurried event into something special. "He loves me."

"He's a fine man—one in a million," Reba agreed.

A short while later, Reba tucked one last flower into Miriam's hair, fussed to make sure the skirt hung just so, and scooted back to admire her. "Lovely. Just lovely! I'm going to go on out now."

Polly scrambled down from the chair over by the window. "They gots benches out there like for church. Lotsa men are here."

"It sounds as if everything's ready." Miriam retied Polly's sash and gave her a hug. "You're so pretty, Polly."

"Amazing what wonders a woman's touch can do." Laughter tinged Reba's voice. She took Polly by the hand, then looked at Miriam and asked, "Who's going to walk you down the aisle?"

"We talked it over, and I want Gideon to come claim me. There's no one present to give me away, and it just seems right to hold fast to his arm from the start."

Reba and Polly scooted out, and Miriam dabbed on a little perfume. *Lord, Thou art so generous. Thou knowest my heart and hast blessed me far beyond my wildest dreams. Thank Thee for Gideon and the love we share. Help me to be a good wife to him.*

A single, solid *thump* sounded. Gideon. It was his knock.

It's time.

She opened the door.

Gideon took a long, slow look at her—from the flowers in her hair, down her bridal gown, to the tips of her shoes. "Sweet pea, you make me believe in miracles."

"You take my breath away."

He winked. "Save enough to speak your vows, darlin'. There's nothing I want more in this world than for you to be mine."

"I love you, Gideon." She accepted the bouquet of wildflowers he handed her and stepped out to meet her future with him by her side.

SECOND CHANCE

Prologue

San Francisco, 1871

"I'm leaving the house and the money to Alisa."

Standing with her back pressed against the wall outside the library, Alisa touched her fingers to her throat. Alarm inched its way up her spine. What could Mrs. Worthington possibly be thinking by telling her son such an outlandish tale? She inched around so that she could peer through the small crack where the door wasn't quite shut all the way. The dear woman sat regally in a black leather chair behind her husband's desk, her fingers laced together as she conversed with her son.

"Surely you're joking, Mother. Leave our money to a foundling?"

"A foundling who should never have been lost in the first place."

"Please, Mother." The sound of Mr. Worthington's long-suffering voice rankled Alisa. He should show his mother more respect, in her opinion. "Must you always throw that little indiscretion in my face?"

"That darling child is much more than an indiscretion in my eyes. I'm so thankful to God that we found her before she left the orphanage. My only heartbreak is that it took so many years to locate her. Now that I have all the legalities taken care of so that you can't prevent it from happening, I am ready to tell her of her true heritage and welcome her into the family."

Alisa shifted her gaze so that she could see Mr. Worthington. He stood by the stone fireplace, one of his elbows resting on the mantel. He leaned his forehead into the palm of one hand and gave a short laugh. "And what of me, Mother? You raised me accustomed to a certain standard of living. How do you expect me to fend for myself? Have you love only for the girl? None for your son?"

"Of course I love you, my boy. And it's true, you were much too spoiled for your own good. As for your well-being, you still own 75 percent of the shipping business. Alisa will own the other 25 percent so that she may live in comfort the rest of her life."

Frustrated by her obscured view, Alisa dared to push at the door, widening the crack so that she could see both Mrs. Worthington and her son. What was the elderly woman saying? Had her mind suddenly become unhinged? In the three months since she'd come to work for Mrs. Worthington as her companion, she'd noticed peculiarities in the way she was treated more highly than most servants.

But what possessed the woman to even consider leaving her a penny, let alone part of a company? And this beautiful home?

Mr. Worthington stalked across the room, his boots clacking on the hardwood floor. He leaned across the desk. "I'll have you declared incompetent, Mother. I don't want to, but I will if you force me to."

"I thought you might try that one." She sighed. "Why do greedy children always think it's so easy to declare an old woman feebleminded? Son, I've already made the changes to the will in the presence of five witnesses, just to be safe."

Robert's fist came down hard on the sleek mahogany desktop. "I'll contest the will. I'll make the courts believe the girl tricked you into leaving her an inheritance. My inheritance."

Mrs. Worthington pushed back from the desk. Leaning heavily on her cane, she lifted herself from her chair. She limped to Robert's side. "There is nothing you can do. If you contest, the entire city will see you as a cad and a fool."

"If reputation is so important to you, why are you leaving everything to that..."

Alisa gasped at the vile word he used to describe her. While growing up in the orphanage, all of her dreams included a beautiful mother and a handsome father. They were dressed in white each time they returned to get her. What a joyous reunion it was every night while she slept. Her mother's soft kisses, her father's strong arms. Never once had Alisa considered that she might be illegitimate. Her wonderful dream had turned to a nightmare with one filthy word.

Mrs. Worthington struck with her veiny, bony hand and left a print on his cheek as a loud slap resounded through the library. "You've no right to call her that. No right at all. I've made arrangements to legitimize her. She will be given the family name."

Alisa *Worthington.*

"I'll not stand for it!"

"I'm afraid you've no choice in the matter. You should have done right by her years ago; then I wouldn't be forced to bring this embarrassment on you now. She will be introduced into society as my granddaughter during the Christmas ball."

"Never!"

Still trying to grasp the enormity of what Mrs. Worthington had just spoken, Alisa watched in horror as Mr. Worthington took the elderly lady by the shoulders and shook her hard.

"Stop it!" Alisa leapt from her hiding place. "Turn her loose!"

Startled by the sudden interruption, he released her. Mrs. Worthington stumbled back, grabbing the edge of the desk to steady herself.

"How dare you eavesdrop on a private conversation!" the man spouted.

Ignoring him, Alisa gently took Mrs. Worthington by the shoulders. "Are you all right, ma'am?"

A smile creased the lined face. She reached up and patted Alisa's cheek. "You may call me Grandmother, my dear."

Tears sprang to Alisa's eyes. "You don't know what you're saying, Mrs. Worthington. Let's get you settled back into your chair."

"Wait." She pressed her fist to her heart and grimaced.

"Are you all right?"

"I will be. Listen to me now, darling girl. I've searched for you since you were a baby."

"Me, ma'am?"

"Yes. Your mother was the daughter of a laundress who worked out by the docks. She caught Robert's eye, and. . .well, you can imagine how you came to be."

"But I don't understand how you could possibly know I am the child of that union."

"But I can and do. When your mother's time came, she bravely came to our home for help. You were born soon after she arrived. I was privileged to assist in your birth. Afterward, I held you and rocked you while she slept. You were ever so precious."

"Mother, stop filling her head with this nonsense."

Alisa stared at the man standing next to her. All of her dreams of someday having a father died, and without warning, tears sprang to her eyes. Mr. Worthington's face reddened, and his gaze faltered.

Mrs. Worthington touched Alisa's cheek to regain her attention. The old, tired eyes held a look of such love that Alisa knew the precious lady believed every word she spoke. "I wrapped you in your father's baby blanket and placed you next to your mother. Then I retired to my own room. When I awoke to your mother's screaming, I knew Robert had taken you away. He returned later that evening and told me he had given you to a childless couple and that you were sailing for England that very night. I was heartbroken but powerless. The next morning your mother was gone, and she never returned."

"Then. . .how did you. . . ?"

"A maid from the household had disappeared the same night you were born. In those days, we took in all sorts. About a year ago, she came back looking for work. I couldn't hire her, for she stank of spirits, and she told me, out of spite, about taking my grandchild to an orphanage. I hired a detective agency, and they combed the city. A few months later, we found you."

Alisa's thoughts went to the worn blanket she kept tucked away for safekeeping. "And when you described the blanket, Mrs. Perryman knew I was the one?"

"Yes. That is exactly how we came to find you."

"I can't believe it. I have a grandmother?"

"No, you do not."

Alisa shrank from the man she now knew to be her father, as he towered over her.

"I refuse to allow you to take advantage of an old woman's delusions."

A gasp escaped Alisa's throat. "But I would never take advantage."

"Of course she wouldn't. And I'm far from delusional. Leave the girl alone, Robert. She most certainly does have a grandmother." Mrs. Worthington moaned softly and pressed her hand more tightly against her chest. "I. . .believe I. . . must. . .sit."

Filled with alarm, Alisa tried to tighten her hold just as Mrs. Worthington stiffened, clutched her chest, and slipped from Alisa's grasp. Time seemed to slow as she watched in horror. The elderly woman crashed to the ground, her head hitting against the edge of the desk as she fell.

"I am sorry to interrupt, but. . . Madam!" Marietta, Mrs. Worthington's housekeeper of forty years, stood just inside the room. Her silver tray clattered to the floor as she rushed to her mistress's side.

"Mrs. Worthington!" Alisa dropped to her knees. Blood ran from a gash on the elderly lady's forehead.

"What have you done, girl?" Mr. Worthington grabbed her roughly and flung her away. He knelt beside his mother.

"Is she going to be all right?" Tears streamed down Marietta's face.

"Mother? Mother, please open your eyes and talk to me."

The elderly woman lay motionless.

Alisa caught her breath as Mr. Worthington's venomous gaze swept over her. "Marietta, go fetch the doctor and the police. My mother has been murdered."

Chapter 1

"Throw down that six-shooter, mister. Then empty out yer pockets."

Titus Chance glared at the two men—not men really, but cowards, who had to cover their faces with bandannas. Cowards who couldn't win in a fair fight, so they had to sneak up on him while he dozed beside his campfire. But lily livers or no, they had two guns to his one, and he wasn't riled enough to be a fool.

He tossed his Colt to the dusty earth. Reaching slowly into his pockets, he pulled out twenty dollars and a gold money clip and pitched those on the ground, as well.

The burly leader fingered the bills. "That all you got?"

" 'Fraid so." At least that was all he had in his pockets.

Piercing eyes bored through him. Titus stared back, careful to keep his expression as innocent as a newborn babe's.

Titus balled his fists as he watched the thief shift his gaze. "That's a fine little horse you got there. I'd say it'll make up for you not having enough cash to make this worth my time. Amos, get the horse."

The other rider jerked his head toward the leader. "But we can't jest leave a feller out here in the middle of nowhere without a horse, Bart. Besides, stealing a little money is one thing. I ain't no horse thief. They can hang a man for that."

"They can hang ya for stealing money, too. Now do as I say." He expelled a frustrated grunt. "And what have I told you about calling me by my name while we're robbing someone?"

"Well, I don't like it," Amos said, but he dismounted his horse and headed toward Titus, his pistol pulled and threatening. "Back off easy-like, mister, and don't make me use this."

If the situation hadn't been so grave, Titus might have laughed at the bumbling crooks. But bumbling or no, they still had the guns, and he didn't. And if he had a prayer of a chance of getting out of this situation alive, he had to be smarter than they were. Which actually didn't seem all that far of a stretch.

He backed away from the mare he'd raised since birth. He'd named her Raven for her beautiful black coat. Swallowing hard, he kept a cautious gaze on the men as Amos took Raven's reins. The horse reared only for a second, long enough for Titus to dive for his Colt. He landed with a painful thud on his stomach and slid until he reached his gun. But he wasn't fast enough. One of the ruffians kicked dirt into his eyes, blinding him. "Yer lucky we don't kill ya fer that stunt. Mount up, Amos, and let's git."

When they'd gone, Titus crawled sightless until he reached the lake. After he'd washed the dirt from his eyes, he sat back and slapped his thigh in frustration.

Now what was he supposed to do? He'd left home a few days ago—directly after Priscilla White had refused his proposal. It had been at his sister-in-law's insistence that he'd left for a few days. "One grouch around here is plenty," Miriam had said, waving a wooden spoon in his face. She jerked her head at Daniel. "And my other brother-in-law already has that position filled." She said it with a twinkle in her eyes to remove the sting, but Titus knew she was right. He'd been moping long enough.

Daniel—who really was a grouch like Miriam said—had gotten up and stomped out of the house, while her husband, Gideon, laughed uproariously. Titus hadn't necessarily thought it funny, but Gideon was a new husband and thought anything his new bride said or did to be brilliant and inspired.

So Titus had taken a few days to pull himself together, mourn the loss of the woman he'd convinced himself he was destined to wed, and generally shake off his foul mood. San Francisco wasn't too far away. Close enough that he could make it there in a few hours if he started walking now. He could catch the stage out to Reliable. From there he could rent a horse to ride to the ranch.

He walked back to the campfire and sat down, knowing he'd have to wait until dawn to head back to the city. Feeling like a fool for letting himself get robbed in the first place, he stretched out on the ground and spent the night listening for noises that might indicate the thieves had returned.

By first light, he was up and headed back to San Francisco, relieved beyond measure that the thieves hadn't been smart enough to tell him to empty his boot, the place where he'd hidden most of his money.

Alisa eyed the mother and son sitting next to her on the seat.

"Davy, please, eat your bread for Mama." The woman's soft, pleading tone filled the inside of the stagecoach, annoying Alisa more than the boy's constant kicking against the seat.

After two days without a decent meal, she gladly would have snatched at the bread and gobbled it down in front of the ungrateful child. He kicked the bottom of the seat with the backs of his heels over and over and over until Alisa was tempted to place her hand gently on his swinging legs and order him to stop.

He held his bread in one hand and rubbed a chubby little fist over his eye.

"Oh, is Mama's boy sleepy?"

"No!" he yelled and kicked his feet higher and harder.

"Of course you are. That's why you're acting so unruly."

Alisa ventured a glance at the dark-haired cowboy sitting across from her. His head rested on the back of the seat, and his hat covered his face. His shoulders rose and fell with an almost unbelievable rhythm. How on earth could he sleep through all the racket that annoying boy was making?

"I'm truly sorry," the young mother intoned.

Alisa tore her gaze away from the handsome man. The mother's lips curved into a weary smile. "He's really a lovely child," she tried to explain. "We've been traveling several days, and he's so very tired."

"I'm not tired!" the boy insisted at a feverish pitch.

"Mama believes you."

Despite a deplorable lack of disciplinary action on the young mother's part, Alisa had to admire the woman's calm. Her own patience had worn thin an hour ago. The young mother looked at the boy and patted her thighs. "How would you like to sit on my lap?"

She winked at Alisa, and Alisa couldn't resist the dimples flashing in the young woman's cheeks. She smiled back.

Davy set his bread down on the bench and climbed into his mother's lap. Before long, both were dozing.

Alisa's empty stomach rumbled in protest as she stared at the half-eaten bread still sitting where it had been flung. It was all she could do not to snatch it up and wolf it down. After two full nights and a day of wandering around San Francisco in case she was being followed, and then half a day so far on the stage without food, her head felt light, and she almost wept from hunger. She'd been holding her reticule, about to visit the orphanage, when she'd heard Mrs. Worthington's voice from the hallway outside of the library door. The only money her reticule held was the donation she'd intended to leave with Mrs. Perryman, the woman who ran the orphanage. The amount was just enough for her stage ticket.

The chubby five-year-old boy was now fast asleep in his mother's arms, and the bread just sat there like a shiny pot of gold at the end of the rainbow.

She slid her hand along the bench, then snatched it back as the child shifted, causing his mother's head to snap up and her eyes to fly open. "Are we there yet?"

"No. You've only just dozed off," Alisa said, guilt searing her heart. *Thank you, dear Lord, for not allowing my hunger to cause me to sin.* She shuddered to think how close she'd come to stealing a little boy's bread.

The woman's eyes had drifted shut once more. Alisa ogled the bread for one last second, then willfully turned her entire body away. As she shifted, she came face-to-face with the cowboy. Only this time he wasn't sleeping. He stared at her with oh-so-blue eyes. Eyes filled with. . .pity.

Horror sank into the pit of her stomach. He must have seen her almost take the bread. Heat flashed to her cheeks. She covered her face with her hands, too ashamed to look him in the eye. He tapped her forearm. Shaking her head, she flexed her muscles to press her face harder into her palms. Oh, she had never been more humiliated.

"Look at me," he whispered.

Reluctantly, she glanced up, tears already pooling in her eyes.

He gave her a gentle smile. "Take this."

She looked down at the beef jerky in his hands. "I. . .I couldn't." She *couldn't* look away. Before she could stop herself, she licked her lips like a wolf eyeing a tasty rabbit just before it pounced.

"Take it, miss," he urged. "I have more."

Unable to resist a second longer, she took it. "Th–thank you," she whispered.

He nodded. Then he leaned back and covered his face once more with his hat while she gnawed the dried meat, savoring it as though it were a juicy chicken leg.

San Francisco

"I am sorry, Mr. Worthington, but there is nothing we can do. Your mother left no detail to chance. I assure you, her will is binding."

"I can fight it in court. Then we'll see how binding it is."

Frank Chadwick, Mrs. Worthington's long-standing attorney, glowered, and Robert could tell he was fighting to stay calm. "I seriously doubt any judge will be inclined to award you the estate, particularly after you tried to frame the girl for your mother's murder."

"How was I to know Mother's heart failed?"

"To say the girl pushed her and demanded money was a deliberate ploy so that you could contest the will."

Yes, and it would have worked if the housekeeper hadn't seen Mother slip out of Alisa's grasp and the girl try desperately to save her.

"So I'm left with only the company?"

"Seventy-five *percent* of the company." Mr. Chadwick leaned forward. "The girl, should she be found, will be awarded the house and all of its contents, 25 percent of the shipping company, and the money in all the accounts, with the exception of two thousand dollars. Your mother thought you might need it to tide you over for a few weeks. By then you should be receiving revenue from the shipping company."

Robert leaned back against the brown leather chair. Mr. Chadwick smiled—most smugly—his fingers steepled in front of him.

Two thousand dollars. That wouldn't pay for much of anything. Robert knew Mother had at least three million dollars sitting in those accounts. Nausea nearly overwhelmed his stomach at the thought of all that money going to the girl. It would take him thirty years to make back that kind of cash with the income from

75 percent of the business. What right did she have to it? He felt no responsibility, no affection for the girl who carried his blood in her veins. Truth be told, there could easily be a dozen more just like her between here and England. He didn't know, nor did he care.

"And if the girl isn't found?" He could make sure she wasn't, if necessary.

Chadwick narrowed his gaze. "The money will stay in an account for ten years, at the end of which time it will be given to charities."

"Charity?"

"Your mother was quite firm about the matter."

"What are my choices if I am to prevent this young woman from stealing my inheritance?"

The lawyer's lip curled in poorly disguised disgust, but Robert didn't care. Let *him* lose three million dollars and his childhood home and see how he'd behave.

"Well?" Robert demanded.

"You can always find her, speak with her, and if she is willing to sign over her rights to the house and the money, then I suppose they would go to you."

Hope flickered anew in Robert. Then that's what he'd do. Put out ads all over the state. Post a reward. One thousand dollars. No, he only had two. On the other hand, if the girl was found, he'd have more than enough to pay a reward. Five hundred.

He stood and extended his hand. "Thank you, Frank. You've been most helpful."

Chapter 2

A cramp in his leg pulled Titus rudely from sleep. He sat up straight, rubbing at the knot in his thigh, and took his hat from his face. After being awake throughout the night and walking all the way to San Francisco, he was worn clear through. But at least he wasn't hungry. Not like the girl sitting across from him. He hadn't offered her another strip of meat. No sense adding to her humiliation. Poor thing. His heart clenched at the memory of her staring at the kid's bread.

She slept, her head resting against the wall. The open window sent a breeze through the stagecoach and lifted wayward strands of auburn hair from her forehead. Titus swallowed hard at the sight. Her long lashes framed beautiful, enormous eyes and brushed the tops of her cheeks as she slept. His brow furrowed at the sight of the dark circles. She'd undoubtedly lost as much sleep as he had. But why? What possessed a woman to spend her last dime on a stage ticket? She had no luggage that he'd seen. Only a small reticule that she clutched tightly even in sleep. Everything about her indicated a woman on the run.

The stage hit a hole and jostled. A shuddering breath lifted her shoulders. She opened her eyes, sitting up as she did so. She looked straight at him, and her eyes widened.

Caught staring, Titus sent her a sheepish grin. He thought he detected a twitch of her lips before she averted her gaze to the window.

"How long until we reach Reliable?" The low, sleep-induced huskiness of her voice was alluring, he had to admit. A bit of guilt niggled at him for thinking it; after all, he'd been jilted less than a week ago.

He glanced out the window, barely remembering to answer her question. "I'd say no more than three or four hours." He tipped his hat. "I'm Titus Chance. My family owns a ranch not far from Reliable. You got family there?"

She shook her head. "N–no."

"Mail-order bride?"

Her face reddened. "No."

"So no folks, no husband waiting?" For some reason his heart lightened at the last bit of information. Still, he hated the thought of her being alone. "Do you have friends? Or at the very least a position of employment waiting?" His throat dried out in a split second as he mentally ran through a list of possible employers.

"I have no one and no job."

"Well, if you don't mind my saying so, Reliable might not be the best choice of a town for a pretty young woman all alone." He smiled to take the sting out of his words, but what happened next filled him with horror.

Her lovely brown eyes filled with tears.

He swallowed hard and fumbled in his pocket for a handkerchief. "Please don't cry, miss." He should be shot. Why did he always have to blurt out the truth?

"Oh, it's not your fault. I cry far too easily. I. . .I don't know what I'll do if there's nothing for me in Reliable." She eyed him. "I mean respectable employment."

It was Titus's turn to blush. He couldn't think of anything that she could do. In a young town the size of Reliable, there weren't many positions available for a decent woman. But he planned to see what he could do. He knew enough people that surely someone would take her in.

"You didn't tell me your name."

"Alisa."

He smiled. "Alisa what?"

She hesitated, then squared her shoulders. "My name is Alisa Worthington." She said the words like an announcement.

"Nice to meet you, Miss Worthington. Would you care to have dinner with me?"

"Dinner?"

He grinned and reached into his bag. "It's not much," he said, offering her a strip of the jerky.

"You've been too kind already." She eyed the meat hungrily.

"Nonsense." He offered it again. This time she took it.

"Thank you."

"I hate to eat alone."

A pretty smile lifted the corners of her lips.

Titus almost choked on his bite of jerky. He hadn't realized how badly he'd wanted to see her smile. The sight of it brightened the entire inside of the stagecoach, as far as he was concerned.

A giggle from the other side of the stagecoach captured his attention. He turned to find the woman next to Miss Worthington grinning at him. She sent him a broad wink. His ears burned to have been so transparent.

To his profound relief, she didn't dwell on the situation. Instead, she stretched and moved the still-sleeping little boy onto the seat. He mumbled and shifted and finally ended up with his head resting against Miss Worthington's shoulder.

"Do you mind?" the child's mother asked. "I'm worn clean through. He sure isn't the teensy baby he once was." With a weary huff, she glanced out the window, then back to Titus. "How far do we have to go?" she asked.

"Only a couple more hours."

"Oh, I will be so glad to be done with trains and stagecoaches. I never plan to travel again."

"Do you have family in town?" Titus asked, more to be polite than from a desire to know.

"My brother, Aaron Bladdel. Do you know him?"

"The blacksmith? Sure. I didn't realize he had a sister."

She laughed, and her twinkling blue eyes set in a chubby-cheeked face made him feel more at ease. "I suppose I should be insulted that he hasn't mentioned me."

"We talk more business than anything."

"Then I suppose I'll forgive him."

Titus returned her smile. "Will your husband be joining you?"

Her expression crashed. "No. I'm afraid my Henry passed on a few weeks ago. That's why Davy and I are here."

Miss Worthington reached around Davy and patted her hand. "I am so sorry, Mrs. . . ." She glanced at Titus for support, but he hadn't caught the woman's name, either.

"Ah, well." The woman pulled a lace handkerchief from her bag and dabbed at her eyes. "There's no point in crying. It only upsets Davy. And my name is Mrs. Greene. Violet Greene." She smiled. "Henry always laughed at my name. Two colors."

Titus had to admire her spirit. He didn't want to bring it up, but he doubted seriously she'd be long without a husband. Not in a town where the men outnumbered the women about twenty to one.

Of course that applied to Miss Worthington, too. Now that thought stuck in his craw, and it was mighty uncomfortable!

Alisa's arm was growing numb by the time Davy woke up and glared at her as though she'd been the one to pull him from the safety and warmth of his mother's lap.

"I'm thirsty, Mommy."

"I know, sweetheart. We will be in Reliable very soon, and I will get you a drink."

"I'm thirsty now!"

"I'm sorry, but the water is all gone. You drank it to wash down your lunch, remember? I told you that was all."

Mr. Chance slipped his hand into his saddlebag and produced a canteen.

"Oh, we couldn't," Mrs. Greene insisted.

"I have plenty." He winked at Davy. "Can't have the boy thirsty. Take some for yourself, as well, and pass it to Miss Worthington."

The little boy gulped noisily, then heaved a sigh and began swinging his legs, thumping the bottom of the seat as he had earlier.

Alisa pressed her fingertips to her temple, trying to ward off the mounting ache.

"Hey, little fella," Mr. Chance said, smiling at Davy. "How about not kicking that seat?"

The child scowled and turned his face to his mother's arm, but he continued to thump the seat. "I'm so sorry," Mrs. Greene said. "It's difficult for him to keep still."

"It's all right," Alisa said. She'd never seen such a poorly behaved child. Growing up in an orphanage had taught her obedience. Though her upbringing had not been harsh, it was most definitely strict.

Trying to ignore the pain in her head, now throbbing in time to the kicks of Davy's boots against the seat, she glanced out the window. In the distance, she saw riders coming. She turned to alert Mr. Chance, but his gaze, too, was focused toward the horizon. A muscle jerked in his jaw.

A sense of unease crept through Alisa as she felt his tension. His hand went to his gun belt. It was empty. Frustration crossed his features.

"Is everything all right, Mr. Chance?"

"The men coming are not the welcoming party from Reliable," he said in a matter-of-fact tone.

"Oh, Reliable has a welcoming party?" Mrs. Greene asked.

Alisa fought the urge to roll her eyes. "I believe Mr. Chance is saying the men coming are up to no good."

Mr. Chance nodded gravely. "You're right, Miss Worthington. I'm afraid those are the same men who robbed me last night. They took my gun and my horse and all the money I had in my pocket."

Mrs. Greene let out a little shriek and grabbed Davy close. "Oh my."

"Mr. Wayne?" the cowboy called to the stage master.

"I see 'em," came the rough reply. "Yaw!" he yelled to the horses, and the stage sped up.

But even Alisa could see there would be no outrunning two men on horseback. "What should we do, Mr. Chance?"

"Unless you have a pistol hidden in that bag of yours, I suggest we pray." He hesitated; then he gave what Alisa was sure was supposed to have been a reassuring smile. However, it fell short of doing any such thing. "If they were out to truly do any harm, I'm sure they would have done more than kick dirt in my face and steal my horse."

"They kicked dirt in your face?" Mrs. Greene asked. "How awful."

"Not so awful as a bullet," Mr. Chance retorted absently. Alisa had to agree.

Gunfire sounded, and the stage master pulled the stage to a stop. The two bandits held pistols upright. A series of shots fired into the air. They ordered the wagon master to throw down his weapons and climb down. Then a gravelly voice called out, "All right. Get out. All of you."

Alisa looked to Mr. Chance for instruction. He nodded and opened the stage door. "I'll go first." He climbed down, then turned and offered his assistance to Alisa. Next he lifted Davy from the stage, then helped Mrs. Greene.

"That all of ya?" one of the bandits asked.

"Yes." Mr. Chance stood, fists clenched.

Recognition flashed in the bandit's dark eyes. "Well, Amos, looky here. This feller jest ain't very lucky."

The other man chuckled. "Didn't we make yer acquaintance last night? Yep, that's one nice Colt ya give us." He patted the sleek neck of the horse he had just dismounted. "And this girl here is one beaut of a horse."

The cowboy grinned back, and Alisa frowned. What was he up to?

"I suppose this surely isn't my lucky day, but I have to tell you. . .it's not yours, either."

"How do ya figure that?"

"Well, considering you forced me to empty my pockets last night, you won't find anything of value on me. And this young lady didn't even have. . ."

Alisa drew in a breath. Would he humiliate her just to prove the point that if she couldn't feed herself, she probably couldn't give them anything of value?

"A trunk," he said, completing his observation. Despite her precarious situation, Alisa's heart swelled with gratitude. Mr. Chance personified all the heroes in her dime books—the stories she hadn't been allowed to read when she lived at the orphanage. But since becoming Mrs. Worthington's companion, Alisa read everything she could get her hands on, dime books included.

He continued goading the thieves. "The other young lady is widowed and traveling to Reliable to live with her brother because she can't raise her son alone."

"I thought you said there was a senator on this here stage, Bart."

"Can I help it if that drunk varmint back at the Lucky Hand Saloon lied to me?" The man eyed his partner. "And what have I told you about calling me by my name?"

"Sorry, Bar. . .Joe."

Alisa stifled a giggle behind her hand.

"All right, gimme whatever ya got," the one called Bart said. He held out his hat as though passing around the offering plate.

Scurrying to obey, Mrs. Greene opened her satchel and tossed a wad of money into the hat. Alisa's eyes widened, and she stared at the woman. "M–my husband was well off. I never said I came west because I was poor. Although, after today, that is certainly going to be my circumstance."

"Yee-haw!"

Alisa jumped as Amos grabbed the hat away from Bart. He stopped in front of Mr. Chance. "Not our lucky day, huh? Well then what do you call this?"

The cowboy glared but kept his mouth shut. Alisa couldn't help but be relieved. A man capable of robbery might also be capable of violence if provoked.

The man came to her. "Well? Whaddaya got, girlie? Or am I gonna have to search ya?"

Mr. Chance stepped forward. "Keep your filthy hands off her. She has nothing."

"I'll see that fer myself."

Alisa showed him her reticule. "A–all that I have is a handkerchief."

"That all? Well, maybe I'll take a kiss instead."

Shrinking back in alarm, Alisa felt the blood rushing to her head. She grabbed Mr. Chance's arm to keep from losing her balance.

"I thought I told you to leave her alone!" He reached out to grab Amos just as Bart's gun fired.

Alisa stared in horror as Mr. Chance slipped from her grasp. He landed with a thud on the ground, blood spilling from a wound in his temple.

Chapter 3

Titus slowly came to, pain slicing his temple. Pebbles ground into his back—evidence he was lying on hard ground. His head, however, was pillowed in something soft and elevated off the ground. Gentle fingers pushed back the hair from his forehead and pressed a wet cloth to his temple. He opened his eyes.

Miss Worthington?

"Oh, thank You, Lord," she breathed. "He's coming around."

Was he dreaming? Or was Miss Worthington even prettier from this angle? He started to sit up, but a wave of dizziness sent him back to. . .Miss Worthington's lap? If this was a dream, may he never wake up!

"How are you feeling, Mr. Chance?"

He offered her a wobbly smile. "Like I've been shot. What happened? I'm obviously not dead. Unless, of course, you're an angel."

A beguiling blush darkened her rosy cheeks. "I'm afraid you're still mortal, Mr. Chance. And I most certainly am, as well."

A shadow blocked the glow of the retreating sun. The stage master stood over him. "Well, if that bullet had been a little more to the left, he wouldn't be with us. As it is, he's going to have a monster of a headache for a few days from that nick." His gravelly voice held not a trace of sympathy. Like a grizzled Westerner, he stated the simple facts. "Them varmints took off like a couple of scared jackrabbits after you pitched to the ground. Lucky for you they couldn't hit the broad side of a barn with a sawed-off shotgun."

It had nothing to do with luck, he thought, at the same time Miss Worthington said, "Luck had nothing to do with it, Mr. Wayne. God surely had His hand on Mr. Chance."

Hmmm. He gazed into her suspiciously moist eyes and smiled. She smiled back. "Are you able to get up now?"

He'd rather just stay there forever, close his eyes, and relieve the pain in his head, but he couldn't take advantage of her generous spirit and soft lap any longer. He sat up again, this time with her assistance. The world spun for a moment. Miss Worthington handed him the wet handkerchief she'd been holding against his head.

"Thank you."

His gaze locked onto hers, and he felt time stand still. How could he have ever believed himself in love with a woman like Prissy White? He couldn't even remember what she looked like, except for the ridiculous false blond curls she'd recently taken to wearing. Funny, two weeks ago, he'd found them attractive. But that was before he'd met Miss Worthington. And right now she seemed to be having as much trouble looking away as he was having.

Mr. Wayne stepped forward and offered his hand. "Well, let's get you back into the stage. I got a schedule to keep."

Titus groaned as pain stabbed his head. Movement wasn't necessarily a good thing, but he gritted his teeth and closed his eyes as the stage master hefted him to his feet. Miss Worthington stood on one side of him. He swayed as the world spun. The gentle pressure of her palm heated his back. "It's all right, Mr. Chance. I won't let you fall."

Her gentle, sincere voice made him smile, despite the pain. If he'd been feeling better, he'd have asked her who would hold her up if he started to fall. Instead, he accepted her assistance to the stage. She climbed in ahead of him and then offered her hands while Mr. Wayne helped him from behind. When he was finally settled into the seat, his head throbbed. All he wanted was to lie down and sleep. Since the cramped interior and narrow seat prevented him from doing so, he stretched out sideways as much as possible and slumped against the window.

Mrs. Greene gasped softly. As she had been earlier, she sat next to Miss Worthington, clutching Davy tightly in her grasp. "Oh, I am so relieved that you are all right, Mr. Chance. I just knew that bullet went through your head. I had to bring Davy inside so he didn't have to see all the blood. He's very sensitive. I feared for his peace of mind."

"The bullet only grazed Mr. Chance," Alisa broke in, much to Titus's relief. He didn't feel like talking, as his stomach was beginning to rebel against the jostle of the stagecoach, not to mention the vivid image of his blood spilling on the ground. *Thank You, Lord, for steering that bullet away from my skull.*

Regrettably, Mrs. Greene didn't take the hint. "Oh, that is fortunate for you. I once knew a man who—"

Titus closed his eyes against the pain.

"Perhaps we should let Mr. Chance rest." Titus heard the sweetness of Miss Worthington's voice just as he drifted to sleep.

He awoke to the same sweet voice. "Wake up, Mr. Chance. We've arrived in Reliable."

His head throbbed, but he smiled. He could get used to waking up to that sound every day. When he opened his eyes, she was leaning forward, concern plainly written in her expression. As he met her gaze, relief replaced concern. His first attempt to sit up straight failed as a bolt of pain sent him back to the seat with a moan.

"Sit up slowly," Miss Worthington admonished.

It felt good to have a woman fuss over him. And even more so when she placed her hand on his side and gently helped him to an upright position. Gideon's assessment of things sure had been right. There was nothing like a woman's touch. Of course, Gideon was a happily married man. Not just any woman's touch would do. Take Prissy for instance. Her hand tucked inside the crook of his arm had never sent shocks of warmth down his spine. Now, Miss Worthington was a different matter altogether. He could barely remember where he was when he was so close to this woman. And he was almost certain the near-amnesia was due to the sweetness of her touch and not his wound.

Clarity slowly replaced his confusion, and he glanced through the window as the stage rolled to a halt in front of an eating establishment.

"I have never been so happy to see a dusty old town in my life!" Mrs. Greene said, and Titus had to agree with her. The stage master opened the door.

"Everyone out. We're behind as it is. Other folks are waitin'. There's dinner waitin' inside iffen you can pay for it."

"My, oh my, I am famished." Mrs. Greene climbed out of the coach and reached around for Davy. "Are you hungry, darling? It's a good thing Mommy had some money hidden away from those bad, bad men." She turned to Titus and Miss Worthington. "It was so nice meeting you both. I am sure in a town this size, we will meet again. Say good-bye, Davy."

"Bye." The farewell was hardly discernable as the chubby little boy's attention was averted to the source of food. He yanked on his mother's hand. "Come on, Mama."

With a final dimpled smile, Mrs. Greene stepped inside the diner. The dinnertime smells wafting from the building tempted Titus's stomach. He could only guess how the aroma of roasted meat and freshly baked bread was affecting Miss Worthington.

She looked around, her lip clasped between her teeth, brow furrowed. Titus's heart went out to her. What was she going to do? Where on earth would she sleep? The sun had set two hours earlier. Even if she were to find work, it certainly wouldn't be tonight. At that moment, chivalry was born in Titus's heart. There was no getting around it. He would help her. His heart had already made the choice for him, and there was nothing to do but follow along.

He would need help getting home; there was no question about that. If it was daylight, the solution would be obvious. Hire a team and buggy from the livery and appeal to her sense of pity. But no decent woman would agree to spending so much as an hour in the dark traveling out to the ranch. And no decent man would dare ask. As badly as he'd like to find a place to sleep for the night, he knew Miss Worthington couldn't afford to rent a room, and he was loath to leave her alone.

"Well. . ." Her shoulders trembled as she took a shaky breath. She turned to him, her lips curving into a half smile. "Be careful not to overexert yourself until that gash heals. And you, um, might want to get out your hanky. You seem to be bleeding again."

He fished out his handkerchief and pressed it to his temple.

"Good-bye, Mr. Chance. Thank you for your kindness earlier." She walked away. Heart in his throat, Titus watched her go, trying desperately to think of a way to make her stay.

"Miss Worthington." He hurried to join her.

"Yes?"

Gulping like a schoolboy who, for the very first time, figures out that girls aren't a nuisance, Titus clenched his hat tightly. "It would be my honor if you would accompany me inside for a meal." Holding his breath, he awaited her answer, all the while allowing his mind to think ahead.

Her eyebrows pushed together into a deep frown. "I appreciate your kindness, Mr. Chance, but I cannot accept charity." She gave a stubborn jerk of her chin. The show of dignity shot like an arrow, piercing Titus's heart. The tremor in her bottom lip as she desperately fought for control beckoned to be kissed away. Though everything in him begged to comply, he knew better.

Charity. She thought that was what he was offering? How did he tell her that he'd been born the moment he looked into her eyes? That the sky was bluer, the air fresher? That all he could think about were her beautiful, fawnlike eyes and silky auburn hair?

She cleared her throat, and he realized he'd been staring. "Good-bye, Mr. Chance. Once again, thank you for your kindness."

Knowing it was now or never, Titus gently took hold of her arm. "Miss Worthington, I would never insult you by implying you would accept charity." He pressed his hat over his heart. "The truth is, I'd love the chance to repay *your* kindness."

She hesitated, the lamplight reflecting the doubt in her eyes.

"Humor me? Please?"

A smile played across her lips. "All right, Mr. Chance. You've talked me into it."

Relief flooded him. For the next hour and a half he would enjoy her company, during which time he would try to figure out a way to help a woman who refused to take charity.

Alisa was forced to use all her restraint not to slurp the delicious vegetable soup or wolf down warm slices of buttered bread. Slowly, much too slowly, her stomach began to lose the empty ache that had plagued her for two days and two nights. She ventured a glance at Mr. Chance. The gash on his temple still didn't look too good. "How's that feeling?" she asked.

"I guess if I said, 'Like I've been shot,' you'd just think I was trying to make you laugh again."

Laughter bubbled from her.

"Ah, and I see it worked."

She'd never met anyone quite like Mr. Chance. A smart, funny man with a heart of gold. She wasn't so silly as to think he really had asked her to dinner to repay her kindness. He knew she was famished and had no money. So far God had taken care of her, but even she knew that she couldn't allow Mr. Chance to do anything else for her. Not only was it not proper, but it simply wasn't fair of her to presume upon his good nature. But she had a suspicion that he felt responsible for her. Though the thought sent a thrill from her heart straight down to her toes, she knew she had to relieve him of that sense of duty before it went too far.

Just as she opened her mouth to insist they part company as soon as they finished their meal, the door opened.

A muffled groan came from Mr. Chance's side of the table. She arched her brow and stared at him a moment. He sipped his milk but stared at the door over the rim of his glass. Alisa followed his gaze and almost gasped. A young woman with ringlets of blond hair that didn't look entirely real sashayed into the room ahead of an older couple. She worked the room like a politician, nodding to the men who sat around the four long tables. Every eye watched her, and as far as Alisa could tell, the young woman enjoyed the attention. She batted her lashes and touched shoulders as she passed. Then her eyes lit on Titus. And Alisa. All merriment fled her expression. Her face turned three shades of red, and her green eyes narrowed to slits. She looked like a cat about to pounce.

"Oh no," Mr. Chance muttered. "She's coming over."

"Why, Titus, sweetheart, this is quite a surprise."

Titus stood. "Hello, Priscilla. We just got off the stage from San Francisco and decided to get a bite."

"Sit down and eat, you silly goose." She turned to Alisa, and her ruby lips—was the color stained on?—curved into a sly smile. "He's such a gentleman."

Like a queen granting favors, she offered Alisa a slight nod of her head. "I'm Priscilla White. My parents are over there talking with some of the old folks in town. We own the dry goods store. And you are?"

Alisa hesitated. She glanced at Titus, who looked as perplexed as she felt. "Alisa Worthington." Loving the sound of her name, Alisa smiled.

"Titus, darling, aren't you going to ask me to sit down? I must admit I am totally famished. Mother ordered me an entire new wardrobe, and it arrived today. From New York! I plumb wore myself out trying things on." She motioned to the ridiculous pink gown she wore. "Do you like it, Titus? I know you love me to wear pink."

"Uh, yeah, Prissy. And do sit down."

Alisa's heart sank for two reasons. One: This woman obviously had a claim on Mr. Chance. And two: Nothing about Mr. Chance so far in their short acquaintance had indicated that he had such bad taste. Alisa locked in on his gaze. He spoke a silent apology with those warm blue eyes. But some things were beyond apologies. Extending a dinner invitation when one has a prior commitment to another girl, for instance. She glared at him and sniffed her disdain. If she'd been strong enough, she'd have left the plate of chicken, potatoes, and fresh garden peas and told him, "No, thank you." But her mouth watered at the sight and smell of the wonderful food, so she picked up her fork instead. The nightmare in fake ringlets and frightful pink spoke faster than an auctioneer, paying very little attention to Alisa.

So Alisa shoveled bite after bite into her mouth, making no attempt to follow the conversation.

"And where are you from, Miss Worthington?"

Alisa nearly choked. She glanced up from her plate, met the catlike gaze, and chewed hard. The silence at the table seemed palpable as she swallowed down the bite with a gulp of milk.

Sensing the other girl's impatience, Alisa couldn't help but prolong the silence a bit. Deliberately, she dabbed her mouth with her napkin. "I'm sorry. What was the question?"

A long-suffering sigh blew from Priscilla's lips—which Alisa was now convinced were painted. "I simply asked where you're from."

"San Francisco."

"And what, may I ask, are you doing in our quaint little town?"

Calling this dusty hole-in-the-wall a town was a bit of a stretch, but "quaint" was absolutely laughable. Still, the girl had her. What could she possibly say? *My father accused me of killing my grandmother, and I narrowly escaped imprisonment by running away?*

Though she couldn't explain why she did it, Alisa found herself glancing at Mr. Chance for support. He caught her gaze, and the shining armor began to sparkle in the light of the lamp.

He cleared his throat, looked Priscilla squarely in the eyes, and said, "Miss Worthington is coming to work at the ranch."

Chapter 4

Titus had set a new record. This was the first time in his life he'd ever made two women gasp in horror simultaneously.

"Whatever do you mean, she will be working at the ranch?" Prissy's eyes had narrowed dangerously. "Miss *Worthington* hardly looks like a ranch hand to me."

Miss Worthington's face turned deep red, and the question in her eyes echoed Prissy's concern.

Clearing his throat, Titus glanced from one bewildered woman to the other. "Miriam could use the help. She has a pretty heavy workload with all of us men plus Daniel's two youngsters."

Finding her voice before Prissy could jump in, Miss Worthington managed to croak, "I don't understand."

A smug look flitted across Prissy's face, and Titus knew she'd caught him in his—if not a lie, then definitely—stretch of the truth. It was obvious Miss Worthington was hearing about her new job for the first time.

"That's right. I never got around to explaining things to Miss Worthington."

Prissy's haughty expression faded to one of humility.

"I should say you didn't." Miss Worthington's frown spoke for itself, compelling Titus to speak up quickly before she could ruin his developing plan. Why *not* hire Miss Worthington? Miriam could certainly use the help. And he'd rather chew off his arm than leave Miss Worthington to the mercy of the slew of fellas staring at her from around the four neighboring tables.

"Miss Worthington," he appealed to her, hoping she'd take the hint and simmer down while he explained.

She scowled and sent him an all-right-but-make-it-good expression, folding her arms for emphasis.

"Okay, it's like this. My brother Daniel lost his wife in childbirth almost two years ago."

"Oh, I'm so sorry."

"Thank you. Anyway, Miriam showed up a few months later, not knowing her sister had passed on. Daniel and Gideon wanted to send her right back, but we all voted that her cooking was the best we'd ever tasted, and besides, Polly and Ginny Mae needed a woman's care."

"Polly and Ginny Mae?"

Titus grinned at the very thought of his young nieces. "Daniel's girls. Polly's four, and Ginny Mae's not yet two."

"I see." She chewed her bottom lip and stared at the table as though trying to gather the information into something that made sense. "I'm afraid I don't understand—"

"The fact of the matter is that Gideon snatched up Miriam pretty quick and married her before the circuit-riding preacher left to take on his own pastorate. But there are an awful lot of us out there for one woman. This is a rough land and really not fitting for a woman. At least not one alone on a ranch with. . .all of us."

"Oh, honestly, Titus." Prissy's outburst reminded him of her presence. She turned to Alisa. "What he's trying to say is that those brothers of his are utter ruffians. Miriam has done wonders taming Gideon, but there are just too many of them for her to handle alone."

She turned back to Titus as though he should thank her. How could he have ever thought he wanted to marry such an indelicate woman? For all her pink and ribbons and lace, Prissy White had the manners of a bawling calf, and up close to another woman, she wasn't even all that pretty. That fancy finishing school she'd attended back east had been a colossal waste of time and money. But that was none of his business. He was just thanking the Lord that she'd turned down his proposal. Now he was free to court. . .

"Miss Worthington. Perhaps I was a mite deceptive in letting on like you were already coming to the ranch to work, but truth be told, we need all the help we can get. We can't pay much, but you'd have a roof over your head and plenty of food."

She hesitated, averting her gaze to her clasped fingers. "I don't know. . . ."

"I can assure you there's nothing improper at our house. We're God-fearing folks. Even hold the Sunday meetings at our ranch. So you have nothing to worry about."

The door crashed open. Miss Worthington jumped as a wolf whistle blistered the air. "Looky there, Logan. Titushhh brung us another woman. Gideon got the lasssht purty girl, but I got dibs on thisssh one."

Titus's stomach dropped at the sight of Miss Worthington's bewildered, accusing glare.

His two brothers staggered up to the table, obviously inebriated. "Hiya, Titus," Logan said, pounding Titus's back until it felt bruised. "Shhhaw the stage come in. Wuz you on it?"

Titus shot to his feet, snagging each young man by the collar.

"Hey!"

"Whachhhha doin', Titusshhh?"

"I can't believe you two have been drinking. If there weren't a couple of ladies present, I'd thrash you good. Right here and now."

"Awww, Titushhh."

Titus's anger hit him on two levels. One, the boys hadn't touched a drop in months. And two, by the look of utter horror on Miss Worthington's face, no amount of cajoling was going to convince her to come work at the ranch.

"Why, Titus," Prissy said, poorly concealed amusement dripping from her painted lips. "Aren't you going to introduce Miss Worthington to your brothers? After all, she *will* be helping to take care of your wonderful *God-fearing* family." With a triumphant laugh, she stood. "So very nice to meet you, Miss Worthington. Don't worry. There are plenty of men in town who will offer you marriage. A single woman in Reliable doesn't stay single for long, unless she's choosy." She gave Titus a pointed look. The boys hee-hawed.

"Be quiet," Titus ordered, tightening his hold on each collar. "Do you two have the buckboard?"

" 'Courshh. Miriam shhhhent usssh for supplies."

"Good. Get to it. Stay there, and wait for me."

"We're shhorrry, Titushh," Logan slurred. "It'll never happen agin."

"Yeah, we promishhh."

"Well, you should be ashamed. Miriam sent you to town in good faith that you'd behave yourselves. How do you think she'll feel when she finds out you've been hanging out at the Nugget? And you've upset Miss Worthington."

"Aw, Missshhhh W. . .wor. . . Misshhh, please accept my apolozhyyy." Bryce bent at the waist, trying to be gallant, and pitched forward. He caught himself just before falling into her lap—which Titus knew from experience was a wondrous thing. Still, he didn't want the boy, or any other man, for that matter, knowing it firsthand.

"You two go on to the wagon. I'll be there soon."

The boys staggered back across the room and left the diner, banging the door behind them.

Rarely did Titus feel nervous, but there was no denying the trembling in his gut as he dared to meet Miss Worthington's gaze. She arched a brow. Titus recognized the challenge. She'd let him explain but wasn't promising to believe a word he said.

"All right. Logan and Bryce are the youngest of us six brothers."

"I thought you said you were a God-fearing family." Miss Worthington's voice remained soft and calm. Again, Titus felt optimism rise.

"They got a little rowdy last year until our older brother Gideon threatened to tan their hides if he ever caught them at it again." He glanced in the direction his younger brothers had gone, then looked back to Miss Worthington. "I don't know what's gotten into them to end up at the Nugget again after such a long time."

"The Nugget?"

Titus cringed. "The saloon."

"Do you really need help for your sister-in-law, or were you only trying to keep me from being humiliated in front of your girl?"

Titus started. "First of all, yes. Miriam needs help, and I'd be obliged if you'd consider coming to work on the ranch. Second, Prissy White is not my girl. Not really."

"Not really?"

"Well, I asked her to marry me, but she was considering a few other proposals at the time. I guess my pockets weren't deep enough for her."

"All right, Mr. Chance. I do need a job, and I'm used to large numbers to feed and care for. So I suppose I will accept your offer."

Titus nodded, aware of the curious stares coming from everyone in the room. "Will you consider the boys as proper chaperones? The ranch is an hour's ride east of here. No one in these parts would consider you compromised. But if it makes you uncomfortable, I'll make other arrangements for you."

Again her expression revealed her conflicting emotions. No doubt she realized she had no place to sleep but weighed that reality against the fact that night had fallen in earnest and she would be forced to ride with three strange men, two of whom were inebriated.

Gathering a shaky breath, she nodded. "I suppose they'll have to do."

Relief rushed over him like an ocean wave.

"I'm in your debt."

"No, Mr. Chance." She spoke so softly, he had to strain to hear.

Titus's heart leapt to his throat. "No?"

She kept her gaze steady on his. "We are both well aware that the debt owed is mine. Not yours."

⁂

Despite her nervousness, Alisa couldn't help but gather a deep breath and drink in the fresh smell of pine wafting from the trees lining each side of the well-worn path. Nighttime usually frightened her, but out here the black sky shaded with rolling gray clouds appeared like a painting created by a master. The fragrance of the coming rain hung in the air.

Calm slowly replaced her jitters. She cut her gaze to Mr. Chance. He stared ahead, watching the road. Her stomach turned a flip just observing his profile. Black stubble formed a pattern across his jaw. To Alisa, the unshaven roughness only added to his good looks. As though unaware of the effect he was having on her, Mr. Chance absently hummed "Shall We Gather at the River," his rich baritone adding to the pleasure of being in his company.

He turned his head as though aware of her perusal. A smile curved his full lips, and Alisa had trouble looking away. "Everything okay?" he asked.

"Yes." Cheeks burning, she forced herself to stare ahead into the darkness.

He jerked his thumb toward the back of the wagon. "Listen to those two."

The two lanky boys snored happily. She knew they wouldn't be so happy when they awoke, and she took satisfaction from it. "Perhaps their condition in the morning will discourage them from indulging in spirits." Her cheeks burned as she realized she'd spoken her musings aloud. What would he think of her even knowing about headaches and sick stomachs—consequences of too much alcohol?

"I hope so. Only the Lord can deliver a person from a hankering for the temporary pleasures of sin."

Impressed with his astute observation and obvious love for the Lord, Alisa began to feel much more at ease. "How is your head feeling, Mr. Chance?"

"Well, let's just say I probably won't be in any better shape than those two in the morning, but at least I got mine honestly."

Alisa gave a soft laugh, then sobered as she remembered that Mr. Chance had been robbed. "Will you go to the sheriff?"

He nodded. "Mr. Wayne will also inform the marshal in San Francisco."

"I hope you get your horse back."

His smile nearly stole her breath. "That's sweet of you, Alisa."

Alisa started at his use of her given name.

"Do you object to being called that? I won't do it if you feel it's inappropriate."

"N–no, of course you may use my name. I will be a servant in your house, after all."

Without speaking, he tugged the reins, and the horses stopped. He turned to give her his full attention. "Look at me," he ordered.

Alisa did as he commanded, meeting his stern gaze. "I want you to get that notion out of your head right now."

"N–notion? I thought I would be working for you."

"Well. . ." He hesitated, then scowled deeply. "You'll be helping Miriam and will be compensated for it, but that doesn't make you a servant."

"It doesn't?"

"No," he growled.

"Then what does it make me?" Alisa fought the giggle rising in her at his discomfiture.

"Part of the family."

"You marryin' her, Titus?"

"Shut up and go back to sleep, Logan," Mr. Chance growled. "I'm trying to explain to Miss Worthington that she isn't a servant."

" 'K," he mumbled and resumed snoring.

"Alisa. . .Miss Worthington. . ."

Alisa decided to quell his discomfort. She placed her palm on his arm, then lifted it off again when his muscle twitched. "I know what you mean. I appreciate your generosity. Please do call me Alisa, as it will be much easier if we are to see each other often."

"We'll most definitely be seeing each other." His eyes searched hers, and he smiled, once again revealing straight, healthy teeth. "Every breakfast, lunch, and supper." His lazy, husky voice created pleasing word pictures. Warmth slithered across her belly at the thought. "During family devotions, long walks by the creek, Sunday meetings."

"Picnicsshhh. I like picnicsshhh."

He glared over the seat. "Mind your own business, Bryce."

Still tingling from the moment that had just passed between them, Alisa released the laughter bubbling up, grateful for the opportunity to ease the tension.

"Well, I suppose we should get moving, anyway."

Alisa nodded. Pins of nervous energy pricked at her spine. Would the rest of the family welcome her? If not, where would she go? She'd be right back in the same situation she was in before Mr. Chance came into her life. Only this time. . .this time she wouldn't have a champion.

Chapter 5

Alisa tilted her head to one side like a curious puppy and stared at the group of buildings in front of her as Titus pulled the reins, and the wagon halted. "It's like a small town," she said in amazement.

Titus's low, throaty chuckle pulled her attention from the view.

"How many brothers did you say you have?"

"We're a close bunch." He pointed toward the structures. "On the left is the main cabin. Gideon and Miriam live there, and that's also where we share our meals. Next is my cabin. We built it for Miriam, but when she and Giddy married, I took over. Next to that, those two knuckleheads in back bunk together. My brother Paul has the next cabin. I used to bunk with him. And up there on the far right is my brother Daniel's cabin. He's the one with the two little girls."

"It's wonderful you have such a large, close family."

He cocked his head and gave her a lazy grin. "It's not always wonderful. But usually it is. We don't want to split up the land, but we knew we'd need our privacy as each of us marries. Besides, Daniel keeps us in logs."

"One man cut down the trees to build all of this?"

"Pretty much. After his wife died, he needed something to occupy him so that he didn't go crazy. Felling the trees seemed to be his way of working things out."

Pity warmed Alisa's heart. "I understand."

Titus looked at her sharply. "My brothers are going to be curious about a woman traveling alone with no extra money or even a change of clothes. Do you feel like you want to tell me your story?"

"I. . .don't think I can just yet."

Not until she was certain he would believe her and not send her back to San Francisco to be arrested for her grandmother's murder.

Her grandmother.

"I understand." He climbed down and headed to the back of the wagon. "Hey, knuckleheads. Wake up."

Alisa's mind moved past the grumblings and mumblings of the drunken young men. For at least the thousandth time in the past two days, she shook her head to rekindle the memory of her dear grandmother's words. She truly wasn't alone. Or she wouldn't have been if Robert Worthington had been the sort of father a girl could be proud of. Growing up, she'd always thought if one had money, that person must be truly above all others in manners and grace. After all, would God reward someone who was truly wicked? But her father had certainly proven her wrong.

She shuddered at the memory of his steely, hate-ridden glare as he accused her. Despite his wonderful mother, somehow cords of evil had slithered around his heart and squeezed the decency from him. For the first time, Alisa understood that the love of money could, indeed, be a root of all evil. She'd almost rather have no father than to have one who was wicked. But that hadn't been her choice, and now because her dream of finding a family had been granted, she had to run to escape the injustice of being falsely accused.

Before she could succumb to ready tears, Alisa noticed that Titus was at her side of the wagon, holding his hand out to help her down.

Titus swallowed hard as he approached the door. Alisa's warm hand tucked in the crook of his arm made it difficult for him to think, let alone formulate a logical reason that he hired a girl to help Miriam without a family vote. He could imagine the backlash.

Alisa released a shaky breath, the first sign she'd displayed that she was less than confident. Titus covered her hand. "Don't worry. Miriam will love you."

With a barely perceptible nod, she squeezed his arm. "I'll be all right."

"Let's go in." He knocked on the door of the main cabin. Miriam appeared in short order. She smiled broadly when she saw him. "Titus, I'm so glad you made it back." Then she seemed to notice Alisa. Rather than asking questions, she opened the door wider. "Come in, please. Your guest looks worn to a frazzle."

Alisa's lips curved into a weary smile. "Thank you."

Gideon stood when Alisa entered—manners compliments of his new wife—and offered her his chair at the table. "Please, have a seat." He held her chair and stared at Titus over her head. His expression clearly spoke his disapproval and his curiosity.

Titus cleared his throat, suddenly aware of the silence in the room. Silence he was expected to fill. "I'd like you both to meet Alisa Worthington. Alisa, this is my brother Gideon and his wife, Miriam." So that took care of the names.

"And where did you meet Titus, Miss Worthington?" Miriam's pleasant voice broke through the silence.

God bless Miriam.

"On the stage from San Francisco."

Titus inwardly cringed in anticipation of the next obvious question.

"Oh? And what brings you to Reliable?"

Alisa's gaze faltered, and a pretty blush crept to her cheeks. "I. . .well. . ."

"I hired her to help Miriam."

"What?"

"How thoughtful!"

Gideon and Miriam spoke as one, then looked at each other. Alisa glanced from one to the other, then to Titus. He nodded, hoping to reassure her, but from the crestfallen expression clouding her face, he knew he'd fallen abysmally short of accomplishing his goal.

"Miss Worthington, you must be dead on your feet," Miriam said. "Have you eaten supper?"

Alisa nodded. "At the station in Reliable."

"Well, how about coming with me? I'll get you tucked into my bed. You can sleep with me tonight."

Gideon choked on a sip of coffee. "What?"

Miriam smiled sweetly at her husband. "You and Titus have some talking to do, and Miss Worthington looks just about ready to fall asleep sitting up."

Titus had to fight the urge to slap his brother on the back and laugh out loud. But Alisa's concerned voice halted him.

"Please, don't put your husband out for my sake. I can sleep anywhere. The floor is perfectly fine. I've done it plenty of times."

Alarm seized Titus, and he wanted to pound Gideon for not being more gracious. Who was Alisa that, by her own admission, she'd slept on the floor plenty of times?

At Miriam's loud clearing of the throat, Gideon's face grew bright red. "Like Miriam said, my brothers and I have some talking to do tonight."

"About me?"

Titus grinned and waited to see how his brother would respond.

"Yes, Miss Worthington."

The smile she displayed was so sweet, Titus wanted to sweep her up in his arms and protect her from all the heartache she'd suffered. Wanted to kiss away the trembling of her lips, the worry in her eyes. "I understand, Mr. Chance," she said to Gideon. She lifted her gaze to Titus. "I'll not hold you to your offer. You've been more than generous, and I appreciate your kindness more than I can express."

Anger burned in Titus. "You're staying." He glared at Gideon. "She's staying. Vote or no vote. Even if I have to marry her. She's not going anywhere."

Silence thickened the air. Alisa pushed back her chair and stood. She faced Titus, her face white. "If your brothers vote against my employment here, I'll leave without a fuss. But make no mistake. No man *has* to marry me."

"That's not what I—"

Miriam stepped forward. "How about if you two go on and call the boys to a meeting?" She rose to her tiptoes and kissed her husband soundly on the mouth. "Be sure to invite God's opinion in this decision."

Gideon nodded, cupping her cheek. The love flowing between them made

Titus's heart ache as it always did. He wanted that feeling. With Alisa, he was closer to it than he'd ever been before. And now like an idiot, he'd somehow insulted her and had most likely lost her before she was even his.

"Let's go." Gideon clapped him on the shoulder.

Shaking off his brother's hand, Titus reached out to touch Alisa's arm. "Wait a second, Alisa. Let me explain."

"Explanations aren't necessary," she murmured.

Miriam looked at him with silent appeal. "I'll cook you some flapjacks in the morning, Titus. We have fresh honey and strawberry preserves. But for now, why don't you go?"

With a final glance at Alisa's crumpled face, Titus nodded.

"Don't worry," Miriam said for his ears only. "I'll take good care of her. You concentrate on swinging the vote in your favor. I have a feeling Alisa's been through a rough time and needs us."

"Great hoppy toads, this looks good, Miriam!"

Alisa's eyes popped open at the sound of voices in the other room. Light streamed into the room, blinding her for a moment.

"You boys hush before you wake up Miss Worthington," Miriam hissed.

Alisa smiled. After a refreshing sponge bath, she'd changed into a borrowed nightgown and had been asleep practically before her head hit the pillow. Now she knew she must be frightfully late to breakfast, but her muscles ached so badly from the past two days' activities that she couldn't bring herself to hop right out of bed and face the day.

"When do you think the new gal's gonna wake up?"

Alisa's ears perked at the sound.

"Wish I could remember what she looks like. Titus says she's just about the prettiest thing he's ever seen."

He did? Alisa's heart thrilled to the information.

"Well, I like that!" Miriam's teasing voice filtered through the thin wall.

"Well, he didn't mean nothin' by it, Miriam. I think he's smitten, that's all."

This conversation was getting better and better. She'd certainly awakened at just the right moment.

The only question on her heart and in her mind was whether or not she would be allowed to stay. Spurred on by the thought, she pushed back the quilt and swung her legs over the side of the bed. For certain she wouldn't be hired if her potential employers thought she couldn't even get out of bed at a decent time in the morning.

"So when do you reckon she'll get up?"

"You asked that already, Logan."

Her gown was gone. Panic swelled her throat. She had laid the dress across the chair last night. Now it was gone. Whatever was she to do? Shoulders slumped, she sat back on the bed and listened to the conversation coming from the other room.

"I don't remember what she looks like."

Something clattered, and the sound of boot steps clacked brusquely across the wooden floor. Miriam's voice sounded sharp and firm. "You would if you hadn't imbibed. I'm so ashamed."

"We're sorry, Miriam. But sometimes when his friends want to socialize, a man just can't help it."

"A man of character can always help it. God promised we would not be tempted beyond our ability to do the right thing. So spare me your excuses."

Respect for the woman rose inside of Alisa. Suddenly she desperately wanted to be allowed to stay. Her stomach quivered at the thought of a vote against her. She slid to her knees and rested her elbows on the bed. Sometimes her heart felt so full, she couldn't form the words beyond, "Oh, please." And now she found her vocabulary once more limited to those words. "Please, dear Jesus. Oh, please, please let me stay." Slowly the pounding of her longing heart slowed to normal, and she rested her cheek against the back of her hand.

In a stranger's room, peace flooded her soul, and the words of entreaty became words of praise. "I thank Thee for giving me a name. For taking care of me so far." The fact was, she didn't have to stay at Chance Ranch for God to meet her needs. Whether He chose for her to leave or stay, her heart calmed to the fact that He was well able to take care of her. With a smile, she gathered a deep breath and opened her eyes.

Whatever happened, God was in control.

Chapter 6

Robert Worthington surveyed the two-story frame home critically as his boots clicked on the cobblestone walk. Paint was cracked and peeling off just about every board. He gave two solid raps on the door. A moment later, a girl of perhaps ten years appeared.

"May I help you?"

"I'm looking for the woman who runs this place."

"Would you like to come in?"

"Yes. Thank you."

The child stepped aside. "I'll tell Mrs. Perryman you're here."

Robert looked around at the dingy furniture, chipped tables, and worn curtains and rugs. His daughter had grown up in this dump? He pushed aside the thought as soon as it came. No. She wasn't his daughter. Alisa was the unfortunate result of a few nights of fun on his part. She never should have been found.

Anger burned within his breast as it did whenever Alisa's heart-shaped face and innocent brown eyes came to his mind. Why should he lose everything to a daughter he'd never wanted in the first place?

The sound of footsteps captured his attention, pulling him from his thoughts. An attractive, middle-aged woman smiled as she entered, followed by the young girl. A girl who might have been Alisa a few years ago. He shook the thought from his mind and scowled. The woman cocked her head to the side, the twinkle in her green eyes replaced with caution.

"May I help you?"

"You run this place?"

"I'm Mrs. Perryman. Yes, I care for the children. Are you looking for a child to adopt?"

Robert recoiled at the thought. "No!"

"I see." She turned to the girl. "Sarah, please let the children know to continue with their lessons."

"You teach them here? Why do they not attend public school?"

"Children can be cruel. Most of these children find they prefer to be taught at home."

Robert shrugged off the concern. Why should he care if a bunch of orphans received a proper education or not? He was here for one reason only. To find Alisa.

"I'm looking for my daughter. I believe you raised her here."

The woman's eyes lit up. "You've traced your child to us? This will be the second family reunion this year."

Realizing she was talking about Alisa, Robert felt his ears burn. "To tell you the truth, Mrs. Perryman, Alisa is my daughter."

Confusion clouded her face. "Perhaps you'd better come into the kitchen, and you can explain over a cup of tea."

"Really, that won't be. . ." Robert sighed as she turned and headed down the hallway. All he wanted was information, not a tea party, but he followed her swishing gray skirts, nostalgia filling him at the familiar sound. There were times when he missed his mother so badly his throat ached. Unpredictable moments such as this. He cleared his throat to ease the tightness.

"Is Alisa missing, Mr. Worthington?" she asked over her shoulder.

"Yes."

She opened the door to the kitchen and entered, stepping aside as she waited for Robert to follow. He did.

"Please have a seat at the table while I prepare our tea." She moved to the stove with a quiet grace and began preparing a kettle of water.

Robert sat in the chair she'd indicated. The wood felt wobbly beneath him, and he wondered if it would hold his weight. "It seems there are plenty of things around here in need of repair."

She sighed, pumping water into the kettle. "I'm afraid you're right. Since Mr. Perryman passed on four years ago, I haven't been able to keep up with much. Some of the boys are handy with tools and can help with repairs, as long as the jobs don't require funds we simply don't have."

Robert knew she wasn't hinting. But he knew how to play a situation to his advantage all the same. "How many children do you care for here?" First rule of thumb when trying to weasel something out of a person—make them think you care.

She turned to him and smiled. "Right now we have seven boys ranging in age from four to sixteen. And ten girls approximately the same ages." She took in a slow breath. "Unfortunately, Seth, my oldest boy, will have to be moving on soon."

She sounded so sad, Robert was prompted to ask, "Why is that?"

"Once they reach the age where they are able to find work, we must make room for new children. It breaks my heart to see them go. I was little more than the oldest among them myself when we started the orphanage. But they understand, and most come back often to visit. Some even help out. Alisa always brought her pay over here. I tried to protest, but she left it with one of the children when I refused to take it."

She poured the tea and set a chipped cup in front of him, along with a creamer. "I'm afraid I don't have any sugar at the moment. Little Judith turned eight yesterday, and I used the last of it to bake a cake."

"Plain is fine." Robert detested the way his heart constricted at the thought of anyone being so poor as to make a choice between having sugar for tea or using the last to bake a cake. He gathered himself together. All the more reason for her to take him up on his forthcoming offer.

"Mrs. Perryman, I can see you care deeply for these. . . orphans."

"You see correctly." She stirred a drop of cream into her cup. "My husband and I were never blessed with children of our own. The children God brings to us . . .to me. . .become part of a family. Now what of Alisa? We missed her yesterday for Judith's birthday."

Armed with confidence, Robert flashed a smile. "I'm afraid she's run away."

A frown creased Mrs. Perryman's already wrinkled brow. "That doesn't sound like Alisa. Was she in danger?"

"Of course not. I'm afraid my mother passed on very recently, and my. . . daughter took it rather hard."

"Oh, how sad." Her green eyes drew him in, and he almost forgot his objective. Almost. Not quite.

"Yes. Alisa and I are all the other has in the world now."

"How long has she been gone?"

"My mother passed away two nights ago. I haven't seen Alisa since." Robert sipped the weak tea. "The reason I bothered you is that I hoped you'd seen her. I take it you haven't?"

"I'm afraid not. But if I do, I'll be sure to tell her you're looking for her."

Robert inwardly cringed. That would be the worst thing she could do. Alisa would run and never return if she knew he had come here to look for her. "There's more to it than that."

Mrs. Perryman frowned. "I don't understand."

"Alisa is under the impression she is somehow responsible for my mother's demise."

"However would she have gotten such an idea?"

"I'm as much at a loss about that as you are, Mrs. Perryman. But it's very, very important that I find her." He leaned forward, his hands wrapped around the teacup. "If Alisa contacts you, I would appreciate it if you would send word immediately." He reached into his coat pocket and pulled out ten dollars.

Mrs. Perryman's eyes narrowed. She squared her shoulders. "Sir, if you are trying to pay me to betray Alisa, I would like you to leave my home this instant."

"Please, Mrs. Perryman. You misunderstand. I am simply donating to your cause."

"The Lord provides for our needs. We do not need your donation." The woman stood. "You may show yourself out."

Frustration shook Robert to the core. He looked toward the door and saw a dark head peeking around the corner.

"Come out here," he ordered.

Slowly a small boy moved to stand in front of him.

"What's your name?"

"Spencer." The freckles on his nose crunched together as he grinned, a wide, gap-toothed smile.

Robert found himself responding. He walked by, ruffled the boy's head, and handed him the ten dollars. "Give this to Mrs. Perryman and tell her to buy some sugar. No strings attached."

He berated himself as he stalked down the walk away from the nearly dilapidated orphanage.

What kind of a fool was he?

Titus felt his stomach respond to the smell of bacon frying and flapjacks staying warm in the oven. True to her word, Miriam had cooked all of his favorites. He scanned the room but didn't find Alisa present. His gaze traveled to Miriam. Her lips curved. "She's still asleep."

"Good. That was quite a stage ride yesterday. I'm sure she needs her rest."

"In the meantime, we can take our vote." Gideon kept his voice low.

"What vote?" Bryce reached for a flapjack, then turned his gaze to Gideon.

"About Miss Worthington staying."

"Why do we need to vote on that? I figured she was staying."

Daniel wiped the jam from Ginny Mae's chin. "This life is too hard on a woman. I think we ought to do her a favor and send her back where she came from."

Frustration chewed at Titus. He raked his fingers through his unruly hair and glared at his widowed brother. "We're all sorry Hannah died, Daniel. But that doesn't mean no woman is cut out for this life. Alisa should have the right to decide for herself."

"You could always marry her like Gideon married Miriam," Logan suggested. Bryce passed him the plate of bacon. Logan's face blanched, and he shook his head.

"He's right," Bryce offered. "Then we wouldn't have any choice but to let her stay."

Paul and Gideon cackled. "She already turned him down," Gideon informed them.

"All right." Miriam set another plate of flapjacks on the table. "If you don't lower your voices, you'll wake her up. Take the vote, and get it over with."

"We already know what Daniel thinks," Titus said.

Daniel grunted and gulped his coffee.

"I vote yes. Now can I go back to bed?" Logan held his head in his hands. "I'm not hungry."

"I vote yes, too." Bryce forked another flapjack. "If Logan's not eating, I'll take his."

Titus shook his head at his brother. So much for his morning pain teaching him a lesson.

"Paul?"

Paul sipped his coffee. "I haven't even met her yet. Where will she sleep? She can't stay with Miriam."

"You'd better believe she can't."

Miriam's face grew red at her husband's outburst.

"I have that all worked out," Titus said quickly. "How about if I move back in with you, Paul? Alisa can have my cabin."

Paul shrugged. "That'd be all right with me."

"So you vote yes?"

"I reckon so."

"That settles it, then. We don't need Gideon's vote. We have a majority." Titus felt a smug grin tug at his mouth.

Miriam walked by and patted his shoulder. "Do I get a vote?"

No one said a word.

"After all, I'm part of the family now, too, aren't I?"

"Well, sure." Even if she voted no, the four of them had a majority. Titus smiled to encourage her.

"Well, of course I vote yes, but that isn't the point. From now on, I wish to be included in these decisions."

"Miriam's right," Gideon said. "She's an adult member of the family and deserves a voice when we vote."

"I think we should vote on whether Miriam should vote or not," Bryce said between bites.

Miriam sniffed and tossed a dish towel at him. "How about if I vote to stop cooking flapjacks just the way you like them?"

"Just kidding. I think Miriam should have a vote, too."

Gideon slapped him on the shoulder. "You'll agree to anything if it means the difference between Miriam's cooking or going back to Paul's."

"Can't say as I blame him," Paul said through a grin just before he shoveled another bite into his mouth.

"All right," Titus said with a nod. "Then we're agreed. Miss Worthington stays, and from now on, Miriam gets a vote."

Daniel grunted his disapproval but didn't speak.

Logan rose. "I'm going back to my cabin," he said a bit thinly. "You'll have to do without me today."

"Get some rest," Gideon said sternly. "But when you get up, we're going to have another talk about you two and your drinking."

Logan nodded and slunk toward the door.

"Then it's settled. Alisa stays." Titus glanced toward the other room, his stomach churning with anticipation at seeing her again.

"Someone's coming," Logan announced from the open door.

"Who?"

"Looks like Miss White."

All eyes turned to Titus. Bryce snickered. "Guess she wants to marry you after all."

Chapter 7

Alisa's heart sank at Bryce's theory about Prissy and her matrimonial intentions. Guilt pricked her that she'd been eavesdropping the whole time, but the truth was, she couldn't leave the room without clothes, and so far, hers hadn't materialized. She could only assume Miriam had taken them to be washed—which was sweet of her—but what would Alisa wear in the meantime?

She jumped a moment later when Miriam slipped into the room. The other woman's lips twitched. "I guess you heard the vote."

Warmth flooded Alisa's cheeks. She nodded.

"I took your dress to wash. But naturally it isn't dry yet. I brought you one of mine. You're a bit taller than I am, but it should work until yours is dry." Miriam deposited the clothing on the bed. "I see you tidied up in here. Thank you. You are going to be handy to have around."

Alisa smiled at the praise.

Miriam walked to her wardrobe and pulled out some white lacy articles. "You'll need these as well."

"Thank you."

"Just hurry and get yourself presentable. Prissy White just pulled up."

"I—I met her last night, I'm afraid. I—I don't mean I'm afraid. I mean. . ." She cleared her throat. "Well, I made her acquaintance at dinner."

Miriam laughed. "It's all right. I completely understand. Prissy takes a little getting used to. Poor Titus."

"Poor Titus?"

"Obviously, Prissy's predatory nature took over when she saw you with him. She turned down his proposal—and she wasn't too nice about it—but it looks like she's changed her mind. It'll be interesting to see how Titus gets himself out of this bind."

"Why would he want to get out of it? If he asked her to marry him, he must love her." The very words left a bitter taste in Alisa's mouth.

Miriam waved her hands. "Nonsense. Love rarely has anything to do with marriage in these parts." A lovely smile tipped her lips. "There are exceptions, of course. Anyway, I will admit Titus was smitten for a while. But that's all changed. I can see it in his eyes. You've definitely caused the glow of Prissy's presence to dim. He lights up like a Roman candle every time he looks at you."

Alisa tried not to allow her heartbeat to speed up. She couldn't put too much stock in a man whose heart switched allegiance so quickly. "I see."

If a man could get unsmitten with Prissy White that quickly, what was to say Titus Chance wouldn't meet a prettier face in a few days and get unsmitten with Alisa as well? A chuckle from Miriam pulled her back to the present. "Well, I'll go greet our guest while you get ready."

Alisa donned the underthings and the blue gown, which was slightly too short. After pulling her hair back into a loose chignon, a style her grandmother had mentioned was quite attractive, she stepped into the other room. All eyes turned to her, but she locked onto Titus's gaze and couldn't look away. His smile started at his lips and spread upward until pleasure glowed in his eyes. "Good morning," he said, leaving Prissy's side and walking across the room to meet Alisa. He offered his arm. "May I escort you to breakfast? There's still plenty on the table. I could heat it up for you if you like."

A snort from Bryce brought a scowl to Titus's nearly perfect features.

Alisa felt her cheeks warm at his obvious attempt at. . .something. His gallantry wasn't lost on Prissy. The girl looked as though steam might blow from her ears at any second. Alisa took his arm and walked with him to the table. "Thank you, Titus. I'm sure the food is plenty warm."

"Would you like some coffee, Alisa?" Miriam asked.

"Yes, thank you."

"I'll get it," Titus offered.

"Perhaps I'll have a cup after all, Titus," Prissy said in a slightly falsetto voice.

"Uh, okay. Two cups of coffee coming right up."

Prissy flounced to the table and plopped down in the wooden chair next to Alisa. "Miriam," she said, "I'm surprised to see you doing all the work. I thought that's why Miss Worthington was hired."

Alisa gathered a steadying breath. She recognized the challenge and refused to take it up. She wouldn't embarrass herself by insulting her employer's guest.

Titus set two steaming cups on the table in front of Prissy and Alisa. "We're giving Alisa a day to rest from the stage ride and to get her bearings."

"Oh, of course. She must be exhausted. Poor dear." Prissy gave her the once-over and then dismissed her. Alisa felt the slight to her toes but again chose to let it go. As an orphan she had gained a lot of experience with once-over looks from townsfolk. She'd never been very good at swallowing the insults without resentment, but she had at least learned to keep her mouth shut.

She felt a warm hand squeeze her shoulder and looked up just as Titus moved around her to the end chair. "Did you sleep all right, Alisa?"

"I did." She smiled. "Thank you."

"Good!" He smiled back, and Alisa felt the background fade. They were the only two people in the cabin. "Today we'll get you all moved into my cabin."

A gasp from the ruffly, ribboned, pink-clad Prissy caused Alisa to jerk around. "Did you burn your mouth on the coffee, Miss White?"

"I am mortified that you will be sharing a cabin with my fiancé!" Prissy glared around the room, taking in the brothers and Miriam. "And quite frankly, I'm shocked that any of you would allow such an abomination."

Now it was Alisa's turn to gasp. She shot to her feet, knocking over her coffee cup in the process. The liquid made a brown trail toward Prissy's pink gown.

A scream escaped Prissy's painted lips as she tried in vain to jump up out of the way.

Alisa watched, horrified as the liquid trail met the fabric. Titus groaned. The rest of the men grunted with dread, and Miriam gasped. Prissy spun, her face red with fury. "You, you did that on purpose. You ruined my new gown from New York."

"I most certainly did not do it on purpose," Alisa said, fighting to keep her temper in check and respond quietly. *"A soft answer turneth away wrath,"* she reminded herself.

"You did, too, you immoral girl." Prissy's hand shot out, landing across Alisa's cheek with a resounding *smack* and an explosion of pain. Alisa stepped back, palm over the stinging area. The girl's hand came up again. Too stunned to defend herself, Alisa watched the hand descend.

Titus stepped forward, grabbing Prissy's hand before she could strike a second time. "That's enough, Priscilla."

Tears pooled in her eyes. "Did you see what she did, Titus? She poured her coffee on my new gown on purpose. She's afraid you'll come back to me and turn her out."

"Don't be foolish," he ground out. "Miss Worthington will not be sharing the cabin with me, and I can't believe you'd think so little of me as to even entertain the notion."

"But you said—"

"I'm moving out of the cabin, and Miss Worthington will occupy it alone, of course."

Her trembling lips curved upward into a pouty smile. "What a relief. I was afraid she had corrupted you."

"Miss Worthington is completely devoted to her Christian faith. So you have no need to fear the corruption of my morals at her hands."

Humiliated by the entire conversation, Alisa stepped back. "Excuse me, please." Unable to meet anyone's gaze, she fled out the front door, around the house, and toward a path cut through the woods. As an orphan, she'd been ridiculed and falsely accused often, but never had she been accused of loose morals. The spiteful woman.

Titus dropped Prissy's wrist and stomped outside in pursuit of Alisa. How could he ever have imagined himself in love with that frilly, flouncy, spiteful young woman? Standing next to Alisa's quiet grace, Prissy was obviously inferior in quality of character. He certainly didn't want her to be the mother of his children.

Remembering Miriam's bout with poison oak last summer and her subsequent weeklong recovery, he hurried along the path behind the house, hoping Alisa would stay away from the woods.

If she stayed on the path, she'd come to the creek and be forced to wade or stop. He figured she'd stop. He was right. After a few more yards, he came to the clearing. Alisa stood along the bank of the creek, her arms wrapped around her.

A twig snapped beneath his feet. She turned her head at the sound.

Tenderness swelled Titus's heart at her red-rimmed eyes and tear-streaked cheeks. He went to her quickly and wrapped her in his arms without asking permission. Times like this called for comforting, and he didn't have to be an expert on women to realize his arms would be welcome.

She wilted against him, her head resting on his chest. Her arms were tucked between them. And while Titus might have preferred to have them wrapped around him, he understood her need to be cuddled. "Shhh, honey. Everything is going to work out fine."

He stroked her silken hair, wishing it was loose and flowing instead of pulled back into a knot at the nape of her neck.

"What if she goes back to town, telling tales?"

"Who's she going to tell them to?"

"What do you mean?"

"Honey, this isn't San Francisco. There are only three decent women in Reliable, four if you count Prissy. You know that. The men aren't going to cotton to a woman's gossip."

She stayed in his arms, but he could feel her relaxing against him. When she pulled away, he took her chin between his thumb and forefinger and gently forced her to look up at him. Her lovely brown eyes were wide and innocent, filled with unshed tears. Her moist lips still trembled. Titus swallowed hard, fighting for control. Instinctively he knew kissing her would be a disastrous move.

"If it'll make you feel better, we could get married." The words came out of nowhere, sending a jolt through him.

She drew a sharp breath and stepped back.

"Titus?" Prissy's falsetto voice rang from the trail.

Alisa's eyes crinkled with amusement. "Don't you think you have enough fiancées for now?"

"Prissy's not my. . ."

"Oh, thank goodness. There you are."

"Yes," Alisa said, with a smirk. "Here he is. If you two will excuse me. I'd best go see if I can help Miriam clean up." She gave Prissy a sidelong glance as she walked by. "It's never too early to start earning my keep."

Prissy's sniff was the only response. Titus felt as though a cloud had drifted across the sun as he watched Alisa walk away. The warmth of her slender body wrapped in his arms filled him with a longing to go after her and tell her he was serious about the proposal. Out here it didn't matter if he'd only known her for a couple of days. They were both single adults. The attraction between them couldn't be denied. He frowned. Or maybe he was only assuming Alisa wasn't already spoken for. She hadn't seemed to even consider his proposal. Titus grimaced. How could he have blurted it out like that? This was the second time in less than twenty-four hours he'd suggested marrying her. The first time he'd made her angry. This time he'd amused her. She must think he threw out proposals at the drop of a hat.

Prissy's touch on his arm brought him back to the annoying situation at hand. "Titus, please. The ground is so soft from last night's rain, my heels keep digging in. I'll need you to carry me back to the wagon."

Was she serious?

Her lips trembled, but rather than tempting him to move in for a kiss as Alisa's had moments before, Prissy's lips made Titus recoil.

He softened when her eyes filled with real tears. "Please, Titus. My gown is already ruined. Mother's going to be fit to be tied as it is. I—I only came out to see you. To tell you that I. . ."

Dread clenched his gut. Then sympathy filled him as he observed her gown. A large coffee stain covered the skirt, and the bottom edge was wet and covered with mud.

"It's all right. Tell your mother I'm sorry about your gown, and I'll be happy to compensate her if you're unable to get it clean." He swept her into his arms as she'd requested and headed back toward the yard where her buggy was tethered.

A contented sigh escaped her as her arms wrapped about his neck. "Oh, Titus. You're such a gentleman. I was a fool to turn you down. And that's what I came to tell you."

They were reaching the clearing, and all he wanted was to put her down on the firmer ground so that no one would see him carrying Prissy.

"Are you listening, Titus?" Her emotion-filled words were spoken softly against his ear.

Waves of dread washed over him, and a knot lodged in his throat at her next words.

"I have reconsidered your offer, my darling. I will marry you after all."

He stopped dead in his tracks and turned his head to look at her. The movement brought them face-to-face—much too close for retreat. Obviously mistaking his action as an invitation, Prissy closed her eyes and pressed her lips to his before he could make a move.

He pulled quickly away and set her down.

"Prissy. . ."

"Oh, Titus. Our first kiss." She wrapped her arms through one of his. "Was it all you'd hoped it would be?"

More than he'd bargained for was more like it. As he walked her to the wagon, he tried to formulate the words to let her down gently.

"Prissy, listen to me." He disentangled himself from her solid grip. She was quite strong for a woman.

"Yes, my darling?"

"I'm not still. . .I mean, you honor me with your decision. But. . ."

"Oh, Titus." She patted his cheek. "You are just too sweet. Please come by tonight and speak with my father, all right? Then mother and I can begin planning the wedding."

Without giving him another chance to speak, she held out her hand. Dumbfounded, Titus took her hand and assisted her into the buggy.

"Don't forget now. Come to dinner tonight. Six o'clock."

Not sure what had just happened, he stumbled into the house.

Bryce whistled. "Guess Prissy changed her mind."

Titus jerked his head up. "Huh?"

"We watched the whole thing from the window."

Panic exploded inside of him. Titus searched the room until he found Alisa at the counter washing dishes. She kept her gaze focused on the dishpan. Ignoring the rest of the family, he strode across the room and cupped her elbow, turning her to face him. "It wasn't what it looked like."

Her gaze settled on his lips, and she arched an eyebrow. Taking the dish towel from the counter, she handed it to him and walked toward the bedroom. Frowning, Titus watched her leave. He turned a questioning glance on Miriam.

Her lips were tight. "You have Prissy's lip stain smeared all over your mouth." She shook her head. "I don't know how you're going to fix this one. But Alisa is worth ten of Prissy."

Bryce tossed his napkin on the table and leaned his chair back on two legs. "If Titus is going to marry Prissy, does that mean Alisa's fair game?"

Gideon's booted foot shot out, knocking Bryce off balance. Chair and all, he landed with a thud on the floor.

"Hey! I just meant Titus don't need two women. I want one of them."

Miriam patted Titus's shoulder. "You have a decision to make. You'd best make it fast before you lose Alisa. Bryce isn't the only man around here who's going to be coming around wanting to court her. She'll have ten proposals before the week's out."

Alarm shot through Titus. She was right. He had to get out of this predicament with Prissy. The sooner the better.

Chapter 8

Loose strands of hair flew up, tickling Alisa's cheek as she lifted the quilt and let it settle back to the bed. True to his promise, Titus had removed his things from the cabin just before mounting a horse and riding toward town.

Miriam had provided her with fresh bedding and instructed her to take as much time as she needed to make this little cabin her own. The thought of being all alone sent an ache of loneliness through Alisa. She'd never been alone before. It had been difficult enough to grow accustomed to sleeping in a vast house with only Mrs. Worthington, Robert, and Marietta. She wondered if she would ever fall asleep without the sounds of children snoring, the sounds of the city moving about outside her window. The Chance family bewildered her. They were a close-knit bunch, given to arguing at the drop of a hat and just as quick to defend one another.

Throughout the afternoon, one by one she'd had a visit from each brother, with the exception of Daniel. And of course, Titus. Each assured her that Titus thought he liked Prissy until he met Alisa. Though she appreciated their thoughtfulness, she'd felt compelled to remind each in turn that she'd only just met Titus. She certainly had no hold on him, and furthermore, she wasn't looking for a husband.

But whether she was looking for a husband or not, it was difficult to push aside the memory of Prissy White in Titus's arms and the sight of that kiss. He'd tried to explain that he was an innocent recipient of the kiss and that he was relieved Prissy had turned down his proposal and that he had no intention of going through with a wedding.

But if that was the complete truth, then why had he headed toward town with the instructions not to hold supper for him? She felt safe in assuming he would be eating with Prissy and her parents. And newly acquainted, notwithstanding, the thought didn't sit well with her. So she poured her energy into cleaning her new home.

Titus wasn't the most meticulous housekeeper. The multicolored rag rugs were in desperate need of washing. The wooden planks, too, needed a good scrubbing. She opened the window to let in a bit of chilly autumn breeze to freshen the air inside the room. Her favorite discovery was a wooden slab that folded down and became a desk.

At lunchtime, Miriam knocked on her door. She looked about and nodded appreciatively. "This room hasn't sparkled so much since I lived here."

Alisa laughed. "I believe it."

"The Chance men have their good qualities, but neatness isn't among them. I suppose that's why God sent us."

Alisa glanced down, embarrassed.

"May I give you a bit of advice?"

"Of course."

"Don't discount Titus because of this misunderstanding."

"I don't know what you mean. I can't discount someone I never counted in the first place. Titus is a nice man. So is Paul and—"

A frown creased Miriam's brow. "Do you fancy Paul? I just assumed Titus was the one."

"Well, no. I mean I don't fancy Paul. I don't even know him." Alisa dropped to the bed and looked up at Miriam. "My point is that Titus is free to marry Prissy or anyone else he chooses. I don't have any hold on him any more than I do on Paul or Bryce or Daniel."

"I see." She cleared her throat. "Well, I came to tell you lunch is just about ready."

"Oh, I should have helped cook."

"Nonsense. Today was your day to settle in. Tomorrow we'll get you acquainted with the ranch and discuss what chores you can take over."

Miriam's warm smile eased Alisa's tension. She nodded. "All right. I'll wash the dirt off my hands and be right over."

Paul had just said the prayer when the rattle of a wagon outside drew attention away from the venison stew.

"Looks like word's gotten out already."

Daniel grunted. "That's all we need. To feed half the men in town again."

Miriam's laughter filled the room. "When I first came to the ranch, the men of Reliable took to dropping by at mealtimes. Often up to ten at a time."

"Until I put a stop to it," Gideon said, taking his wife's hand. He gave it a squeeze and stood.

"It's Marv Wall."

"Titus ain't going to like this," Logan said around a bite of bread.

"Titus has his own mess to clean up right now," Daniel grumped. "Serves him right."

Alisa could feel herself slinking further into her chair, wishing she could just disappear altogether from this meal and this conversation. It was too late to slip out the door and to her cabin, as Gideon had already invited the man in. Alisa tried not to look away, but the man's steady gaze and wide eyes made her uncomfortable.

"I heered ya got another one," he said, remembering to slip his beat-up, greasy hat from his head. Sweat stained his armpits all the way down his sides. A grizzled beard stubbled his face. Alisa thought she might be ill.

"Good afternoon, Mr. Wall," Miriam spoke up. "Would you like to join us for lunch? We just finished saying grace."

His face lit up. "Don't mind if I do, Mrs. Chance."

Alisa had never been more aware of anything as she was of the empty seat beside her. Apparently that suited Mr. Wall, for he nearly leapt toward the seat. Miriam took his arm and steered him to the other end of the table.

"Fine. Why don't you take Logan's seat? It's really the best seat at the table."

"Oh, but I was just going to—"

"Nonsense. Logan doesn't mind scooting over." A sweet smile curved Miriam's lips, and Alisa wanted to hug her. "After all, you are a guest."

Logan grinned at Alisa and winked. She couldn't help but return the scamp's smile as he scooted next to her. Suddenly her heart grew light. Thanks to God's intervention, she had landed smack in the middle of a large, loving family who seemed bent on helping her. And Titus or no Titus, she felt as though she belonged.

Titus swallowed hard and tried again, wishing desperately Whites' wasn't the only store in town. "I need enough material for two dresses for Miss Worthington."

Prissy's scowl only deepened. "Why should you be buying clothes for your servant?"

"First of all, she isn't a servant. And second, she needs clothing and a warm coat. As long as she's living under our roof, we're responsible to see that she has everything she needs."

"I should think you'd care more about your fiancée's feelings than about your hired help."

"Well, about that. . ."

Her smile could have lit up the room. Titus swallowed hard. How had he gotten himself into such a mess?

"Prissy, I came to tell you that I—"

"Hi there, Titus." Reba White entered from the back room. "Nice to see you. Is this business, or couldn't you wait until supper tonight to see my girl?"

Prissy giggled. "Mother, you're embarrassing me."

Sure she was.

"To tell you the truth, we've hired a young woman to help Miriam around the ranch."

"Now why would you go and do a thing like that when you'll be adding my Priscilla to the ranch soon?" Reba waved toward Prissy. "She'll be plenty of help."

"Now, Mother, I'm not much good at cooking and cleaning. You know that."

"Sure, but once you marry, you'll need to take care of your man. We discussed this. Remember?"

"Yes, but with Miriam doing the cooking—"

"You'll have to learn, just like every other woman does." Reba's voice had taken on a hard edge, and she glanced sharply at Titus. "So this young woman. Is she the one you had supper with last night at the station?"

"Yes, ma'am. She came in on the stage."

"I figured that. What's she needing?"

"As I was telling Priscilla, enough material for two dresses and any other things women need. You'll be a better judge of that than I would. And a coat."

Prissy gave a harrumph and flounced toward the back.

With a shake of her head, Mrs. White jerked her thumb in the direction the girl had gone. "Don't mind her. She'll learn the ropes in no time."

"Yes, ma'am."

Mrs. White peered closer. "You havin' second thoughts, Titus?"

Was he that transparent, or was Mrs. White a mind reader? Whatever the case, it was too bad her daughter wasn't as astute.

"No need to answer. I can see she doesn't take your fancy anymore. Is it the new girl?"

Titus felt his cheeks warm, and he averted his gaze.

"Never mind. I can see it written all over your face."

"I'm sorry, Mrs. White. I tried to tell Priscilla the truth, but—"

"Oh, I know. Once she gets something into her head, there ain't no convincing her. I wondered why she'd gotten herself all fired up to go out to the ranch this mornin'." She gave a dismissive wave. "Don't you worry yourself none about it. I'll take care of that daughter of mine. She has a dozen standing proposals. I'm sure one's just as good a catch as another. She won't be upset for long."

Relief flooded Titus from his hairline to his toes.

"Guess you'd best not come to supper, though. Mr. White might not take this as rationally as me."

"Yes, ma'am."

"All right. You come back in an hour, and I'll have your order ready."

Titus thanked her and stepped outside. "Titus, hold up!"

He turned to find Todd Dorsey striding toward him. "What are you doing off the ranch today, Todd?"

"Thought I'd come in and get a haircut and a shave."

The saloon keeper doubled as a barber, and from the nicks on Todd's face, Titus figured the man had been drinking before he took the razor in hand.

"I. . .uh. . .thought I'd come over for a visit this evening. Heard you're breaking a new colt."

"That's right. Bryce is working on it." Titus eyed the man suspiciously. He was no fool. A new colt being broken was no reason to go visiting, especially when the same thing was going on at his own ranch. Alarm bells rang inside of him. He didn't even have to ask the question on the tip of his tongue.

"I hear you're hidin' a real pretty girl at Chance Ranch."

"We're not hiding anyone."

"Then there ain't a girl out there?"

"I didn't say that."

Todd's eyes narrowed. "Then what *are* you sayin'?"

Expelling an impatient breath, Titus shrugged. "Miss Worthington came in on the stage and needed a place to stay. Miriam could use the help, so we offered her a job in exchange for room and board."

Satisfied?

Todd wasn't satisfied. Not by a long shot.

"So no one's got dibs on marrying her yet?"

"Dibs? You make her sound like the last piece of chocolate cake." Titus cringed at his analogy.

Todd grinned. "Well, ain't that sorta like what she is? I'm moseyin' on out there to get my offer in 'fore someone beats me to it."

"Now hold on just one minute." Anger began to rise, and Titus took a steadying breath to control himself. "No one said she wasn't already called for."

Todd frowned. "Ya mean she's already promised to one of ya?"

"Well, no, but I—"

"Then she's fair game. You Chances got the last woman, and that was only fair seein' as how she's your brother's wife's sister and all, but it's someone else's turn, and I plan for it to be me."

With that, he mounted his horse and took off at a gallop toward the ranch.

Titus hurried to his horse and mounted quickly. Wishing he still had Raven, he turned the sorrel toward home. His faithful old horse would have gotten him home before Todd could get there. As it was, he knew a couple of shortcuts.

He was halfway home before he remembered the dress goods he'd ordered from Mrs. White. With a groan, he whipped back around. Hopefully Alisa wouldn't take a fancy to Todd or anyone else before he could get back and announce that his wedding was off once again.

Chapter 9

Choosing her words carefully, Alisa smiled at Mr. Wall. "Yes, Mr. Wall. I can see how a woman would be blessed to marry a man with a ranch as vast as yours." He'd spent the last few minutes spouting every acre of land, every piece of livestock, and his future plans.

The man's chest swelled. Indeed, his modest acreage, though it couldn't be compared with Chance Ranch, was quite impressive. Of course, a woman would have to look past the excessive sweating, the missing teeth, and the layer of dirt on his neck for him to find someone to share his life with. And she certainly wasn't that woman. Mr. Wall had come for lunch and had stayed for the entire afternoon, despite Miriam's hints that he surely had work that needed attending at his own ranch. He seemed intent upon staying at Alisa's side. They'd been sitting on the bench just outside the door to the main house since lunch.

Alisa was having trouble keeping her eyes open, and the smell was beginning to give her a headache.

The pounding of a horse's hooves drew her attention toward the road.

"Well, if that don't just beat all." Mr. Wall's disgust was clear.

"Is something wrong?" Alisa asked.

"There sure is something wrong. I was here first, that's what. Todd Dorsey must have caught wind of you. Now he's coming to try and take you away."

"I beg your pardon?"

"Someone must've been yappin' about you being here at the ranch." He put a protective arm around her shoulders.

Alisa gasped and pulled back sharply. "Please keep your distance, Mr. Wall, or I'll be forced to ask you to leave."

"Sorry, miss," he muttered. "Just don't want there to be no mistakin' who was here first."

The horse pulled to a halt, and a young man dismounted. He removed his hat and grinned, showing a much more promising set of teeth. "Hello. My name's Todd Dorsey. You must be Miss Worthington."

"Why, yes, I am." Alisa found herself responding to his manners.

Miriam appeared on the porch like an answered prayer.

"Good afternoon, Mr. Dorsey. What brings you all the way out here?"

"You know good and well what brung him," Mr. Wall accused.

Mr. Dorsey gave a sheepish grin. "I saw Titus in town. He mentioned that Miss Worthington here was as pretty as a flower and hadn't been picked yet."

"Hadn't been picked yet!" Alisa squared her shoulders and narrowed her gaze.

"Well, in a manner of speaking. He said you wasn't spoken for."

Alisa's heart sank. Titus was shuffling her off to other men? He must have decided to marry Priscilla White after all.

"Titus was wrong," Mr. Wall declared, stepping forward. "I picked her. I'm claimin' her right now. So you kin just go on and get outta here."

"You can't claim her. I'm claimin' her." The two men stood nose to nose. Alisa feared they might come to blows.

"Gentlemen, please," Miriam's voice remained low and conciliatory. "Don't you agree that Miss Worthington has the right of choice in the matter of who will be her husband? Marv, you were here first, so you were certainly at an advantage. But Todd rode all the way out here to meet Miss Worthington, so the least you can do is step aside and give him a chance to get to know her as well."

Marv turned to Alisa. "You choose, then. Me or him."

Alisa gasped. "I—I—I don't know what to say."

"Now, gentlemen. Don't be silly. Miss Worthington isn't going to choose one of you right here and now. She doesn't even know you."

"That's right." Alisa's relief that Miriam was here knew no bounds. She only wished she could escape the men who seemed bent on getting her to an altar.

"Now a real gentleman would realize that Miss Worthingston is dead tired from her long trip from San Francisco. I should think a man might show his consideration by letting her rest. That sort of man might make a good impression."

Luckily, Alisa was forced to stifle a weary yawn at just that moment.

Understanding flickered in Todd's eyes. He gave a gallant bow. "Miss Worthington, may I call on you tomorrow evening?"

"Now wait just a cotton pickin' minute. I was about to ask."

"Why don't you both come to supper tomorrow night?" Miriam suggested. Alisa glanced at the woman. Whose side was she on anyway? Surely she realized Alisa would never be interested in either of these men. Both paled considerably in comparison to Titus. Of course, he'd called her an unpicked flower! Apparently he had no interest in her after all.

The sound of a horse's hooves interrupted once more, and with great trepidation, Alisa lifted her gaze toward the sound. "Titus," she breathed.

"Yes," Miriam said, a smile crossing her lips as she nodded. "I guess he'll be home for supper after all."

Unpicked flower.

Suddenly the humiliating situation of having two unsuitable men fighting over her while the one she admired was handing her to them on a first-come, first-served basis was more than she could manage. "Excuse me, please." Turning on her heel, she fled to her cabin. Once inside, she leaned against the closed door and shut her eyes.

Tears slowly pushed past her lashes. She flung herself across her bed. Wave after wave of images rolled over in her mind. Discovering her grandmother only to lose her in a flash. Being implicated by her own father, having to run away before the police arrived, wandering all night and all the next day unsure what to do but knowing she couldn't go back. Nor could she return to the orphanage. After buying a half-rotten apple from a street vendor, Alisa had found the stage station and bought a ticket to take her as far as she could go. Reliable was the end of the trail for her.

Were her only options to marry the likes of the men represented here today? Or should she go back to San Francisco and hope that the police would believe her? But wouldn't they take Robert Worthington's word over hers? After all, he owned a prominent shipping company, and she was merely an orphan working in the Worthington household. Despair filled her, and the tears became a river until sobs shook her.

Titus paced the floor. Alisa had been in that cabin all afternoon, and now she'd failed to show up for supper.

"Titus, please be still. You're making me nervous."

He glanced up in surprise at Miriam's words.

She shoved a filled plate at him. "Why don't you take this to her?"

Relief flooded him. "Good idea."

Letting the door slam shut behind him, Titus headed for Alisa's cabin. He frowned. It was completely dark; not even the soft glow of candlelight filtered through the window. He stopped at the front door and knocked.

No answer. He knocked again, harder this time. "Alisa?"

Finally, a muffled sound assured him that she was inside. The lump began to dislodge. He'd been afraid that perhaps she'd left without telling anyone.

The door slowly opened. She stood before him, her hair and clothing disheveled, but she'd lit a candle.

"We were worried when you didn't show up for supper."

The soft flame highlighted her drowsy smile. "I must have fallen asleep."

"I brought you a plate."

Her smile widened. "That was thoughtful of you."

So entranced was he at the vision she made, Titus said the first thing that popped into his mind. "It was Miriam's idea."

Her expression fell. "I see. Well, be sure to thank her for me." She started to close the door. Titus put his hand out to stop it. "I'm not marrying Priscilla."

"Oh, I'm sorry."

"You are?"

"Aren't you?"

"No."

"I see."

She saw a lot but never the full picture as far as Titus could tell. "The fact is, I don't love her."

Staring mutely, she seemed to be waiting for him to expound. Titus was at a loss for words, but he wanted her to be clear that he intended to court her. "I know it's awkward. And we haven't known each other long, but I'd like to. . ."

Her eyes widened.

"Do you think you'd be willing to allow me to court you?"

A light flashed in her eyes. At least he thought it was a light. He couldn't be sure, because whatever it was left almost as fast as it had shown up.

She shook her head. "I'm sorry, Titus. You've been so kind to me, and I truly appreciate all you've done."

Disappointment seeped through him. That didn't sound like she was building up to "Thank you, I'd be honored." She was about to turn him down flat.

"Alisa, I thought there was something between us."

"It's just not possible. I. . .you don't know me."

"Then let me *get* to know you." Stepping forward, he cupped her cheek. "I can see in your eyes that you feel the same thing I do."

She covered his hand for a second, then stepped back. "You're mistaken, Titus. I plan to stay only through the winter. That should give me enough time to earn a train ticket east."

"East? What's back east?"

"My future." This time Titus didn't stop her as she closed the door. What could he say? If she didn't want him, there was nothing he could do about it. With a scowl, he strode to the cabin he shared with Paul, pulled three packages from his saddlebags, and carried them back to Alisa's cabin. He knocked on the door.

"Titus, please," she said when she answered. "I thought I made myself clear."

He shoved the packages toward her. "To make you some dresses."

Her lips opened slightly as she took in a sharp breath of air. "For me?"

"Yes. That dress of Miriam's is too short."

"You're right. Thank you, Titus. Please deduct it from my salary."

He opened his mouth to object, then realized the longer it took her to pay off the things she needed, the longer it would take for her to raise railway fare back east.

"All right." With that he spun around and walked away. Including the cost of the coat, that ought to be an extra month that she had to stay. And during that time, he would do everything in his power to convince her not to go.

Chapter 10

Robert Worthington had no time or patience for games. During the past two weeks, the posters with Alisa's sketch had brought out every thief and lowlife from the very dregs of society in and around San Francisco. Most demanded more money or else. In every case, it hadn't taken long to realize that none had truly seen her.

He had no reason to believe these two men standing in his office were any different. Hope deferred caused him to eye the two men, disheveled and dirty, with suspicion. He had become adept at pegging the liars within five minutes. So far, he hadn't made a decision about these two.

The one who seemed to be the leader tossed a frayed poster onto Robert's desk. "You lookin' for this gal?"

Alisa's heart-shaped face stared back at him. "That's right. And I'm sure you've seen her." His tone was laced with sarcasm, but the men didn't seem to notice.

"Maybe." Black eyes bore into Robert, making him uncomfortable. "You still offerin' five hundred dollars?"

"Not for information."

"How much for information?" the other man piped up.

"Shut up, Amos. That ain't what we're sellin'."

"What exactly are you selling, then?" Robert's interest piqued. He kept his voice calm. His muscles twitched beneath the woven fabric of his white shirt like a restless horse impatient for a race to begin.

Something flickered in the man's dark eyes, and Robert braced himself for a demand of more money.

"We saw this girl." He jammed his forefinger down on Alisa's image. "Like the poster said, we want five hundred dollars to bring her in."

"Where and when did you see her?"

"About two months ago. She was on a stage about a half day's ride east of here.

"You sure it was her?"

"Yep."

Robert steepled his fingers atop his desk and scrutinized the pair. "She probably won't come willingly. As a matter of fact, I can guarantee she won't. Are you willing to kidnap her in order to bring her home?"

"Would we be here if we weren't?" His sneer grated on Robert, igniting his ire. This idiotic pair was the first real lead he'd had in the past two months that Alisa was alive and still in California. He didn't want to anger them, so he gulped down the sarcasm and forced a tight smile.

"All right. Then I suggest you get to it."

"Now hang on a minute. We want half of the money up front. By my calculation that's two hundred dollars."

Idiot.

"The poster clearly states the reward for bringing the girl home is five hundred dollars. When she is sitting across from me, you'll get your pay. Not a penny until then."

Those dark eyes narrowed. "Then maybe we'll just mosey on and do somethin' else."

"I thought you said we need this money, Bart," the other man said, the look of confusion in his sunken eyes nothing short of comical.

Bart scowled. "Shut up, Amos."

Robert reached into his pocket and pulled out fifty dollars. He tossed it onto the desk. "This is all you're getting until you bring Alisa home."

With a black-gloved hand, Bart reached forward and snatched up the bills. "All right, you have a deal. But first I want to know something."

"And that is?"

"What's the girl to you?"

From the way the man seemed poised to strike, Robert surmised any information would be used against him. If he said she was his daughter, the reward would become a ransom and most likely double or even triple. If he acted nonchalant, even a couple of fools like these two would assume he was bluffing. So he arched his brow. "That's my business."

"She's quite a looker."

Amos snickered. "Almost stole me a kiss from her."

Darting his gaze to the simpleton, Robert felt the blood leave his face. "What do you mean?"

"She didn't have nothin' to steal, so I was going to steal a kiss."

"Shut up, Amos," Bart snarled.

"Well, looks like I'm gettin' a second chance at that kiss," Amos persisted.

Alarm clenched Robert's gut. "You'll keep your filthy hands off her. Do you hear me?"

A sly smile curved Bart's thin lips, revealing missing teeth. "So she means more to you than you're letting on."

Why couldn't he just think of her as a maid who was stealing his inheritance? Robert inwardly kicked himself for being a softhearted fool. "The girl means nothing to me, but I'm telling you not to harm her or I won't pay a dime."

"Or maybe you'll pay anything to have her back no matter what shape she's in."

For the first time in his life, Robert felt real fear for someone else. If he didn't get his bluff in on these two outlaws before they walked out the door, Alisa might be in more danger than he'd bargained for. He didn't want the girl violated or hurt in any other way. And until now he hadn't thought about anything leading up to her return. He might be a desperate man, but he wasn't a monster. The thought of what could happen to her at the hands of immoral bandits sickened him. Leaning forward to make his point, he curled his lips into a deliberate sneer. "Or maybe the marshal would be real interested in knowing who's been robbing stagecoaches and unsuspecting riders between here and Sacramento."

"Hey, Bart. Maybe we better get goin' and forget the gal."

"Shut up, Amos."

Bart pressed forward, leaning his weight on massive hands, and practically came across the desk, closing in on where Robert sat. The outlaw's putrid breath fouled the air between them. "I don't like threats."

Forcing himself to stand on trembling legs, Robert clenched his fists to control his fear. "Neither do I. Do we understand each other?"

The man glared but nodded. "We will bring her back untouched."

"What about the kiss she owes me!"

"Untouched!" Strangely, Bart's growl reassured Robert.

As the two men stalked to the door, Bart called over his shoulder, "We'll be back."

The door slammed shut behind them. Robert's legs refused to hold him another second, and he sank back into his chair. The paltry sum Mother had left him was about gone. Thankfully, part of her wishes had stated that household expenses be paid automatically through Mr. Chadwick's law firm until Alisa was well versed in household management.

If he didn't find Alisa soon, he'd be destitute. For now, no one could kick him out of the house. At least not until the time came for it to be sold and the proceeds given to charity as Mother had stated in her will. The thought sent a shiver of anger through him, renewing his determination. Alisa would be found, and one way or another she would relinquish control of the inheritance that was rightfully his in the first place.

"Aunt Miri-Em, Ginny Mae's doing it again. Hurry!"

At the sound of Polly's shrill, four-year-old voice, Alisa leapt up from her desk and flung her door open. Miriam had already exited her cabin and had made a beeline for the garden. It didn't take much to guess what the child was up to. She sat in the middle of the harvested garden, her hands caked with black dirt. From chin to nose, her face bore the evidence of her latest venture. The child just couldn't stay away from worms.

Miriam's face blanched. "Ginny Mae, dumpling. Please come out of the dirt." Her thin voice seemed to come from far away, and Alisa grabbed her arm.

"Are you all right? You're as white as a ghost."

Miriam's head moved slightly in a weak nod. "I think I'd better go lie down. . . . Will you please take care of her?"

"Of course. Do you need some help getting inside?"

Miriam shook her head. "I can make it." She headed toward the house but made a detour and disappeared into the privy.

"Miss Alisa, she's got another one. Stop her!"

Alisa grabbed Ginny Mae just in time to keep her from popping another fat worm into her rosebud mouth.

"Little girl," she said, sweeping her up and out of temptation's way. "Worms are not a proper meal. And I fear you've made your poor auntie Miriam ill."

"Mum?" The little girl's wide eyes were hardly concerned, but they held a world of questions that Alisa had no doubt would begin bursting out as soon as her mind could form enough words.

"Yes, Mum." Alisa tickled the little girl's belly. Ginny giggled, pushing her hand away.

Miriam appeared a moment later, her face void of color, and she clutched her stomach. It didn't take a doctor to figure out that she'd lost her breakfast. "Come on, girls. Let's get your auntie into bed, and then we'll get Miss Ginny Mae all cleaned up."

Obviously too weak to protest, Miriam accepted the assistance, and they got her settled into bed. Next, Alisa lifted the washtub down from the wall. She grabbed two buckets and headed out to the pump. She returned to the cabin, settled Polly at the table with a picture book, and started the water warming on the stove.

The sun was almost directly overhead, so she knew she'd have to move fast to finish up Miriam's lunch preparation for the men, bathe Ginny Mae, and have everything looking presentable by the time Titus and his brothers came in for their noon meal.

While she peeled and sliced potatoes for frying, Alisa kept an eye on Ginny, who sat on the floor playing. Thankfully, the two women had just made bread the day before, so there was plenty of that left. By the time the potatoes were peeled and sizzling in the frying pan, Ginny was splashing in her bathwater, and Alisa was ready to start frying the fish Bryce had left in the sink after his early morning trek to the creek.

The girls were angels, obedient and cooperative, as Alisa moved between tasks in order to accomplish everything in a timely manner. She was just lugging the dirty-water-filled tub outside when the men rode in from the woods.

The sight of Titus dismounting and striding confidently toward her sent a ripple of pleasure up Alisa's spine. There was no denying it. Titus was one good-looking man. Everything about him was appealing, and somehow she couldn't help but wish her life wasn't so topsy-turvy.

"Let me get that for you," he said, taking the tub. "Who had a bath?"

"Ginny Mae."

Daniel scowled. "What's this all about on a Monday afternoon?"

Intimidated as she always became by Daniel's surliness, Alisa cleared her throat. "I'm afraid she got into the dirt. I'm sorry."

"Why wasn't Miriam watching her?"

"She's not feeling well. So perhaps Ginny toddled outside without her knowledge. I was in my cabin writing a letter."

Titus glanced at her sharply, and Alisa cringed, knowing he would ask her whom she was writing to.

Gideon's voice spared her the drill for now. "Miriam's ill?" His face clouded. "Where is she?"

"Lying down."

He tossed Logan his reins and dashed into the house.

"How sick is Miriam?" The concern in Titus's eyes touched Alisa. What would it be like to have him worrying over her?

She gave him a reassuring smile. "I'm sure she'll be better after she rests awhile. In the meantime, lunch is ready."

"You gave Ginny a bath, looked after Polly, and cooked for all of us?" Admiration shone in his blue eyes, and Alisa drank it in.

She laughed, waving aside his praise. "I learned to take care of a lot of people at the orph—" She stopped and clamped her mouth shut. From the very beginning, she'd determined not to reveal anything about her past. Even a little information might bring disaster on herself and this family. If the law found her and took her back, at least the Chances could honestly say they knew nothing about her.

Unfortunately, Titus wasn't one to let things go. He raised his eyebrow. "The orph? I assume you were going to say 'orphanage'?"

"I'd best get inside and put lunch on the table for your brothers."

"They can get it themselves." Titus took her arm gently. "Tell me about the orphanage. Were you mistreated growing up? Is that why you don't want to talk about it?"

"Oh, no!" The very thought of Mrs. Perryman raising her voice or lifting her hand in anger was ludicrous. A kinder woman never existed. Before Mr. Perryman had passed away, he had on occasion produced the strap but only under strict provocation.

"So you were going to say 'orphanage.'"

"Yes."

"Won't you finally tell me about yourself?" He let his hand slide down her forearm until his fingers tickled her palm just before they laced with hers. "I want to know everything. Sometimes I think I'm going to go crazy if you don't open up and give me some clue into who you are."

The warmth of his hand sent waves of longing through her. How she would love to tell him about growing up without a real family and how she'd prayed every day and every night for someone to claim her. And how when she finally learned she wasn't alone, her grandmother had died. She longed to tell him that she was wanted for murder, but that she wouldn't, couldn't hurt anyone, let alone the wonderful woman who had given her a name.

"Alisa." Titus pulled her to him, releasing her hand as he snagged her about the waist. "I don't have any intention of letting you go. Not now. Not ever."

"Titus, please," she whispered, though she could barely hear her own voice through the pounding in her ears. "You don't understand."

"Then make me understand. You've been here for two months, and all I've learned about you is your name. Now I know you're an orphan. Did you think that would matter? Is that why you've been so evasive?"

Alisa wanted to laugh, a short, bitter laugh devoid of humor. He didn't even know that much, because she wasn't an orphan after all. But she couldn't tell him that. Instead, she shook her head.

"Then what is it? Why can't you trust me? Don't you know how much I care for you?" The pleading in his tone nearly undid her resolve. If he only knew how much she truly cared, he would understand why she couldn't risk making him an accessory to her perceived crime.

"I can't. I wish I could. But I can't."

His face clouded with disappointment, and he released her. "All right. Have it your way. But I'm still not letting you go." He stomped away toward the barn.

"Aren't you going to eat lunch?" she called after him.

"I'm not hungry. Let Logan and Bryce fight over my share."

Defeated, Alisa trudged to the cabin. She knew how he felt; her own appetite had fled, as well.

She entered the house amid shouts of laughter. Her brow rose in surprise to find Miriam out of bed. Her face, though still peaked, shone with joy. Gideon's chest puffed, and he was grinning as Paul, Logan, and Bryce pounded him on the back.

"What's going on?" Alisa asked, her lips twitching at the merriment.

"Oh, Alisa." Miriam stepped forward and took her hand. "I'm so happy you've come to be with us. I'll be needing you more than ever now."

"What is it?" She frowned, searching Miriam's face for the answers. "Are you all right?"

"I will be." A bit of color tinged her cheeks.

Suddenly Alisa gasped. "Miriam! A baby?"

Miriam nodded again. "I've thought so for a while, but I didn't want to believe it. Gideon finally convinced me."

Daniel shot up from his chair and slammed out the door. Gideon scowled after him. "I'm getting tired of his moping."

Placing a gentle hand on her husband's arm, Miriam shook her head. "Have some compassion. Remember, Hannah died shortly after Ginny Mae was born. You can't blame him if memories are tormenting him. Please be kind and just pray for your brother."

Tenderness, or maybe more accurately a look of cherishing, washed over Gideon's face, and he cupped his wife's cheek. After pressing a soft kiss to her forehead, he nodded. "You're right." His eyes clouded as he peered closer. "You look tired."

"Don't worry about me, Gideon. Everything will be fine."

"I want you to be careful." He glanced up at Alisa with silent appeal.

The sight of the exchange between these two filled her heart with longing. Would she ever be able to share that sort of love without fear of having it ripped away from her? Pushing back the ache, she smiled at him over Miriam's head and nodded her reassurance.

Miriam turned, her eyes shining. "Well, what do you think of my news, Alisa, dear?"

Alisa threw her arms around the other woman's shoulders. "Oh, I'm so happy for you. I can't wait to hold your new son or daughter. Babies are wonderful."

Laughter bubbled from her lips. "They are, aren't they?"

"Now you mustn't overdo it. I'll take care of all the heavy chores from now on."

Miriam looked from husband to Alisa and back to Gideon. "Oh, you two are conspiring already, aren't you?"

Alisa grinned as Gideon winked at her. "We certainly are, and you may as well get used to it until the baby arrives."

It was only later that Alisa realized she had practically promised to stay as long as Miriam needed her.

Chapter 11

Standing in the foggy barnyard, waiting for Sunday service to begin, Titus gave an inward groan. He should have known Prissy wouldn't give up so easily. Staring into her tear-filled eyes brought about a myriad of emotions in his chest—none of which was love or desire. Pity maybe. Irritation, a little bit of guilt for his changing affection? What was it about a woman that if a man lost interest, suddenly she wanted him more than air?

Those were her words. "I can't breathe for wanting you, Titus."

"Prissy." *Please give me the words to end this once and for all.* "You were the one who turned down *my* proposal, remember?"

"I know," she whimpered. "But I was so wrong. I see that now. Won't you give me another chance?"

A second chance. That's what he felt like he'd been given. A second chance with the right woman. He shuddered to think where he'd have ended up if Prissy hadn't rejected his proposal in the first place. Stuck is where. Up a creek without a paddle. In a sinking boat. In a pasture with a riled bull. On a bucking horse with a broken saddle strap. Not one scenario he could imagine made him a happily married man. Not even one.

Maybe a man with stronger character would take one look at her ashen face and give in, seeing as how he *had* proposed, but Titus couldn't bring himself to consider it. He couldn't bear the thought. Besides, what woman would want a man who was in love with someone else?

Before he thought better of the question, he heard his own voice. "Prissy, I'm in love with someone else. Would you really have me marry you just to keep my word?"

As soon as the stupid words left his mouth, he knew he'd made a big mistake. Her eyes narrowed and her nostrils flared, and for a second, that bull-in-the-pasture scenario was looking a bit less dangerous.

Amazing how fast tears dried when fanned by red-hot anger. "Titus Chance, you are a liar and a cad, and I never want to lay eyes on you again. If you prefer that silly, dowdy-looking servant girl to me, then I suspect more is going on out here than meets the eye."

Instinctively, Titus reached out to snag her arm. He'd never been tempted to hit a woman before, and he wasn't seriously tempted now, but if she spread one word of lying gossip about Alisa. . .

"Turn me loose!" She tried to jerk free, but Titus held her fast.

"Not until we get something straight."

Her lips trembled, and he loosened his grip.

"There isn't one improper thing going on at this ranch. Alisa Worthington is a morally upright, Christian woman, and I'll not have her name smeared by a jealous female. Is that clear?"

Again, wrong thing to say. Horrified rage flashed in her eyes. Titus inwardly kicked himself. What kind of an idiot was he?

"Jealous?" she sputtered. "You take my love for you and throw it in my face and then have the audacity to call me jealous?" This time when she jerked away, he released her.

"Of course I didn't mean you were jealous, exactly."

But it was too late. Her hand was poised to strike, and before he could grab her wrist, her palm made contact with his cheek so hard his ears rang. She was beyond reasoning with. "I could have any single man in Reliable, and I chose you, fool that I was. But never fear, Titus Chance. I will not bother you or the woman you love ever again."

She whipped around and flounced quickly toward the barn where benches had been set up in the makeshift church for their Sunday meeting.

During the warm months, they simply stayed outdoors and worshiped together under God's blue sky. There was something awe-inspiring about being surrounded by nature while seeking God. But when the weather turned cold or rainy, the barn was second best. And their neighbors looked forward to the Sunday meetings. The men took turns sharing scripture, and they always sang hymns to the strumming of the guitar.

"You having troubles?"

Titus turned to find the circuit preacher standing next to him. The parson motioned in the direction Prissy had stomped. The skinny fellow stood a head shorter than Titus. His black suit was just a bit crumpled, and his wide-brimmed black hat seemed a little too large for his head. But he had the kindest, sincerest eyes Titus had ever looked into. Heaving a sigh, he nodded. "I asked her to marry me, and she turned me down."

"I'm sorry. But God allows things to happen for a reason. I'm sure He has another woman for you."

"Oh, I know. That's the problem."

The preacher's brow lifted. "How's that?"

"I'm in love with a different woman."

"I'm sorry. I don't understand. Perhaps it isn't my place to inquire, but why did you ask one woman to marry you if you care for another?"

It seemed almost too much trouble to go over it again. But Titus needed to talk to someone, and in the absence of a regular preacher, he had to take counsel when he could get it. So he spilled out the entire story, beginning with his proposal to Prissy and ending with the slap that still smarted.

The preacher's expression remained impressively passive throughout Titus's discourse. When Titus finished, Parson Abe nodded his understanding of the situation. "So the woman you don't love anymore has changed her mind and is begging you to allow her to reconsider, but the one you now want to marry won't even consider accepting you?"

Giving a curt nod, Titus rested his forearms on the corral fence and released a frustrated sigh. "I reckon that pretty much sums it up."

"Sounds like we have some praying to do."

That was it? Where were the words of wisdom? The comfort? Encouragement? Where was the reassurance that God had surely brought Alisa into his life and that it was only a matter of time before she saw the truth and ran into his arms?

He couldn't restrain a scowl. The preacher gave a short laugh. "You were looking for a different answer?"

"I'd hoped."

"Sometimes the answer is easy and obvious. Other times, particularly when other people are involved, we have to pray and trust God to answer in His time, knowing He might just say no."

As much as Titus hated the thought, he knew in his heart the preacher's words held a large measure of truth. He couldn't force Alisa to come to him, and God wouldn't force her. He still didn't know anything about her past, what had brought her to Reliable. Why had she been running away from San Francisco? Whatever the reason, he knew it wouldn't change his feelings for her.

The barn door opened, and Gideon motioned for them to come in.

"Well," Parson Abe said, "I guess it's time to start the service. You folks got any music?"

Titus nodded. "I play guitar and lead a few hymns."

A broad smile lit the round, red-cheeked face. "Wonderful. Do you know 'Amazing Grace'?"

"Yep."

"Good. You planning to sing that one today? I'm kinda partial to it."

"You got it, Parson."

Alisa closed her eyes and listened to the gentle strumming of Titus's guitar. One thing she loved about Titus was that he always seemed to be whistling, humming, or singing.

Through many dangers, toils, and snares,
I have already come;
'Tis grace hath brought me safe thus far,
And grace will lead me home.

His rich baritone rose above the rest of the men's voices. Alisa's heart lurched as he sang. She'd come through danger, toils, and snares. Tears burned her eyes beneath closed lids. The thought of home seemed so unlikely. She had never had a real home. Mrs. Perryman had done her best, but everyone knew that by the time they were eighteen years old, they had to leave and make their own way in the world.

They were blessed. All of the children at Mrs. Perryman's home. Most children in their circumstances were on their own much younger, but Mrs. Perryman felt a child needed to be taken care of years longer. Many did leave by the time they were fifteen or sixteen, but most stayed as long as they were allowed. Alisa had stayed a bit longer because she helped so much with the little ones. God's mercy had stepped in just in time, and Mrs. Worthington had offered her the job as companion.

If only her grandmother had lived, Alisa would have a home. Living at the ranch the last couple of months had made her feel like part of a family for the first time ever. Against her better judgment, she allowed herself a moment to dream. She dreamed of Titus. Of staying here at Chance Ranch. Marrying Titus. Giving him a half-dozen babies. Really being part of a large, wonderful family.

"Let's begin with a word of prayer."

Alisa's eyes flew open as she realized the music had ceased and the parson was now standing at the front of the barn. Her gaze shifted to Titus. Rather than having his head bowed with the rest of the group, he returned her stare. Her face flushed hot. The concern in his eyes made her feel as though he had read her thoughts.

But how could he know that she longed to call the ranch her home? Longed to return his attention? She had done all she could to keep her distance, though she had to admit to herself that it was becoming more difficult. Deep inside, she knew it would probably be best for her to leave, but how could she go now when Miriam needed her? Poor Miriam was sick morning and night. Halfway through the service, she left the barn, looking peaked.

The parson preached a beautifully poignant message about walking in the will of God. Alisa accepted it as God's speaking directly to her, commissioning her to stay at the ranch to help Miriam until she could manage on her own. Tears ran freely down Alisa's cheeks as Logan and Bryce, too, seemed to be listening to the call of God. Both boys slipped from their seats and knelt before a makeshift altar while the parson prayed for them.

By the time service was dismissed, the pig slow-roasting over the barbeque pit was beckoning with its smoky aroma. Alisa headed for the main cabin to check on Miriam and set out the pies.

Gideon had beat her to it and sat next to his wife on the bed.

"How is she?" Alisa asked.

Miriam moaned. "The barbeque smell is making me so ill I can scarcely stand to breathe."

"Oh, I'm so sorry. Can I bring you anything to help?"

She shook her head as though the effort to speak was suddenly too great.

Gideon seemed to forget Alisa's presence as Miriam rolled to her side, curled into a ball. He rubbed her back, crooning words of love and reassurance.

Feeling like an intruder, Alisa turned away and nearly collided with Titus. She gasped, stopping short. He reached out to steady her, the warmth of his hands steaming through her sleeves. She could feel the heat from his body, smell the smoke from the barbeque pit on his clothes.

With him standing this close, Alisa had trouble concentrating. Apparently he had the same trouble, for he stared mutely down, his face a profusion of emotion. Everything within Alisa screamed for her to pull away, to run outside to the safety found in the numbers of people cloistered in the barn and beginning to make their way into the yard. As she began a retreat, Titus drew her close until she was forced to stand on her tiptoes. "Stop running from me," he said, his voice close to a growl. "You're driving me crazy."

"Titus," she whispered. "I don't mean to run. . . ." She couldn't finish. Instead, she stared into his blue eyes, becoming lost in the sea of emotion as they silently locked gazes. Only when her lungs began to burn did she realize she'd been holding her breath. Her lips parted slightly to allow an intake of air. Titus's gaze flickered to her mouth, and Alisa knew in a heartbeat what was about to happen. Her stomach trembled as his head dipped closer.

"Well! Nothing is going on, is it?"

Titus released her in an instant and spun around at the sound of Priscilla's indignant voice.

"No wonder you changed your mind about me. Why marry a decent girl when you can have an indecent one at your disposal?"

Alisa gasped, and the world began to spin as she noticed several neighbors, including Reba White, Prissy's mother, standing nearby, listening to the girl's lies.

This was the last straw. From far away, Alisa heard Titus call her name just before her world went black.

Chapter 12

A cool cloth swept across Alisa's wrists and neck. She shifted, trying to move away from the wetness, but it followed her. She moaned.

"That's it, girl, open your eyes."

Frowning, she obeyed. Mrs. White's face hovered above her.

"What happened?"

"You fainted dead away. Titus brought you home, but considering Prissy's big mouth, I thought it best if he not be in here alone with you."

Clarity came rushing back, bringing with it the humiliation she'd felt at Prissy's outburst. "Oh my."

"Now don't you worry. I know these Chances. They're decent folks." She went on without waiting for Alisa to comment. "Everyone around here knows Titus is a God-fearing man, and he'd marry you before he got close enough to compromise you. So don't you go thinking anyone believes there's anything improper going on out here."

"Th–thank you, Mrs. White." Alisa studied her hands, embarrassed by the entire topic.

"By the way, when will you and Titus be tying the knot?"

"I beg your pardon?"

"Getting hitched? My Prissy says Titus won't marry her because he's in love with you."

A flame of joy flared inside Alisa at the honor of a man like Titus Chance being in love with her, but the truth of the matter came behind like a cold, soaking rain and quickly quenched the flicker of happiness. "Oh, that's not true. I don't know why he isn't marrying Prissy—except she did refuse him first."

A pained look crossed Mrs. White's face. "I know. That girl can't seem to make up her mind. I told her she was being mighty foolish for turning down a Chance man. But she wouldn't listen. Now she decides she wants him after all, and it's too late." She peered closer. "When did you say you two are getting married?"

"We're not." Alisa averted her gaze to the quilt.

Mrs. White's work-roughened hand covered hers. "Unless I miss my guess, that decision is yours, not Titus's." The bed shifted with her weight as she turned slightly. "Do you want to talk about it?"

Alisa bit her trembling lips but shook her head. "I can't."

Somehow Alisa found herself enveloped in comforting arms, crying out her hurt and disappointment. When her tears were finally spent, Alisa took the handkerchief Mrs. White pressed into her hand. She wiped the wet, salty trails from her cheeks and blew her nose. "Thank you, ma'am."

The older woman took hold of Alisa's shoulders. The look she gave her could only be described as motherly, and Alisa bit her trembling lip to keep from sobbing all over again. "Now listen, honey," Mrs. White said. "I know things can look pretty desperate out here. It's a man's world. That's for sure. But if you're thinking of leaving because of the difficulties, I urge you to reconsider. Take Miriam for instance. She came out here and took over her sister's children, took on six brothers and their messiness and big appetites. Even in the family way and feeling sickly, she glows like a candle. Happiness is finding where you belong."

"What if you don't belong anywhere?" The question left her before Alisa could rein it in.

Understanding flickered across Mrs. White's features. Her chin jutted upward in a short nod. "I see. You've been dealt a bad hand, and you're running from something."

With no strength to deny it, Alisa merely sighed. "I can't stay here indefinitely and build a life with Titus when my past may bear down upon us one day."

"Maybe you should come clean with him. Give him the choice to decide if it's worth the risk or not."

Alisa shook her head. "He can't know anything about how I ended up here."

"Honey, I can see the weight of the world is nearly more than your skinny shoulders can bear. If you don't tell someone soon, you're going to crack beneath the load. Now anything you tell me is going to stay right here in this room and in the throne room of God."

How good it would feel to tell someone her troubles. Alisa's heart began to pound against her chest. "You promise you won't say a word? Because if the Chance family knew, it could cause them harm if I was ever found."

A deep frown created twin ruts between Mrs. White's eyes. "You have my word."

Even before she began to speak, Alisa felt the burden lifting. Just knowing she could trust her plight to another human being made her feel a thousand times better. When Alisa finished up with Titus bringing her to the ranch, Mrs. White gave her a tender smile.

"So you see, Titus would move heaven and earth, even at the risk of crossing all five of his brothers, to help someone in obvious need. I think you should open up to him. Tell him the truth. If his feelings for you run as deep as yours do for him, I think he has a right to know."

"My. . .feelings?"

"Every time you say his name, your face softens. You care for him. And I can't say that I blame you. Now I believe every word of your story, and Titus will, as well. He's saved you once, and unless I miss my guess—and I rarely do—he'll do whatever it takes to prove your innocence."

"But it doesn't seem fair that he should be placed in that position. Wouldn't it be better if I left and gave him the chance to turn to another woman? Prissy, for instance, cares for him a great deal." The very thought of Titus ending up with that girl left a bitter taste in Alisa's mouth. But perhaps if he were to fall back in love with the other girl, Alisa's leaving, once Miriam was back on her feet, wouldn't be so hard for him to swallow.

Mrs. White expelled a short laugh. "Once a man like Titus Chance finds real love, he won't settle for anything less." She stood. "Honey, I understand why you don't want to open up to Titus, and I admire your reasons, but if you leave, I have a feeling he'll come after you. Men like him don't come along very often, and when they do, they don't give up very easily."

The thought of Titus coming after her sent a tremor through Alisa's stomach. The memory of being held in his arms just before Prissy burst in on them made her heart slam against her chest.

He'd almost kissed her. There had been no question that she would have allowed it to happen. Not only allowed it, but most likely kissed him back. Weakness spread over her. If she was going to stay at the ranch for a few more months, she could never, ever let that almost happen again. No matter how she might long to feel his arms around her. Feel his kisses.

"I'll leave you to gather yourself together." Mrs. White stood.

"Oh, but I should get up and put the food out on the tables."

Mrs. White patted Alisa's shoulder. "I'll take care of that. You can come out and help when you're ready."

Alisa lay back on the bed and stared at the ceiling.

Through many dangers, toils, and snares,
I have already come;
'Tis grace hath brought me safe thus far,
And grace will lead me home.

Tears trickled down the side of her head and dampened her pillow.

Hiding behind a large oak tree in front of Mrs. Perryman's orphanage, Robert Worthington felt like a Peeping Tom. And he hated that feeling. But after two weeks, he'd still heard nothing from those two outlaws, Amos and Bart. Rage burned inside of him at the very real possibility that they'd taken the fifty dollars he'd paid up front and forgotten all about Alisa and the five-hundred-dollar reward.

With a self-deprecating chuckle, he continued to watch the house. Why should he be surprised that a pair of thieves stole? But that left him to form another plan of action. And that plan just walked outside.

A boy who appeared to be in his late teens trotted down the steps, leaving the door to bang shut behind him.

"Jonesy, really!"

"Sorry, Mrs. Perryman."

Robert knew the boy would be headed toward the ice warehouse where he would work loading blocks of ice into the ice wagons all night. He'd been watching him. The kid worked hard. He had to hand it to him. Maybe too hard for the measly salary he was sure the boy earned. Robert had a hunch Jonesy might be leaving the orphanage soon and would be looking for a way to make more money.

Able to draw funds from the shipping company, Robert had formed the idea. He stepped out just as Jonesy reached the tree.

"Yeow!" The lad jumped back and assumed an attack stance.

"Settle down," Robert said, holding up his hands.

"What are you doing sneaking around in the middle of the night?" Jonesy asked.

"I could ask you the same thing." No sense letting the boy know he'd been watching him. That would definitely put him on the defensive.

"Going to work, not that it's any of your business." He turned and resumed his gait.

Robert followed and quickly caught up to him, easily matching him stride for stride. "Where do you work?"

"At the icehouse."

"Sounds cold."

A shrug lifted his shoulders. "I guess."

"How would you like to earn a month's pay just for a little bit of information?"

The kid gave a mocking laugh. "And end up with my neck in a rope? Forget it."

"Now this isn't something that'll get you into trouble. I just need someone I can count on not to double-cross me. That's all."

"What makes you think you can trust me?"

"I have a gut feeling."

"What would I have to do?"

Robert bit back his grin. Now that he had the kid's attention, it was only a matter of time before Alisa was back at the house. And she would turn her inheritance over to him. . .one way or another.

He placed a fatherly arm around Jonesy's shoulders and smiled. "Tell me, son. Who collects the mail for the orphanage?"

Foggy mist chilled the December air as Titus helped Alisa from the wagon and walked her through the muddy street to the boardwalk in front of the mercantile. He stopped short of escorting her inside. "All right. I'm going over to the feed store. You stay put until I get back to take you home. You hear? This town isn't safe for a woman alone."

As if to punctuate his words, two shots sounded from the end of the street. Alisa gasped. Titus glanced in the direction of the gunfire, then turned back to her, giving her hand a comforting squeeze. "Looks like just a couple of cowboys making their presence known. Nothing to worry about. I'll wait for you to get inside before I head to the feed store."

A smile curved Alisa's lips, and she nodded. "Thank you for your thoughtfulness."

"I'm not being thoughtful." His blue eyes sizzled with emotion as he looked down at her, his hand still clutching hers. "I'm doing everything I can to make sure the woman I love is safe."

Titus was making a habit of sharing his feelings openly. No one could doubt his sincerity. All the more reason Alisa felt she had to discourage his attentions and remind him often that she would be leaving as soon as Miriam recovered from childbirth. She opened her mouth to once more make the announcement, but Titus stopped her with a well-placed finger to her lips. "I know. Don't say it." He lifted her hand and brushed a soft kiss to her knuckles. "Get inside. I'll be back in less than an hour."

Still reeling from his soft touch, Alisa could only nod. He reached around her and opened the mercantile door. He was so close she could feel his breath warm on her face as he shifted back to allow her entrance.

She stepped inside, and he closed the door after her. Alisa watched through the glass as he sauntered away, each step sure and confident.

A snort behind her alerted her to Mrs. White's presence. "That man has no intention of letting you go."

Sighing, Alisa nodded. "You're right about that, I'm afraid."

"Still being stubborn, are you?" A scowl pinched her face. "I think you ought to just tell the whole truth of it and let Titus decide."

"So you said last week," she replied, distracted as Titus glanced back at the mercantile just before disappearing inside the feed store.

"And so I'm saying again, young lady," Mrs. White snapped. If possible, her frown deepened. "They took you in when you had nowhere else to go, made you part of the family. They deserve your honesty."

"You're more than likely right, and if my being honest didn't have the potential to cause them trouble, I'd have told them everything from the first day. But as it is, I can't do it."

"So what brings you into town on such a dreary day?"

Was it a dreary day? Seated shoulder to shoulder with Titus during the hour-long ride had felt like a sunny day in paradise, despite the drizzle. But of course she couldn't tell that to Mrs. White. The woman knew far too much as it was. Only her promise not to reveal Alisa's past gave her peace. Reaching into her reticule, she pulled out the letter she'd composed and a coin to pay for postage.

"I'd like to mail this."

"San Francisco, eh?"

Alisa nodded. She had no secrets from Mrs. White. "I'm sending Mrs. Perryman a donation for the orphanage. Christmastime is always rather worrisome. She tries to buy a little something for each of the children to open Christmas morning. Whenever possible she buys a ham and sweet potatoes and makes apple pie."

Mrs. White's face softened. "I'm sending a donation, as well. Those children are going to have a wonderful Christmas this year."

Alisa watched through quick tears as Mrs. White opened Alisa's envelope and slipped some bills inside. After resealing the envelope, she set it aside. "This will go out in the morning and should get to San Francisco in plenty of time."

Clasping the other woman's hand, Alisa looked into her lined face and smiled. "You have no idea what this will mean to them. Thank you."

Mrs. White smiled in return. "I'm glad to do it. You didn't leave a return address, I see."

"No. It's better if she doesn't know where I am. I assured her that I am safe. And I told her all about what happened to my grandmother so that she never thinks I did anything to harm her."

"Anyone who knows you as well as Mrs. Perryman must will know you aren't capable of harming a soul. But I'm sure she'll be relieved to hear that you are safe."

The bell chimed above the door. Alisa turned, expecting to see Titus standing there.

"Well, looky here, Amos. We don't got to look no farther."

"I told you two weeks ago we shoulda come here in the first place, but you had to take us hither and yon."

"Shut up, Amos."

"What are you talking about?" Mrs. White asked.

"The girl. She's wanted in San Francisco, and we come to fetch her back."

"You the law?" Mrs. White eyed the two.

Hysterical laughter bubbled from Alisa's lips. "The law? These are the two men who robbed the stagecoach the day I arrived."

"Then they can forget taking you anywhere."

Bart took a menacing step forward. "Now you just be a nice old lady and don't cause a fuss, and no one'll get hurt. One way or another, we're taking her with us."

"In a pig's eye."

Before Alisa or either of the two men could react, Mrs. White reached beneath the counter and pulled out a shotgun. Bart stopped dead in his tracks. Fear leaped across his grizzled features. "Now, lady. There ain't no need to get jumpy."

"I'd say there is a reason. We don't much care for thieving snakes around here."

"That's right." Mr. White's deep voice coming from the storeroom made Alisa's knees nearly buckle with relief.

"Listen here." Bart stepped back but encompassed them with a dark glare. "I have five hundred dollars riding on taking that girl back to San Francisco, and I don't aim to leave this town empty-handed."

"I aim for you to leave this town in the marshal's wagon, mister." Mr. White snatched the shotgun from his wife's hands. "Now the two of you toss down those sidearms."

"What are we gonna do, Bart? I can't go back to jail."

The bell jangled once more, and Prissy flounced through the door. "Hi, Mama. Mr. Wall just dropped me off. We had a dandy lunch." She stopped, her eyes growing wide in the silence. "Wh–what's going on?"

Mrs. White gasped as Amos reached out and put Prissy in front of him. Too swift for anyone to react, he produced a hunting knife and pressed it against the young woman's neck. "Well now. This appears to be my lucky day." He leveled his dark gaze on Alisa. "I'll be back, my sweet. You can count on that."

Chapter 13

Titus hummed along to the tune of "Amazing Grace" as he guided the team back toward the mercantile. He looked forward to the long ride home with Alisa. Even toyed with the idea of stopping somewhere along the way and insisting she open up about her past. There was no denying she knew where he stood. Every day he fell more deeply in love with her. Her sweet willingness to help out during Miriam's bouts of illness—though they were becoming fewer and farther between—never failed to send a rush of tenderness through him. Even after a hard day of doing her own chores, she was willing to pitch in and help take care of the girls, cook supper, and clean up—generally do everything Miriam used to do alone. He shook his head. The whole group of brothers, himself included, had been nothing but insensitive knuckleheads.

His heart leapt as he pulled up to the mercantile. Maybe he'd carry Alisa to the wagon. This mud was enough of an excuse that she probably wouldn't protest too much. Just as he hopped down, he heard a scream coming from the alley between the mercantile and the next building over. Alisa?

His heart lodged in his throat, and he took off at a run, drawing the newly acquired Colt that his brothers had graciously agreed he needed to replace. In the alleyway, he saw Prissy struggling against a man. The sight of her false curls brought Titus a flash of relief that it wasn't Alisa until chivalry took over, producing the indignation he needed to trot down the alley, careful not to make noise.

"No!" Prissy's muffled voice shrieked.

"Let her go, Amos, and come on!"

Amos? Rage flared within Titus's chest. The thieving, no-good outlaws. What were they doing in Reliable?

"Not before I get my kiss."

"We don't got time for that. Let the girl go. She'll only slow us down."

"I ain't lettin' this one go." He gave up the struggle for a kiss and hauled Prissy toward his horse. *My horse!* Titus moved into full view, his pistol pointed in the direction of the outlaws.

"Let the girl go."

"Titus, help me!"

"See what you done, Amos? Get yerself outta this." Bart slapped his horse and took off at a gallop, leaving Amos behind. Keeping his gun fixed on the outlaw, Titus walked forward. "That's right. Step away from the girl."

"Or maybe I'll just keep her, and you can either shoot her or let me go."

"This is going to end badly for you, Amos. Look, Bart didn't even stick around to back you up."

He sneered. "Bart did exactly what I'd have done. A man's gotta look out for hisself."

So much for honor among thieves.

"Titus, do something!"

With a grin, Amos shoved her forward so that Titus had no choice but to catch her or let her fall. She filled his arms, and he watched helplessly as Amos dashed to Raven and rode away after Bart. Regret filled him. If he could've kept Amos, he'd have sent a thief to jail and would have gotten his horse back.

"Oh, Titus. Thank you." Prissy's shivering body brought him back to the present. She looked up at him with tears flooding her green eyes, and his heart softened. He held her close and allowed her to cry. "Th–that horrible man tried to kiss me."

"I know, but he didn't succeed," he soothed.

"B–but, Titus. He said I l–looked like I wanted to be kissed."

Her eyes were filled with question. And that filled Titus with indecision. Should he be honest and tell her that when a woman wore rouge and painted her lips, it gave a man certain ideas about her willingness to be kissed?

Just as he dismissed the idea, she asked him flat out. "Was he right, Titus? Do I look like I want to be kissed?"

Caught between the temptation to lie and spare her feelings or tell her the truth so maybe she would take measures to correct her actions, he hesitated.

"You can tell me the truth," she urged.

"Well, Prissy, you do sort of. Still, that doesn't mean a man has any call to go stealing a kiss, but—"

"Are you saying I look like I want to be kissed?"

Swallowing hard, he nodded.

She closed her eyes and pressed closer, rising on her tiptoes. "Then kiss me, Titus. I want to be kissed by you." Before he could shift back in alarm, she pressed his head down until their lips touched. He took hold of her arms and held her away from him.

Triumph gleamed in her eyes. "I know you must care for me, Titus. You're my hero. You came after me."

"When I heard you scream, I thought you were Alisa. I care for her." Anger over her kiss caused the words to come out more sharply than he would have allowed under normal circumstances. "Please, Prissy. I don't want to hurt you, but will you please get it through your head once and for all that I plan to marry Alisa?"

Her eyes narrowed dangerously. "I wish they had taken her like they intended all along. And good riddance."

"What do you mean?"

"They wanted your precious Alisa. I came in at the wrong time, and they used me as a hostage to get away."

She swept past him and headed back to the mercantile.

Titus followed her, rubbing his mouth with the back of his hand and hoping there were no traces of Prissy's red lip rouge on his mouth. He had to resist the urge to toss her into the mud. Instead, he opened the door for her. One glance at Alisa's stricken face melted his anger. As Mr. and Mrs. White rushed to their daughter, Titus opened his arms to Alisa. She walked toward him slowly, as though her legs had little strength, and allowed him to enfold her in an embrace. Her soft sigh told him all he needed to know about her feelings for him. She had been waiting for him to return, had been waiting for his arms.

Robert Worthington stared at Jonesy in surprise. Less than two weeks had passed since they'd made their arrangement, and here the boy was already in his office, holding an envelope in his hands.

"Well, give it to me," Robert said.

"Not until you hand over three dollars and twenty-five cents."

Robert reached into his pocket and gave him five. Jonesy's eyes widened.

"Consider the rest a bonus."

"Thank you." Rather than leaving, he stood watching Robert.

"Well? What are you waiting for? Don't you have to go home to supper or something?"

"I'm waiting for you to be finished so I can take the letter to Mrs. Perryman."

Leveling a firm gaze at the boy, Robert fingered the envelope. "I just paid you five dollars for this letter. It's mine now."

The boy frowned. "She's been worried sick about Alisa. If you think I'm going to give her letter away and let her think Alisa is hurt or dead or something like that, you're crazy. I sold you the right to read it. Not keep it." He tossed the five dollars back on the desk. "Forget the deal. Give me back the letter."

"Now just hold on. I'll read through the letter and perhaps I'll allow you to take it."

"Read it," the kid said through clenched teeth. "Then hand it over."

Without a reply, Robert glanced at the postmark. Reliable. He'd never heard of such a town, but it shouldn't be very hard to locate. He slid his letter opener beneath the seal and quickly scanned the letter:

Dear Mrs. Perryman,

Please forgive the amount of time that has gone by with no word from me. I am fine and staying with a wonderful family on their ranch. I have become a fugitive, unjustly accused of murder, and though I know the stamp on this letter will reveal my whereabouts, I couldn't bear the thought of the holidays going by without wishing you and the children a Merry Christmas.

I know you would never believe me capable of harming anyone, let alone my grandmother. That's right, Mrs. Perryman. Mrs. Worthington revealed to me that she was my grandmother. Unfortunately, she died very suddenly, and I was accused of her death. I did not cause her death, of that I can assure you, but my father has accused me anyway. I suspect this is because my grandmother was set to give me an inheritance. If only she had lived. A relationship with her would have made me the richest woman alive.

I have enclosed some money. It isn't much, but I hope it will give the children a bit of a Christmas. Perhaps you can buy that goose this year. Annie whispered to me just before I left that she secretly longs for a new pair of pink ribbons like the ones her mother wore the night she died. Do you remember the white dress I always longed for because the mother in my dreams always wore white? I can't help but hope Annie will get her ribbons.

I will try to write again soon.

Kiss the children for me and ask them to pray for me, as I am praying for each one of you.

All my love,
Alisa Worthington

Robert folded the letter, tucked it back into the envelope, and stuffed the bills inside as well. After another cursory glance at the stamp on the front, he tossed the letter back on the desk. "Take it and go."

He shifted his gaze to the window until he heard the door open. "Wait just a minute."

"Yes, sir?"

Scowling, Robert pulled his wallet from his coat pocket and removed some bills. "Give this to Mrs. Perryman," he said. "Tell her to buy the little girl some ribbons and Christmas presents for all of the children. And tell her to buy a goose for Christmas dinner."

Jonesy's face molded into a look of utter disbelief. "What are you trying to do?"

"Nothing. Can't a man give a bunch of orphans a decent Christmas?"

The boy gave him a dubious look. He glanced at the bills in his hand and shrugged. "Whatever your reason, the children deserve a good Christmas. Mrs. Perryman will appreciate this."

Averting his gaze to the desk, Robert gave a dismissive wave. "Close the door behind you."

With a frustrated grunt, he sat back in his chair. The letter held not one clue as to where Alisa might be. It had, however, given him a clue into Alisa. She'd dreamed of her mother wearing white? Robert felt a tremor of guilt, then pushed it away with a short laugh. Perhaps her mother would have worn a white dress and married a good man if he hadn't spotted her and lusted after her. Truth was, he couldn't even remember her face. He could, however, remember his daughter's heart-shaped visage. The image haunted him. Reaching into his drawer, he pulled out the sketch of Alisa. What if he'd never taken her away? What if he'd been a father to her as his father had been to him?

He raked his fingers through his hair and laughed at his sentimentality. "You're a fool, Robert Worthington. An utter fool."

Alisa peeked around through the window to make sure the girls weren't inside the main house before she tapped on the door.

"Come in," Miriam called. Her voice sounded strong, and Alisa smiled as she stepped inside. Miriam was just pulling a pie from the oven. The spicy, cinnamony aroma filled the cabin.

"Mmm. Smells heavenly."

"Thank you. It's apple.

"My favorite. You sound like you're feeling better."

"I am! Praise the Lord. I was beginning to think I might be sick for the rest of my life."

Laughter bubbled from Alisa's lips. Even at the orphanage, Christmas had been a time of joy and expectation. This year, despite her situation, her childlike optimism had returned within a week of the ordeal in Reliable, and it continued to permeate these days leading up to Christmas.

"Did you get them finished?" Miriam asked.

"I did."

"You didn't wrap them yet?"

Alisa grinned and shook her head. "I wanted to show them off first."

"Let me put some water on for tea, and I'll be right over."

Miriam wiped her hands on a towel and came over to the table. Alisa pulled out the gifts she'd been working on for the past two weeks in her spare time. She'd had to use Miriam's sewing kit, as she'd left her own back at the Worthingtons' home.

The girls had been such good little helpers that Alisa had made them each an apron. Polly's was made of red gingham, and Ginny Mae's of blue gingham.

"Oh, how darling!" Miriam exclaimed, holding each item close to her heart. Her eyes filled with tears. "I can't wait to begin sewing for the baby."

"It'll be such fun."

Miriam folded the aprons carefully and set them back on the table. She moved to the stove and pulled the teapot from the fire. After pouring two cups, she brought them back to the table, then moved back to the kitchen shelves. She fumbled around for a moment, then produced some paper and string. "You can use this to wrap them. Their little faces are going to light up when they see those."

"They'll have quite a Christmas. Polly and Ginny Mae are going to adore the dresses you made them."

"Yes. I only wish Hannah were here to see how special those two are."

Alisa covered her hand. "She knows. I'm sure God allows mothers to look down from heaven and see the ones they left behind."

Miriam gave a short laugh. "Then better for Daniel if he never remarries. Because Hannah would never stand for it."

Despite the slight irreverence, Alisa laughed outright. Miriam joined her, and if for no other reason than to relieve the tension of the past few weeks, the two women laughed until tears streamed down their faces. Gideon and Titus entered the cabin to the howling.

"What's this?" Gideon demanded, dropping an armload of wood into the bin.

"We were just talking about Hannah."

"And that made you laugh?" Titus asked.

At the look of bewilderment on the two men's faces, the women laughed even harder.

Still chuckling, Alisa rose. "I'd best put these under the tree and head back to my cabin."

"I'll walk you," Titus said.

Alisa's pulse quickened. "Thank you, Titus, but it isn't necessary."

"I'd say those two outlaws looking for you make it plenty necessary."

Alisa finished tying the string around the packages and walked to the tree. "Honestly, Titus. It's been more than two weeks since we've seen them. Do you really think they are still hanging around these parts?"

"I don't know. But I'd rather not take any chances."

"I agree with Titus," Miriam said. "No sense risking it."

"Oh, all right." She took her coat from a peg by the door and shrugged into it. They stepped into the chilly night. Titus took her elbow to guide her. She gathered a slow breath of the crisp air. "I love Christmas," she whispered.

"So do I. It seems like it makes the world fresh and new again. Like an innocent baby."

"Like Jesus."

"Yes."

There was no need for them to say more. But Alisa couldn't help but feel the wonder of sharing a love for Jesus with a fellow believer. She didn't understand why her life had taken such a topsy-turvy turn, but God did. And even in the difficult times, He had taken care of her so far. She knew that nothing could separate her from His love. Christmas was a good reminder of that.

As though reading her thoughts, Titus gave her elbow a little squeeze. She smiled at him as they reached the door.

He stepped closer, and for an instant, it seemed as though he might kiss her. Alisa braced herself, unsure whether her heart would lead her head this time or not. A shrill scream tore through the air, taking the decision out of her hands.

She gasped. "That sounded like Polly."

Titus sprinted toward Daniel's cabin, with Alisa close on his heels.

He burst inside. Daniel held his trembling daughter in his arms. Fat tears rolled down Ginny Mae's face as she sat on her bed. Alisa's heart constricted, and she went to the child. She lifted her, cuddling the warm body close.

"What happened?" Titus demanded.

"Polly said she saw someone at the window."

"A man. A big ugly man with a big hat."

A knot thudded in the pit of Alisa's stomach.

Titus stomped to the door and grabbed the lamp from the rail just outside. "I'll be back. Stay put, Alisa."

In a minute, Alisa noticed the lamp's glow from the window. Then Titus came back. "Daniel, I'd like to talk to you on the porch."

Daniel turned his gaze to Alisa. She nodded. "I'll put them back to bed."

That moment, the rest of the family showed up. "Did I hear a scream?" Logan asked.

"What's wrong? Are the girls all right?" Miriam bustled into the room and looked from one of her nieces to the other. Then to Alisa. The men stayed outside with Daniel and Titus.

"Polly saw someone outside the window."

A flash of concern crossed Miriam's face. "Was she dreaming?"

Alisa shrugged. The door opened. The brothers stomped in. "Here's what we've decided. Alisa's going to bunk with Miriam tonight."

"Good idea," Miriam said.

"Gideon will bed down in the other room instead of going to one of the other cabins."

Miriam smiled at her husband. "We'll feel safer that way."

"And I'm staying, too."

Gideon scowled at him. "I can protect my wife and Alisa."

"Probably." Titus kept his gaze fixed on Alisa so intensely she couldn't breathe. "But I'm not taking any chances."

Chapter 14

Alisa watched with satisfaction as the stack of pancakes waned. She set another platter on the table amid the oohs, aahs, and grateful grunts from the brothers. Miriam replenished the platter of bacon and rolled her eyes at Alisa, grinning affectionately as she did so. The holiday seemed to have doubled the men's already healthy appetites. Even Miriam, Alisa noted, nibbled on a bit of bacon and managed to tackle a pancake.

Little Polly seemed to have forgotten the previous night's terror in anticipation of the promise of gifts to be opened directly after breakfast.

Alisa smiled at the two little girls, and her heart ached with longing to see the children at the orphanage. How she wished each one of them could experience this large, loving family. She turned to the tub of dishwater to hide the tears simmering just beneath the surface.

"You didn't eat much." Titus's soft voice next to her ear made her jump. He set his plate down on the counter.

"Gracious, Titus. Don't sneak up on a body."

"Sorry. Why didn't you eat?"

"I did. I'm just too. . ." She was going to say nervous, but one look into his worry-filled eyes convinced her that it wasn't the best thing to say. "Too excited to eat. Christmas is the best day of the year."

"For now."

"For now? What's that supposed to mean?"

He scooped up a fingerful of bubbles and brushed her nose. Alisa could feel the bubbles tickling her. She gasped. "I can't believe you did that!"

A chuckle left him. "Your life with me will be filled with little surprises."

Alisa wiped away the bubbles with the back of her hand. "We've already—"

"Shh. Don't spoil it. This is the last Christmas that will be your favorite day. So you'd better enjoy it."

"Titus." She gave him an exasperated look, wiping her hands on the nearest towel. "You aren't making any sense."

He leaned in so close she could feel the warmth of his breath against her cheek. "From now on, your wedding day will be your favorite day of the year. Every anniversary, you'll have a surprise better than the year before."

Alisa wanted to reprimand him. To remind him that she would be leaving in a few months. But she also wanted to wrap her arms around him and beg him to marry her right now. He seemed to understand her conflicting feelings, for he leaned forward and brushed soft, warm lips against her cheek. Then he pressed a box into her palm. "Merry Christmas, Alisa."

"You're supposed to wait until after breakfast, Unca Titus."

Polly's indignant voice rose up between them.

"You're right, sugar dumplin'," Titus said, swinging the four-year-old into his arms. "But I couldn't wait." He danced her around the room amid giggles and pleas for more. Alisa watched, her mind conjuring the image of Titus holding their own laughing daughters in his arms.

"He'll make a wonderful father, won't he?" Miriam's voice evaporated the fantasy.

Alisa tucked the box into the wide pocket of her apron, determined to return it unopened at the earliest opportunity. "I'm sure he will."

"And a wonderful husband, too. I just love a man who hums and whistles. That's a sign of contentment, which in my opinion is a sign of character."

"Yes, he's definitely going to make some woman a good husband. Titus is a great man. There's none better."

Miriam chuckled. "Well, I could argue with that. But then, I could never convince you. A blessed woman knows there's no one like the man she loves." Her expression grew soft. "Isn't that true?"

Sighing gently, Alisa nodded. "I suppose it is."

"Honey, why don't you give up this notion of leaving us after the baby comes? We all love you and want you to stay. Even if Titus wasn't madly in love, the rest of us adore you."

"Even Daniel?" Alisa laughed at her own joke.

A smile tugged at Miriam's lips. "Well, I'm sure he does in his own way. But let's leave him out of this for now."

"Are you ladies about ready to join us?" Gideon called. "These girls aren't going to be able to restrain themselves from tearing into these packages much longer."

"Just a few more minutes and we'll have everything cleaned up."

"I'll help," Bryce piped in. Not to be outdone, Logan grabbed a stack of plates. Alisa held her breath until they were safely deposited into the water. In no time, amid laughter and teasing, all traces of breakfast were cleaned up and put away.

Alisa's heart soared as she watched the girls open their gifts. When Ginny Mae toddled over to her carrying her new little apron, Alisa's heart melted.

"Put on?"

"Of course. Turn around." Alisa wrapped her arms around the child and pressed the apron to the girl's tummy, then tied the strings in back into a large blue-gingham bow. "There. Now you're ready to cook Christmas dinner." Ginny Mae giggled and threw her chubby little arms around Alisa. It was all the thanks she needed. She drank in the sweet baby scent as she rubbed her cheek against the child's silken hair. "You're welcome, precious."

Paper littered the small room a few moments later. The girls, dressed in new outfits Miriam had made and wearing the aprons over them, looked like little princesses. Daniel surveyed his daughters, and Alisa could have sworn there was mist in his eyes. "You look like little ladies," he said.

"You sure do, sugar dumplin'." Logan swung Polly up into his lap. "You haven't seen the present your uncles got for you. You ready?"

"Yes, Unca Logan."

"All right, Bryce," he called. "Bring it in."

Bryce opened the door and stomped in, carrying a load covered with a blanket. Polly jumped up and down. "What is it? What is it?"

"You have to open it, dumplin'. That's the rule at Christmas."

He set it down in front of her. Alisa gathered her breath at the lovely pint-sized saddle.

Polly's face grew serious, and she glanced at Logan and Bryce. "This is a nice saddle. Thank you very much."

The boys laughed along with the rest of the adults in the room. Ginny Mae had become fascinated with the dollhouse their uncle Paul had crafted.

Daniel grabbed his daughter's coat. "Let's go see what your daddy got you for Christmas, sweetheart."

Alisa knew the girl was getting a pony. But as the rest of the family trekked outside to witness the child's joy, she hung back, needing a few moments of solitude. She began picking up the papers and spreading them out to be put away and reused. The box from Titus was burning a hole in her apron. She reached for it but pulled her hand away as though she'd touched a hot stove. No. She couldn't accept a gift from him and then leave. It sent the wrong message.

Oh, God. If only there was a way I could remain at the ranch with Titus.

What if she were to go back and proclaim her innocence? Even if the authorities didn't believe her, would it be better to run for the rest of her life or sit in jail? Possibly get hung for murder? She shuddered.

"You cold?" This time Titus's hands on her shoulders and the sound of his voice didn't startle her.

She shook her head. "Just thinking an unpleasant thought."

"On Christmas morning?" He turned her to face him. "That's not right. You're supposed to save unpleasant thoughts for the day after."

She smiled in spite of herself.

"You haven't opened my gift yet?"

"No." She pulled it from her pocket and offered him the box. "I can't accept this."

His face clouded with hurt. "But you don't even know what it is yet."

"It doesn't matter." She placed it in his hand and curled his fingers around the cardboard edges. "It isn't proper for me to accept a gift when I'm leaving in a few months. It's not fair to you."

He scowled and tossed the box onto the table. Then he took her by the shoulders and captured her gaze. "I want to know why you think you have to leave. I don't care what you have done in the past. I don't care who you're running from. I love you, and I'm not letting you go." His frown deepened. "You're not already married, are you?"

"Of course not!"

"All right. Then tell me what's wrong!"

"Oh, Titus. . ." Suddenly, it all came tumbling out as it had weeks earlier with Mrs. White. Anger flared in his eyes as she ended her story with the account of her boarding the stagecoach.

"I'm so sorry, Alisa. I can't even imagine what it must have been like for you to finally find your father only to discover he's lower than a slug's belly. I'd like to—"

"Oh, please, Titus. God has given me the grace to forgive him. I even pray that God will give him a new heart. But now do you see why I can't stay here? Especially now that you know the truth. You are keeping a wanted woman from justice."

"It wouldn't be justice to send you back. As far as I'm concerned, you're not going anywhere. We'll get married the next time Parson Abe rides through."

She allowed herself to relax against his broad chest, wishing for all the world that she could accept his proposal and live her days building a life with this wonderful man of her dreams.

Apparently taking her silence as a yes, Titus relaxed as well. His large hand cupped her head. When she pulled back, he commanded her gaze with eyes filled with love and passion. Suddenly he crushed her to him, his mouth covering hers. Slowly he softened the kiss, but his warm lips continued pressing against hers until she became breathless. The sensations flashing through her surprised and delighted her. . .and broke her heart. Unless she could clear her name, he would never be hers. She pressed closer and allowed herself another heady moment of being in his arms.

He pulled away as voices from the others came closer.

"I love you," he whispered.

Her lips trembled. "Titus Chance, I love you, too."

Tears clogged her throat. There was no choice now. She had to leave him before she lost the power to do so. With difficulty, she maintained a normal demeanor throughout the rest of the day.

That night after everyone had gone to bed and she was reasonably sure they slept, she rose and dressed with trembling fingers. Then she grabbed her coat and reticule and wrote a note for Titus, promising the return of his horse. Quietly she left the cabin amid Daniel and Titus's snoring and made her way to the barn. Ten minutes later, she knew she'd made the biggest mistake of her life as two riders blocked the path in front of her.

"Amos, it looks like this is our lucky night."

"It sure is, Bart. It surely is."

Titus jerked awake. Something didn't feel right. The fire had gone out, but that wasn't it. He stood and walked around the room. Glanced outside. Everything seemed quiet enough. Stepped back inside.

"What's wrong?" Gideon's sleepy voice asked.

"Not sure." He lit the lamp on the table and knocked on the post next to the bedroom. "Miriam, Alisa?"

"What are you doing, Titus?" Gideon was on his feet. "Miriam needs her sleep. Don't go waking her up on a hunch."

She appeared, clutching her robe about her, her face white. "Alisa's not here."

A lump lodged in Titus's throat. "We've got to go after her. If those two hurt her, I'll—"

"Titus, she left a note. She wasn't kidnapped."

He looked down at the paper she pushed into his hand.

"It's for you."

"Let's get you back to bed," Gideon said to his wife, but Titus knew they were giving him the chance to read the letter from Alisa in privacy.

His heart sank as he read the words:

Titus,

These last few months have been the happiest of my life. God used you as a sort of knight in shining armor to rescue me and bring me to the ranch. I don't know what I would have done without you. And I thank you from the bottom of my heart. Falling in love was the last thing on my mind, but I don't suppose we have a choice where our hearts are concerned. For I do love you, my Titus. I hope to return to you soon, but if I am not back within a year, I beg of you to forget me.

Yours,
Alisa

Forget her? How could she even suggest that was possible? No matter how many years went by, he'd never forget her. Didn't she understand that? Panic swelled his chest. Where could she have gone? He pulled on his boots and grabbed his hat.

She'd gone to turn herself in. And if she was right, her worthless father would see that she hung.

Oh, Lord. Help me find her.

He saddled Logan's horse, a stallion and the fastest of the horses on Chance Ranch since Raven had been stolen. Titus rode hard, the rising sun at his back. He only prayed she wasn't too far ahead for him to catch her before she turned herself in.

Chapter 15

"You men could have saved yourself the trouble. I was going back to turn myself in anyway."

Alisa knew she should probably keep her mouth shut, but she couldn't help goading the two bumbling thieves.

"Maybe so, sister, but I know a man who's willin' to pay five hundred dollars to see you handed over." Bart snarled. "And that's what we're gonna do."

Five hundred dollars? It could only be Robert Worthington. But why was Robert, rather than the law, offering a reward for her?

"How did you two find out about me?"

Amos reached into his filthy coat pocket and produced an equally filthy paper. He pushed it toward her. She scowled and lifted her bound wrists for his perusal. "My hands are tied; you'll have to open it for me."

"Oh, yeah," he muttered. He unfolded the greasy paper.

Alisa's eyes went wide at the sight of her image staring back. "This isn't an official wanted poster, though?"

"Nope." Amos refolded the paper and replaced it in his coat pocket. "How come you're thinking the law's after you? You steal this feller's money or something? Looked like he has a lot of it."

"That's none of your business." She averted her gaze to let him know she was through speaking with him.

"Spunky little thang, ain't ya?"

"Not really."

"Can't we just keep her, Bart? I really like this one. She ain't so pretty as the one with all the curls, but at least she don't scream and cry like that one did."

Stung by the negative comparison to Prissy's painted beauty, Alisa felt the heat rise to her cheeks. She resisted the temptation to defend herself and concentrated on staying atop the horse despite her bound wrists—which were beginning to chafe along with other parts of her anatomy. She had never ridden before coming to the ranch and had only had a couple of lessons as it was. That she'd managed to avoid falling headlong to the muddy ground was a miracle indeed.

"You heard what Worthington said. No one touches her."

Robert didn't want her harmed? Surprise and gratitude combined inside of Alisa to form a tender spot in her heart for her father.

"Yeah, but he wants her back pretty bad if you ask me. I'd bet my half of that reward that he'd take her however he can get her."

From his place in front of the two of them, Bart turned in his saddle and glared at Amos. "Keep yer hands off her, or I'm gonna put a bullet through yer heart. I ain't takin' a chance on losing five hundred dollars because of somethin' you can get at just about any saloon in San Francisco."

Heat flared in Alisa's cheeks as she listened to the two argue, knowing there was nothing she could do about her predicament at the moment and praying fervently that Bart kept the upper hand on the other man.

Droplets of water splashed from the sky and hit her hands and her head. Soon the sprinkles became a soaking rain. A miserable rain that wouldn't let up. With muddy conditions being added to the already soft road, the ground soon became difficult for the horses to trudge through, and the going became nearly impossible.

Finally, Bart muttered a loud oath. "We're gonna have to hole up somewhere."

The thought of being "holed up" anywhere with these two immoral men made Alisa sick to her stomach. "I need my hands untied if I'm going to handle this horse without falling off," she said.

Her words were met with silence as the two concentrated on keeping their own horses upright.

"Bart!" Her voice shot through the steady stream falling from the sky. "I can't ride in this with my hands tied."

"Untie her so she'll shut up."

The other man made no move to obey.

Frustration and a real fear she was about to fall emboldened Alisa. "Bart!"

"Amos!"

"I can't. My horse ain't doin' so well."

"Fine," the brute growled. "Take my place at the front of the line. I'll untie her."

He maneuvered the animal around and rode back to Alisa's position. Amos moved carefully ahead, fighting for control. Alisa stopped her horse and held out her bound wrists.

Bart's dark gaze focused on her with an intensity that made her want to shrink back. Pure evil lurked beneath the surface of that gaze, and she silently prayed for protection. This man might be keeping Amos in line, but when he stared at her and roughly took hold of her clasped hands, she had trouble thanking the Lord for him. He brandished a ten-inch blade and sliced through the ropes. Alisa gasped as the knife's edge nicked her. Blood trickled down her hand toward her fingers. She winced at the pain. With a scowl he made a grab for her skirt.

"What are you doing?" she demanded, outrage suddenly eclipsing fear or pain.

He sliced a patch of the muslin and handed it to her. "Wrap this around that cut. And don't flatter yerself. Ain't no woman alive worth five hundred dollars—not to me anyways. I'm warning you," he snarled. "If you take off, I'll come after you and let Amos test that theory that Worthington'll take you however he can get you back. Understand?"

Unable to speak for the terrifying image conjured up by his words, Alisa nodded and grabbed on to the reins.

After another tense hour of concentrating on keeping the horses from slipping and falling, the trio spotted a farmhouse in the distance.

"We'll hole up in the barn," Bart announced.

"We can't just ride up to a person's barn. Someone's gonna see us."

"If you don't act stupid, no one'll suspect we're anything more than three travelers needin' a dry place to rest. I'm gonna knock on the door and ask."

Relief swept over Alisa at the thought of getting out of the rain. But along with the relief came the worrisome thought of spending any time alone with these two. On the other hand, if the people who lived in the farmhouse knew she was there, perhaps she could somehow convey her predicament and find a rescuer.

As if reading her thoughts, Bart curled his lip. "Don't make me slice your throat."

She swallowed hard and nodded. Only God could get her out of the situation. As long as Bart was in charge, she felt reasonably safe.

The next seconds seemed as a dream. As Bart urged his horse forward, the animal lost its footing in the mire. The burly outlaw's arms flailed as he went down. He landed with a thud, and the mount landed atop him, then quickly righted itself. But Bart remained where he'd fallen. Alisa dismounted quickly and slogged through the mud until she reached him. Her stomach roiled at the sight of his leg, twisted under him in an unnatural position. One didn't need to be a physician to recognize the severity of his broken leg.

"You gettin' up, Bart?" Amos called. "Yer the one who said we need to get goin'."

"He's badly hurt. He won't make it without our help."

Amos cursed and dismounted. He stomped back to where Bart lay. His face drained of color. "This is bad, Bart."

"You ain't sayin' nothin' I don't already know," Bart grunted, then clenched his teeth.

Alisa stared at Amos, waiting for him to instruct her as to how they would get his partner the next couple of hundred yards to the farmhouse. Confusion spread over his face.

"We'll have to help him," she prompted.

Amos scowled. "I know that!"

Obviously threatened by her instruction, the man turned his attention once more to Bart, who was beginning to lose consciousness. Alarm filled Alisa. She knew it would be difficult enough to move Bart with his help, but his dead weight in these conditions would be next to impossible.

"Bart," she said, kneeling beside him, "try to stay with us. We're going to need your help supporting part of your weight while we move you. Do you understand what I'm saying?"

Without opening his eyes, he nodded. "I'm tryin'."

Compassion rose inside of Alisa. "I know you are," she soothed. "I'm going to try to straighten your leg." She glanced at Amos. "Is there anything he can bite down on to help control the pain?"

"Ya mean like chewin' tobacco?"

Alisa sighed. This idiot would be no help. "No. I mean something hard that he can't bite in two. Like a heavy branch or something."

Amos slogged to the nearest tree and luckily had the presence of mind to hack off a branch thick enough for their purposes. He whittled away the leaves. "Will this do?"

Nodding, Alisa took the heavy stick. "Open your mouth, Bart. I want you to clamp down on this while we straighten your leg."

Fear lit his eyes, but he nodded and did as she instructed.

"Will you help me?" she asked Amos.

"He's gonna kill me if I hurt 'im."

"He'll be grateful you cared enough to help him."

Amos sneered. "Don't think this nursin' business is gonna make us let you go. 'Cause it ain't."

"That's the last thing on my mind. Let's get Bart out of this mud for now."

A scream of agony tore from Bart, and the stick fell to the ground as he passed out. Despair filled Alisa. How on earth would they get him to the barn now?

"We're going to have to go for help."

"No, we ain't, girlie." Amos grabbed her arm and yanked her to her feet. "Leave 'im. He's more than likely gonna be dead by mornin' anyways."

A gasp escaped her throat. "We can't leave him. What if it were you? Would you want us to leave you?"

He gave a short, bitter laugh. "Mark my words. If I was dumb enough to fall off my horse, Bart'd leave me without lookin' back."

Alisa had to admit to herself that he probably had a point. Still, she had to try to make him see reason. "Amos, Jesus said we are to do unto others as we would have them do unto us. If you were hurt, you'd want Bart to help you."

He frowned as though the words were too much for him.

Help me, Jesus.

"If you had fallen off your horse, I would be interceding for you just as I am now for Bart. Please reconsider."

"Stop yer yammerin'."

Alisa's shoulders slumped in defeat, until none-too-gently Amos hefted Bart up and slung him over his shoulder. She nearly gasped in surprise at the strength he demonstrated. She followed as he muscled Bart over the horse, who seemed not to be injured from the ordeal.

"Thank you, Amos. You did the right thing."

He grunted. "Probably the dumbest thing I ever done. Get back on your horse, and let's get goin'."

Fingers of fear crawled up her spine as his gaze slid over her. A slow smile lifted his mouth.

What was she going to do when her only protection was injured and unconscious?

Titus spoke gently to the horse, urging it forward. "I know you want out of this rain, and I don't blame you. Fact is, so do I. But Alisa needs me, and I'm going to find her. And you're my partner." It hadn't taken long on the trail for him to realize that though Alisa had started out alone, two other riders had quickly joined her. He felt nearly strangled by the thought of who those two men most likely were. They were ruthless men, and he prayed for strength not to act out of vengeance if they hurt Alisa.

He knew the danger of plodding on in this mud and rain, especially now that night had fallen. All day he'd seen signs of the three horses trying to stay afoot. But he knew the outlaws would have to hole up eventually. And that was when he planned to make his move.

Father, lead me to her.

Alisa smiled and handed the middle-aged woman a tray containing the swept-clean plates. The gracious couple who owned the farm had helped set Bart's leg and had offered Amos and Alisa a place in the house for the night. Amos had declined, stating the foolish lie that he and Alisa were on their honeymoon and preferred to be alone in the barn. Mortified, Alisa tried to be impassive, but she was almost certain the woman's eyes flickered with concern. If only there was some way to clarify her position as a hostage without taking a chance that Amos might harm the couple.

After lighting the lantern, the woman, whose slightly graying hair was pinned neatly into a bun at the nape of her neck, smiled. "Well, I brung you some extra blankets. I set 'em over there in the corner. Wish I could offer you some dry clothes, but my only other dress is wet, too."

Alisa smiled. "I appreciate all you've done. You've been very kind."

The woman flushed. "Ain't no more'n anyone else woulda done. Yer welcome to stay 'til it's safe to travel in this mud." She glanced at Amos. "If you'd like to follow me to the house, I can spare a fresh shirt of my husband's."

A grin stretched Amos's mouth. "Don't mind if I do."

Resisting the urge to beg her to stay, Alisa watched the woman slip through the barn door with Amos on her heels.

Bart moaned from his bed of hay at the end of the barn. Amos refused to allow even Bart to stay in the house. "I'm in charge now," he boasted. "Bart ain't gettin' no soft bed if I ain't."

Alisa hadn't reminded him that he'd had his chance for a real bed and turned it down. She didn't want to encourage his memory as to the real reason he was sleeping in the barn.

She lifted a blanket from the stack and spread it over Bart's shivering body. If they could have built a fire, she would have insisted he get out of the wet clothes, but again, no sense giving Amos any ideas.

She sat back against the wall and watched Bart's white face and trembling body. He needed a doctor. Had the horse's landing on him injured more than just his leg? He'd begun to awaken by the time their hosts had begun the task of setting the leg, and the woman had offered laudanum, which Alisa had encouraged. Now Bart slept and didn't have to endure the pain.

It was almost certain that Amos would leave him behind. She prayed the five-hundred-dollar reward would be enough to discourage Amos from keeping her captive. She stood on legs wobbly from the day's ride. Why hadn't she snuck out when Amos left? Hurrying toward the door, she paused only a minute to grab an extra blanket. Heart in her throat, she reached the door and flung it open. She stepped into the night. She gasped as Amos's stubbly face loomed in front of her like something from a nightmare.

"Get back inside," he ordered.

Silently she obeyed, tentacles of fear clutching her belly.

"You know what I want, girlie. And Bart ain't in no position to keep me from it."

"Amos, please," she croaked, backing up. "Don't do this."

"Save yer breath," he snarled. In a flash, he grabbed her arm and pulled her roughly to him. Alisa fought wildly, flailing her hands and feet. She screamed. Amos clamped his hand over her mouth. She twisted and shook her head until his hand slipped enough for her to bite down.

"Yeow!" His hand came up in a terrifying moment.

She saw the sheer hatred in his eyes just before his hand slammed into her face and pain exploded in the side of her head.

Chapter 16

Titus heard the gut-wrenching cry tear from his throat as though it came from outside his body. The sight of that filthy, foul man touching Alisa, manhandling her, attempting to violate her, was more than his very soul could take. Everything in him wanted to draw his pistol and shoot, but he couldn't take a chance on harming Alisa.

He rushed forward and clamped down on Amos's coat with both hands and, with strength he didn't know he possessed, flung him away from Alisa and onto the ground. Titus grabbed his gun from his holster and pointed it toward Amos, using all of his control to refrain from squeezing the trigger and sending a bullet into the man's skull.

A stream of profanity flew from the outlaw's mouth, fouling the air as much as his stench.

"Get out of the way, Alisa," Titus ordered and, from the corner of his eye, noted that she backed toward the other side of the barn.

Amos quickly regained his footing and started to go for his gun.

"I wouldn't," Titus warned. "Real slow-like. Take the gun out and toss it this way."

Keeping his hate-filled eyes fixed on Titus, Amos reached for his gun and eased it out of the holster. "I shoulda killed you the night I took this Colt off of you."

"Probably," Titus replied, matching him sneer for sneer.

"Bart, no!"

At Alisa's scream, Titus's world slowed its spinning. Just as Titus turned to the woman he loved, he saw Amos lunge from the corner of his eye.

Horror filled Alisa, and she made a dash for Bart. She kicked at his arm as hard as she could. Gunfire filled the barn as his pistol flew from his hand. He hollered and reached for her, but she jumped back in time to avoid his massive hand.

The sound of Titus's grunt brought her about, a sense of dread knifing into her gut. He lay on the ground, Amos stretched sideways across him.

She rushed to his side. He pushed at Amos's lifeless body. "Help me get him off of me," Titus said.

She helped him roll Amos aside. "You killed him, Titus. I'm so sorry." Her heart nearly broke for him at the necessity of taking a man's life.

He took her into his arms and held her tight, as though clinging to life. "I didn't," he whispered against her hair. "I would shoot him to protect you. But I didn't fire my gun. I didn't have time."

Frowning, Alisa pulled away. "What do you mean?" Then she turned to Bart as realization dawned. "You shot your partner?"

Bart grimaced. "I'd rather take my chances in jail than be at the mercy of that snake."

"I—I thought you were trying to shoot Titus."

He responded with silence, his eyes closed.

Alisa turned in Titus's arms. "Are you all right?"

"I am now. Did they hurt you?"

Heat rose to her cheeks. "No."

"Praise the Lord."

The barn door opened, and Mr. Meyers stood, rifle in hand, ready to defend his home. "What's going on in here?"

Titus quickly explained the situation. Mrs. Meyers slipped her arm around Alisa's shoulders. "I could just kick myself for not following my instincts. I knew a sweet young thing like you wouldn't take up with the likes of those vermin."

"It's all right," Alisa assured her. "But if you don't mind, I will accept the hospitality of your extra bed."

"Of course." She bustled Alisa inside while the men tended to Amos's body.

They spent the next four days waiting for the rain to stop and the ground to firm up enough for safe travel. Alisa avoided time alone with Titus as much as possible. She knew by his possessiveness that he considered their future sealed. But the fact still remained that she had to turn herself in and hope for God's justice to prevail. Otherwise she would never have a life with Titus. But she didn't bother to tell him. She knew it wouldn't do any good.

On the morning of the fifth day, he found her on the front porch enjoying a glorious pink and blue sunrise. He slipped his arm about her waist and pulled her against his side. A sigh escaped her as she gave herself to the moment and rested her head on his shoulder.

"This is just the first of many sunrises we'll share," he said, his voice wrought with emotion and longing.

Oh, how she wished that were true. And it could be, but only if God willed. First she had to take care of anything that might cause them or their children harm.

Titus shifted, and Alisa raised her head from his shoulder. He turned her to face him, his hands warm on her arms. "Alisa," he said, capturing her gaze with blue pools filled with love. "I want to talk to you about something. . .ask you. . ."

Her heart lurched, and she quickly pressed a finger to his lips. "Now isn't the time."

Disappointment evident in his features, he dropped his hands and nodded. "I suppose you're right."

"Are you going for the sheriff or taking Bart in?"

"I've been working on a travois to carry him. That way he can lie down, and the horse can drag him along behind. I don't want to burden the Meyers with him until the law picks him up."

"It's probably for the best."

"I plan to leave this morning. But I've already spoken to Mr. and Mrs. Meyers, and they'd be pleased to have you stay on until I come back. I'm leaving Logan's horse as well as Raven here. San Francisco is only a few hours away. It'll take me a little longer, having to go slow so as not to cause Bart any more pain—not that he doesn't deserve it."

"You're considerate," she said softly. "God must love that about you."

Tenderness softened his features. He reached out and trailed a line from her cheekbone to her jaw. "There are so many things God must love about you, I can't even begin to name them all." He stepped closer, and Alisa had neither the strength nor the desire to protest as he pulled her to him. He pressed his forehead to hers. "There are so many things I love about you, too," he whispered. "So many things."

She took in the wonder of his gaze sweeping over her face as though he were memorizing every contour. His mouth settled on hers, and before she could summon a thought, Alisa felt his lips on hers, warm and so very soft. His tenderness brought tears to Alisa's eyes. How she loved this man. She allowed herself the sweetness of his embrace, and in that moment, for the first time in her life, she felt cherished.

Titus pulled away, and concern filled his eyes. "You're crying."

She nodded, unable to speak for the emotion clogging her throat. He pulled her into his embrace once more. Cupping her head, he pressed it against his shoulder. She was so relieved that he didn't demand an explanation for the tears. Didn't condemn himself unnecessarily for kissing her. It was as though he understood her feelings, understood she was overwhelmed with all the events of the past months that had led to this moment—the moment she understood once and for all that she was precious and worthy of the love of a good man. And of the love of God as He'd displayed time and again, watching over her with loving care, guiding her to the people who would be His hands to her.

She wrapped her arms around Titus's waist and snuggled into his warmth. They remained locked in a tender embrace until the smells of frying bacon and brewing coffee wafted onto the porch, serving as a reminder that the world didn't belong only to them.

Titus blinked at the sheriff, fearing for a moment he hadn't fully understood the wonderful words coming from the man's gravelly throat. After delivering the outlaws, one dead, one alive, to the sheriff, Titus had been compelled to ask about Alisa. Now, faced with the answer, he couldn't believe what he was hearing. "You mean Alisa Worthington isn't wanted for murder?"

"Already told you. The old lady weren't murdered. Doc says her heart gave out. She hit her head on the way down."

"Then why would Alisa have thought she was wanted?"

The sheriff gave a heavy sigh and leaned his chair back on two legs. He laced his fingers over an ample gut and frowned in concentration. "If memory serves, it had something to do with the old lady's son accusing the girl. Seems she was holding on to Miz Worthington when the lady died. The whole thing was a mite confusing if you ask me."

"How so?"

"Seems the girl was raised an orphan. . ." The sheriff launched into the tale, his story matching the one Alisa had shared with him. But then he continued, "Miz Worthington left her big, fancy house and all her money—loads of it—to the girl. That son of hers gets most of the shipping company, which will bring him enough to be one of the richest men in town, but he wants it all. I guess that's why he offered the reward for the girl."

Trying to assimilate the information that Alisa was now a wealthy young woman, Titus pressed his fists to the desk and leaned forward. "Do you think he intends her harm to get his hands on her inheritance?"

The sheriff dismissed the concern with the shake of his head. "Naw. He's not dumb enough to do that. I figure he's going to try to talk her out of it."

Fury ignited Titus at the thought of this man trying to weasel Alisa's inheritance from her.

"Where can I find this Robert Worthington?"

The sheriff eyed him. "I don't want no trouble."

"Neither do I. But it just so happens that I'm in love with his daughter and plan on marrying her as soon as I get back home. I just want to see that he cancels the reward for her return. I don't want to be constantly looking over my shoulder, afraid some lowlife like Bart is going to try to take my wife away."

The sheriff nodded. He gave him directions to the street. "Can't miss it. It's the big brick house—covers most of the block."

Alisa guided Raven down the familiar streets of San Francisco. She'd waited until the morning after Titus left before borrowing Raven and heading west toward the city. He'd know where she was going, but by the time he got back to the Meyers' and back to San Francisco, it would be too late for him to stop her from turning herself in. She had had time to reflect while she rode the few hours alone. A curious sense of peace enveloped her, a reassurance inside that all was well. That God would forever remain on His throne in her heart regardless of the struggles she might have to endure.

She refused to allow herself to think of the possibility that she might go free, refused to hope for the best. Time had taught her that. Time and one disappointment after another. Mr. and Mrs. Perryman had been kind guardians, but they never pretended they were mother and father. They had a calling to place children with good Christian parents. Their love was evident, but even so, they couldn't shield any of their young charges from the cruelty of other children or the pain of being rejected by possible parents. Over and over again—more times than Alisa could, or cared to, remember. But all in all, Alisa had been happy, especially during her later years at the orphanage when she finally understood that she wouldn't be adopted and she might as well throw herself into making life a little sweeter for the younger children.

Alisa pulled Raven to a stop in front of the orphanage. Before she did anything else, she needed to see her little family. To tell Mrs. Perryman all about Titus. To tell them all good-bye just in case she was locked up for a long, long time. The front gate groaned as she opened it and groaned again when she shut it behind her. Her heart nearly broke at the sight of the sagging porch, the house that had been her home in such need of repair and painting. She knocked and waited. And waited. Then tried the knob. Locked? The orphanage doors were never locked. Not even at night. Worry flashed through her. Had the orphanage been closed down? Where were Mrs. Perryman and the children?

"You looking to adopt?"

Alisa turned to find Miss Smithers, the woman who occupied the home next door.

"No. I'm—"

"Why, Alisa! I recognize you."

"Hello, Miss Smithers." She walked down the steps and met the elderly woman at the gate. "Where are Mrs. Perryman and the children?"

"Gone. The roof at the back of the house finally caved in."

"Oh my." She hadn't noticed the roof from her view.

"It was a blessing in disguise if you ask me. Those children are better off now."

"What do you mean?" Alisa asked, gently touching the woman's arm to bring her back to focus.

"Don't you know?" She smiled broadly. "They're staying at the Worthington house. Can you imagine those orphans running around that big place?"

Chapter 17

Alisa rode Raven as fast as she could all the way across town until she reached the Worthington home. She stared at the massive brick structure and shuddered at the memories it conjured. Tears stung her eyes as she realized that Mrs. Worthington's beautiful smile wouldn't greet her when she entered the ornate foyer.

She climbed the steps, her heart beating wildly in her ears. Grabbing the brass knocker, she hesitated. An image of Mr. Worthington's face, red with fury, passed through her mind. Would he order her from the house? Her hands trembled as she slowly lifted the ring and brought it down, then lifted it again and knocked once more.

Marietta, Mrs. Worthington's longtime housekeeper, opened the door. Her face split into a smile. "Alisa! You've come home." Stepping aside, she allowed Alisa to enter the familiar home, the home her grandmother had left to her, though Alisa knew it would never be hers.

"How have you been, Marietta?" she asked, catching the woman into a quick embrace.

"Lonely." The simple word brought tears to Alisa's eyes. She reached for the older woman's hand.

"I know what you mean. This house seems much bigger without her, doesn't it?"

Before she could answer, a crash sounded from the parlor just beyond the foyer.

"Look what you did," a child's voice cried. "We're going to get thrown out of here now."

Marietta huffed. "I'm much too old to run after children."

Alisa followed her toward the parlor. "Why are they here?"

"Young Robert has taken a liking to them, I suppose." She scowled and opened the parlor door. A vase—one that looked expensive—lay in pieces on the floor. Sarah and Sammy Baker, six-year-old twins who had come to the orphanage two years earlier after both parents succumbed to influenza, trembled before Marietta. "We're sorry," Sarah whispered. "It was an accident."

Sammy's gaze darted away from Marietta's stern face, and his brown eyes widened, then a smile pushed his chubby cheeks out even farther. "Alisa! You've come back. We live here now."

Alisa returned his tight hug. "I'm so glad to see you."

What did he mean, they lived here now? She turned her questioning gaze on Marietta. The housekeeper clapped her hands together and gave the children a stern frown. "Run along and find the broom and clean up this mess. It's a mighty good thing for you the ugly vase was already cracked." Alisa hid her smile as the contrite children slid by. Sammy looked back at her before heading out of the room. "You still going to be here when we get back?"

She nodded. "I'll be here."

When the children had gone, Marietta shook her head. "Those two get into more trouble. . . ."

"How long have they been living here, Marietta?"

"Since Christmas Day."

"Christmas?"

She knelt and began picking up the big pieces of the vase. "Mr. Worthington was invited to the orphanage for Christmas dinner, seeing as how he donated a sizable amount of money for the children's Christmas."

"He did?"

She sat back on her heels. "Wouldn't have thought it of him, would you?"

Too stunned to speak, Alisa shook her head.

"Anyway, while they were enjoying a Christmas goose—"

"A goose?" Oh, God was so good. Every year since she was a child, Alisa remembered Mrs. Perryman's lament over the lack of a Christmas goose.

"Goose. Anyway, the way the children tell it, they were just finishing up their dinner when all of a sudden the roof gave way under the weight of all that rainwater. It flooded the kitchen and ruined the pies."

"And Mr. Worthington brought them here?" It was a little hard not to question his motives, given their last encounter.

"That's right. Packed up the lot of them and tucked them into bed upstairs."

The place certainly was large enough. She could imagine the thrill the children must be feeling to have gone from a dilapidated old home to this mansion. When she'd come to be Mrs. Worthington's companion, Alisa had felt as though she was living in a palace. She frowned. But just as in her situation, this arrangement wouldn't last. The children would be on the streets if Mrs. Perryman couldn't fix the roof. And how could she? She could barely feed the children, which was why the house was in such desperate need of repair in the first place.

"Alisa!"

Alisa turned toward the door at the sound of Mrs. Perryman's voice. She rushed toward the only mother she'd ever known and ran into her arms. Mrs. Perryman's voice shook with tears. "It's true. You really are here."

"Yes. But I don't understand all of this. Marietta explained why you're here. But how. . ."

"I invited them, of course."

Alisa gasped and took an instinctive step back as Mr. Worthington strode into the room. "And I hope they'll stay as long as necessary."

Mrs. Perryman fingered her collar and averted her gaze to the Turkish rug on the floor. Her cheeks grew pink as Mr. Worthington came to stand beside her. Alisa's eyes widened, then narrowed in suspicion. "What are you playing at, sir?" she asked, indignation beginning to build within her.

"I'm not playing at anything. I'm merely offering this good woman and the children in her care a home since theirs is unlivable." He frowned. "I would have thought this would make you happy."

"It would. . .I mean it does." Alisa looked from her father to Mrs. Perryman. "May I speak to you in private, Mr. Worthington?"

"Of course." He turned to Mrs. Perryman. "Please excuse us for a few moments. My daughter and I have some things to discuss."

Alisa's throat tightened, and she felt suspiciously close to tears at his words. If only this scoundrel really meant what he said. She followed in silence as he led her to his office. "Please have a seat," he offered, motioning toward a pair of brown leather chairs.

"Thank you," she replied stiffly. To her surprise, he took the other chair rather than walking around the desk and sitting as she'd seen him do many times with guests and business associates.

"You're all right?" he asked. Was that guilt hiding in his eyes?

She sniffed. "If by your inquiry you mean did Bart and Amos harm me, no, they did not—no thanks to you."

That was most definitely relief washing across his face. What was he playing at?

"I understand Amos is dead and Bart has been placed in jail?"

Alisa frowned. "That's right. How did you know that?"

"Your young man came to see me yesterday."

"My young. . .Titus was here?"

"Yes, and he seems to be under the impression that you're safely tucked away at a farmhouse between here and his ranch." He peered at her closely. "Why have you come back?"

"To turn myself in."

His eyes widened, and he sucked in a sharp breath. "For something you didn't do?"

"I hope to plead my case to the authorities. Perhaps the judge will be lenient."

Moisture formed in his eyes, and his shoulders slumped as he leaned forward and reached for her hands.

Alisa shrank back.

"Don't be frightened," he said.

At the soft, almost defeated tone, Alisa allowed him to take her hands in both of his. "What's come over you, Mr. Worthington? I don't understand."

"I know. Bear with me for a few minutes, and I'll explain."

Alisa nodded, praying that God would give her wisdom to know the truth.

"When Mother announced she was giving you the house and the money already accrued from the shipping company, I was furious. Shocked. Betrayed."

"But, Mr. Worthington, I never—"

He nodded. "I know. You didn't even know that you're my daughter."

Hearing him say the words sent a jolt through her. She stared at him and for the first time saw the truth. This man was her father; his blood flowed through her veins. They had the same nose that turned up slightly at the end, the same brown eyes, and the same creases in their cheeks that hinted at dimples when they smiled. Which he did at that moment.

"It's a little overwhelming when it comes to you, isn't it?"

"Yes, sir," she whispered.

"Over the past few months, my life without my mother has been lonely, and I realized that I would gladly give up everything, including the shipping company, to have her back." He gave a short laugh. "She would love to hear that. Mother always believed I had great potential, but I never believed I could make it without the allowance she bestowed upon me each month.

"But as lonely as I've been, I started thinking what it must have been like to grow up without either a mother or a father."

"I had Mrs. Perryman."

His expression softened. "I have high regard for Mrs. Perryman. She's a rare jewel indeed."

A rare jewel? Alisa peered closer. Was her father falling in love with Mrs. Perryman? She captured her bottom lip between her teeth in order to stave off a smile.

He smiled, obviously reading her amusement. "As I said, she's a remarkable woman."

"What about Bart and Amos?"

"They came to me after reading the poster. At the time, I still hadn't come to grips with everything, and against my better judgment, I gave them the okay to find you."

"You instructed them not to harm me."

"You're my daughter. I couldn't bear the thought."

"Why were you looking for me?"

He heaved a sigh. "At first, of course, I wanted you to sign away your rights to the house and money."

"I never wanted—"

Again he silenced her. "I know you didn't ask for anything. But Mother loved you. I wish the two of you could have established a familial relationship. Even so, she had grown to know you over the months you worked for us while she was making arrangements for your future. It was her desire to give you the house and the money. And in doing so, she did me a great favor."

"A favor?"

"I'm learning the shipping company. Even gave Jonesy a job there in the office running errands and learning the books."

"What a wonderful position for Jonesy! He's so good with numbers."

Her father nodded, and Alisa felt warm all over. "I discovered that pretty early on. He has a head for sales, too. I expect he'll move up and be a successful man himself someday."

The pride reflected in her father's face piqued her curiosity. He answered her question before she asked. "I'd like to know how you would feel if I were to adopt Jonesy. Give him my name—our name—and ask him to join me in the business."

"Oh, Mr. Worthington." Tears burned her throat and eyes. "Have you spoken with Jonesy yet?"

"No. First I wanted to see how you felt."

"But why?"

"I've denied you—my flesh and blood—the right to a father for twenty years. I would spend the rest of my life making it up to you if you want me to. Devoting all of my attention to you and any grandchildren you give me."

"You mean you want to be sure I don't mind sharing you?" Alisa laughed.

He reddened. "I understand. It was a ludicrous thing to even suggest you might want a relationship with me. Forgive my presumption."

"No, that's not it. I'm amazed by all of this. Really."

"So am I, to be honest. Now to get down to business matters. I assume you will live on your husband's ranch?"

"Oh, well, Titus and I do need to speak of matters now that things have changed." And she wasn't going to jail. Joy welled up inside her and curved her lips into a smile. There was nothing keeping them apart now. It was all she could do not to jump back on Raven and fly all the way home to the man she loved.

"Will you be selling the house?"

"Sell Titus's house? There are several cabins all together. It wouldn't be right to sell one of them to a stranger. Besides, Titus would never leave his family."

His mouth twisted to one side in a smile. "I meant this house," he drawled.

"How could I? I mean, why would I sell your house?"

"Alisa," he said, keeping his gaze steady on her. "It's your house. Mother left it to you."

"Oh." Was it really true? She hadn't been dreaming it all this time? Even in her wildest imagination, it never occurred to her that anyone would actually let her have it.

"Do you want it?" she asked her father. Something flickered in his eyes.

"I am preparing to buy my own home. The company brings in much more than I realized, and I am financially secure."

"But wouldn't you rather stay in the home where you grew up?"

"I must admit I would. But the house is large. Much too large for a man alone."

Alisa smiled as understanding dawned. "You've offered Mrs. Perryman and the children a place to stay for as long as they need."

"Yes."

"Would you object if I turn the house over to them for good?"

He expelled a breath and smiled as though relieved. "I had hoped you would consider that an option."

"D–do I have enough money to maintain the house for them?"

He chuckled. "My dear, you have enough money to maintain a hundred houses for them. You are an extremely wealthy young lady. Not to mention the fact that 25 percent of the shipping company belongs to you, as well."

Alisa's eyes widened. "Oh." If she hadn't already been sitting, she would certainly have felt the need to do so. She remembered the conversation between Robert and Mrs. Worthington before the horrendous scene that followed. All the inheritance talk had been eclipsed by the appalling aftermath.

"You're remembering." He said the words as a statement, not a question. "I'm so sorry."

"Mr. Worthington, I forgive you for accusing me. I know your mother sprung the news on you as suddenly as I heard it myself."

"I want to know you, Alisa. You're so much like your grandmother." He squeezed her hands. "I know I don't deserve the opportunity to know you. But I've changed, and I pray God will give me the chance to prove it."

"I. . .I would like the chance to know you, too." It was too hard to say 'Father' just yet. She wasn't ready. But someday she hoped their relationship would be such that her children would have the benefit of a real grandfather.

"Where is she?" A roar from the foyer interrupted them. Robert shot to his feet, releasing Alisa's hands. The door burst open, and Titus strode through.

Alisa gasped. "Titus!"

"Why did you leave?" he demanded. "I thought I told you I'd be coming back."

"If you'll excuse me," Robert said, coughing into his fist. "I'll leave you two alone to talk things over."

"Well?"

Alisa frowned. "If you'll calm down, I can explain."

His breathing slowed a bit, and he looked into her eyes, tenderness replacing the hard edges of only a second ago. Alisa smiled. This was the Titus she knew.

"I was worried sick about you riding alone to San Francisco. When Mrs. Meyers told me you'd ridden here, I thought you had come to turn yourself in."

"There's no reason for me to."

"I know. I talked it over with the sheriff yesterday."

"Robert said you came to see him, as well."

Titus nodded. He stepped forward and gathered her around the waist, pulling her close. Alisa didn't resist. On the contrary, she willingly stepped into his embrace and wrapped her arms around his neck.

"Why did you come to see Robert?"

He brushed her upturned lips with his. "I wanted to be sure no one else was going to be coming after my wife."

Alisa grinned. "Have you a wife, Titus Chance?"

"I will have before the day's out, if you're willing to marry me before we go home."

"So soon? Won't your family be upset?"

"We can throw a barbeque for all the neighbors to celebrate. But if we wait, there's no telling when Parson Abe's coming back. If weather keeps him from his appointed time next month, it could be another three months." He dipped his head and brushed her lips again. "I don't want to wait that long to marry you." His husky voice sent a shiver down Alisa's spine, and she found herself nodding in agreement when he said, "Let's go find a preacher."

"Perhaps we could find one to come here? I'd love to have Mrs. Perryman and the children in attendance."

"And your father?"

She nodded. "Yes. Him, too. And, Titus, before I become your wife, I would like to ask a favor."

"Anything, my love."

"I want to sign this house over to Mrs. Perryman."

"The house?"

"My grandmother left it for me."

His eyes grew soft and thoughtful. "I think it's a wonderful idea to leave it to the children."

"There's more. I. . .I, well, we'll never have to worry about money, Titus."

"I've never been worried about it." He grinned and kissed her. "But I have the feeling you have more news."

"According to Mr. Worthington, I'm apparently quite wealthy. Please say I can share it with you."

"My brothers are pretty determined to make the ranch a success on their own. But I'm sure if we get in a bind, they'd agree to take a little help. At any rate, the money will be there for our children."

"Yes, our children."

His gaze captured hers, revealing all the love she could ever have imagined possible. When he lowered his head and pressed his lips to hers, his arms tightened about her. Locked in his embrace, Alisa returned his kiss, knowing that God had truly taken the horror of the past few months and turned it into something good.

Epilogue

Alisa's eyes misted with tears as she and Titus waved good-bye to the group at the doorway. Her father and Mrs. Perryman and all of the children, including Jonesy, were on hand to wish them well.

Titus grabbed the reins, then hesitated. "We could stay one more day if you want."

Alisa smiled at her new husband and leaned her head against his shoulder. They had been married for a little over a week, staying at one of San Francisco's finest hotels during most of that time. She'd met with Mr. Chadwick, the lawyer handling her grandmother's estate, and had settled everything so that Mrs. Perryman would never have to worry again. Best of all, with the new home, they could accommodate up to ten more children. Alisa had loved every moment of her time with them all, and a seed had been planted for a loving relationship with her father, but she was eager to begin her life as Mrs. Titus Chance in their own home. She squeezed his arm. "No. It's time to go home."

"I agree," he said, taking his attention off the road for a moment to kiss her soundly. "It was generous of your father to insist you take a few things of your grandmother's."

Alisa twisted in the seat and eyed the pile of furniture she was taking back. Two beds, one for her and Titus to share and one for Miriam and Gideon—a belated wedding present. Poor Miriam's back was beginning to hurt her from the uncomfortable straw mattress she'd had to endure. Then there was the pie safe she'd fallen in love with from the moment she entered the kitchen, and the Turkish rug from the library. Some chairs. She loved the idea of being able to contribute to the home somehow.

"Did you mention the furniture we're bringing back when you telegraphed the family?"

Titus grinned. "Nope. Just told them I was bringing home my bride and to move my things back into the cabin."

Alisa's cheeks warmed, but she snuggled closer to her husband. "Good. Then it will be like Christmas all over again."

"That reminds me." Titus stopped the wagon and reached into his pocket, producing the box he'd offered her at Christmas. "Merry Christmas."

"Oh, Titus." She opened the box, and a soft gasp escaped at the sight of the lovely cameo pin inside. "It's beautiful. I love it."

Despite the fact that they were stopped on a crowded street, Titus pulled her close. "You're beautiful, and I love you." He lowered his face to hers and kissed her. As they resumed their journey, Alisa's heart sang with thankfulness to God. Though she'd been raised an orphan, He hadn't left her fatherless forever. He'd sent her to a large, loving family and, more important, to a man who would love and cherish her for the rest of her life. She knew she'd never be alone again.

TAKING A CHANCE

Chapter 1

Reliable, California, early spring 1872

Stop your squawking, Dan. You know she's staying—just like the last two." Bryce brought up a good point, Paul reflected. The family did have a history of keeping unexpected females. *Wonder who'll get hitched to this one.*

"Dibs!" Apparently Logan's thoughts followed along the same line. All six brothers turned toward the window where the woman in question could be seen from a distance.

It was no mystery why Logan claimed her. No one could mistake the curves beneath her travel-worn clothes. Glorious hair, darker than midnight, gleamed as the soft waves captured the last rays of the setting sun—along with the interest of every man within a square mile. Paul almost wished she didn't have her back turned, so he could see her face. Almost.

"She's taller than you, Logan," Bryce contested. That wasn't exactly true, though her slender build did bring her closer to heaven than any other woman Paul had seen. That presented a welcome change. Paul always felt a little awkward around bitsy Miriam, and Alisa wasn't much better. He didn't see how Gideon, the only one of his brothers to top him in size, managed being married to the pretty pipsqueak. Even Logan, the youngest and smallest of them all, knocked her over the first time they met.

"Why's she here, Gideon?" Paul's question stopped the beginnings of a squabble. The heavy sigh that came before the response wasn't encouraging.

"She's in a fix." The enigmatic comment set off a new round of exclamations.

"With the law?" Logan bolted upright. "What'd she do?"

"And she knows Miriam?" Titus couldn't quite keep the incredulity from his tone.

"I'll bet she's expecting. I told you if we kept taking in strays we'd end up regretting it." This from Daniel, who hadn't quite gotten over the bitterness of losing his own wife, Hannah. Personally, Paul didn't see how anyone with a set of eyes could think that slim waistline concealed a baby.

"You hush. Even I know the difference 'tween ladies and strays." Bryce, who boasted the least social graces of them all, took a stand. At last the clamor subsided, and they all stared expectantly at Gideon. He'd explain. Then they'd vote on whether or not the mysterious woman would stay.

Delilah Chadwick kept her back to the house, trying not to reveal how anxious she felt. *I don't have anywhere else to go if the men don't let me stay.*

"Don't worry, Delilah," Miriam said in a reassuring tone. "They're good men who'll make the right decision."

"Maybe the right decision is to say no. I don't want to be a burden, but I don't see how I can contribute to a place like this. . . ." Who could want more than the beauty of the surrounding land? Blue sky stretched on forever over the rich, solid earth beneath her feet. The well-crafted house and barn built near it promised a cozy haven—and a garden. She'd always wanted a garden.

But Papa chased other dreams. He'd gambled his way from town to town all the way across the country until they'd finally ended up in California. He'd always said they'd get some land of their own as soon as he won a big enough pot, but then he'd turn around and "invest" his winnings in another game. She'd come along to take care of him, but she'd failed miserably. *Oh, Papa. I miss you so much.*

Miriam's voice interrupted her reverie. "But there's plenty to do around here, I'll tell you that much! With the baby coming, I need more help than Alisa can provide. Cooking for and cleaning up after six men isn't as easy as you'd think!"

Delilah knew she could feel herself turning red. "Miriam, I—I can't cook. We never had a stove. . .and when we were on the go, we just ate hardtack and jerky." This would never work! If she could offer them nothing, she'd be sent packing. That's just how the world worked.

"That's all right. You'll learn soon enough. I'll enjoy teaching you. Besides, I wasn't finished yet." Miriam began ticking off chores. "There's still the washing and mending—enough to keep a small army busy—so your needle will be appreciated. Then there're the girls and the weeds in the garden, which both grow far too quickly if you ask me! Of course, we can't forget the livestock. Every day there are eggs to gather, chickens to feed, pigs to slop, and cows to milk—"

"All right! All right! I get your point. I'm a quick learner and a hard worker. You'll just have to teach me everything." Well, not everything. She already did laundry and mending. As a matter of fact, she handled a needle well. Maybe she'd finally have the chance to make a real quilt.

"Will they really let me stay, Miriam? They've been in there for a while."

"Oh, they're just being Chance men. Like I said, they'll make the right decision. And if they don't, they're in for it. They've always been staunchly democratic about making major decisions. They voted the same way about letting me and Alisa stay. But they're going to have to factor in the Chance women now. We've already weighed in on the subject. Right, Alisa?" Miriam tacked on as the only other Chance woman rejoined them. Alisa had just made a quick trip to check on Dan's girls, who were playing with their dollhouse in a cabin.

Alisa laughed. "That's right. If need be, we'll have our say, too." She sobered a bit and turned to Delilah. "How are you holding up?"

Delilah offered a halfhearted smile. "I've been better."

"I'm so sorry you lost your father."

Delilah tried to tamp down the tears that sprang to her eyes. She still couldn't believe they'd buried Papa earlier that week. But now he was gone, and she was all alone. There hadn't been very many options since she only owned her clothes and sketch pads. Very little money and some worthless stock Papa had won the night before were stashed in the false bottom of her valise, but they wouldn't get her very far, and only one profession opened to unclaimed women on the frontier.

The pot he'd had the winning hand for last night went to fund the burial, such as it was. She and the sheriff stood side by side, the only ones at the grave site. The circuit preacher hadn't been in town, but that was all right, since Papa didn't hold with much religion. It seemed sort of fitting, because since Mama's death, it had been only her and Papa wherever they went—and occasionally the law when one of his games got too heated.

Some of the more spiteful townspeople had muttered that it was only fitting a gambler should meet such an end: shot in a saloon for cheating. Delilah knew Papa didn't cheat. While her father couldn't stop gambling away everything they owned, Delilah came to understand a long time ago that he couldn't really help it. He made promises he never kept, but he'd always meant to. He was a man of integrity in his own way, and he never cheated. *Maybe if he had, he'd've won more. . . .* The nasty thought crept by before she could stop it. She hadn't really been herself since she found out they'd let his murderer get away. Was there no justice?

Not for Papa, but maybe for me. The men began coming out of the house to issue her verdict. Six behemoths, but she had Miriam's word that they were all "good men." She believed it about Gideon, since her cousin had married him, but she maintained reservations about the rest. They all stood fairly tall, each boasting dark hair and startling blue eyes. As they came closer, she tried to gauge what their answers would be.

She'd already met Gideon but couldn't read his expression. As for the others, one gawked at her past all reason, one gave his attention to an ecstatic dog at his side, and another looked politely curious. None of these gave any indication of a warm welcome. The brother with flowers in his pocket absolutely radiated hostility. The incongruity would have struck her as funny if she weren't so anxious. As things stood, his glare made the possibility that she'd be turned away far too likely.

That left only one man, but he was different. She'd endured men gawking, scowling, leering, or being disinterested before, but this man's gaze stayed steady. It wasn't openly assessing like the others, but his scrutiny somehow made her feel as though he could take her measure better than any of them. His glance didn't feel judgmental but was disconcerting, nevertheless. She wasn't sure what to make of him, which left her completely in the dark as to whether or not he'd have voted for her to stay. That meant she knew the opinion of only one brother, and that wasn't encouraging.

"Well?" Miriam's tone sounded as both a question and a warning.

All of them except the scowler grinned as Gideon pronounced, "She stays."

Paul watched as Delilah let out the breath she probably didn't even know she'd been holding. The stunning creature's smile managed to be both gracious and grateful as she thanked them for their kindness. Delilah was a lovely temptress, indeed, but her eyes truly captivated him.

From a distance he'd thought them brown, but upon closer inspection, they were no mere brown. Amber. Golden, pure, sparkling amber is what came to mind. Not that a gal possessed any power over her eye color, but the beauty of it snagged him just the same. He got the impression eyes like that should be full of joy and mirth, reflecting the beauty around them, but hers seemed deeper with some hurt that didn't let her smile reach them. He wondered what she'd look like when she put those heavy cares on the Lord.

He'd watched her since the moment he'd stepped out of the door, seen her size up each of his brothers. Obviously she'd heard something of them from Miriam and was trying to label him and his brothers. Had it been his imagination, or had her glance lingered a bit on him?

He realized Gideon still spoke. "You haven't met most of us yet, so I'd better introduce my brothers. This one here is—"

"Titus, right?" Her soft interruption stunned them.

"Miriam, did you already point out who's who?" Logan demanded.

Miriam laughed. "None but Gideon!"

Delilah spoke again. "Miriam and I have been writing to each other for years. From the letters I managed to receive, I've pieced together some things for myself. Even so, Titus gave himself away since he went straight to Alisa."

Logan nodded. "All right, which one am I?"

"You must be Logan, who I'm told is the most sociable and outgoing." Paul noted she showed the tact not to mention to the infatuated youth that he stood the shortest.

"That's pretty good, Miss Delilah. Now do him." Logan jerked a thumb in Bryce's direction.

"Well, I've been told one of you has a special way with animals, so since the dogs followed him, I'd have to name him as Bryce." She looked around for confirmation, and when they nodded, she turned to Dan. "You have to be Dan. The flowers in your pocket are a dead giveaway you're a father." Again, she demonstrated enough prudence not to point out the ever-present scowl. The moment those spectacular eyes trained on Paul, a bolt of heat shot through him.

"So you must be Paul."

"She pegged every last one of us, Gideon. Even old Gus White down at the general store can't keep the older four of you straight, and he's seen us more'n once."

Dan's voice put a damper on things. "All right, so we know she's stayin', but *where* is she stayin'? Gideon and Miriam got the old bunk room, and the two rooms connecting the old ranch house and my place each have a bachelor or two in 'em. Titus and Alisa are newlyweds with the latest cabin. Where's she gonna fit?" Obviously, he had worked himself into a temper.

Alisa tried to avert the coming storm with a gentle request. "The girls have their own room now, and so do you. Maybe for a while Delilah could share the old cabin with the girls and you could use their room?"

The scowl softened only slightly, but that was something. "I figured you all were fixin' to kick me outta my own house. I won't leave my girls, you hear?"

"I won't take anyone's home from them. A man deserves his own place, and so do couples." Her voice caught as she went on. "And parents should never be separated from their children. If it's all right, I'll just bed down in the barn."

She'd hardly finished speaking her piece before the menfolk gave their collective opinion of that harebrained scheme. Miriam and Alisa didn't manage to get a word in edgewise.

Surprisingly, Bryce spoke up first. "That's fine enough for me when one of the animals is ailin', Miss Delilah, but it ain't fittin' for you."

"That'd be an insult to our hospitality," Titus protested.

Gideon gave a flat, "No."

"Don't you listen to old Dan when he's sour." Logan shot Dan a heated look. "That's just his way."

Even Dan seemed taken aback. "I didn't mean that, miss. What kind of example would that be to my girls?"

Apparently, Delilah nursed a stubborn streak. "I've done it before, and I don't want to be a burden."

Miriam opened her mouth, but Paul beat her to the punch. "We appreciate how you don't want to put anybody out, miss, but you need to be close at hand. It's the only way you'll be able to help Miriam while she's in her condition. I'll bunk with Dan, and you'll take my room—it's closest to Miriam's."

She looked at him intently, and he had to remind himself to steadily meet her gaze instead of getting lost in it. After what seemed an eternity, she slowly nodded.

"Well, if that's settled, I'll just take your things on in." Dan reached out a hand.

"Oh, it's no problem." She hefted the large bag at her feet. "I've got my valise right here."

"I'll take you, Miss Delilah," Logan offered gallantly.

"This is all I brought, gentlemen. If you'll just show me the way. . ."

"Well, you beat me!" Alisa exclaimed.

"Not me," Miriam confessed. "I'm afraid I brought along half of the islands with me!"

While the women took her to the house, Paul pondered what he already knew about their pretty guest.

"From the letters I managed to receive. . . I'll bed down in the barn. . . . I've done it before. . . . This is all I brought. . . . " Her father was a gambler. The poor thing must have been dragged all over creation. What kind of man moved his daughter from place to place, not providing a decent roof over her head and making it so almost everything she owned could fit into one bag?

Chapter 2

Delilah woke up the next morning and stretched groggily. As her eyes grew accustomed to the darkness, she tried to pick out a few details to remind her of where she was. It definitely didn't look like a barn or stable, nor did it seem like a hotel. The room contained only one window covered by a flap of fabric. The sun wasn't completely up yet, so everything stayed cast in varying degrees of shadow. She lay ensconced in a snug bed and could make out a chair against the wall. A small potbelly stove graced one corner, with a washstand taking up residence as the only other furniture in the room. She remembered placing her drawing supplies in the washstand's convenient drawer and filling only a few of the many pegs on the walls with her clothes. Long ago, she'd learned unpacking was the only way to make a strange room more comfortable.

The door opened quietly, bringing in a blast of frigid morning air. Miriam poked her head in the room to whisper, "Delilah?"

Yes, she remembered clearly now. She'd buried Papa and gone to Miriam's ranch, taking the home of one of the Chance brothers. She swung her legs over the side of the bed.

"I'm awake." Leaving the snug warmth of the bed, Delilah padded across the cool floor in her bare feet.

"I need to make breakfast, so I thought you'd like to watch before you have your first real lesson later today," Miriam invited.

Delilah nodded. "I'll be dressed in a minute." Miriam carefully closed the door, and Delilah crept over to the table where her valise sat. She changed out of her nightgown into her yellow cambric day dress. The dress she'd worn while traveling here currently boasted more dust than cloth, and she only owned one other. The primrose satin evening gown her father had purchased in a spurt of indulgence after a good gaming streak wasn't appropriate for ranch work. She'd brushed and braided her hair before bed last night, after Polly and Ginny Mae let her do the same for them. She quickly twisted the braid on top of her head and pinned it into place. She left the cabin as Alisa walked across the yard toward her.

"Good morning, Alisa."

"Good morning, Delilah. Did you sleep well?"

Delilah took enough time to assure the kindhearted woman that she had slept very well before hurrying into the main cabin.

"What are you going to make?" Delilah wanted to know what she was getting herself into.

"The men can hardly crack their eyes open without their morning coffee. Then I thought we'd start with something easy—scrambled eggs and diced ham." Miriam handed her the coffeepot. "If you'd like, you can pump this full of water."

Delilah did as she was asked, then pulled out plates, glasses, knives, and forks to set the table.

Miriam brought out a salted ham hock. "Why don't you watch as I cut the first bit? Then you can try your hand at it." This seemed easy enough—Delilah didn't lack competence with a knife.

"All right, you try it." Miriam nodded her approval as Delilah started shaving and chopping. "You have a sharp eye and a steady hand. That's good." Together they finished the ham, and Delilah, starting to feel more comfortable, waited for further instructions. Miriam brought out a huge bowl.

"I still have plenty of eggs left from yesterday, so we're all set. You tap 'em on the edge of the bowl, like this." She demonstrated in one swift movement. "Then part the halves and let the egg run into the bowl. See?"

Miriam made it look absolutely effortless. Heartened, Delilah resolutely picked up an egg and brought it down on the rim of the bowl. With a crack that all but echoed in the morning stillness, the shell split completely and yellow goop slimed the tabletop.

Miriam started laughing. "Gently!" She wiped up the table with a rag and handed Delilah another egg. "All right, give it another shot."

Delilah put down the egg. "I don't want to waste them."

Miriam smiled. "That was just your first try. I did the very same thing. Try again."

This time, Delilah tapped it so gently, the shell didn't boast so much as a crack. She looked helplessly at Miriam.

"Just keep tapping it a little harder each time until you get the feel for it. Be careful, and you'll get it right." In no time at all, Delilah got the hang of it, and three dozen eggs floated in the bowl.

"Now what?"

"We stir it until the clear and the yellow run together. Here." She gave Delilah a wooden spoon, and Delilah followed her instructions, then poured half of the mixture into a large, greased skillet waiting on the stove.

"Mix it periodically and add in the ham." Miriam demonstrated. It cooked until a mess of scrambled eggs and ham sat ready to be put on a platter.

"Now try cooking the other half while I warm some bread." Miriam pulled two loaves from the bread box and began slicing.

Delilah took the pan and poured the rest of the eggs into it. She watched intently for it to bubble, then pounced to stir it as soon as it began. Some of the goop seemed stuck on the bottom.

"Miriam? Why do mine stick to the pan when yours didn't?"

Her cousin hustled over to take a look. "I forgot to tell you that you need to regrease the pan. It'll be difficult to scrub clean, but your eggs'll be fine. Just keep moving them around until they look like mine."

Pretty soon, they looked finished, and Delilah emptied the contents of the pan onto the platter. Following more advice, she filled the dirty pan with water from the pump.

Miriam had just finished placing butter and preserves on the table when Gideon wandered in. "Sure smells good in here, sweetheart."

"Thank you. Fresh coffee's on the stove, and Delilah here helped me make ham 'n' eggs for breakfast."

Gideon turned to Delilah. "Good morning, Delilah. If you're half the cook my Miriam is, we'll keep you busy for sure."

Delilah confessed. "Actually, this is the first time I've cooked anything. I hope it tastes all right."

Logan and Bryce stumbled into the room toward the basin, followed by Dan and Paul. Dan started cutting toast into little strips and putting them on a tiny plate. Paul grabbed the milk and filled two small glasses. He turned to her.

"Miss Delilah, would you like milk, water, or coffee this morning?" His gaze was as penetrating as the day before, and her nerves tingled as heat spread through her.

"I'd like the milk, please." She loved fresh milk. "And please just call me Delilah. No 'miss' is needed." That was for sure. With her twenty-first birthday fast approaching, she knew most girls her age had already started families. Somehow, she didn't want this intriguing man to think of that every time they spoke.

"Delilah." He said it softly, testing it out, but the way he said it made it sound beautiful.

Titus came in, leading Alisa and their nieces. Everyone took a seat. Gideon presided at the head of the table, with Miriam on his right. Delilah hastened to sit on her other side. Dan sat to his left with Ginny Mae on his lap and Polly beside him, flanked by Alisa and Titus. Paul sat next to Delilah, with Logan beside him and Bryce at the end of the table. Delilah tried to ignore the fact that they were packed so close, she could feel Paul's warmth.

After everyone settled in, Delilah jumped a bit when Paul clasped her hand in his until she realized they had all joined hands for prayer. She only wished she could be a part of something so special.

For now, she'd just pretend that she wasn't someone they'd taken in out of charity. She listened as Gideon spoke of his appreciation for all of their blessings and asked God to be with them during the day to come. It seemed strange that they'd think God, who was so big and busy, would be right beside each of them all day long. *Perhaps it just feels that way because they have each other to care about.*

Paul's hand swallowed hers. It almost made her feel dainty and feminine sitting next to him with her hand cocooned in his warm, work-roughened palm. She stifled a pang of regret when the prayer ended, and after a slight reassuring squeeze, he let go. She sat as an outsider once again amid morning chatter as everyone passed around platters of eggs and bread with the coffee.

I don't want to let go, Paul realized. He didn't even know why he'd sat next to her. Usually he took the place at the end of the table where Bryce sat today. Logan sent him a peeved look, but Paul watched Delilah hop like a frightened rabbit to be next to Miriam, and before he knew it, he squeezed beside her at the table. He'd felt her quick intake of breath when he'd first grasped her palm. Now he didn't want to let go of the warm, soft, slender hand nestled so sweetly in his.

She towered over Miriam on the other side of her, but the crown of her head came about equal to his nose. She reminded him of that old fairy tale Alisa told the girls. The one about the girl who walked into the bears' house and tested everything out. Delilah felt not too big, not too small, but just right. She smelled so feminine and delicate, but he didn't feel like he crushed her hand, either, which brought him back to the odd little war going on inside of him.

Paul knew the prayer would end any minute, but he just hadn't quite convinced himself to let go. Her dress—the color of marigolds—made her look like a ray of sunshine, and he wanted to enjoy her warmth a little longer. When everyone said, "Amen," he compromised and gave her hand a slight squeeze before withdrawing.

"Your breakfasts make it worth gettin' up, Miriam." Bryce's praise was well earned.

"Thank you, Bryce, but I think Delilah deserves most of the credit this morning. It's the first time she's ever cooked." Miriam's response had everyone peering at their new houseguest.

"You did a fine job, a mighty fine job." Logan shoveled eggs with gusto as everyone congratulated Delilah.

Even Polly chimed in. "Yeah. I haven't ate crunchy eggs since Auntie Miri-Em came."

Silence fell as the menfolk became intently interested in their coffee, and Delilah blushed. "I must've gotten some shell into the bowl. I'm so sorry."

"It's all right," Alisa assured her as she inspected Polly's plate. "A little bit never hurt anyone, I'm sure."

"What are you doing, Auntie Alisa? I like my crunchy eggs!" Polly snatched back her plate. Paul couldn't help it; he started to chuckle. Soon everyone joined in, even Dan.

"Crunchy eggs!" Dan grinned at his little daughter. "Well, Princess Polly, if you like your crunchy eggs, you can go ahead and eat them. Won't do you any harm."

After the laughter stopped, Paul faced Delilah. Her cheeks flushed. "Maybe little Polly got a bit of shell in hers, but I've never tasted better eggs 'n' ham." He couldn't remember the last time he'd enjoyed breakfast so much.

After breakfast, the men went out to their usual duties while the women cleaned up. It took Delilah half of eternity to scrub the skillet clean, but finally she finished.

"Delilah," Miriam offered, "since you arrived yesterday evening, you didn't have much of an opportunity to wash up after traveling. I'll bet your hands are pretty well soaked after that pan, but if you'd like, we can fill the tub so you can have a bath. After you're done, we'll dunk the girls."

"That would be wonderful, Miriam. I'll start pumping the water." While Miriam dandled Ginny Mae on her lap and worked with Polly on colors and numbers, Alisa and Delilah heated pots of water and hefted them to the old washtub they'd hauled in from the barn. When they'd set everything up, Delilah hurried to fetch her soap.

Once behind the screen, she got out of her clothing as quickly as possible and slid into the bath. She supposed the tub was barely big enough for the largest of the brothers to hunch into, but it gave her enough room to lean back as long as she bent her legs. Mindful that the little ones would be next, she picked up the soap instead of soaking. It wouldn't be fair to leave them with a cold bath after she luxuriated in the relaxing warmth. After she filled her hair with suds, she reached for the basin of fresh water next to her. When she'd scrubbed out all the dirt and achiness, she reluctantly climbed from the tub to help Miriam and Alisa with the girls.

When she came out from behind the partition, Miriam looked at her in surprise. "That was awfully fast."

"Usually we enjoy a soak for as long as we can. It's one of the comforts around here." Alisa spoke as she helped Polly undress.

"I enjoyed every minute," Delilah praised. "I just didn't want the water to be cold for the girls. I feel so much more like myself now that I'm clean again."

"Why don't you try to dry your hair and braid it while we take care of the children?"

Delilah gratefully took Miriam's advice and toweled her hair a bit more, only to realize she'd forgotten her brush. She excused herself and went out once more. The sun glowed cheerfully in the blue sky, so full of life she slowed her pace to enjoy the beauty of the day. Rather than braid her hair alone in the small cabin, she picked up her brush and trekked back to the kitchen. After living without the company of women for so long, she found herself eager to spend time with Miriam and Alisa. *I might as well enjoy it while it lasts.*

Paul shaded his eyes and scanned the sky. It could only be about ten o'clock, but for some reason, he hankered for lunchtime. At any rate, he needed to head back for some more tacks. The stretch of fence they'd been fixing needed more help than they'd thought, considering they'd worked on it a few weeks before.

He strode over to where Speck, his brown and white paint, calmly grazed. He swung into the saddle and trotted over to Titus. "I'm heading back for some more tacks." At his brother's nod, he turned Speck toward the barn and cantered off. As the house came into sight, he spotted a flash of yellow as Delilah came out of the kitchen. He watched as she slowed her pace, enjoying the sun. Her head tilted back for a moment, and black waves tumbled over her shoulders. His throat went dry.

As she disappeared into the room he'd given up for her, he spurred Speck over to the barn before hitching the horse. *I'm parched,* he told himself as he headed toward the kitchen for a cup. Yep. Being so close, it made sense to go get a cool drink from the pump rather than slug some of the tepid water from his canteen. That was all there was to it. Who could blame him if he stayed a couple of moments to tickle the girls? Good uncles needed to spend time with their nieces, and since the women had arrived, he missed having a day a week with the girls. If Delilah happened to come back into the kitchen while he was there, it'd do no harm to see how she was getting along. He lengthened his stride toward the door.

"Hello, Paul." Alisa didn't hide her surprise at seeing him. From the damp towel on the floor by his barefooted niece, he reckoned she'd hauled Ginny Mae from the tub and was just buttoning up the last button. When she made as if to hand the toddler off to Miriam, he quickly intercepted.

Delilah glided into the room like a beam of sunlight carrying a brush. She stopped cold at the sight of him.

"Don't mind me. I came by for some tacks and thought I'd grab a drink before I got back out there." He ignored the knowing glance Miriam sent him and forgave her amusement when she jumped in.

"That's right, and he's lending a hand with Ginny Mae here for a moment until you're finished fixing your hair. Take a seat by the fire so your hair will dry a bit faster."

Delilah nodded and took a seat. Paul busied himself by drying Ginny Mae's hair, but he watched Delilah gently guide the brush, stroke after stroke, through her magnificent mane. When she started braiding, nimble fingers slipping through and weaving those black tresses, he became transfixed. The agility with which she performed the ritual showed it was a common one, but it seemed intimate since it was something usually done in private. By the time she'd finished putting her hair up, he wanted nothing more than to pull out the pins and run his fingers through it, testing its weight and silky texture.

She went out to the pump and filled a glass with water. As soon as she'd finished, she walked around the table. His breath caught as she stooped beside him and gently took Ginny Mae from his arms, giving him the cool water. She smelled wonderful—like fresh snow and violets.

As he walked back to the barn, he decided that lunchtime couldn't come soon enough.

Chapter 3

After breakfast the next morning, Delilah followed Miriam into the barn with trepidation. She'd meant it when she said she wanted to learn everything about running the household, but somehow she'd never figured milking cows fit into it. She'd rather be in the vegetable garden with Alisa. Now she'd just have to make the best of it. *I like milk, so that's something, at least.*

The two creatures shared a large stall. Delilah watched as Miriam set a stool beside one of the beasts, then sat down and motioned for Delilah to come closer. Determinedly, Delilah strode over.

"Ready? First, take hold of one of Mister's teats, and—"

"Mister?" Delilah cut Miriam off. Even she knew this cow couldn't possibly be a male.

Miriam grinned. "Polly named them. This one's 'Mister' and the other's 'Sir.' Since she practiced her manners so well, the guys just didn't have the heart to tell her no."

It made perfect sense, so Delilah only giggled for a couple of minutes. Then they shifted their attention back to the lesson at hand.

"After you grab a pair, you tug and squeeze. Like this." A stream of white milk ran into the bucket. "Want to try?"

Not really. Delilah eyed Mister doubtfully but nodded anyway. Miriam got off the tiny stool so Delilah could perch on it. At least the cow wasn't moving. She hesitantly reached for the udder.

"That's it. Now tug downward and squeeze." Delilah did, and a squirt of milk splashed off the side of the bucket.

"Try to aim it into the bucket."

Well, why didn't she say so? Aiming posed no problem. Delilah compensated and caught the hang of milking in no time. While Delilah finished Mister, Miriam milked Sir, and before long, they completed the task.

"We'll make fresh butter today," Miriam decided as they carried their milk pails to the kitchen. They'd just set the buckets on the table when they heard voices outside.

They'd finished driving the herd to the next grazing pasture and were moving the bulls when a raven caught Paul's eye. Its wings shone the same smoky black as

Delilah's hair. Unfortunately, an ornery bull chose that moment to break free and charge straight for him. After years of tending a ranch, Paul handled this sort of thing often enough, but for once it caught him off guard. He spurred Speck to zig when he should have zagged, and by the time he realized his mistake, he lay on the ground with a sharp pain throbbing up his arm.

Logan and Dan took charge of the bull, and Bryce reached Paul first, only to immediately check on how Speck fared.

"Anything other than a few bumps and bruises?" Gideon's concerned tone brought little comfort as Paul nodded.

"My arm." He gritted his teeth and awaited the pronouncement as Gideon prodded.

"Probably broken. We'll have to take you back to Miriam so she can have a look." Gideon hefted him up. It took both Bryce and Gideon to help get Paul into Splotch's saddle; then Gideon gave him a wary look. "You okay to ride?"

"Yeah."

"You lie just as lousy as you look." Gideon swung up behind him. Bryce followed with Speck as they rode back to the house.

After the men had gotten off the horse by the house, Miriam and Delilah dashed out to see what had happened. Paul left the explanations to Gideon.

"Speck lost him when they dodged an angry bull. I think he's broken his arm."

"Take him on into the kitchen," Miriam said. Everyone trooped behind, and Paul felt like a first-rate numbskull. How on earth would he prove himself a good protector and provider if he couldn't manage to stay on a horse? He'd decided after supper last night that Delilah was the woman for him. Maybe it seemed like a quick decision, but Papa had been the same way with Mama, and besides, there were dozens of men to every one woman out here. He needed to act fast. Of course, he'd be going slower now if he'd managed to break his arm. His forearm had already puffed up. Yep, that was attractive, all right.

He took a seat and grimaced as Miriam gently turned his arm. "Can you wiggle your fingers?" He complied, then sucked in a quick breath at the fresh flash of pain. Stupid arm hurt like anything, but the last thing he was gonna do with Delilah standing right beside him was holler about it. He snuck a peek at her face and gained some satisfaction at the expression of compassion on her delicate features.

"I broke my wrist years ago." She reached out and clasped his good hand. Warmth shot through him, but this time, he enjoyed the tingling sensation.

While he'd been distracted, someone had brought in some straight pieces of wood and bandages. Miriam confirmed Gideon's assessment.

"You've broken your arm, but it seems like a clean break near the wrist. I'll have to splint it and put you in a sling, Paul. You won't be able to ride for at least a couple of weeks. For today, I think you should take some of this." She plunked a glass of water on the table in front of him. From the way Miriam said it, he knew she'd laced it with laudanum. He shook his head.

"I'm not taking that." Since Delilah had begun holding his hand, the pain had stopped being so sharp.

Miriam retreated. "Paul, we all know you're a strong man who gives as good as he gets." That sounded better. He nodded his agreement.

She continued. "Do you remember the first night I came here?" Uh-oh. She'd tricked him. He scowled at her.

"You gave me laudanum after Logan brained me, right?"

He had no choice but to admit it. "What of it?" Now he sounded surly—typically more Dan's territory than his.

"So if you can give as good as you get, you should be able to take what you give to others." The pronouncement held no logical flaws, but he gave one last argument.

"I'll be fine—just fine—without it." He felt Delilah squeeze his hand, and he turned to her.

"Wise men can admit when they need a little help. There's no shame in that, but there is some in causing yourself more pain than necessary." From her serious tone, he realized she spoke from watching her father's addiction to gambling ruin his life. It also crossed his mind that being stuck around the homestead wouldn't be such a bad thing for the next month or so. Staying close to the house meant sticking close to her—but only if he wasn't asleep the whole time. This called for a compromise.

"I'll be sure and take it before bed to make sure I sleep, but not now. If your argument holds, Miriam, that's fair since I only gave you laudanum at night."

Miriam gave in graciously. "I'll hold you to that, Paul."

After trussing Paul up like a turkey—his words, not hers—Miriam sent the rest of the men back out to the grazing fields and handed Paul a bucket of slop for the pigs.

"This morning I intended to teach Delilah how to take care of the yard livestock. We'd just finished milking Mister and Sir when you rode up. Alisa's watching the girls, and I need to start on lunch. I hadn't gathered the eggs this morning so I could show Delilah. It still needs to be done. The chickens need to be fed and the pigs slopped, too. If you feel up to it, take Delilah with you and teach her. She's a quick learner." With that, Miriam shooed them both out of her kitchen.

Delilah found herself standing outside with Paul, trying to decide whether or not she felt happy with the situation. She'd learned long ago not to let herself be caught alone with a man—they couldn't be trusted. But here she stood. She couldn't do or say anything to get out of it without insulting Miriam or Paul. Not to mention that of all the brothers, it had to be Paul—the one she was most drawn to and least comfortable around. Well, Dan probably made her more uncomfortable, but Miriam wouldn't push her into spending time with him.

Why couldn't it be Bryce, more concerned with his animals, or either Titus or Gideon, who couldn't keep their eyes off their wives? She'd even prefer Logan, who couldn't seem to stop himself from staring. Nope, she wasn't that lucky. Paul, the unexpectedly intriguing giant, broke his arm. She'd even held his hand for some reason she couldn't recall. The man who gently held Ginny Mae and dried her duck fluff hair, whose touch sent tingles down Delilah's spine, would teach her to slop pigs.

A lot of thoughts raced through that pretty head. Paul wondered what those thoughts might be. He figured they had something to do with the fact that Delilah wasn't comfortable being alone with him. As unencouraging as that might be, she'd held his hand earlier while Miriam looked at his arm, which meant that even if chances were slim, they existed. He should say something to set her at ease.

"Shall we go?" It wasn't exactly a proposal, but it was a start.

Delilah looked at the basket of chicken feed she held. "Do you want to feed the chickens first?"

"Sure. The henhouse is this way." They walked over to the coop. Actually, calling it a chicken cupboard would be more accurate since its two doors swung on hinges that opened outward. Bryce had invented it years ago. Given that all of the brothers were too big to squeeze into a small aisle in the middle of a crowded coop, he simply made a structure about six feet high with a single wall filled with rows of nesting boxes in the back. As usual, the doors stayed open so the flightless birds could peck around their fenced-in yard during the day.

"The eggs are in those boxes. You just have to stick your hand in and find them. First, we scatter the feed in the far corner of the yard, so the hens will be distracted. This is springtime, though, so a few of 'em are bound to be setting."

"Setting?"

"Yep. They just sit on their eggs day in and day out and don't want to move except to snatch some feed. If you run across one that comes back before the others or won't move, just let her be. It's actually best if you can sneak a few extra eggs into her nest so she'll hatch them, too. In a little bit, she'll have a brood of baby chicks."

"All right, so first we scatter the feed. Over here?" She started tossing handfuls in front of her.

"That's it. Now when you've scattered some, be sure to scoot back—" His instructions came a bit too late, as the hungry clutch of chickens converged on the feed. . .and Delilah. She backed up against a fence. Paul waded through the squawking mass of feathers to help her edge away from the ravenous birds pecking very close to her feet.

"Thanks." The smile she shot him singed his heart like a lightning bolt. "They managed to corner me."

"You just didn't count on them being such greedy birds. The second the feed hits the ground, they're on their way. Now that they're good and distracted, we'll fill the basket with eggs."

He understood distraction all too well. She wore the same dress as yesterday, but the golden fabric hinted at the worth of its wearer.

They stepped into the coop and started rooting around for the eggs. "It's more like hunting eggs than gathering them, isn't it?" Delilah asked. "They hide them pretty well under all that straw and such."

"True. It's always like that when they're nesting. Sometimes a really determined hen will go into the taller weeds and build a secret nest for her eggs."

"I understand that. It's natural to want to protect what's yours, and who doesn't want to have some small space just to call their own?"

He'd like to call her his own, and he knew of a cozy little cabin they could share.

As the basket filled, one or two of the hens came back to settle on their nests again. He took some of the eggs and tucked them under the birds; then he led Delilah away from the coop. They dropped off the eggs in the kitchen, where Miriam was checking on a roast. Paul picked up the slop bucket with his good hand, and they headed off again. It wasn't until he reached the hog pen that he realized they had a slight problem.

"Usually I just grab the handle with one hand and the back of the bucket with the other and pour it into the trough. . . ."

She understood the problem. "Need a hand?"

"Literally." He smiled.

"Here, I'm the one who's supposed to be learning, anyway."

He looked at her, then the bucket. "It's kind of heavy."

His angel squared her shoulders and gave him a determined look. "I carried buckets of milk this morning. Besides, if Miriam can do it, so can I."

So she had an independent streak. Good. He didn't want some gingerbread miss who'd crumble at a word. He handed her the bucket and watched as she dumped its contents over the side of the pen and into the wooden trough.

Accustomed to dining at an earlier hour, the pigs were hungrier than usual. They snuffled over to plunge their snouts into the mess of grub. Delilah watched them thoughtfully.

"You know, they're kind of cute. Almost reminds me of. . ." Her voice trailed off, and he thought he knew why.

"Yep. They get almost as much food on themselves as in their mouths—just like Ginny Mae." That brought on another smile.

"I thought so, too, but I didn't want to compare such a precious little girl to a bunch of pigs."

"Well, since we both thought the same thing, there must be truth in it," he pointed out. "There's no harm in plain speaking."

"True, but honesty isn't a very common quality, is it?" She stated the observation with such quiet certainty, he wasn't sure how to respond.

"Why do you say that?" Though he wanted to know, he also aimed to fill the awkward silence as they walked back to the house.

"I'm not saying there aren't good people out there." Her eyes filled with resignation and regret. "You and your brothers seem to be some of them. But on the whole, people lie, or cheat, or hide things from others. Everyone makes decisions based on their own needs. That's the way of the world."

Paul knew she'd hopped from town to town with her father, that she didn't own much and wasn't married because of it. He hadn't thought of the people she'd been exposed to along the way—probably all drunks, hustlers, gamblers, and crooks. Little wonder she didn't have much faith in the general honesty of humankind.

"Everyone makes mistakes. It's a matter of how we deal with them before God. 'If we confess our sins, he is faithful and just to forgive us our sins, and to cleanse us from all unrighteousness.'"

"If He's able to do that, then why doesn't He help the people who can't help themselves but want to?" Her wistful tone hinted that she thought of her father's addiction to the gaming tables, but her statement chilled Paul to the core. Could it be that the woman he wanted to make his wife didn't even trust the Lord?

Dear Lord, am I wrong in thinking this is the woman Thou hast made to be my helpmate? She's been hurt in so many ways, but I see Thy grace in her smile. Please give me the words to soothe her and bring her closer to Thee.

"He works in mysterious ways, Delilah, so we don't always know when He's working in us. That doesn't mean He's not with us, but it doesn't mean He necessarily makes things the way we want them."

She refused to meet his gaze any longer. "Then what's the point of believing in Him?" she whispered sadly before turning and walking away.

Chapter 4

Two mornings later, Delilah eyed her primrose evening dress with distaste. Today was laundry day, so at least she'd get her traveling frock clean, but she'd been wearing the yellow one for three days straight. Unfortunately, she couldn't very well don the primrose satin evening gown to do laundry. That meant the yellow wouldn't get washed.

Well, one clean dress was better than none, and she'd take what she could get. As she prepared to get dressed, she heard a knock on the door.

"Who is it?" She tried to make her voice loud enough for the person to hear but soft enough so that it wouldn't wake Bryce and Logan in the next cabin.

"Alisa. May I come in?"

Delilah hurriedly put on her robe before unlatching the door.

Alisa walked in. "You know it's wash day today, right? Well, I know the dress you wore when you arrived was done in from traveling, and you've been wearing the yellow one all week. I've got plenty of dresses, so I thought this might fit." She held out a deep green day dress.

Despite knowing from Miriam that Alisa had recently inherited her wealth and that Alisa probably did own plenty of dresses, her kind gesture touched Delilah. "Thank you, but I really couldn't. You've already done so much for me."

"This shade looks awful on me, but with your coloring, it'll look fabulous on you. I only brought it back because I thought we could make something from the fabric—it's a bit long. Luckily, you're taller than I am. Why don't you try it on while I go set the table?" With that, Alisa placed the dress on Delilah's just-made bed and whisked out of the room.

It would be rude to refuse the beautiful garment. Delilah pulled it on, relieved to notice the small pockets concealed in the skirt. The sleeves and hemline both fell a bit short, but otherwise it fit perfectly. She always rolled up her sleeves, anyway, so that hardly mattered, and hopefully she could let down the hem. For now, it was passable. She put up her hair and hurried to the kitchen to see if she could help with breakfast. Thanks to Miriam, she knew how to make eggs and ham, stew, biscuits, cobbler, coffee, bread, bacon, and oatmeal. Well, she didn't remember how much flour and so forth by heart just yet, but she could follow the instructions well enough. Today she'd learn how to prepare flapjacks.

When she entered the kitchen, Alisa smiled. "See, it would be positively criminal for you not to wear that shade. Other than it being a little short, it's perfect for her, isn't it, Miriam?"

"She's right. Somehow the forest green suits your dark hair and light eyes. It's very becoming. I've already put on the coffee and made the flapjack batter. Are you ready to cook them?"

Delilah stifled a pang of disappointment over missing how to make the batter. She enjoyed cooking, even though she'd made a few minor mistakes—like with the eggs. Soon enough, she started ladling batter onto a large skillet, pouring smooth circles. Watching vigilantly for the circles to start bubbling, she lifted the edge of the flapjacks to make sure they'd cooked enough before flipping them.

Even though she tried to be careful, one slid off the griddle onto the stove, and somehow one ended up on the floor before she really got the hang of it. Miriam and Alisa laughed with her when she made a mistake and helped her make what had to be more than two dozen good-sized pancakes.

By the time the men wandered in, everything was ready. They all took their places, and this time, Paul said grace. Delilah sat at his injured left side, so she rested her hand on his shoulder. She might not believe all of what they said during prayer time or even at nighttime Bible readings, but she relished the feeling of closeness and the warmth of family.

"Dear heavenly Father, although we cannot see Thee, we know Thou art always with us. . . ."

How can we know He is always with us if we can't see Him?

"Please guide us through this day and bless the food Thou hast placed at our table. . . ."

Humph. Paul must mean the food Miriam, Alisa, and I placed at the table.

"Let us feel Thy presence and remember to thank Thee for the blessings Thou hast given us. . . ."

Well, she didn't know about feeling God's presence, but she did feel blessed to be with Miriam and Alisa and Polly and Ginny. . .even Paul. She hadn't made up her mind about the rest yet.

"And a special thanks to Thee for bringing Miriam's cousin here. We're glad to have her with us. . . ."

Miriam's cousin? His words warmed her heart until she really thought about it. Paul thought God had brought her to Chance Ranch? Wouldn't that mean He'd let her father die? How could that be right?

Maybe it was a kind thing to let him go, a tiny voice inside her spoke up. *You know how much unhappiness he felt that he never lived up to his promises to you. Traveling all the time and the pressure of not winning were slowly killing him anyway. Papa loved you. He'd be relieved to know you ended up here safe and sound.*

Delilah tried to choke back her tears. She couldn't think about that now. After taking a deep breath, she realized the prayer was over. Belatedly, she removed her hand from Paul's shoulder. To give herself something to do, she picked up the syrup jug and started passing it around.

"Are you all right?" Paul's quiet question unnerved her even more. When she faced him, she needed to take a deep breath.

"I'll be fine. I'm just. . ." She paused. "Why don't you let me cut up those pancakes for you? You'll have to tell me if they're any good. Miriam made the batter, but if they're burned, it's my fault." She busied herself with her fork and knife.

"All right." Again, he spoke softly so the others wouldn't easily overhear. "I won't push you, but we'll talk sooner or later."

She didn't want to think about what that meant and strengthened her resolve not to get too close to this man. He understood her far better than he had any right to, and it flustered her.

"Alisa, Delilah, and I would like to go to town tomorrow." Miriam's voice thankfully pulled her attention away. "Paul should go with us so Doc Morris can have a peek at his arm."

For some reason, Gideon didn't look too happy. "Normally, that'd be fine, but since Paul only has one good arm, I'd prefer you wait until one of the rest of us can go with you."

Everyone listened in, and Titus, Bryce, Logan, and even Dan nodded their agreement.

Miriam stood her ground. "Without Paul, you already have fewer hands to take care of the ranch, and we need to get some supplies."

"I'm sorry, sweetheart. I don't want the three of you women going to town alone. It's not safe."

Alisa chimed in. "We're just going to the Whites' general store. With Paul along, we ought to be fine. Even with only one sound arm, he's still stronger than any two of the town boys."

"I agree with Gideon." Titus threw in his two cents' worth. "You'll have to wait a bit."

"Besides, you know it isn't often we get to go to town." The hangdog look on Logan's face made Delilah smile, it was so comical. Bryce focused on his plate.

Paul studied the women. "What is it you need?"

Miriam seemed to welcome his practical question. "We're low on sugar and could use some baking soda and flour, too. I wanted to teach Delilah how to make baked apples, but we don't have enough. I need some oil for cooking and a new scrub brush, and I'd like to pick up a few things for the baby before I can't make it to town anymore."

"I love baked apples." Bryce's hopeful comment earned him black looks from his brothers.

"I don't take any offense at what Gideon said," Paul stated. "It's a matter of protection."

"What if I proved that we could protect ourselves?" Guffaws met Delilah's question.

"Well, if you can prove that, missy, you can go wherever you want." Dan obviously thought she couldn't, or he wouldn't have made the promise.

"Do you all mean that?" In her experience, men thought women were helpless. That made dirty, paunchy, foul-breathed drunks dangerous—which is precisely why she'd learned how to protect herself at an early age. Now as the strapping Chance men winked slyly at each other and gave hearty "Oh sure's," that assumption finally worked in her favor.

"All right, then. As soon as you're all done with your flapjacks, we'll go outside," Delilah decided.

Miriam tugged on her too-short sleeve. "Do you know what you're doing, Delilah?"

That tiny whisper reminded Delilah of how different they really were. "Trust me, Miriam. I have a few tricks of my own."

Dan threw his napkin on the table. "I'm ready. I can't wait to see this. I'm going to go put Polly and Ginny Mae in the play yard."

"If you're ready, I'd suggest you all get your pistols and meet me on the south side of the barn." The men stared at her.

"What for?"

"You'll see soon enough. Miriam, Alisa, would you join me, please?"

After the three women exited the room, Paul looked at his brothers. The expressions ranged from surprised to confused. Dan clearly expected to be entertained, but Paul held a few suspicions. Competency with a firearm became a necessity on the frontier—even for women—but marksmanship denoted long practice of the skill.

He stood up and strode to the door. Logan, Bryce, Titus, and Gideon quickly followed. Dan stayed to the back, with a girl tucked under each arm. When they got to the barn, Delilah quickly outlined the plan.

First, the girls would watch from a safe distance, tucked into a large shipping crate pushed against the barn. Then everyone participating in the makeshift "contest" would take turns shooting at a large knothole in a slab of wood Bryce leaned against the fence. They all inspected the target up close. Gideon cleared his throat. "Couple of close shots, and that board is going to be nothing but toothpicks."

"We'll use a bale of hay." Dan hiked toward the barn door and called over his shoulder, "Just stick a paper on it and stab a hole as the bull's-eye."

Soon a pencil dot marked the center of the knothole.

"There won't be a bull's-eye left after seven holes are put in it," Logan protested.

"Six," Dan smirked.

"We'll be able to declare a winner, at any rate," Bryce decided.

"How many paces?" Titus asked.

"I'd think ten would be enough, since the test is about self-defense. Agreed?"

Paul figured she was a fair shot, but so were all the Chance men. He resolved not to let her win, no matter how disappointed she'd look later. It wasn't good for a woman to get the idea she could go scampering off wherever and whenever she liked. He'd rather beat her this once than have her run into trouble later.

"Who goes first?" Miriam asked.

"You'll go from youngest to oldest," Alisa directed.

"What about ladies first?" Paul broke in. It would be nice to gauge the competition.

"I'd prefer to go last." Delilah ruled that out. "Logan, you're up."

Logan measured off ten paces, turned, and aimed. A few heartbeats after he fired, everyone rushed to the paper to see how he'd fared. Alisa whipped out her measuring tape.

"Two and a quarter inches left of center," she proclaimed as Miriam made a tiny L by the hole.

"Stupid thing always did shoot a bit to the left," Logan muttered about his Navy Colt. Bryce took the next turn. His bullet hit too far right but did slightly better.

"One and seven-eighths inches from center," Alisa announced, and Miriam scribbled a minuscule B.

Titus managed to shoot a bit high. "Best yet, darling," a not-quite impartial Alisa congratulated. "One and a quarter inch from center."

"I object," Logan broke in. "Titus sweet-talked the judge!" Miriam assured him Alisa measured correctly, and the competition continued. Paul's turn came quickly.

Now he'd take his chance to prove that even though he'd gotten thrown from his horse, he could still hold his own. He issued a swift prayer. *Lord, I know pride goes before a fall, but since I already fell this week, I'd be mighty obliged if You'd consider it even and let me do well today.*

He counted off ten long paces and aimed. While Alisa and Miriam hustled over to the target, he held his breath.

The call of "a half inch right from center" was music to his ears. Anyone would be hard pressed to beat that—even Gideon, whom Paul viewed as his only real competition. He risked a look at Delilah. Her appreciative smile took him by surprise, because she seemed completely unruffled. Could she possibly beat him?

Dan shot a little low, "one inch from center," and Gideon matched Paul's shot with "a half inch left from center." The only way Delilah could possibly win would be to shoot dead center between the holes Paul's and Gideon's bullets made.

"Would you like to borrow my gun?" Gideon offered.

To the astonishment of everyone present, Delilah pulled a small Derringer from a pocket in her dress.

"I always carry one of my own." The brothers watched, flabbergasted, as she took ten strides, hardly bothered to aim, and fired.

Paul prayed fervently as Alisa measured. "A quarter inch from center, low." Delilah had won.

She couldn't remember the last time she'd had so much fun, Delilah decided. Logan seemed awed, Bryce eyed her with a new respect, Dan looked downright mutinous, and Gideon and Titus moped. As for Paul, she averted her face from his piercing gaze.

"I suppose that means we get to go to town after all, ladies," she said, addressing a beaming Alisa and grinning Miriam.

"I don't think so," Dan growled. "You needed to prove that you three women would be protected. What happens after your one shot?" To underscore his point, he snatched the compact gun from her grasp.

"It won't do you much good, and I don't like the thought of you carrying this around my daughters." He stalked off.

Quick as a flash, Delilah grabbed the small knife she kept strapped to her ankle. "Daniel Chance, you will return that." Her voice held a warning even he couldn't completely ignore.

He stopped and turned around. "I don't think so." The next minute, Daniel groped the top of his head and started looking around. Obviously he didn't understand—no sudden breeze had snatched his hat.

His much-used hat hung pinned to the barn behind him by a small knife with a mother-of-pearl handle. As he gaped at it, Delilah swept past, pulled the knife from the wall in a single jerk, and turned to face Daniel, holding his hat behind her back.

"My gun, if you please." She held out a commanding hand.

Daniel all but gnashed his teeth before giving in and getting his hat in return.

A pleased smile spread across her face. "Thank you."

"My hat. My poor hat." Dan sat on his bed, looking mournfully at the hat he held.

Paul bit back a grin. "You shouldn't have tried to take her gun, Dan."

"A girl like that has no business owning a gun. Or being able to handle a knife like that."

"Think about it, Daniel. Her father gambled his way from town to town, dragging her along with him. Who knows what kind of trouble a pretty woman like her ran into? I hate to think of it, but she probably did have occasion to use them." Paul saw the light dawn in Dan's eyes as his habitual scowl deepened.

"Well, she won't need 'em here, that's for sure. And neither will my girls. If anyone comes near a-one of them, I'll skin him alive. Her papa didn't do right by her, poor thing."

Dan's words just about summed up Paul's own feelings on the subject. Paul punched his pillow into shape with more force than was absolutely necessary.

Maybe her father didn't, but I will.

Chapter 5

Long before the sun came up the next morning, Delilah awoke to someone knocking on her door. Apparently the Chance clan didn't think she'd get up on her own, as this was the second time in as many days. Hastily pulling on her wrapper, she heard Miriam's urgent whisper.

"Delilah? Delilah!"

Delilah wrenched open the door, and Miriam, clad in only her nightgown and robe, scurried in.

"What's wrong?" Delilah demanded, dozens of scenarios in which one or more of this precious family were gravely injured.

"Nothing's wrong!" Upon closer scrutiny, Miriam's face, flushed with cold, seemed more excited than frantic.

"Do you remember how we made butter the day Paul broke his arm, since we could get store credit for it?"

Delilah nodded, confused. "Yes, but it's so early in the morning, Miriam! What's going on?"

"Well, Gideon said last night that any credit I managed to wrangle from Mr. White could be ours to spend however Alisa and I choose!"

"That's wonderful, but my mind's not working well enough this early to figure out why you're jumping like a grasshopper." Obviously her cousin had lost her mind.

"I need your help, and the sooner we start, the better off we'll be. I don't want to go to Alisa and Titus's cabin, so it's up to us to fetch the cream from the springhouse and make as much butter as we can this morning!"

Suddenly all became clear. Miriam wanted the extra currency for their trip to town. Even Delilah knew that pregnant women sometimes had odd starts, but apparently Miriam hadn't gone mad after all.

"All right. Go get dressed, and I'll meet you in the barn so we can milk Sir and Mister."

"Thank you, Delilah!" Miriam rushed out of the room.

Delilah put on her freshly laundered blue serge traveling frock. The widest of her skirts, it permitted her to easily get in and out of the buckboard. Besides, they were setting out early, and the heavy fabric would afford more protection against the sharp morning air.

Throwing on a heavy shawl, she tromped out to the barn. Miriam was already there, starting on Sir. Delilah set a stool next to Mister and started milking. When they'd finished, they hauled the fresh milk to the springhouse.

They brought the cream back into the kitchen, where the paddle churn waited. Delilah scooped in some cream and started churning while Miriam scurried about, feeding the chickens and pigs and gathering eggs—until Alisa came into the kitchen.

"Is it time to start breakfast already?" Miriam couldn't disguise her disappointment. They usually began breakfast at about five o'clock. Since she and Delilah had started working almost two hours before, they'd expected to get more done.

"No, I just woke up early and couldn't get back to sleep. It's about half past four now." Since Alisa had brought back a mantel clock from her old home, she alone knew exact time. "You wanted to get an early start on packing things for town, too?"

"Gideon said we could spend all the credit we get for eggs and butter on whatever we like!"

"Let's get going, then!" Apparently Alisa was quicker on the uptake than Delilah early in the morning. "Where do we stand now?"

Delilah did some quick tabulating. "We made eight bricks on Thursday, and there are still nine in the springhouse from before that. I've finished one this morning, and this batch is ready for rinsing." Alisa took over the churn while Delilah rinsed and pressed the butter.

"Miriam, how are we for eggs?"

"The day Paul broke his arm, we didn't collect the eggs until after breakfast, which was about three dozen. Yesterday we had flapjacks, so I saved another dozen. This morning I collected another three, so we have seven dozen to take to town." Miriam finished packing the eggs and started to pick up a crate. In a few quick steps, Delilah took it from her.

"You shouldn't be lifting anything in your condition. If I catch you trying to haul anything today, I'm going to side with the men and say you shouldn't go to town." She made the warning as ominous as she could, but Miriam just shrugged and started the coffee before getting to work on the oatmeal. Delilah stacked the crates outside the door.

"Not bad," Alisa said approvingly as she plopped the butter into the bowl for the next washing. "I'll have another load of butter done this morning. We should leave one in the springhouse since we'll be wanting to do some baking and one more for the oatmeal this morning. Delilah, how does that add up?"

"Nineteen for town." They didn't have much time left, so everyone buckled down. Delilah just started pressing the final brick of butter when the men began trickling in. First came Gideon, with a smile and a peck on the cheek for Miriam. Logan and Bryce came in next. Logan looked suspiciously at the pot on the stove.

"What's that?"

"Oatmeal," Delilah answered. Logan groaned and grumped about for the remainder of breakfast. Not only was he stuck at home while Paul and the women got to go to town, but he couldn't look forward to the standard three feasts a day. Delilah thought the oatmeal deserved more credit. Miriam added generous amounts of sugar during the cooking, and the butter and preserves on the table let everybody doctor theirs as little or as much as they liked.

During breakfast, the women handed out last-minute instructions. Dan would watch Ginny Mae and Polly. Miriam set out bread and meat for them to make sandwiches for lunch. As soon as the meal ended, the men loaded half of the steer they'd butchered yesterday into the buckboard, along with the eggs Miriam packed while the other women did the dishes.

Usually one of the men would drive, but since Paul had a broken arm, the responsibility fell to the most competent woman. Alisa took the reins because Miriam's delicate condition excluded her from taking on any strenuous activities.

Paul insisted Miriam sit beside Alisa rather than ride in the back with half of a dead steer, which left Delilah to share the cramped space with him. She took care to sit on his right side so she wouldn't bump his injured arm. Still, it didn't do much good if he was as uncomfortable as she felt. Her arm pressed against his, and they hunched so close, even their legs touched. As usual, sitting next to him made her feel almost petite, but the crowded seating arrangement wasn't to her liking. *Why did I ever put on this shawl?* Delilah wondered. The morning was nothing if not overly warm.

Usually Paul opted to ride Speck rather than pile into the wagon, but for once, he didn't mind being packed in like a sardine. Despite the butchered steer sharing the space, he relished Delilah's company. Noticing how she took special care to sit on his right gave him an idea. He casually moved a crate of eggs between him and the side of the wagon, pretending to rest his arm on it. Hopefully, she'd never suspect he did it intentionally so they'd have less room.

It worked. The length of her leg pressed against his, her arm against his, and he could catch the scent of violets in her hair. He bit back a grin and leaned back to enjoy the next hour as they rode to town. Yep, he reckoned breaking his arm was probably the smartest thing he'd ever done.

They reached Reliable far too soon to his way of thinking. Miriam and Alisa hitched the horses while he jumped out of the wagon and swept Delilah down with his good arm. The men on the street jabbed each other and gawked at her.

If he could, he'd have held on for a lot longer, but he needed to help Miriam. By the time they reached the back of the general store, a horde of bachelors straggled in behind them. Paul glared at each and every one of them, wishing he could make them all leave.

Reba White bustled out to the counter, beaming from ear to ear. "Miriam! Alisa! It's so good to see you again. How've y'all been?" She caught sight of Delilah. "And who's this pretty young thing?"

That let loose a torrent of remarks from the rabble behind them. "Yeah! Who's she?"

"Where'd she come from?"

"Marry me!"

"No, me!"

Paul stepped in front of the women and spoke in a low voice. His tone served as a warning. "This here is a guest at the Chance Ranch. If anybody wants to speak to the lady, they'll have to act like a gentleman. If you can't behave yourselves, you'll have more trouble than you can handle." Out of the corner of his eye, he saw that Delilah stood in front of Miriam, her hands in her pockets.

"Aw, you Chance boys have all the luck."

"It's not fair. There weren't no decent women in the town but Reba and Priscilla when Miriam came," another interrupted.

"And Gideon got her, and Titus snatched Alisa. You Chance men can't go round taking all the women to be found. Ain't neighborly."

General mutters of agreement rumbled as the throng moved closer. "Ya oughta introduce us proper-like."

Gus White came out from behind the curtain in the back of the store, brandishing a broom.

"Get out, you lazy good-fer-nothin's. You can't stick around hasslin' my customers."

"But, Gus, we just wanna—Hey!"

Gus thwapped the dirty ruffian on the head with the broom. Paul didn't remember the last time he'd felt so much brotherly love for any soul as he felt for Gus at that moment.

"I said git!" Gus punctuated his words with a well-placed prod to another man's backside as the crowd beat a hasty retreat.

"All right, all right. We're goin'. We didn't mean nothin'."

As soon as they left, Gus turned, his scowl replaced by a genial smile. "Hello, Mrs. Miriam, Mrs. Alisa. Ma'am. Howdy, Titus. What'dya do to your arm?"

"This un's Paul, Gus." Reba shook her head, then spoke to the women. "I declare, if there really were more women around here, he'd probably forget my name, too. Well, seems to me you've got some news to tell." She waited expectantly.

"Paul broke his arm, Reba, and this is my cousin, Delilah," Miriam quickly explained.

Reba gave Delilah an assessing once-over. "I'm right glad to see you, Miss Delilah. Don't worry none about that bunch—they're lonely, and you'll probably get more decent offers than indecent, if you take my meaning." She straightened her shoulders. "I'm afraid Doc Morris is out of town, Paul. Will you be all right?"

"Miriam already set the break, and it hasn't been troubling me too much. My arm'll be fine, Mrs. Reba. And how've you been?"

"Can't complain," Gus remarked. "What can we do for you folks today?"

Alisa rattled off a list of goods—rice, beans, flour, meal, sugar, spices, apples, cocoa, maple syrup, canning jars, buttons, and vegetable seeds—then turned to Paul. He added tacks, ammunition, spring tonic, and a salt lick to the list.

"We slaughtered a steer yesterday, Gus. It's out in the wagon." The Chance family never bothered with store credit if they could avoid it.

"Fair enough." Gus turned when he heard the door creak open. "I told everyone to get outta here."

"We heard." A wiry man made his way to the back of the store, followed by two others.

"Howdy, Paul," one of them greeted. "We done heard you broke your arm and figgered ya'd need a hand with unloadin' your wagon."

"Perfect." Gus ushered them back out the door and called to Paul, "That ought to be about even, after what you brought me last time," before turning back to the ladies.

Delilah watched Paul leave with some regret. He'd been so strong when he stood up to that awful pack of men. True, they'd been more curious than dangerous, but there were some rough characters mingled in, and you never could tell when a crowd could turn into a mob. She knew how to take care of herself, but she'd never been up against a dozen men, and she couldn't forget Miriam and Alisa. Paul had immediately placed himself between them and the townsmen; even with a broken arm, he'd had an air of power and control she could only admire.

Her reverie was interrupted by the sound of Miriam's voice asking Gus for peppermint sticks and licorice for the girls. The whitewash she listed surprised everyone.

"You're gonna whitewash your cabin, Miriam?" Reba asked, smiling. "You'll be surprised at the difference."

Miriam nodded. "I've been wanting to for a while now. That's it for the Chance account, Reba, but there are a few other matters to settle. I've got some eggs and butter out in the wagon."

"Butter? Nobody round here bothers to make it." Gus's voice betrayed his eagerness. "I can give you, say, twenty cents a pound, Miriam."

"Oh, I'd say twenty-three is fairer. We both know you'll sell it for more than that. Anyway, I've got ten bricks I can sell you, and I'll take the other nine to Mr. Scudd at the restaurant."

"I'll give you twenty-five cents a brick if you sell it all to me."

"Deal. You'll make a tidy profit when you sell it to the restaurant, too."

"We've also brought seven dozen eggs," Alisa chimed in.

Gus nodded. "I can give you twenty cents a dozen for those. It's a bit high, but nobody around here really raises chickens, and the ones as do eat their own eggs. There's plenty who will pay for 'em. Let me see, that's nineteen bricks of butter at two bits each, and seven dozen eggs at twenty cents a dozen—that'll be six fifteen, total. Did you want cash?"

"I'll tell you what, Mr. White. Why don't you and Paul haul in the goods from the wagon while we women discuss what we'd like to do."

"I need about five yards of flannel and six of the green gingham, Reba, and a special order for baby buttons." Reba, busily writing down the order, broke her pencil.

"Did I hear that right? Did you say 'baby buttons' just as innocently as could be? You're in the family way! So that's why your cousin is here! Oh, this'll be the first babe since your sister's, God rest her soul. And you hiding it behind your cloak! You give old Reba a hug this minute!" She came around the counter and all but smothered Miriam in a jubilant embrace. She shared an amused glance with Alisa, but Delilah felt the same way Reba did. Miriam loved Hannah and Dan's girls, but she had told Delilah in her letters how much she wanted children of her own.

Maybe someday I'll finally have a family, too.

"How far along are you? Are you feeling all right?"

"I'm doing just fine, and I expect the baby in about four months."

"Oooh. 'Four months,' she says. That means you're five along and haven't told me. Shame on you! Oh, but it doesn't matter, I'm that happy for you. Which pattern of flannel would you like?"

"The blue plaid, please."

"You've already got an inkling that your babe will be a strapping boy, do you? Small wonder when your husband has five brothers. There you are. What else can I get you?"

Miriam turned to Alisa. "We earned about three dollars each, and I've spent mine. What would you like to spend your share on?"

"I brought back everything I needed from San Francisco, but it seems to me that Delilah did an awful lot of churning. You'll need a good cape and skirt for the winter—it's never too early to think about these things. I'd say we should get some good wool."

"Wonderful idea. I thought the same thing." Miriam laughed. "We'll use most of the green gingham I'm buying for a work dress."

"No. That's your money. You should spend it on yourself, both of you." Delilah didn't want any handouts.

" 'The labourer is worthy of his hire,' the Bible tells us. You've done a lot of work on the homestead, and you'll need heavier clothing when it snows. Since the Lord blessed me with everything I need, I want you and Miriam to split it." Alisa was rapidly becoming the most generous person Delilah had ever known. If she refused the gift, it would hurt Alisa's feelings. Besides, they were telling her that they wanted her to stay through winter—that would mean a whole year here!

"All right." Delilah gave in as graciously as she could. "What will I need?"

"I'd say three yards of the gray plaid with black and red shooting through it for a skirt and about four yards of black for a good warm cape. You're tall but slender, so it will be enough," Alisa decided.

"Wool's the most expensive fabric for good reason. You'll be nice and cozy in it," Reba said with approval. "The seven yards comes to about two dollars' worth. What else?"

Delilah looked to Miriam and Alisa. "I'd like a charcoal pencil for my drawing and a few packets of flower seeds to plant in front of the cabin, if that's all right."

"I'd forgotten you draw, Delilah. You'll have to show me some of the pictures you've made when we get back," Miriam exclaimed.

"What a wonderful idea! We've tried, but the place still seems more masculine than anything else. Some flowers would be welcome." Alisa's approval made Delilah decide on the spot she'd plant some in front of her new friend's cabin the moment she got a chance. For now, she had a home—and they wanted her for a whole year. She might as well enjoy it while it lasted.

Chapter 6

Delilah stepped into the kitchen with four dozen eggs and a smile. She'd now been at Chance Ranch for an entire week—longer than at any residence she'd ever known. She'd come to look forward to waking up and joining Miriam and Alisa in the kitchen, where she'd learn how to make something new and delicious.

"Are we getting started on the baked apples?" She remembered promising Bryce his favorite treat.

"No. We'll make those so we can have them right after lunch. Everybody gets one, so it wouldn't be enough for breakfast." Miriam placed a towel over a bowl of dough. "This morning we'll make French toast."

"For the Lord's Day." Alisa moved a stack of thick slices toward the stove.

"Oh." Delilah felt the smile slide off her face. The Lord's Day? For Papa, that was just a day to sleep off the effects of Saturday's revelry since the saloons were closed, but she knew that wasn't how most people behaved. When she was a little girl, Mama would read from the Bible or, if the town were big enough, take her to hear a preacher. The very thought of listening to someone expound on the idea of what a sinner she was for hours on end made Delilah's stomach lurch.

"The rain's wiped away any chance of anyone coming over for the service, so the men can relax a bit instead of setting up outside the barn."

Miriam's words lifted Delilah's spirits. No preacher and a day of relaxation didn't sound bad at all. Besides, at least for today, Paul wouldn't have to feel bad about not being able to help his brothers until his arm healed.

"What can I do to help?" Time passed quickly as she got swept up in making breakfast. Mixing eggs with cinnamon and milk and then dipping bread into the mixture before frying it to a golden brown was much easier than she'd thought it would be, and soon the men began filtering through the door, noses twitching appreciatively.

After breakfast, everyone pitched in to clean up. The table was cleared and the dishes done in record time. Surveying the sparkling kitchen, Delilah wondered what the men would do all day. Her question was answered when Gideon brought in a worn Bible and settled to the right of his usual position at the head of the table. As though the action were an unspoken command, the rest of the family flocked to join him. Reluctant to join in for reasons too numerous to count, Delilah wondered whether there was any way to excuse herself. Obviously this was a family religious gathering. Since she didn't believe as they did and couldn't count herself as a member of the family, there was no place for her here.

She watched as Paul took the seat at the head of the table, waited until everyone else was situated, and beckoned for her to sit at his left. When she hesitated, Gideon shot a glance at Miriam, who rose from her seat, walked over, and took Delilah's hand.

"Come on, it's time for worship. It's all right if you don't know the words to the hymns Titus will lead us in. Gideon will be praying for our family and friends, and Paul has chosen the scripture for today."

With that, any hope of wiggling out of the situation disappeared more quickly than the French toast had earlier. Pasting a smile on her face, Delilah slid onto the bench and bowed her head as Paul and Ginny Mae each held one of her hands. Clinging to the comfort of Paul's warm, steady grasp, she blinked back tears at Gideon's prayer.

"Lord, we come before you happy and whole and blessed beyond what we deserve. Right now, we know that across the world some people are not so fortunate. Please be with those who lost their homes and loved ones when Vesuvius burst open and rained fire upon the land. We know Thou art there, keeping watch over Thy children. Please help us never to lose sight of how blessed we are by Thy love. Amen."

Titus asked if anyone had any particular hymn they'd like to sing.

"I'd love to sing 'Holy, Holy, Holy,'" Alisa offered.

Delilah closed her eyes as everyone followed Titus's deep baritone. Although she tried to ignore the lyrics, instead silently reciting recipes she'd learned or the kinds of flowers she'd plant in the garden, the lovely music broke through her thoughts. She didn't want to listen because she didn't agree with what was said.

How can they think that God is "merciful and mighty"? If He really exists, He took away Mama and didn't help Papa overcome his weaknesses.

"Early in the morning, our song shall rise to Thee. . . ." The words and melody were so lovely! Even Daniel's scowl faded as Polly's little voice piped in, trilling the words in slightly off-key exuberance.

After another song Delilah didn't recognize, Paul started the lesson.

"Here we sit, surrounded by friends and family in a solid home on good land. These are only a few of the blessings God has bestowed upon us. But I've been thinking about Mama and Papa a lot lately, how proud they'd be to see how much our family has grown. They built the foundation on faith and love, and it has withstood hard times. But in chasing the past, we can easily lose track of all the wonder of the present"—his eyes met hers—"and the promise of the future.

"The Bible reading is about following the Lord wherever He sees fit to lead and giving thanks for the blessings He provides, rather than looking back on things that are no more."

The lump in her throat swelled at Paul's words, and anger pulsed at her temples. *Is he talking about me? It's only right and natural to grieve when a loved one is lost!* Taking a deep breath, she listened as Paul read about a city given over entirely to sin. Only one man in the entire city found favor with God. Well, she could easily believe that. After all, as far as she could see, God was mighty selective about the people He looked after. Mama prayed and read the Bible every day and did her best to be a good wife and mother. She begged for God to help Papa stop gambling and longed for the security of a home. Instead, she died in a strange town with no money to see a doctor. If Mama, whose heart held no selfishness, wasn't good enough for God, there was precious little hope left for anyone else.

Paul read on. " 'And when the morning arose, then the angels hastened Lot, saying, Arise, take thy wife, and thy two daughters, which are here; lest thou be consumed in the iniquity of the city. . . . And it came to pass, when they had brought them forth abroad, that he said, Escape for thy life; look not behind thee. . . .' "

Ah, so there's the part where he was talking about not thinking on the past. Comforted that Paul hadn't been pointing her out, she listened more carefully as he continued.

" 'Behold now, thy servant hath found grace in thy sight, and thou hast magnified thy mercy, which thou hast shewed unto me in saving my life. . . .' "

Wait a minute. God saved Lot's life from whom? From Himself? That doesn't seem very benevolent. So He saves one man and destroys entire cities, and that is magnifying His mercy? Maybe there's a turn in the middle, and He saves the cities to show His mercy! Delilah listened intently to the next verses.

" 'Then the LORD rained upon Sodom and upon Gomorrah brimstone and fire from the LORD out of heaven; and he overthrew those cities, and all the plain, and all the inhabitants of the cities, and that which grew upon the ground. But his wife looked back from behind him, and she became a pillar of salt.' "

Nope. He destroyed the cities. Even Lot couldn't depend on God to protect his family. No, this God who smote entire cities and turned a woman into salt simply for watching can't be the God of love, too. It just doesn't fit. Where is the lesson here?

"So the lesson here"—Paul's voice mimicked her thoughts almost exactly—"is stated by Christ Himself in Luke 17. This tale is specifically used by the Savior to remind us that we need to make Him the focus of our lives.

" 'Remember Lot's wife. Whosoever shall seek to save his life shall lose it; and whosoever shall lose his life shall preserve it.' "

That makes no sense!

"Now this may seem to contradict itself," Paul clarified, "but Jesus isn't just talking about life as we know it, but eternal life, too. The only way to gain eternal life is by giving Christ this one."

His words sent shivers up Delilah's spine. *How can I be asked to give my life to the control of someone when everyone I've depended on has let me down?*

"Once we acknowledge God as the one who created us and give ourselves to Him, we will live forever in His grace. Let's pray."

Thoughts whirled through Delilah's head as the family joined hands once more. *How could anyone live forever? It just isn't possible.* She'd seen death in all its horrible finality—no one could escape the threat that came and stole all smiles and laughter and life.

Mama gave her life to Jesus. How can I trust Him when He took Mama away and didn't save her? And how can I tell these people who believe in salvation they're wrong when I don't understand it? Why do they have the same peace and joy in God that Mama had? Delilah's heart ached as the others sang another hymn she didn't recognize. *Why can't I understand what they believe and be as happy as they are? What am I missing?*

Her thoughts came to a halt as she recognized the melody everyone sang. As the words poured forth, Delilah remembered the hymn as one of her mother's favorites. Despite her resolution not to take part, she mouthed the words:

"Blest be the tie that binds
Our hearts in Christian love. . ."

She snuck a glance at Paul, only to find him watching her. At his encouraging nod, she raised her voice and joined in:

"The fellowship of kindred minds
Is like to that above."

Amid the deep voices of the brothers around her, Delilah could almost hear her mother's clear soprano. By the third verse, she blinked back tears at the memory.

It was no use. God had abandoned her long ago, and there was no tie to bind her to these good people, no matter how much she wished for one. At least there was one thing she could take away from Paul's lesson. She didn't have to keep reliving the past and regretting what she couldn't change. Instead, she'd focus on these people who opened their home and hearts to her. For now.

Paul smiled as he remembered the service that morning. His lovely little lady couldn't carry a tune in a bucket, but somehow that added to her charm. After all, no one was perfect. And if he wasn't mistaken, the Lord had begun answering his prayer about softening her heart to the truth. He'd watched her reaction to the hymns and the Bible reading and seen a woman lost in deep thought and longing. It was too much to think she'd already come completely to God, but the seed was planted. *Thank You, Father.*

"Hey! It's your turn, Paul!" Titus called.

Logan waved a horseshoe as his brother walked across the barn.

"If I were you, I wouldn't be so eager to lose first place," Paul joked.

"What?" Logan joined in the good-natured ribbing. "I know you always said you could beat us with one hand tied behind your back, but I never thought to see it tested!"

Paul stifled a groan as he remembered his arrogant boast from last month. He hadn't expected to have to prove it! Pulling his good arm back, he tossed the horseshoe at the spike, only opening his eyes when he heard a promising clang.

"Well, I'll be." Gideon laughed. "I reckon he was right after all. Don't suppose you'd care to repeat that performance?"

"What, and lose my moment of victory?" Paul protested. "Nope. I think I'll just stroll inside for some cool water and see how supper is coming along." He headed for the house, ignoring the taunts aimed at him by his brothers about how he just didn't think he could make that shot twice in a row.

Truthfully, he probably couldn't. But he had a powerful thirst to quench. He opened the door to a mix of tantalizing smells.

"Need some water?" Miriam handed him a cupful.

"How's supper coming along? Smells good enough in here to tempt the angels."

"We just put the roast in the oven. The biscuits are rising and the apples are ready for baking, but we'll put them in later so they don't get cold." Alisa smiled. "Did Titus put you up to throwing horseshoes regardless of your arm?"

Holding back a grin at how well Alisa knew her husband, Paul tried to think of an answer that wouldn't get them both in trouble.

"Just one to defend my place. Besides, it's not my throwing arm."

"I warned you to take it easy!" Miriam chided, but she couldn't hide the laughter in her tone. "You'd think first place in an ongoing horseshoes competition wouldn't be as important as your health."

"Are you all right?" Delilah gently adjusted his sling, her fingers brushing his forearm when she made sure his sleeve was still rolled up. He knew she meant to keep his sling as dry as possible in the rainy weather, but the heat following her touch succeeded more than she knew.

"Fine." He turned to Polly to mask the gruffness of his voice. "What do you have there, baby girl?"

"Lilah's going to teach me a game!" She held up a pack of cards.

"Cards?" He raised an eyebrow.

"I said it would be fine to have a hand of Old Maid," Miriam cut in. "Would you like to join Delilah and Polly? I'm sure Polly would love to have you on her team."

"I got Unca Paul!" Polly crowed, then her face fell. "But who have you got, Lilah?"

He saw a flash of sadness cross Delilah's face and knew she thought about her parents again. He stepped in. "Ginny Mae, of course. Come on and take a seat."

Delilah had Ginny Mae on her lap and held the cards, taking out all the queens but one. She held up the remaining female face card. "All right, Polly. This is the Old Maid. Every other card has a match—fours go together, nines go together, and so on. You want to find a match to all of your cards, because the first one who does, wins. The Old Maid doesn't have a match, though, so whoever has her in their hand at the end of the game loses, all right?"

"Okay. How do we get the matches?" Polly's tiny brow furrowed in serious concentration as she dangled her feet off the edge of the bench.

"First, I'm going to split the cards." Delilah dealt the hand. "Now you need to look at your deck with Uncle Paul and take out all the matches while Ginny Mae and I do the same thing."

There was silence as Paul helped Polly match cards while Delilah's partner helpfully stuck peas in the box with the extra queens and waved it in the air.

"I gotta question. What if we got three cards that are the same number? Like these?" Polly held up two sixes and a nine.

"Well, honey, that's close, but not quite. Do you remember how Auntie Miriam's been teaching you numbers? Well, you haven't gotten to these yet, but a six looks like an upside-down nine. See?" He turned the cards for her inspection.

"Oh." Polly nodded sagely, her braids bouncing. "That's why there's more spots on this one, right?"

He and Delilah shared grins over that astute observation as Polly waved the nine of clubs.

"Right. But see, here we have three fours. So we'll take out the two with the same color," he plunked two down on the table, "and keep this one until we get another four. Got it?"

"Got it." Polly beamed at him. "We got rid of lots of cards, so"—she lowered her voice—"we're gonna win, right? 'Cause we don't have the one with the lady on it?"

"That's where it gets tricky," Paul warned. "See, Delilah should have the same number of cards we do, so we have to pick one from her to try and make another match. But if we pick the Old Maid, and we still have it by the end, we'll lose. Are you ready?"

Polly stretched across the table toward Delilah's hand, and the game began. The Old Maid traveled from team to team until finally, Polly sat with one card while Delilah held two.

"All right, Polly. You've got to pick one. We're looking for a two, but if you get the Old Maid, Delilah might still win."

Polly grasped a card and turned it around. "We won, Unca Paul! Look! Lilah's an o–old ma–aid, Lilah's the o–old ma–aid," she singsonged, then stopped suddenly to tug on his sleeve. "Whatsa old maid?"

"Well. . ." Paul was at a loss for words.

"It's a lady who's not married even though she's been old enough to be for a while, Polly." Delilah's tremulous smile twisted something inside him.

"So you really *are* an old maid!" Delighted, Polly scooted off the bench to go tell Miriam.

"No, you aren't," Paul stated firmly, holding Delilah's gaze.

"Yes, I am. It's all right," she assured him as she picked up Ginny Mae and went after Polly.

Not for long, if the Lord's will and mine are the same.

Chapter 7

Later that week, Delilah looked at the small plot of land she and Paul had been working on. Together, they'd watered the soil for three days before Logan and Bryce could hoe it up easily and turn the dirt to let in air. Her nose wrinkled at the memory of the fertilizer they'd used the previous morning.

Today would make it all worthwhile. Today they'd finally begin planting the seeds and bulbs.

I wonder whether I'll be here long enough to see them bloom. I hope so. It will be beautiful next year with all those colors. And Polly and Ginny Mae want to help me water and weed. They may pull up the plants when they begin sprouting, so I'll have to teach them which ones are flowers.

Delilah went to her cabin to fetch the flower seeds. She stepped around the cabin to find Paul playing patty-cake with the girls. Ginny Mae followed the pattern as Polly sat in Paul's lap and tried to fill in for his left arm. As giggles floated through the air, Delilah's breath caught at the homey scene.

"No, Unca Paul. You forgot this one!" Polly gestured in the air.

Delilah let loose a peal of laughter at Paul's abashed expression, catching everyone's attention. His handsome face broke into a grin.

"Looks like Delilah's here just in time to save me from any more mistakes." He stood up. "Are you ready to plant the flowers?"

"Yea!" Polly grabbed Ginny Mae's hand, and they both raced toward the garden.

Paul fell in step beside Delilah. "Have you decided where you want everything?"

The humor in his tone almost made her blush. She'd written lists of every kind of flower they had, then sketched where she would plant each variety. She'd taken some jokes about how many times she'd changed her mind but knew they meant no harm by it. Honestly, there were so many things to consider! She didn't want to clump all of the same color together but instead wanted to spread them out so it looked like a rainbow touched the earth. Also, some of the flowers would bloom in different months, and she couldn't leave patches bare while others sprang in glorious blossoms.

Maybe she was going a bit overboard, but the Chances just couldn't understand why she wanted this garden to be absolutely perfect. Even after she left, this garden should stay beautiful, a lasting testament that she'd made a difference somewhere.

"I think so." Delilah smiled up at Paul, the only person who'd been patient enough to help her throughout her quest. Well, Miriam had helped her know when each plant would blossom, but Paul spent hours helping her remove all the rocks and prepare the land. He'd actually chosen the plot for having plenty of sunlight with adequate protection against winter winds. His smile and able advice helped make this project such a joy. Not that she knew how to tell him!

"Do you have the markers?" His deep voice broke into her thoughts.

"Right here." She brandished the small pieces of wood on which she'd painstakingly written the name of each flower she would plant. The clever folding desk in her room had been much used lately.

"All right. I've numbered each stick, and here's a little map for where each number goes, so the flowers will be planted there." The morning whirled by as Paul helped Ginny Mae dig shallow holes while Polly practiced her numbers counting out seeds to drop inside. Delilah gently dusted them again with dirt.

"What will these look like?" Polly's oft-repeated question let Delilah describe the pretty flowers.

"From March to May, we'll see white evening primroses and blue wild hyacinths," she described, pointing to the areas where they'd planted the seeds. "April will bring lavender godetias, spring beauties, and live-forever."

"Like we're going to in heaben?" Ginny Mae's question sent pangs through Delilah's heart. How could she explain now that a flower called "live-forever" didn't really live forever—and neither could she.

"That's right, ladybug." Paul stepped in. "In a lot of ways, flowers are just like we are. They need food and water and sunshine and love and all the good things God made for us. But you won't always be able to see the flowers. You have to know that they bloom and fade away, but they make seeds. See, that's the really important part that makes it so this special flower can bloom again later."

Polly frowned in concentration. "So how's that like us? You can always see me."

"Do you remember what we told you about heaven, Polly?"

"Yes, it's a beautiful place where I'll see Mommy again, and we'll live forever with Jesus!" Her face brightened.

"Do you remember how you have to leave here first?" At the little girl's nod, he continued. "It's just the same as this flower. See, Mommy faded away and left here, but her soul, just like the seeds, is made of something stronger, and it's that part that goes to heaven and makes it so we'll see her again if we believe in Jesus."

" 'Cause she had Jesus in her heart," Polly finished, taking her sister's hand.

Tears pricked Delilah's eyes as she watched the tender scene. If all that was true—and she was by no means certain it was—then Mama would be in heaven because she believed in Christ. *But I won't be there to see her because I can't believe.* The helplessness of it all washed over her in a suffocating wave. Paul's words from the day before echoed in her mind. *"The only way to gain eternal life is by giving Christ this one."*

Polly's voice interrupted her thoughts. "We can't 'member Mama, but she loves us, Ginny Mae."

"Jesus gots Mama," Ginny Mae stated firmly, then reached up to tug on the end of Polly's braid. "Daddy gots us."

Delilah's heart ached. *Jesus has my mama, too.*

"Yep. And we've got lotsa people: Unca Paul, Unca Titus, Unca Logan, Unca Bryce, Auntie Miriam, Auntie Alisa—" Polly grabbed Paul's hand.

"And Lilah, too." Ginny Mae grabbed a handful of Delilah's dress.

Touched at the little girl's gesture, Delilah smiled. "We've all got each other," she agreed.

"And now we're gonna have flowers." Polly brushed some dirt over another batch of bulbs. "So what'll these be?"

"Those will be mariposa lilies. They'll be white, and we'll see them in May with the daisies."

"What color are daisies?"

"They'll be white or yellow. I don't know which!" Delilah confessed. "These'll be wild roses. I don't know what color they'll be, either. The dog roses over here will be pink like the end of Ginny Mae's nose when she's cold." Polly smiled at that, and Delilah pressed on. "The saxifrages are tiny white bunches of flowers that we'll see around the same time. After those, in July or so, the larkspurs will come—they're white and blue. The last flowers to stay will be the red farewell-to-springs, and then we'll have to wait until the next year to plant them again."

"That oughta do it." Paul stepped back and surveyed their handiwork. The bell jangled from the kitchen. "And just in time for lunch, too." He deftly swiped a wriggling worm from Ginny Mae's pudgy grasp and scooped her into his arms.

"Let's go get washed up." Polly slipped her hand into Delilah's and marched toward the house.

Delilah dipped a rag in the washbasin and bent down to wipe Polly's hands and face.

"I can do it," Polly protested, tugging the makeshift washcloth away from Delilah. "But you can help Unca Paul." She gestured toward the washstand with the towel, flinging drops of water down the front of Delilah's dress.

"All right." Suppressing a smile at how quickly little Polly was growing up, Delilah turned to find Paul bouncing Ginny Mae with his good arm. Delilah grabbed another rag to clean Ginny Mae.

"Impressive amount of dirt for such a tiny thing, isn't it?" Paul's voice rumbled with good humor as Delilah grimaced at the dirty towel.

"I'll say. If we covered the seeds with this much, they'd never make it to the surface!"

"Daddy!" Polly skipped to the door as Daniel walked in. Ginny Mae wiggled and held out her arms.

"Hello, sugar dumpling. Let me wash up a minute." He affectionately rumpled her hair.

A few moments later, everyone was gathered at the table. Looking around, Delilah marveled at the fact she knew each and every name and face around her. A sense of contentment at the familiarity of joining hands to say grace washed away her discomfort at the religious practice. She almost felt like family. Out of the corner of her eye, she saw Titus give Alisa's hand one last squeeze before letting go. The obvious comfort they found in one another tugged at Delilah's heart.

Will I ever share that closeness with someone?

"Of course." Paul's deep voice startled her.

Hope and horror warred within her as she stammered, "I—I beg your pardon?"

"Logan asked if you'd like some biscuits, and I said, 'Of course.'" He smiled as he held the basket for her. "There you go."

"Thanks." She somehow managed a smile as she grabbed one of Miriam's warm, flaky biscuits, her heart still thumping wildly. She was grateful when Alisa spoke, drawing Paul's attention.

"Tomorrow morning before you men set off, we'd appreciate if you'd help move the furniture in Gideon and Miriam's cabin so we can whitewash it."

"Sure," Bryce agreed immediately.

"If the weather's fine," Daniel conceded.

"Are you going to need an extra hand, Paul?" Logan offered.

"Delilah and I'll manage just fine." She liked the way he said her name. Paul had a way of making ordinary things seem more beautiful than they really were.

And that's exactly why I have to be careful. A man like Paul could put a woman's head in the clouds, thinking fluffy dreams made castles. But come the next strong wind, they'd blow away and she'd be left with nothing. Better to enjoy what was than to put stock in dreams.

The next day, the women bustled over to the cabin Miriam and Gideon shared. Working as quickly as possible, they removed all clothing from the pegs as well as the small mirror hung above the dresser, baring the walls and taking anything they could from the room. They stored it all in Delilah's cabin, which she'd share with Miriam until the smell from the whitewash stopped lingering.

"There. That ought to do it." Miriam's pronouncement came just in time as the brothers filed in, effectively crowding what had seemed a generous space scant moments before.

"So you're finished?" Gideon gestured to the now-bare walls.

"We've taken everything we possibly could," Alisa confirmed.

"Would you look at that!" Bryce stood beside the small dresser. "They even took the drawers out!"

Titus let loose an amused guffaw. Perplexed, Delilah looked at Paul, only to see him exchange grins with Logan.

"What's so funny?"

"Don't you women think that with all six of us, we could've moved it even with the drawers inside?" It was the first time Delilah saw Daniel smile without his daughters around.

"We knew you could handle it." Miriam put a hand on Alisa's back and steered her, spluttering, from the room. "It's better for the furniture this way. We'll just leave you to remove the heavy pieces."

Delilah followed, glad to see that everyone was comfortable enough with her around to act like a real family—tiffs, teasing, and all. Next thing she knew, she stood in the empty room next to Paul.

"Ever whitewashed before, Delilah?"

"No, but I know my way around a paintbrush." She thought of her precious paint set, safely tucked away in her cabin. Maybe she could start teaching Polly to sketch. . .if Daniel would let her and they had the time. But for now, there was work to be done.

"Have you?" She hoped he had. There were sure to be differences between watercolor strokes and wall painting.

"Long time ago. When I was a lad, Mama, my brothers, and I did the outside of our house."

His wistful smile twisted her heart. "That's the first time I've heard you mention your mother, aside from Sunday," Delilah said softly.

"Yeah, well, she was a wonderful woman—godly and loving and generous. She passed on soon after we made Chance Ranch our home." He visibly straightened as he changed the topic. "First you stir it to make sure the color's blended." Looking up to make sure she was watching, he caught her smile before she could hide it.

"What?"

"Nothing. I was just thinking that's probably about how I look when I'm tending the stew." She needn't have worried he'd be offended.

He gave a grin. "Just about, but I'm nowhere near as pretty, and I hope you never have to try my cooking. I'll just leave it to you."

Warmth filled her cheeks at the compliment, so she turned away to pick up the large paintbrushes. "So we're just coating the walls, right?"

"Yep. No point in doing the floor white—it'd just get dirty faster. And we could do the ceiling, but it'd drip on the furniture." He gestured to the middle of the room, where they'd piled everything.

"So where do we start?" Suddenly the room looked immense.

"We each take a wall. You're going to want to paint along with the wood grain, side to side; otherwise it'll drip down and not look as nice as we want it."

"All right." Delilah dipped her brush and went to a wall. "Like this?"

"Not quite. You want to have a longer stroke." He held her elbow and guided her arm, sending tingles up and down her spine. She pulled away. "I see." To cover the awkwardness of the movement, she pointed to the top of the wall. "But I don't see how I'll manage to reach all the way up there."

"Don't expect you to. I'll get the highest parts. It'll probably be best for me to take care of that first, and then you follow." He grabbed a brush and got going.

Discomfited by his nearness, Delilah focused her entire concentration on the task at hand rather than on starting a conversation. What good would it do to learn more about him? He didn't complain when he broke his arm, loved his brothers, worked hard, spent time with his nieces, and spoke tenderly of his mother. He was a family man and obviously needed to find a wife who could give him as much as he gave to everyone else.

Why couldn't you do that? her heart whispered. She shook the thought away. It would never work. Sure, he was a wonderful man, but he was still just that—a man. If she let herself fall for him and marry him, he'd have the right to make her go anywhere he liked. She just couldn't take the risk.

Chapter 8

The hours passed in a deep silence Paul wasn't about to break. No whitewashing ever inspired a furrowed brow, so he stayed convinced Delilah was doing some deep thinking. He sure needed to.

It had been a mistake to touch her arm. Despite the long sleeve on her dress, his fingertips still sizzled at the memory of that contact. She'd felt it, too, since she'd abruptly pulled away, skittish as a frightened colt. Maybe she was thinking about what it meant. The question certainly plagued him.

Lord, why do I feel so deeply for this woman if it isn't Thy will? How can I help her see Thy hand in the beautiful things she loves? I understand why she's afraid to trust others, but not all of it. Please, Lord, give me the strength not to hand her my heart until she gives hers to Thee. And give us both the time we need.

They finished the last bare patch, and Delilah stepped back to survey their handiwork. "That went faster than I thought it would." She offered a tentative smile.

Grateful for the gesture, Paul grinned back. "Good company can conquer time."

As her cheeks turned pink for the second time that day, he decided her inability to accept a compliment only added to her charm.

To his surprise, she didn't busy herself with something.

"It's not often you can be around another person without having to fill the time with words," he observed.

"I know what you mean," she said softly.

His heart thumped as she agreed. This meant she was becoming more comfortable around him.

They gathered their brushes and walked out to the pump. She held the brushes under the water while he pumped. The hot and dusty day alone couldn't account for the dust cloud they spotted in the distance.

"That's odd. Miriam hasn't rung the dinner bell yet, and your brothers are already coming home. I hope everything's all right."

Paul wondered whether she remembered the day he'd broken his arm and worried for his brothers.

"Wait a minute. They wouldn't be coming from the east. Wonder what would bring someone out on a Saturday?" He shaded his eyes and squinted as the wagon came closer. As soon as he realized the approaching horses carried the MacPherson brothers, he tried to get Delilah in the house. Why else would they come a day before they should for worship—unless they were coming courting.

"Delilah, why don't you go tell Miriam we might be having company for dinner."

"All right." She cast one last look over her shoulder and headed for the kitchen.

Paul started walking out to meet them. Maybe he could find out what they needed and send them away without letting them so much as get a glimpse of Delilah.

Mike pulled up beside him. "Reckoned we was a mite late fer the doin's. Hadda hole smack dab in one o' the fences."

It took Paul a moment to realize they thought it was Sunday, and by then, Obie had chimed in.

"Yeah, and seein's how the gully-washer kept us away week afore today, we figgered we'uns best try an' come anyhow."

"Gentlemen," Paul interrupted, "I'm afraid there's been a mistake. You're a day early. Tomorrow is the Lord's Day." Maybe he could get them to turn around and go home before Miriam rang the dinner bell.

"Aw, you're joshin' us fer shore. Leave off cuttin' up." Hezzy guffawed, but Micah silently counted on his fingers.

"Naw, he ain't! Think on it, Hezekiah MacPherson." Micah glared at his older brother, who scratched his head in bewilderment.

"You're the only one as can cipher, Mike. I reckon ya musta messed up." It seemed as though Obie's well-meaning intervention hadn't helped.

"If'n I done tole ya once, I tole ya agin an' agin. Ya mark the day off after dark! If'n ya cross it off of a mornin', we end up a day ahead 'cause this one ain't o'er yet!"

Hezekiah had the grace to look abashed. "Shore am sorry, Mike. I done fergot agin."

Paul watched the brothers confer until he couldn't wait any longer to get them out of there. After all, once the dinner bell rang, it would be too late to get them to leave.

"Well, if it isn't the MacPherson brothers!" Paul winced as Miriam bustled up.

"Ma'am." Mike respectfully tipped his grimy hat, and his brothers mimicked the gesture.

"Why are you out in the hot sun? Dinner'll be on the table soon. Come on in."

"We don' wanna be botherin' ya, but we shore would be tickled to sample some of those fine vittles o' yourn, ma'am." The three of them beamed down at Miriam even as Paul quelled the urge to glare at all four of them.

What is she thinking? Paul watched helplessly as they all hopped out of the wagon and followed Miriam.

Delilah dropped the edge of the curtain as Miriam headed toward the house. She recognized the three men as ones they'd seen at the general store but didn't quite understand why Paul seemed so displeased to see them. Two were large bears of men, but the third stood shorter and had a wiry build. One thing was clear: They would be staying for dinner. Delilah quickly slid three more bowls on the table as Miriam rang the dinner bell. The men strode inside.

"Delilah, you may remember the MacPherson brothers: Obadiah, Hezekiah, and Micah," Miriam said in introduction.

Obie spoke up. "Back in Kentucky, we don' stand on ceremony. We's just plain Obie, Hezzy, and Mike."

"He's got the right of it," Hezzy added. "Don't make a lick o' sense to call us all 'Mr. MacPherson.'"

"Right nice to make your aquaintanceship, miss." Mike bowed over her hand.

"Aw, wouldja look at the jack-a-dandy come a-courtin'," one of the older brothers crowed.

"Hush your face, Obie," Hezzy whispered loudly as he elbowed his brother.

"Pleasure to meet you," Delilah greeted them, amused rather than appalled by their manners. They seemed well-meaning enough, after all. She didn't like the reference to courting, but the thought that this was the reason Paul seemed so put out lifted her spirits.

"What're you doin' here?" Daniel growled as he stepped up to the washbasin.

Delilah was relieved to see that the MacPhersons didn't seem to take offense at Daniel's curt tone.

"We swapped days, I reckon," Obie explained, then seemed struck by an unwelcome thought. He turned to Mike, clearly the brains of the family. "We kin still come tomorra, right?"

Hezzy's face fell at that, and the pair of them looked for all the world like children about to be denied a treat.

Mike nodded. "We still gotta honor the Lord's Day."

The older brothers broke out in matching grins. As Paul scowled at the blue willow plate Miriam loaded with biscuits, Delilah bit back a smile of her own.

Chapter 9

Everyone began jockeying for a seat. Paul noticed the MacPherson brothers hovering around the table as though waiting for Delilah to sit down so they could swoop in beside her.

His eyes narrowed. Over his dead body would they get any closer to her than absolutely necessary. He plunked down toward the end of the bench and snagged Delilah as she leaned over to put another batch of biscuits on the table. The second he was certain he had a hold of her, he hooked his boot around her foot to make her stumble right onto the seat beside him.

"Oh! Sorry, I must've tripped." She made as if to get up, but he didn't let go of her arm.

"I've never known you to be clumsy. You'd best stay seated—sometimes the smell from the whitewash can make a person lightheaded."

"Just stay put, Delilah," Miriam said with a slight wink toward Paul. "We're just about done anyway."

Maybe Miriam was trying to make amends for inviting the MacPhersons to lunch. Whatever the reason, he'd be glad for any help she'd give him.

There was a brief tussle as Obie and Hezzy both tried to elbow their way to the end of the bench. Hezzy won and got there first. Fortunately, try as he might, he couldn't figure out a way to squeeze his large frame onto the half inch of bench peeking out by Delilah's skirts.

"Ahem." The big oaf cleared his throat. "I'd be much obliged if'n ya could see your way clear ta scoochin' o'er a bit, miss. Don't much fancy perchin' like a jaybird durin' vittles."

His bumbling manners coaxed a smile from Delilah as she obligingly began scooting over. Paul didn't move, which he found yielded double benefits: First, it stopped Hezzy from sitting down, and second, Delilah was now close enough that Paul could catch the scent of jasmine that lingered sweetly in her hair.

"If it's all the same to you, Hezzy, I'd appreciate it if you'd try the other bench. If we're packed tighter than a tin of sardines, my arm'll give me trouble." Paul avoided looking across the table at Daniel, who sat parked next to Obie already.

"Oh, how thoughtless of me!" Delilah interjected. "Paul's been working hard whitewashing, and it certainly won't help to have Logan jostling his arm today, too. Do you mind?"

Paul was gratified to hear the concern in her voice as she neatly made it impossible for Hezzy to refuse.

"Yes'm." Hezzy shuffled over to the other bench, where Polly obligingly bounced over toward her father. Hezzy hunkered down, and the bench gave an ominous creak.

Obie snatched a biscuit and crammed the whole thing in his mouth while the Chance family joined hands. Paul supposed Micah kicked his brother under the table, because Obie let loose with, "Ow," spraying his plate and beard with crumbs before catching on and bowing his head for prayer.

"Wait, that hurts!"

Paul looked over at Hezzy to see him pinching Polly's tiny hand between his forefinger and thumb.

"Open your hand," she ordered, and the giant obeyed without question. Polly placed her hand in the middle of his palm, then used her other hand to fold Hezzy's fingers over, completely engulfing her hand and wrist. "See, like this." Satisfied, she tucked her other hand back in Ginny Mae's and nodded. "We're ready now, Unca Gideon."

Smiling, Gideon closed his eyes and blessed the food before he began ladling the thick venison stew into bowls and passing them down each side of the table. Hezzy grabbed the bowl, looked at it longingly, and tried to give it to Polly before Daniel swiped it from him.

Sitting at the other end of the table, Mike received his stew first.

"Whatcha waitin' fer?" Obie demanded, indignant to see the untouched meal.

"It's good manners ta wait fer everyone else," Mike growled, trying to keep his voice down but failing miserably nevertheless.

"Oh." Crumbs sprinkled from his beard as Obie nodded sagely.

The moment everyone was served, the three brothers picked up their bowls and tipped them to their mouths, downing the stew as quickly as possible.

Everyone else watched in a kind of morbid fascination when all three plunked their empty bowls back on the table. Micah wiped his mouth with his sleeve while Obie and Hezzy made short work of their biscuits. Only when Obie let loose a satisfied sigh scant moments later did they realize no one else had so much as touched their meal.

Micah and Obie seemed uncomfortable, while Hezzy eyed Polly's biscuits greedily. "Ya gonna et this 'ere extry biskit?" He poked the bread with a grimy finger.

Wordlessly, Polly pushed the biscuit toward him, head cocked to the side as she watched him bring it up to his mouth. Then Hezzy caught Alisa staring at him, eyes agog.

"Wha's happenin'?"

No one knew quite how to answer that question. To be honest, Paul didn't mind the way things were turning out. At least they finished sooner so they'd leave sooner.

"How come you eat like that?" Polly asked, only to receive blank looks from the MacPhersons.

"They's hungwy!" Ginny Mae piped up.

"Shore are." Mike latched on to the little girl's assessment. "We bin livin' offa Obie's victuals for nigh on half a year now. Almost fergot how real food tastes."

"Maybe that's 'cause you don't chew." No one knew quite what to do about Polly's helpful suggestion until Mike burst out laughing.

"Reckon tha' might be so, missy," he choked out as his brothers joined in, giving great guffaws. Relieved, the rest of the table gave way to amused chuckles.

"Would you like seconds?" The words were hardly out of Miriam's mouth before the brothers thrust their bowls toward her.

"Use your spoon!" Polly said.

Hezzy picked up one of the spoons, dwarfing it in his huge fist. "I never knew why a body would wanna warsh more dishes. Food's just as good without 'em, so why bother?"

Polly had to think on that for a minute. "So's you don't spill." She reached up her napkin and wiped some soup off of Hezzy's face.

Micah slurped down his first bite and beamed as he plunged his spoon in for a second. Hezzy got his up to his mouth until it clacked against his teeth. Startled by the noise, he dropped his spoon and bent down to pick it up.

"Would you like me to clean that for you?" Delilah offered.

"Naw, what fer?" He rubbed it on the front of his shirt before trying again.

When everyone had their fill, the meal was over. Paul felt pretty satisfied with how he'd handled things. After all, not one of the three brothers had sat beside her or even talked to her directly. To the contrary, they'd fallen on the food like animals and done serious damage if they thought they'd convince Delilah to be their bride.

"Got lotta work ta git ta back home. Can't hardly wait 'til tomorra." Micah once again served as the spokesman for the group as his older brothers nodded in tandem and patted their full bellies. With that, they got up, strode outside, unhitched the horses, and made for home in their wagon.

"So tomorrow the entire town comes over?"

Under any other circumstances, Paul would be unhappy to see Delilah's discomfiture, but here it signified her lack of interest in other men.

"Yes," Alisa confirmed. "So since you're done whitewashing, maybe you can help me. We'll need half a dozen pies and more loaves of bread." Alisa turned to Paul. "Would you mind getting the barn as ready as you can in case it sprinkles and we need to set up inside?"

Paul went to the barn and grabbed a rake. One-handed, it wasn't easy to clear the floor, but it gave him plenty of time to think. What was he supposed to do when every man in the county would find his way over to sniff around Delilah's skirts?

Lord, give me patience, temperance, and a few good ideas!

Delilah stretched before Miriam began helping with her buttons.

"Busy day, wasn't it?" Delilah could hear her cousin's smile even if she couldn't see it.

"I thought so," Delilah confessed hesitantly. "But you just don't know how wonderful it is to have every day filled up. When I was with Papa, I'd paint or embroider to pass the time, but I haven't touched a paintbrush since I got here. I'm not exactly sure how to explain it, but planting the garden, cooking, cleaning, watching the girls, whitewashing. . .it makes me feel. . ."

"Useful?" Miriam offered.

"Yes." Delilah turned around and looked her cousin in the eye, trying to put into words what she felt. "But it's more than that. I feel like a part of something bigger than myself. Does that even make sense?"

"Of course! You're a part of a family now. And you're learning everything so quickly, you have a lot to be a part of. I'm so glad God brought you to us, Delilah." Miriam folded her into a cozy hug.

"You've done so much for me," Delilah whispered.

"It goes both ways. All of those things you've listed are of such great help. I do hope, though, we'll find some time for you to pull out those paintbrushes again!" Miriam scanned the room, seeing the drawers and pegs and quilts she'd brought in. "Where do you keep them?" she wondered aloud.

"In here." Delilah walked over to the washstand and opened the drawer. "Everything I owned that wasn't clothes or my pistol is in here. It's my entire life in one drawer." She pulled out her paint set along with her sketchbook.

Miriam sat down on the bed and ran her fingers over the much-washed tips of the brushes, eyeing the many hues of Delilah's paint set. "So many colors." She picked up the sketchbook. "May I?" At Delilah's nod, she started flipping through the pages, gazing at the charcoal drawings. "You've been so many places! Trains, ships, mountains, fields, wildflowers. . .and you make them all so beautiful!"

"I've seen a lot of things." Delilah didn't bother to keep the sadness from her voice. "But I haven't ever really been anyplace until now. I want to paint Chance Ranch someday."

"Oh, that would be wonderful. After the baby, I can show you the fishing hole and some of the wildflowers—my favorite places to think and pray. You should draw one for every season! That'd keep you busy for a while longer!"

Miriam smiled. "Do you ever draw people, Delilah?"

"No." Delilah looked away. There had been no one special to paint except Mama and Papa. Some of her favorite memories were of Mama teaching her how to paint. They'd started on houses and flowers, full of little shapes to be painted.

The one time Delilah painted a portrait, it was of her father and mother, done from memory. Oh, how she'd slaved over it, hours upon hours, making sure the sketch was perfect before mixing the exact shade of Mama's burnished mahogany locks and Papa's black whiskers. When she'd finally finished, she'd proudly held it up for Mama's inspection. But Mama's delight faded quickly into tears.

At Delilah's confusion, Mama took out another portrait and snuggled next to Delilah. "See, baby. This is your papa right before we were married." But this man with his smooth young face and bright eyes was hardly recognizable in the lined face and tired eyes Delilah had depicted in great detail. "He's changed so much," Mama whispered, tears trickling down her face as she pressed the portrait into Delilah's hand. "Remember him this way, darling." With that, she bustled out of the room, and Delilah furiously painted over her portrait in thick black strokes. She'd never painted another person and told herself she never would.

But how to explain this now to Miriam? "I prefer to paint landscapes. Mama always said things were easier to see and understand than people." Certain Miriam would question her tired smile, Delilah changed the subject.

"What about you? What did you have when you came to Chance Ranch?"

"I brought my clothes, a Bible, a cross one of my island friends made for me, my sewing kit, a writing desk, and a present I never had the chance to give my sister." Now Delilah wasn't the only one swept away by memories of loved ones gone. Miriam knelt by a small trunk. She pulled out a tiny bundle wrapped in cotton.

"This should have been Hannah's. One day it will go to her daughters. I suppose we both brought things we haven't used." Miriam handed the package to Delilah. The loose material fell away from a small wooden box. She opened the tiny hinges to find the inside glowing with mother-of-pearl inlay.

"This is beautiful," she breathed.

"Oh, that's just a teakwood box. Actually, the earrings were for Hannah," Miriam explained.

Delilah unwrapped another strip of cotton to reveal large pearls set in golden earbobs. "They're lovely, and pearls like these are so rare!"

"Not on the islands!" Miriam laughed. "But here they'd fetch a fancy price. I hope to have them reset in rings or pendants for the girls." She gently wrapped everything up again and tucked the treasure in her trunk, then came back and clasped Delilah's hands.

"Lord, we thank Thee for Thy love and blessings and pray Thou wilt keep Thy hand on our loved ones. Thank Thee for friends, family, and all we hold dear. Jesus, Thou knowest what's deep in our hearts, how part of us misses our parents and always will. Please provide us with comfort while we're away from those we love, and help us to remember they live in Thee. Let us not hide behind grief or loneliness but instead concentrate on loving each other. In Christ's name, amen."

The words spoke to Delilah, and for the first time, she truly hoped a prayer would be answered.

Chapter 10

The sun shone brightly with nary a cloud in the sky. *So why do I feel so cold?* Delilah shivered as she listened to Gideon speak on a passage from the book of Hebrews.

Why is it that every time someone reads from the Bible, it seems as though they're talking directly to me? Phrases kept jumping out at her. " 'To day if ye will hear his voice, harden not your hearts. . . . Take heed, brethren, lest there be in any of you an evil heart of unbelief, in departing from the living God. But exhort one another daily. . .lest any of you be hardened through the deceitfulness of sin.' "

Between nighttime devotions and sermons on the Lord's Day—not to mention constant prayers—Delilah felt surrounded by pressure to believe as these wonderful people did.

And for a change, it seemed as though she were one of the few people actually "fixing her thoughts" on the Lord this morning.

Everyone in the township had turned out, and she would have had to be deaf and blind not to realize the vast majority of people were staring at her.

Well, so long as they don't try to talk to me or touch me or anything, I'll be just fine. As they stood for another hymn, she heard a peculiar sound amid the music.

Why won't men carry handkerchiefs when they need them? Delilah's back stiffened as the sound grew louder. Honestly, it was right behind her now.

She heard a muffled yelp and turned her head.

"You're not gonna do that agin, ya hear?" Mike MacPherson growled as he tightened his hold on another man's collar. "Ya jist don' go round sniffin' ladies. And durin' preachin'." He scoffed and released the man, who turned around as though spoiling for a good fight, only to take a small step back as Obie and Hezzy moved closer to their younger brother. He mumbled something unintelligible, shot Delilah a sheepish grin, and realized he'd become the focus of everyone's attention.

"Let us pray." Gideon quickly ended the sermon, allowing the women to escape to the kitchen. Widow Greene took the little girls and her son, Davie, out to the play yard. Priscilla White flounced along behind her, steering clear of the kitchen.

As soon as the door shut, Alisa burst into giggles. Miriam and Reba looked at Delilah with concern until she joined Alisa, and soon the entire kitchen rang with laughter.

"Oh, the look on Scudd's face when Mike grabbed him by the collar and yanked him back," Alisa reflected when she had regained enough control to speak again.

"Do you know. . ." Delilah suppressed a fresh burst of giggles. "I was thinking he should carry a handkerchief if he had a cold. I didn't realize. . ."

"He was sniffing you like a fresh-baked pie?" Miriam filled in.

"Served him right Mike reined him in," Reba observed tartly. "Those MacPhersons sure are an interesting bunch, but they've got their hearts in the right place. Now." She straightened up. "We've got a passel of hungry men out there, so we'd best get stuff on the tables."

Paul glowered impartially at the horde of men around the barn as they gathered to try their hand at horseshoes.

"I'm of a mind to think that the real winner today may not be the man who hooks the most shoes." Ross Dorsey grinned.

"Yep. It's the man who snags that purty little new filly on Chance Ranch," another man agreed.

"Just so's it ain't another one of you brothers," Rusty griped.

"She's not a brood mare, fellas." Bryce joined Paul in scowling.

"Easy enough fer you ta say with three women on your spread," someone scoffed. "You're the best-fed, best-dressed, luckiest men around."

"And you know it!" Nathan Bates chimed in.

"Not to mention the other benefits," someone grumbled.

Paul started toward the men, ready to begin a brawl. Broken arm or not, he wasn't going to listen to them talk that way about Delilah, Miriam, or Alisa. Daniel grabbed his good arm, bringing him to a stop almost before he'd started.

"I don't want to hear that kind of talk. These are good women—ladies." Daniel glowered at all and sundry of the neighbors, whose reaction reminded Paul just which brother was best at this sort of thing.

"Aw, we didn't mean nothin' by it, Danny-boy. We're right glad to have 'em livin' hereabouts."

"They's shore nice 'bout whippin' up a mess o' vittles fer us ev'ry week," Obie piped up.

"And it's nice just to be around 'em."

"Yeah, just enjoying their company, is all," Ross agreed.

"Hey, Scudd," someone exclaimed. "What'd she smell like?"

"Didya get a snootful?" another man eagerly asked.

"I shorely did." Scudd closed his eyes blissfully, then cracked one open to make sure he had a captive audience before continuing. "Smells jist as purty as the little gal looks. Like a flower in spring." Several men nodded and smiled.

Paul shrugged out of Daniel's grasp and stomped nearer. "Don't any of you be getting ideas."

To his surprise, Mike stepped over to his side, reminding Paul just who'd come to Delilah's rescue earlier when he'd been sitting too far away.

"Here I thought I'd learned ya about that. If'n ya need another lesson in manners, I'd be plum tickled ta oblige. Seems ta me you could use a good thumpin'."

Scudd bristled visibly. "It was worth it, and I'd do it again."

"You'd better not," Paul warned.

" 'Course not," Scudd agreed quickly, falling back a step.

Satisfied, Paul turned to face the rest of the town. "We've been through this enough times you all should know better. Any woman under our roof is as good as family—"

"I'll say, seein' as how they become family. You brothers are called Chance 'cause ya don't give anyone else a chance to catch a bride," Rusty complained. "Ya hog 'em all."

"Yeah. Seems to me like we can figger who's got an eye on this one," Ross challenged. "You gonna stake yer claim?"

Paul found himself on the receiving end of several accusing glares but refused to back down. "She's not a piece of land, and well you know it. Listen, she just lost her pa, so you all need to back off."

"So long as you play by the same rules."

Paul pushed back a twinge of guilt at the pointed comment.

"She's Miriam's cousin," Gideon added, "so I'll take it personally if she's bothered."

"And that means she's kin to my daughters," Daniel reminded all and sundry.

"So don't give us reason to ask you to leave," Paul finished.

"That's enough," Gus broke in. "I'm too old to waste what time I've got left listenin' to y'all argue. Now which one of you whippersnappers thinks he can take me on at horseshoes?"

That night, Daniel helped Paul take off his boots.

"Still in a temper, eh?" Daniel broke the silence.

"Just thinking." Paul shrugged, not liking the direction his brother was headed. He'd only heard that tone of voice from Daniel when he was talking to Polly or Ginny Mae. "I don't like every last man in the township circling around her like vultures."

"Well, it seems to me maybe you're doing the wrong thinking. Being sweet on a woman isn't supposed to turn you sour."

Paul looked at his brother in silent disbelief.

"Don't you give me that look. I'm different. It wasn't loving Hannah that took it out of me. It was losing her. And I'm telling you right now, you can't lose what you never had, so you've no call to be looking like somebody put a hole in your favorite hat."

That coaxed a smile from Paul. "Here I thought you were mad about how Delilah threw that knife."

"You got that right. Still, I can't in good conscience send Delilah off to any of the rabble lurking around today. She's one of ours now. And if you aim to keep it that way, you'd best do a bit less thinking and a lot more courting."

"Don't you think I want to?" Paul ran his fingers through his hair in frustration. "I'm praying on it, but she isn't a believer, Dan. You know what the Bible says about being unequally yoked."

"What makes you think she doesn't believe?" Surprise colored Dan's words.

"We've spoken about it."

"I'm glad to see you haven't been sittin' on your hands this whole time, then. Let me tell you what I've learned, because I have something in common with little Miss Delilah. The Lord took loved ones from both of us. And as angry as I am with Him, and no matter how much I disagree with what He does, I still know He exists. I'm just not so sure He's worth trusting anymore. Delilah's the same way. She may not trust Him, but she believes He exists, whether she admits it or not."

Paul mulled that over for a minute. "So you really do believe in Him? You don't just tolerate it for Hannah's memory?"

"Look. This isn't about me. I'm just saying that Delilah's had a rough time of it, and you've got your work cut out for you. But if you're going to convince her to trust you and God, you can't look so surly. Besides," Daniel grumbled as he pulled up a blanket, "the sooner you manage it, the sooner I can get some peace and quiet."

❧

"Mornin'." Any lingering goodwill Paul had toward the MacPherson brothers for their actions two days ago vanished like—well, like a biscuit set in front of one of them! This made the third time they'd shown up in only four days, and Paul was beginning to wish they'd never left Hauk's Fall. Things would be simpler if those brothers had stayed in Kentucky.

"Mornin'." He waited in silence, determined not to make this easy for them. They shifted in their saddles.

"Can we'uns have a word with Miz Delilah?" Hezzy failed to ease the tension. "We brung her summat."

Paul didn't like the sound of that. "Well, I'm sure she's busy right now, so how about I pass it along for you?"

Mike eyed him with a knowing glint. "I don' blame ya fer bein' less'n pleased ta clap eyes on us agin—you bein' clever folks an' all. Still, I reckon we can be civil 'bout this. Ya know we don't mean no harm and won' try an' take no privliges like some."

"Ya know we jist come to give her those seeds fer her garden," Obie protested, obviously missing the new turn of conversation.

Paul didn't like the sound of that at all. The garden was his and Delilah's—a thing shared and fostered like their relationship. Unfortunately, Paul had to admit, Mike had the right of it. The MacPhersons didn't have the best manners, but they did have class where it counted.

"Why don't you come on in?" Paul invited and led them to the house, where they found the women making bacon sandwiches and fixing green beans.

"Hello." Miriam looked up from the table where she worked with Polly on the alphabet.

"Good morning." Delilah smiled and wiped her hands on her apron before ringing the dinner bell.

"We brung ya this." Hezzy thrust a sack toward her.

"Thank you, but I really don't think I can accept it," Delilah said softly.

"How come? Mike says it's proper fer a fella ta take a lady flowers." Obie's brow furrowed.

"Oh, well, thank you." Delilah hesitantly accepted the sack. "This doesn't feel like flowers."

"That's 'cause they's better'n flowers. They's seeds from Meemaw's gardin back home." Hezzy beamed at her.

"I thunk on it when ya tol' us 'bout yer garden, Miz Delilah." Micah fiddled with his hat brim.

"That's so thoughtful." She smiled at all three of them. "But really, you should keep them so one day they'll brighten up your homes."

"Aw, no sense in that. We ain't got much skill fer growin' things. Someone ought to enjoy 'em. It'll do us good ta see sommat from Hawk's Fall, Miz Delilah."

"In that case, I'd be happy to grow some for you. When they bloom, you can take some home on Sundays," Delilah said graciously as the Chance brothers tromped in and started washing up.

"Something wrong?" Gideon went straight to Miriam's side and looked at the MacPhersons.

"No, honey. The MacPhersons were just being neighborly and brought Delilah some seeds for the garden." Miriam turned to their guests. "And of course they'll be staying for lunch."

That does it, Paul resolved as Mike wrangled a seat on Delilah's other side. *I'm making a second table.*

Chapter 11

As before, the MacPhersons dug into the meal with gusto. It really was sweet of them to bring her those seeds, but Delilah decided not to use them all. That way, when the brothers had wives of their own, she could give them back. Delilah certainly had no plans to become one of those women, though.

"You're lookin' mighty fine today, Miz Delilah." Micah almost sounded as though he'd practiced the compliment.

"Thank you." Delilah focused on her green beans.

"Yep. A bit long in the too—" Hezzy broke off as Obie jabbed him in the side with his elbow.

"But we ain't seen a gal so purty since the Trevor sisters back home." Rather than being offended, Delilah choked back laughter with her beans. Surely no woman had ever been faced with such earnest suitors as she!

"What'd they look like?" Logan perked up visibly.

"Oh, hair like a log afire," Obie reminisced.

"Eyes jist as shiny as a mud puddle," Hezzy added. "Nary one single gap from a tooth a-missin'." Delilah fought to keep a straight face at this high praise for the Trevor sisters. And to think, she had the honor of being the next prettiest woman they'd ever seen!

"Sweetest li'l thangs ya could ever hope ta see. Only saw 'em onc't, though."

"Are they nice?" Ginny Mae asked, obviously concerned with issues more important than physical beauty.

"O' course, li'l missy. Their uncle raised coon dogs. That's how we met 'em, gettin' ole Bear. Right fine animal—worth the trip down ta the holler, let me tell you." Obie was clearly lost in his memories.

"If they have a way with animals, there's somethin' good inside them." Bryce nodded his approval.

"Shore as shootin'," Hezzy agreed. "Critters always know. 'Course, some critters are best in a pot."

"They made a fine mess o' squirrel stew. Made the meat so nice it almost tasted like possum." Obie took a swig of water.

"How come you didn't marry them?" Polly asked with a bluntness only a child could display.

"Aw, didn't have nothin' ta offer two fine wimmen like them," Hezzy explained. "That's why we'uns come here—ta make somethin' o' ourselves."

"And we done it." Mike leaned back and crossed his arms over his chest. "Now we gots us a spread o' good land and cattle."

"How many Trevor sisters are there?" Paul asked Mike.

"Cain't say. I ain't never seen 'em," Mike scoffed.

"Two," Obie supplied.

"Anybody you liked better?" Daniel shot Paul a conspiratorial glance.

"Aw, I don' know."

Delilah was surprised to see the tips of Mike's ears turn red.

"Come on, we're all friends here," Miriam encouraged.

"Well, I suppose I've gotta soft spot for Miss Temperance. Her sister was the healer, and she'd come ta help Ma. Tempy would cook for us or sing to Ma ta pass the time. Smart, too. Got a good head on her shoulders."

"You've done well for yourselves," Paul joined in. "Why don't you write to them?"

"Mike's the only one as cain write any," Obie pointed out.

" 'Sides," Hezzy joined in, "they cain't read anywho."

"Tempy can," Mike said softly. " 'Sides, askin' a woman to travel away from her kin has ta be done proper-like. I cain't do that good."

His simple answer tugged at Delilah's heart. Mike obviously held Tempy in high esteem. These were good men, and they deserved good women. *Maybe I can help.*

"How about if I helped you write the letter? You just tell me what you want said."

"Hey, what about our'n?" Obie jabbed a thumb to indicate Hezzy.

"Well. . ." Delilah thought a moment.

"Couldn't we send it to Tempy and ask her to pass along the message?" Paul suggested.

"I reckon that jist might work." After a long silence in which both brothers thought so hard they looked strained, Obie agreed. "Mike?"

"It bears thinkin' on." Mike didn't say yes but seemed to be giving the idea serious consideration. "Are the both of ya set on those gals?"

"As the sun goes down of a mornin'," came Hezzy's solemn vow.

"The sun comes up in the mornin', but I know whatcha mean," Mike allowed. "Which one do ya each fancy?"

Obie and Hezzy stared at each other for a long minute. "Don't recollect their names, Mike."

"Eunice and Lois," Hezzy said.

"Oh, yeah. Tha' sounds 'bout right. Ya got a pref'rence, Hezzy?" Obie generously inquired.

"Not sure I could tell the two apart, come ta thunk on it." Hezzy looked at Delilah. "That gonna be a problem?"

"Um. . ." She seriously wondered whether or not this would work. "I suppose if we worded it right, we could just say you two remember them fondly and would be honored if they'd come and join you in the hopes of matrimony."

"That do sound purty as a poem. D'ya reckon it'd work?" Hezzy beseeched Mike.

"No harm in tryin'." Mike sighed.

"Well, why don't you all think about what you'd like to say. If they're coming, we need to send for them soon enough so they can arrive before winter. Try to make it as personal as you can, and we'll write it up after you've had a chance to think on it."

"And pray!" Ginny Mae piped up. "Auntie Miri-Em always says to think and pray."

"All right. We'll see you later."

Delilah couldn't help but notice the air of excitement surrounding the MacPhersons as they took their leave. In hopes of avoiding their courting, she'd promised to do her best to snag them other women. *What have I gotten myself into?*

"Hang on, we're comin'!" Paul buttoned his shirt and beat Daniel to the door, which he swung open. Miriam faced him, shifting her weight from foot to foot.

"What's wrong?" Panic surged through Paul's veins. Miriam wouldn't bother them in the morning unless it was something important.

"Today's Delilah's birthday! I forgot until last night when I was writing in my diary, and I saw that I'd marked the date."

Relief washed over him, only to be followed by an unsettled feeling as his stomach clenched. He had nothing to give the woman he hoped to wed. Even the MacPhersons had managed to give her something!

"Exactly." Miriam nodded her approval at his reaction. "So here's what we're going to do. . . ."

"Can we have carrot sticks on our picnic, Auntie Lilah?" Ginny Mae tugged on her skirts. "I likes carrot sticks."

Delilah smiled as she wrapped the carrots in a cloth and placed them in a basket. Miriam was so thoughtful to suggest a picnic lunch today. She and Paul would take the girls out for fun and perhaps even a sketching lesson for Polly. Delilah might sketch something worth turning into a painting.

"All right. Have you got Dolly?" Ginny Mae ran to the table, grabbed her dolly off the bench, and clutched it to her chest.

"Uh-huh. And Auntie Miri-Em gots an old blankie." The toddler gave a short hop of excitement. "Can we goes now?"

Delilah held Ginny Mae's hand and grabbed the basket. "Let's go!"

Outside, Paul stood by the wagon where Polly nestled atop the folded old quilt. "Ready?"

Paul helped Delilah and Ginny Mae scramble into the back of the wagon, then took the seat. He'd reassured them he could handle one horse for a short ride without any problems.

He was as good as his word, pulling up under a stand of trees with just enough leaves to offer some shade. They spread out the blanket as Paul tied the horse's reins loosely around a tree.

The girls ran and twirled around for a while.

"It's a lovely day," he commented. "We've got everything we need. Good company, sunshine, shade, and a nice view." His gaze rested on Delilah.

"And clouds! I like clouds!" Polly pointed at the sky.

"That one," Delilah joined in, "could be a little castle, like in fairy tales. See the tower?"

"Oooh," Polly breathed. "I wish our house looked like that!"

"Hmmm. . ." Paul stroked his chin. "That one's white, fluffy, round. . . . I'd say it looks like a biscuit to me!"

"Yummy!" Ginny Mae clapped.

"Can we have some now?" Polly pleaded.

"Well, I don't see why not. What've you got in that basket, Delilah?"

"Carrot sticks." Ginny Mae imparted her wisdom, presenting her treasure with a flourish.

Delilah smiled as the little girl began passing out the carrot sticks. She pulled out a canteen of iced tea, some cold chicken, a wedge of cheese, and some of those renowned biscuits.

She and Paul helped Polly and Ginny Mae make sandwiches, and they all munched happily. After lunch, Delilah pulled out her sketchbook and pencil.

"What're you doing?" Polly scooted over to take a look.

"Drawing that hill over there with the trees."

Polly watched in fascination as the lines became tree trunks and grass. "Why are you only coloring in part of it?"

"It's called shading. It's to show where the light was, so when I paint over it, I get the colors right."

"That's pretty." Polly stood up and walked over to a tree with lots of branches. Reaching up, she grabbed a branch and stuck her foot into a knothole, hoisting herself onto the lowest level. "See? I like trees!" She stretched for the next branch.

"No higher, Polly," Paul admonished.

Privately, Delilah thought even that low branch, close to the ground as it rested, was already too high.

With a gamine grin, Polly scrambled up, only to shriek as Paul grabbed her with his good arm and swung her down.

"That was fun!" She giggled.

"Was it worth disobeying?"

Her smile faded at Paul's tone. "Sorry, Unca Paul." She buried her face in his shoulder.

"You know better. Now you won't get to share some of that apple pie I saw in our picnic basket."

Her head jerked up, and her lower lip quivered. "But I like apple pie." She wailed.

"You'll remember to listen to your elders next time, though. Now go on and play with Ginny Mae." Paul set her down and patted her on the back.

Polly threw one last yearning look at the picnic basket, then trundled off to chase a butterfly with Ginny Mae.

He'll be a wonderful father. Gentle with the girls, but firm in discipline.

He plunked down next to Delilah and tugged the sketchbook out of her hands. He studied the drawing, then the landscape, then held the sketchbook up and squinted. Delilah's heart thumped as she waited for his opinion.

Paul studied the sketch in silence. *How can black and white seem so lifelike? Why does everything she touches gain beauty?*

"If this one weren't in black and white, it'd be just like looking out a window. It's that true to the land. God's given you quite a gift, Delilah."

Her cheeks grew rosy at his praise. "I don't know about that. I draw and paint because I remember Mama teaching me how. When it comes down to it, though, I didn't make the trees or the sky. I enjoy their beauty enough to copy them. This is just an imitation." She tapped the sketch.

"It's wonderful, and I think God will look upon it as a compliment." Paul meant every word. It was a shame she didn't see it that way yet, because her art was an eloquent form of praise.

"Do you have to bring God into everything?" Disappointment clouded her amber eyes.

How do I answer her, Lord? Please give me the words.

"I don't bring Him into anything, Delilah. His hand created all you see before you. All that is beautiful comes from Him."

She was silent for a while; the only sounds were the girls' giggles as they rolled down one of the smaller hills.

"Maybe." Delilah stood up. "We ought to be getting back. Polly! Ginny Mae! Come on back!" Keeping her back to him, she gathered and folded the quilt, placing it and the basket in the buckboard.

Lord, will she ever accept You? Or me?

Chapter 12

Paul's the best man I've ever met—and we're too different to be together. He bases his entire life on something he can't see or touch. Delilah's frustrated thoughts bounced around as much as the buckboard did on the bumpy road they took to return to the ranch.

She put her arm around Polly and snuggled the five-year-old to her side. Ginny Mae crawled into Delilah's lap and fought to keep her eyes open as the wagon swayed over the path. How could anyone not see how precious children and security were? Delilah, for one, intended to make them her priority for every minute she spent at Chance Ranch.

They pulled up to the barn. Delilah cuddled Ginny Mae in the bed of the buckboard as Paul took care of the horse, then helped her out of the wagon before scooping Polly into his arm. It seemed as though he wanted to say something, but he turned away.

She stopped him, only to find herself unsure of what to say. She couldn't let their day together end this way.

"I enjoyed our picnic." It sounded feeble to her ears, but Paul accepted the gesture.

"Someday you'll see that we're not as different as you think." His tender smile lifted her spirits. "Come on, they'll be waiting on us for supper."

Together they walked to the house, where Miriam and Alisa were just setting an enormous pork roast on the table.

"If I'd known you were going to prepare a feast today," Delilah said, eyeing the mashed potatoes, peas, and corn bread, "I would've helped instead of going on the picnic."

"Balderdash." Alisa sat down. "You know very well you helped with breakfast and looked after the girls today."

They all joined hands as Titus blessed the meal and thanked the Lord. Everyone stayed strangely silent, but then again, the food tasted so wonderful, no one seemed too concerned with conversation. Even Polly, having missed her afternoon nap, yawned instead of chattering like a magpie. When everyone had eaten their fill, Delilah rose and began to help Miriam clear the table.

"Oh, Delilah." Alisa stopped her. "There's something the men wanted to show you. Since we've already seen it, Miriam and I will take care of the dishes."

She winked at Titus, who gallantly offered Delilah his arm.

Intrigued, Delilah accepted, following Daniel and Gideon to her cabin.

"Now close your eyes," Daniel ordered.

Feeling slightly apprehensive, Delilah obeyed. She heard the door creak softly as Titus led her forward.

"All right. Open 'em." The words barely left Gideon's lips before Delilah gasped.

They'd whitewashed the cabin while she'd been gone!

"It's wonderful," she breathed, crossing the room and turning around to take it all in. The cabin gleamed, somehow larger and brighter. "Thank you so much!"

Gideon and Titus grinned while Daniel shrugged. "Didn't take long with the three of us."

"We used the whitewash left over from what Miriam bought," Gideon explained.

"Alisa thought you might like it." Titus smiled fondly at the mere mention of his wife.

"I love it." Delilah fought back tears at the thoughtful gesture. "Thank you so much." She saw that they'd done their level best to make this cabin her home.

But it's not my home. It's Paul's.

"Will Paul mind?" she asked, hesitant to make it seem as though she didn't appreciate the surprise, but anxious to hear the answer.

Titus laughed. "Why do you think he took you and the girls on the picnic?"

Happiness blossomed. Paul knew—he'd spent a lovely day with her so she could be surprised when they got back. *He's such a generous man.*

"Miriam and Alisa'll want to know what you think." Gideon nudged her toward the door. Still not quite believing it, she cast one last look over her shoulder, then rushed back to the kitchen to envelop Alisa and Miriam in a hug. "Thank you! It's so lovely—I can hardly believe you did it just for me!"

Alisa laughed. "We thought you might like it."

"It's astounding what a little whitewash can do for a room." Miriam voiced exactly what Delilah thought. "Now it's time to blow out your candles!"

For the first time, Delilah noticed the large cake on the table.

"Happy birthday!" everyone chorused as she took a huge breath and blew out all of the candles.

"Wait a minute!" Logan stopped Miriam as she began cutting the cake. "Bryce and I have something for Delilah, too."

Bryce carried in a crate lined with scraps from an old quilt. He set it down on the bench. Curious, Delilah leaned over to see a small, white and brown ball of fur.

Bryce gently picked it up, and Delilah recognized a kitten just big enough to fit in the palm of his hand. "This here's Shortstack. Normally we keep the cats in the barn, but her mama had a big litter, and Shortstack"—Bryce set her on the table to demonstrate—"has one leg that's a bit shorter than the other three." The little cat started ambling toward the cake. "She can get by but just can't keep up with the rest and might not be able to move fast enough around the cows and horses."

Logan scooped her up and placed the tiny kitten in Delilah's hands. "We thought maybe you'd like to keep her."

Delilah lifted the cat up for a closer view. She gently stroked the soft fur. "Oh, she's adorable!" Delilah lost her heart when the kitten curled up in her cupped hands. "I think she and I will get along just fine."

Logan positively beamed. "You can keep the crate in your cabin—it's where she'll sleep. She's big enough now she doesn't need her mama. She'll do with a saucer of milk."

Feeling as though her heart would burst, Delilah placed her new friend back in the nest of scraps. She'd never experienced such a wonderful birthday. This entire family had given their whole day to making her feel special, and she knew she'd never forget it. Daniel put the girls to bed while everyone else relaxed.

"Well, you certainly had a busy day!" Delilah exclaimed when Alisa held up the forest green day dress with an extra length of black added to the hem and sleeves so it would fit Delilah perfectly.

"Oh, it was nothing," Alisa demurred and pushed a small package toward her. "Open Miriam's!"

Delilah tugged the string and brown paper off to reveal the small teakwood treasure box she'd admired earlier.

"But this is one of the few things from your home, Miriam!" Delilah protested. "You should keep it."

"My home is here now, and so is yours. You should have a few special things in your cabin." Miriam always knew just what to say to put her at ease.

Delilah looked at Paul. "Thank you for letting them whitewash the cabin. I hope you like it, too, so it won't bother you when I leave."

His brow furrowed. "What do you mean, when you leave? That's your cabin now."

"Yeah! We can always build another one." Logan's frown matched his older brother's.

Sorry to have ruined everyone's good time, Delilah tried to backtrack. "Oh, I'm sure you can. But I can't stay here forever. Things will change sooner or later, you know. But I do love it here."

Paul smiled again. "Good, because this week I'll teach you to drive a buckboard. I know it's not exactly a present—"

"Every day here is something I enjoy," Delilah interjected. "And you know I want to learn, so you'll be giving me a new skill. I look forward to it."

Daniel returned, and Gideon began an evening devotional before they all turned in for the night. Delilah brought her new pet into her cabin.

"You'll sleep right here where I can see you." Delilah crossed her arms after pushing the crate right next to her bed.

Shortstack opened her tiny mouth in a feline yawn and kneaded the blanket as she settled in. Delilah smiled and hopped into bed. Tomorrow she planned to paint that sketch she'd drawn today. It couldn't be a grand gesture, but she wanted to give something back to these warmhearted people who'd given her so much.

"Well, at least you don't spoil her," Paul teased Delilah as she set down a saucer of cream on the stoop for Shortstack's breakfast.

"That's what Bryce told me to give her." Delilah grabbed the watering can while the kitten daintily lapped her breakfast.

"Calm down. I think she likes you, too." He watched as Shortstack finished her breakfast and brushed up against Delilah's skirts, trying to twine around her ankles.

"I never knew I could become so fond of something so fast." She smiled as the kitten gave a slightly unsteady hop off the threshold.

Paul waited until Delilah looked at him again to reply. He met her gaze. "I know exactly what you mean." He saw his remark sunk home when she blushed and turned her attention to the watering can, practically flooding a tiny sprout before regaining her composure and moving on.

I can't wait until I give her our first driving lesson.

Later that morning, Paul finished inspecting all the tack and tending to the leather, then went to find Delilah. Garbed in some sort of stained smock, she stood in a patch of sunlight beside the barn, the tip of her tongue between her lips as she concentrated. A speck of green paint dotted her nose, while some stray curls escaped her loose bun to wave in the slight breeze. Paul had never seen a woman look more beautiful.

He just stood there, watching, hesitant to startle her for fear it would ruin her work. Shortstack gave him away, ambling toward him and attracting Delilah's attention with a mewling cry.

Self-consciously, she lifted a hand to smooth her hair, only to stop when she saw her colorful fingertips.

"Hi," Paul said softly.

"Hi." She waved her brush toward the picture. "If you wait for a minute, you can be the first to see it."

More than happy she hadn't sent him away, Paul plunked down to play with Shortstack while she finished.

A few moments later, she stepped back with a satisfied sigh. "I'm done."

Paul got to his feet and strode to where she stood, very aware of her anxious gaze upon his face as he scrutinized the piece.

What he saw almost rivaled its creator in loveliness. "Amazing. It's as though I'm sitting with you on that very same hill!"

A smile spread across her face. "Good. That's just what I wanted—something so the Chance family would remember yesterday for as long as I will." She looked away shyly and confessed, "I'm hoping everyone will want to hang it in the parlor."

"You've got my vote. It's plain to see how talented you are."

"Well, it's about time I wash up and go help with lunch." She picked up the watercolor and headed toward her cabin. Paul noticed her slower pace as Shortstack gamboled along beside her.

Paul stifled a groan when he spotted the all-too-familiar cloud of dust on the horizon just before lunch. This time, instead of trying to dissuade the stubborn clan from coming in, he'd just go inside and let the women know who was coming.

At least this visit from the MacPhersons had one thing in its favor—they wouldn't be trying to woo his woman but rather be soliciting her expert assistance in courting other brides. Come to think of it, the sooner they wrote those letters, the quicker they wouldn't have any reason to barge onto Chance Ranch whenever the mood struck them.

Paul's good humor lasted through lunch and right up until Delilah and the MacPhersons huddled at the table—alone.

"All right, what do you have for me so far?" Delilah eyed the trio of brothers with some misgivings.

Micah reached into his shirt pocket and drew out some grubby paper. He smoothed it on the table and wordlessly slid it toward her.

Delilah looked in consternation at the few words penned across the sheet. "But these are just their names and where to send it."

Micah jabbed it with a finger. "Naw, it ain't. That there's the name of their aunt."

Obie nodded eagerly. "Figgered we oughta pass along our respects an' all."

"That's a wonderful idea. It can't hurt to be on good terms with their family." Delilah desperately tried to think of a way to coax more information out of the would-be swains without discouraging them.

"They's sweet li'l thangs. We done tole Mike to write that down." Obie peered at the paper as though he'd suddenly be able to read.

"Oh yes. I see it here, along with 'nice-sounding voices.' Um, I believe I heard you mention something about how they look?" she prodded.

"Yep. Hair redder'n a rooster's comb," Hezzy complimented.

Red hair, Delilah made a note, omitting the comparison to a rooster. "And you said something about their eyes. . . ."

Obie and Hezzy stared fixedly at the tabletop, so Delilah took a deep breath and pressed on. "I seem to remember you said they were shiny?"

Obie brightened and jabbed a thumb toward Hezzy. "Yep. He said as how they's jist as shiny as a mud puddle."

Delilah bit back a laugh at the extravagant praise. "Hmmm. . .might I suggest something a bit more romantic?"

Hezzy frowned in concentration, then broke into a self-satisfied grin. "Sure. How 'bout eyes jist as shiny as a mud puddle. . . ." He paused to slant a triumphant look at Mike. "In the moonlight."

"Why, Hezzy, that's almost like po'try!" Obie slapped his brother's shoulder.

"Some things just don't sound the same on paper." Delilah diplomatically rejected the entire mud-puddle comparison. "How about 'browner than. . .' " She paused to think, belatedly realizing her mistake when they began offering suggestions.

"Dirt?" Obie supplied.

"Aw, ya don' say she's like dirt." Hezzy spared Delilah having to reject that pearl. "How 'bout bark?"

Her relief faded like a curtain left too long in the sun. "You know, there are different kinds of bark, so maybe you want to be more specific."

"A chaw o' tobaccy?"

"A tater?" Soon the suggestions were flying through the air so fast, Delilah didn't even have to comment.

"Boot leather?"

"Molasses?"

"Fresh coffee?"

"Oh, that's a good un, Obie," Hezzy approved. "But ladies don' always like coffee like we'uns. How 'bout 'the wings of a June bug'?"

With dismay, Delilah realized all three thought this analogy had merit. "Well, I don't know. I don't much like insects, myself."

Mike spoke up for the first time. "How 'bout brown as a fawn's coat?"

"Wonderful," Delilah praised, writing it down and moving on before they could suggest anything else. "And I understand you wrote something to Temperance, Mike?"

"All done with that."

"So they're sweet, with nice voices, red hair, brown eyes, and an aunt we'll need to win over. Is there anything else I'm missing?" She clearly needed to end this session before they backed her into a corner with their woeful wooing.

Hezzy spoke up. "They cook a right fine meal."

"And they's good gals. Not loose or. . .or anythin'." Obie wouldn't meet Delilah's eyes.

"God-fearin' folk," Hezzy affirmed.

"And I've already explained to Tempy about our spread and what's waitin fer 'em," Mike assured her.

"Well, gentleman, I'll write this up and show you a draft next Sunday." She rose from the table, and the brothers followed suit.

"Much obliged," Mike said.

As the brothers made their way out of the cabin, Delilah paused to wonder whether any man would ever write her a romantic letter.

Chapter 13

As most of the town headed back home after church that Sunday, the MacPhersons and Whites lingered at Chance Ranch.

Delilah looked at the three expectant faces before her, and the enormity of the situation sank in like never before. So much hinged on her writing—the dreams of Obie and Hezzy, the futures of Eunice and Lois—her throat went dry. Obie hunkered down to rub Shortstack's tummy as the kitten purred happily.

"I tried to mention everything you shared with me," she began, "so I'll just read it to you, and we'll see if you'd like to change any of it:

> *Dear Miss Eunice and Miss Lois Trevor,*
>
> *I, Delilah Chadwick, am writing this letter on behalf of my neighbors, Obadiah and Hezekiah MacPherson, who pray you are well. These upstanding brothers hold you in high regard and speak fondly of you both.*
>
> *They describe your hair as rivaling a blazing sunset and admire your eyes as being as soft and brown as a fawn's spring coat. They tell me you are good, God-fearing women who will come alongside their men to make a home for their families.*
>
> *They hope you remember the time they visited your home to purchase their hunting dog and ask you to pass along their compliments to your aunt and uncle for raising two such fine young women.*
>
> *If you are agreeable and not already spoken for, the Misters MacPherson will send fare for your journey to their spread as their intended brides.*
>
> *We send this in the care of Miss Temperance Spencer, whose hand Micah MacPherson has requested. They earnestly hope she will be your companion as you travel to Reliable, California.*
>
> *Sincerely yours,*
> *Obie and Hezzy MacPherson*

"Whooeee, if that don't turn they heads, sure as shootin' nothin' will." Hezzy clapped Obie on the shoulder. "We's gonna have us some brides, Brother!"

"Yep. That sounded so fine, I reckon if'n I got it, I'd marry us." Obie beamed at Delilah.

"How soon can we send it?" Mike got straight down to business.

"Oh, I'll take it back to town with me this evening, seal it, and send it out with the next batch of post." Reba White walked over. "So you boys are fixin' to get hitched, eh?"

"Yes'm," Obie and Hezzy chorused.

"All right. I'll let you know just as soon as they write back." Reba took the envelope from Delilah as they all exchanged good-byes.

"So we'll be seeing you on Thursday?" Delilah asked, knowing Miriam had invited the older woman over for a girls' sewing day.

"It's amazing how mending can pile up." Reba laughed ruefully. "And I've even got a quilt that's only half-finished. It'll do me good to spend a day in the company of women."

"All right, now this is just a first lesson, so no need to be nervous." Finally, they were alone. Paul caught Delilah glancing from the reins to the horse and back again.

"Just the same, maybe we ought to wait until your arm is a bit better—in case . . ." Her voice faded as she looked at him pleadingly.

"Any woman who can wield a knife and shoot like you can has no need to fear driving," he consoled. "Besides, you already know how to handle a horse when you ride."

"That's because I can get the feel of the animal. I can touch him or use my voice to calm him down if he gets excited or frightened. I know that an animal that doesn't know you won't trust you. They sense when the person guiding them is hesitant or doubtful."

"Speck is my horse. I trained him up from a colt—that's why he pulls the wagon, too. We understand each other, so he won't give us any trouble."

Delilah eyed the sling on Paul's arm with obvious misgivings but held her tongue.

Appreciating her tact, Paul decided to try it her way. "Would you feel better if you gave old Speck here some carrots and patted him a bit before we go? That way you could get to know him."

"Yes, I think that just might work." Relief colored her voice, and a smile returned to her lips.

"Do you feel comfortable holding his reins while I go grab some of those carrots?" She nodded, and he went to fetch some sugar cubes and carrots.

Lord, if I can say one thing about this woman Thou hast brought into my life, it's that she's consistent. She doesn't trust Thee, and until she does, she can't trust me, and Speck doesn't stand a chance. I wonder whether she even trusts herself. Please be with us today so she'll feel the peace of Thy presence and gain no further reason to withdraw from others.

"You're a handsome fella." Paul squelched a spurt of envy when he realized Delilah was crooning to Speck. She stroked his mane and grinned at Paul when he stepped next to her.

"He's a beautiful animal, Paul. Sweet, too." She took the chunks of carrot and held them out to Speck, giggling when he lipped them from her hand.

"Kind of tickles, doesn't it?" Paul commiserated as Speck chomped his treat and buried his nose in her hands, searching for more.

"Now don't be greedy," Delilah chided. "We're going for a little ride, and afterwards you can have some more. Ready?"

Paul helped her into the buckboard, then jumped in beside her. "Now to get Speck going, you give the reins a bit of a flick and give him the command." To illustrate, he clacked his tongue, and the wagon gave a slight lurch as Speck obeyed. "I want you to hold the reins with both hands." He waited until she had them securely in her hands before letting go.

"And I just hold them?"

"Make sure you don't let the line go slack, or he can have his head and yank the reins out of your hand. Then we have a runaway wagon."

She blanched, and he hastened to reassure her. "Just keep a good grip on them." Her knuckles went white as she clutched on to the leather. "How's this?"

"If you keep on like that, you'll cramp up. Relax a little. Pulling the reins will make him slow down. If you say, 'Whoa, boy,' and tug on them, he'll stop."

"Good. Whoa, boy," Delilah called, tightening the reins. A relieved smile crossed her face as the buckboard came to a halt. "That wasn't so bad."

"Very good," Paul praised. "But if you're going faster, remember you'll need to slow down before telling him to stop, or it'll be too sudden."

"Makes sense." Delilah, obviously feeling more in control, flicked the reins and clacked her tongue, grinning as Speck began to walk forward once again. "I think I've got the hang of it."

"You've got starting and stopping down, but there's a lot more to it," he warned, not wanting her to get too complacent.

"I suppose. How do I get him to move a little faster?"

"If you want him to speed it up, you flick the reins again and tell him to giddyup. Go ahead and try it. Remember if you want him to slow down, just tug on the reins—but don't yank."

Soon she had Speck going at a jaunty trot. "Do you think I should try an even quicker pace?"

"If you ever actually want to get to town, you'll have to step it up a bit. Go ahead and have him go into a slow run—a canter."

"Oh, that's a big difference." Delilah gasped and tugged the reins, breathing more easily when the horse dropped back into a clip. "You did a wonderful job training him. He does exactly what I ask."

Paul refused to puff up like a rooster at the compliment. "Animals are a lot like people. It takes time to earn their trust, but when you do, it's always worth the wait."

She stayed silent for a moment, then asked in a small voice, "Always?"

"Always," he repeated firmly. "Some take more time than others, but those are the ones who are most worth the effort." This time she didn't respond at all.

He reached over and took the reins from her. "We'd best be getting back. Reba'll be here soon."

Lost in thought, Delilah washed her hands slowly. Paul hadn't just been talking about horses.

He wants me to trust him, and I already trust him more than any man I've ever known—even Papa. As much as I loved him, he couldn't keep promises he made to himself, much less the ones he gave to me. Paul has never broken his word to me or anyone else as far as I've seen. But that'll just make it so much harder when he finally does. No one's perfect, so how can I trust him more than I already do?

As she dried her hands, she wiped away the unsettling thoughts, then went to the parlor, where Reba, Alisa, and Miriam waited. Davie had a cold, so Widow Greene couldn't make it, and it was simply understood that Priscilla couldn't be bothered to stitch hems.

"I brought by some flannel for you, Miriam. Thought after we took care of the mending, we could make a few things for your firstborn son."

"So you think the baby will be a boy, too?" Alisa asked, slanting Delilah a victorious look.

"Be mighty surprised if we didn't have another Chance man on the ranch soon, seein' as how his papa has five brothers," Reba confirmed.

"But Miriam's side of the family runs to girls," Delilah protested. "Think about it—there's me, Miriam, and Hannah, and we're cousins because Grandma had two daughters in the first place. Then there's Polly and Ginny Mae, and Daniel has five Chance brothers, too. I'm not saying the babe won't be a boy; I just figure it could go either way."

"I suppose it could, come to that," Reba allowed.

"If you're all finished speculating, I can tell you." Miriam spoke softly, her hand resting on her rounded tummy. "My son will be born in early summer."

"Well, that settles it," Reba finished.

"Have you told Gideon?" Alisa asked.

"We've decided we'll name him Caleb after his grandpa." Miriam looked so content and proud, sitting there in the rocker Gideon had made for her and their babe, Delilah just had to get up and give her a hug. It didn't surprise her when

Alisa joined them, and Reba came over to say a prayer.

"Lord, we thank Thee for Thy many blessings and lift up Miriam and her babe, Caleb, to Thy arms for protection and comfort."

Even Delilah couldn't help joining the fervent chorus of "Amens." If it might help Miriam and her child, she'd pray to their God.

"Why are you all smothering my wife?" Gideon demanded from the doorway.

Everyone untangled as Reba let loose a bark of laughter. "We were just having a woman moment, Gideon."

"Reba prayed for me and the babe." Miriam stood up and walked over to her husband, who put his arm around her and dropped a kiss on the top of her head.

"What are you doing here so early, honey?" she asked. "Supper's hours off yet."

"I knew you were all having a sewing day, so I figured I'd change and hand this over." He held out the brown chambray shirt he'd been wearing earlier that day. "Got caught in some thorny fence."

"Good thinking." Reba bobbed her head. "Nothin' worse than spending a day mending, only to have your man come home with another load."

"I'll just leave you women to it." Gideon left the room, and Alisa giggled.

"What's so funny?" Miriam asked.

"Nothing much. I couldn't help thinking your husband might've felt a bit uncomfortable in here. It's not often the women outnumber the men on Chance Ranch."

Delilah couldn't hold back a chuckle at that observation. "Oh, I don't know. When Paul took me and the girls on a picnic for my birthday, he held his own."

"We all had a nice day." Alisa smiled at the memory. "Gideon, Daniel, and Titus finished whitewashing your cabin in no time at all. Logan and Bryce gave Shortstack a bath, if you'd believe it. Never would've thought dunking a feline would prove a challenge for two young men, but that cat was bound and determined not to get wet. 'Course in the end, Bryce and Logan had their way."

"I don't know about that." Miriam smiled as she threaded a needle. "I thought Shortstack matched 'em drop for drop when they came in looking like they'd been dunked in the fishing hole."

"And all my favorite food lay spread out like a feast when we got home. You two kept yourselves just as busy as the men." Delilah wanted to let them know how much she appreciated their kindness.

"Well, you did right by 'em in return." Reba nodded at the landscape hanging on the parlor wall. "Right before you came in, Miriam and Alisa were telling me how you painted that in thanks."

"Oh, that hardly took any time at all," Delilah assured her. "I sketched it that day while we were on the picnic and filled it in with watercolors the next day. I love painting."

"And it shows in every stroke," Miriam complimented.

"You've got a talent, that's for sure. That's a piece of art any rich man in the city would be proud to hang on his wall. Something peaceful and happy about it." Reba stared at the painting, her fingers darning a sock almost by memory.

"I wouldn't suppose you'd paint another one?" she wondered aloud.

"I don't paint anything in the exact same way twice," Delilah apologized.

"Oh no. I didn't mean the same picture. I just mean another painting. It'd be a real nice addition to the store. I'd hang it right over the counter." The dreamy look on Reba's face faded as she took on the visage of a businesswoman once again. "I'd give you a fair deal in store credit."

"Oh, you're so nice to us. You'll be here for Miriam's birthing, too. I'd be happy to make you one as a gift, Reba."

"Nonsense. I wouldn't feel right about it." Reba looked across at her with a stern expression. "Now you just have it for me some Sunday, and we'll set you up with that store credit. Do we have an understanding?"

"Agreed." Delilah couldn't find it in her heart to argue with the determined woman. "What type of landscape would you like?"

"Whaddya mean?"

"Well, I can paint the barn, or a grove of trees, or the creek," Delilah elaborated.

"Oh, you should paint the fishing hole!" Alisa encouraged.

"I think I'd like something with a bit of water in it," Reba mused. "Well, I trust you. Just go ahead and surprise me."

Chapter 14

Delilah," Paul started to say as Polly and Ginny Mae peered down from the wagon. *How can I tell her that even though she's learning very quickly, I'd rather drive today? She's only had three lessons, and I don't want to risk Polly and Ginny Mae getting hurt.*

While he searched for words, Delilah spoke. "If you don't mind, I think you should drive this afternoon. You're a wonderful teacher, but. . ." She smiled at the girls. "Today we carry precious cargo."

Lord, we are alike in so many ways. Why can't she see it? She values home and family, everything I want to give her. Please help me find the words to reach beyond the wall to her heart.

"We certainly do." He helped Delilah up into the back of the wagon and watched as Polly and Ginny Mae immediately scooted toward her. She wrapped an arm around each of them and listened attentively as Ginny Mae rattled off the beginning of the alphabet.

She'll be a wonderful mother. He let those pleasant thoughts run through his mind until they neared the fishing hole.

"I don't see any water." Delilah gave a slight frown and craned her neck to get a better view. "Is it past that hill?"

"Yep. Just past those trees and bushes." He gestured toward the greenery Spring always touched the pond first. "It's best to leave the wagon right here and walk Speck up so he can have a drink."

Delilah lent a hand in unhitching the horse and held Speck's reins while Paul hefted down the girls and supplies. He accepted the reins and led the way up the well-worn path. Glancing back, he saw Delilah holding the basket on one arm, with Ginny Mae clutching her hand and Polly's in her chubby fists, completing the chain. He hastily tied Speck to a tree and met them at the bushes.

"Before we get any closer, I need you dumplin's to listen to the rules." He knelt to be at eye level with Polly and Ginny Mae. "Neither of you can swim so you'll have to steer clear of the fishing hole—it's far too deep. Do you understand?" The little heads bobbed in unison. "And you're not to run off where Delilah and I can't see you." That way, the girls wouldn't venture toward the creek, which ran a little ways off. "Got it?"

"Yes, Unca Paul," the girls chorused as he took the basket from Delilah.

"All right, then. Let's go!" He started back up the path, only to see two tiny blurs race ahead of him beyond the bushes.

"Hey!" The girls froze at his roar. "What did I just say about running off?"

"Sorry, Unca Paul." Polly scuffed the toe of her shoe in the dirt.

"We got 'cited."

"If you do that again," Delilah said, shaking her finger, "we'll go back home." Her stern demeanor crumbled when Polly's lower lip trembled and tears welled up in Ginny Mae's eyes.

She knelt down and gathered them in her arms. "We love you both very much, and it's our job to make sure you're safe. I'd rather take you home than see either of you get hurt."

"That's why you have to follow the rules," Paul finished for her.

"We'll be good." Polly hugged her.

"Pwomise," Ginny Mae vowed solemnly after a particularly loud sniff.

"Mind that you do," Paul said.

Two seconds later, all traces of crying evaporated.

"It's so pretty!" Polly stared around, awed at the lush vista.

The trees lent cool shade to the newly green hills as rays of sunshine sparkled through the leaves. Wildflowers nestled in clumps of clover, leading to the tall rushes tickling the water's edge. The tiny rivulets feeding the pond gurgled softly, underscoring the chirps of birds lining their nests. A calm breeze chased wispy white clouds across the sky and ruffled the grass along the small hills. Dragonflies skimmed the rippling water, where plump trout eyed them hungrily. Paul couldn't imagine anything closer to paradise than being in this place with the people he loved.

"It's wonderful," Delilah breathed, seeming to drink in her surroundings.

"No, Ginny Mae!" Polly grabbed her younger sister's hand as Ginny Mae toddled after a bright orange butterfly. "We ain't s'posed to go by any of the water." She cast a yearning glance at the cool pond.

"Well now, that's not exactly true." Paul winked at Delilah. "There's one place you can play in the water. See over there?" He strode over to where a bubbling stream of water sprayed over a small outcropping of rocks to form a shallow pool, rolled up his sleeve, and touched the sandy bottom. The cool water lapped halfway up his forearm, not even reaching his elbow, while the stones at the top of the hill would be too high for the girls to touch. Dappled sunlight warmed the water, so he knew the girls wouldn't catch cold.

Polly and Ginny Mae hovered eagerly by his shoulder, anxious to get closer but hesitant to break the rules. They were good little girls and deserved a treat.

"I said you couldn't go where Delilah and I couldn't see you, and you couldn't be near the fishing hole. But as long as you obey those rules, you can play here in your very own pond."

"Complete with a tiny waterfall. It's perfect." Delilah helped the girls strip off their shoes and stockings.

Beaming, Polly scurried to the edge first, only to have her smile fade. "Unca Paul, what're those?" She poked the water with a pink fingertip.

"Hmmm? Oh, those are just tadpoles. They won't hurt you."

"Whatsa tab-ole?" Ginny Mae toddled over.

"They're just baby frogs," Paul explained, taking Polly's hand.

"They don't look like frogs." Doubt still shone in her eyes as Paul slowly, gently guided her hand toward the water.

"They will later," Delilah said, backing him up. "You know, some people call them pollywogs."

"Really?" Polly giggled as the tadpoles flicked around her fingers. "That tickles!"

"Pollywog!" Ginny Mae shrieked in glee, pointing at her sister. "Pollywog!" Together they waded in, the water brushing just below Polly's knees and just above Ginny Mae's. In no time at all, they were laughing and splashing around, throwing handfuls of water in the air to watch the sun catch the droplets on the way back down.

While Delilah began sketching, Paul kept an eye on the girls. When his stomach rumbled, she looked up and quirked a brow. "Hungry?"

"I don't suppose you'd believe me if I said no." He grinned back at her.

"Polly! Ginny Mae! Come on back here. It's lunchtime!" She began pulling sandwiches and apples from the basket while the girls climbed out of the pool and raced each other to the blanket. Paul used the edges of the quilt to dry their legs. Soon they were all munching happily, enjoying the shady quiet.

"I like it here," Polly pronounced. "This is the bestest picnic ever."

"I think so, too." Delilah mopped crumbs off of Ginny's face. "But now I think it's time for a little rest."

"I'm not sleepy," Polly protested, utterly sincere after a satisfying yawn.

"Me, too." Ginny Mae's eyelids drooped as Delilah tucked them both in the quilt.

"Then you'll be awake and playing again before you know it," Paul consoled. In a matter of minutes, the two children were fast asleep, light eyelashes dusting rosy cheeks.

"They're so sweet." Delilah tenderly tucked a stray hair behind Polly's ear.

"Sure are. Best to let them sleep so they stay that way, though." Paul tilted his hat over his eyes and leaned against the tree trunk, breathing in the fresh scent of the grass and the moist earth.

Delilah propped up her sketchbook, and soon Paul heard the rasp of pencil on paper. Readjusting his hat, he watched her record every minute detail with tiny strokes and delicate shading. At last, she breathed a sigh of satisfaction and held the sketch at arm's length for a final viewing.

Paul could scarcely believe his eyes.

"It's perfect." Paul spoke softly but startled Delilah nonetheless.

"Thank you." She made an expansive gesture. "But it doesn't do this justice."

"I disagree. You have a God-given talent, Delilah."

Ugh. Why is it that every time we start to talk, just when I most enjoy his company, he starts going off about God again?

"I get the impression you don't agree with me." Paul's droll comment made Delilah realize she was being rude.

"I don't know."

"Yes, you do. What're you thinking, Delilah?"

"Mama always told me, 'Delilah, if you don't have anything nice to say—' "

"Don't say anything?" Paul finished. She looked at him in astonishment.

"What kind of advice is that?" she asked incredulously. "If someone asks you a question, you can't just ignore them!"

"It's an old proverb. If you only have unpleasant things to say, some people think it best not to voice them." His forehead creased as he gazed back. "What were you taught? If you don't have anything nice to say. . ."

"Say something vague." Delilah jumped when he burst into laughter. "Hush! You'll wake the girls!"

He cast a glance at the snoozing bundle and sobered up a bit—his wide grin still bearing witness to his mirth.

"What's so funny, anyway?"

"Oh, I was just remembering how you dealt with the MacPherson brothers." He peered at her curiously. "You really do live by that rule, don't you?"

"To each her own." She shrugged.

"Aha! See, you just did it again. Not giving a real answer but being vague. Look at me." Paul waited until she stared into his blue eyes before speaking again. "You don't ever have to be vague with me. I want to know exactly how you feel and why you feel it."

"Can't I just try out your way and not say anything?" She gave a weak laugh.

"I never said it's my way—it's an old saying. I tell you what's on my mind, and I hope you feel comfortable enough with me to do the same."

His steady gaze told her he meant every word of it. She sighed and gave in. "I was thinking about how every time the two of us start talking, you always bring up God. Do you remember how I noticed it on our last picnic?"

"Of course I do." With anyone else, the words would have sounded defensive, but Paul remained utterly sincere. "Do you remember what I explained?"

"You said that God made everything beautiful, so whenever you admire something, you think of Him," she recited dully.

"So what's wrong?" He waited, obviously at a loss.

"I've been thinking about that ever since you said it," she began hesitantly, her words gathering strength as she finished. "And I think there's something you left out."

"What's that?"

"You say God created everything, right?" There was nothing she could do but walk him through it.

"Unto the heavens and the earth," he agreed.

"Then what about everything hurtful and ugly and mean? Why did He make those things if He loves us as much as you say?" She blurted out the questions, half-hoping Paul would have an answer but knowing the miserable truth that she was right.

He stayed silent for a long while.

"I should've just let it be. I'm sorry, Paul." She hated to have devastated something so much a part of who he was.

"I'm not. I'm just trying to think of how to put it into words. I stand by what I said—God created everything—but at the same time, the ugly things that cause pain weren't in His plan."

"How do you know? What other reason is there?"

"This is why I was thinking." He rubbed the back of his neck. "I hate to make a mess of explaining, but here goes: Everything God made was beautiful in the beginning, but evil has a way of turning things sour, taking something good and using it for the bad."

"So you're saying that God made the milk, but evil made it go sour?" She couldn't keep the scorn from her tone. "There are worse things than spoiled milk, Paul."

"I know. And I never said anything about milk. Take this example: Knives are incredibly useful tools—they help us cut meat, slice bread, shape leather, skin fish, whittle wood, and more. You even use yours to great effect for protection. These are all noble purposes for the blade, but it can also be used for harm.

"If you've ever read in the paper about someone being taken hostage, you know that a criminal can easily put that same knife to the throat of another human being to hurt or even kill. Either way, that's not why the knife was made, and it doesn't mean the blade itself is evil. Do you understand what I'm saying?"

"So you mean that we can all be tools for good or evil?"

"Exactly." Paul beamed, looking very satisfied with himself for explaining his point.

And I just don't have the heart to ask him my next question. Some things shouldn't be said, but I have to wonder, if we're tools, then who's using us?

Chapter 15

Delilah ignored the twinge in her arm and kept mixing flapjack batter. Miriam and Alisa deserved to sleep late for once. Besides, she wanted to do something, anything, for the Chance family to show how much she appreciated their hospitality and generosity, and the entire Chance family had voted her down when she'd insisted on transferring the store credit Reba had paid her for the painting.

The twinge grew to a full-fledged ache, and Delilah realized she'd been taking her frustrations out on the batter. She set down the bowl and began ladling the goopy stuff onto the skillet, still somewhat amazed to see it become a soft, solid pancake.

The truth of the matter was, she'd finally found a home complete with friends and even family, but it hadn't turned out the way she'd planned.

I want a home and family of my own. She flipped a flapjack perfectly and smiled in satisfaction. *I've learned so much here that I'd make a good wife and mother. As long as I stay here, I'll just be kind of an extra without a say in family business.* Tears gathered in the corners of her eyes. Delilah wiped them away furiously and went after the last pancake.

Spluchh. The source of the disheartening sound was one half-cooked flapjack now dangling from the ceiling. Delilah grabbed the mop, swiped the useless mess to the floor, and wiped up the sticky traces, then bent down to find the ornery little thing.

"Oh! Shortstack!" Delilah couldn't suppress a giggle as the kitten gave a mighty shake to dislodge the well-traveled pancake, then daintily trotted around it, sniffing and mewing plaintively.

"I know, that's not your breakfast." Delilah set down a saucer of cream. "Don't be so upset. You're just lucky it didn't land sticky side down on top of you. We'd never have gotten the batter out of your fur!"

"How much time have you been spending with Bryce?" Logan queried, obviously biting back a grin.

"As though you don't talk to your horse," Delilah shot back, knowing Logan shared Paul's fondness for his mount.

"All right, all right. You've got me." Everyone else wandered in and took their seats.

"Sure smells good." Titus eyed the platter with interest.

"Flapjacks, bacon, and coffee. Can't think of anything better." Paul slid onto the bench beside Delilah. Logan said grace, then began passing around the food.

"Miriam, looks like you outdid yourself this morning," Daniel praised, chopping Ginny Mae's breakfast into tiny bites.

"We didn't help." Alisa drizzled syrup on her plate. "Delilah made all this by herself." She stabbed a forkful and brought it to her lips, chewed for a moment, and proclaimed, "And it's absolutely wo—" Turning faintly green, she clapped her hands over her mouth and ran out of the room.

Titus shot after her an instant later, followed by Miriam, who grabbed a damp towel. Everyone else stared suspiciously at their plates.

"I don't understand," Delilah spluttered. "I know the recipe by heart." She frowned at the table, puzzled.

"I'm sure it's something else." Paul gallantly speared a bite and made as if to eat it when Delilah snatched it from his hand. Despite his bravado, even he seemed slightly relieved when Delilah swallowed with no apparent difficulty.

"They taste just fine to me." The door opened, and Miriam walked in, holding the damp towel to Alisa's forehead.

"Do you want to tell them?" Miriam tried to whisper, but her soft voice carried throughout the silent room. Alisa gave a faint shake of her head, apparently still not trusting herself to speak.

"That's just fine." Miriam patted Alisa's shoulder and looked around. "Titus didn't get back before we did?"

Just then, Titus banged the door and all but flew into the room. "I'm gonna be a daddy!" His smile could've lit the entire cabin, so brightly did his joy and pride shine.

After a chorus of congratulations, Miriam and Titus took a still-green Alisa back to her cabin to lie down for a bit.

"Hey! That means the food really is good!" At Bryce's comment, the men grabbed their forks and dug in with gusto.

"I can't believe Reba's friend saw my painting and commissioned another one," Delilah exclaimed as they drove toward the fishing hole. "I'm so excited, I can scarcely contain myself."

"You're a talented woman, Delilah. It doesn't surprise me at all." Paul watched with pleasure as Delilah expertly turned the horse around the last bend and brought them to a halt.

"Well done," he praised.

"Thanks to you." She smiled warmly as he helped her off the buckboard and they carried their supplies back to the fishing hole. "You're an excellent teacher, Paul."

Maybe in driving, but I haven't gotten the real lesson across yet. We've spent so much time together, and every moment I grow to love her more. Lord, why do I feel as though time is running out? Miriam let me take the sling off the other day, and it won't be long at all before I'm back out on the ranch with the other men. I'll only see Delilah at meals or evening devotions. How do Gideon and Titus stand being away from Miriam and Alisa for so much of every day?

As soon as he'd asked the question, he knew the answer.

They knew their women would be waiting for them when they came back. Delilah liked it at Chance Ranch, but Paul could sense she didn't see it as a permanent home. Besides that, Gideon and Titus could look forward to eternity with their mates, but Delilah still didn't believe.

Lord, help me to reach her today. Please.

"It's amazing how different everything looks from just a few weeks ago." Delilah set up her sketch pad, and her pencil fairly flew across the page.

The light green of spring had given way to deeper, richer shades. Wildflowers peeked out from the fresh-scented grass. Birds no longer fluttered around scavenging for twigs but rather sat cozily in their egg-filled nests, unseen but trilling sweetly. The leaves on the trees had grown and filled out the branches, blocking more of the sunlight and adding an air of cool mystery.

"In My time." The words rustled through the leaves in the breeze, and Paul knew he'd received his answer. Delilah might not accept the Lord today, but Paul needed to trust in his Creator's plan.

He bowed his head. *Lord, what of the desires of my heart? Thou knowest it's difficult for me to stand by. Forgive me for my doubts, Jesus. Give me words as Thou wouldst have me use them, and grant me patience to see them come to fruition. Give me strength to trust in Thy will. Amen.*

He'd been lost in his own thoughts for so long, Delilah had finished her sketch and was peering at him, looking concerned.

"What's running through that head of yours, Paul?"

"How everything comes down to choices."

"True." She seemed to begin saying something but hesitated.

"I thought we agreed we weren't going to be silent or vague," he gently teased.

"I wanted to say that that's one of the reasons I can't put my trust in your God." She spoke the words softly, seeming almost ashamed.

"When you give your life to the Lord, Delilah, He doesn't make your choices for you. That's why He gave mankind free will. It's why we have to choose to accept His love in the first place."

"And that's why some people choose to do harm to others?"

"Yes."

"Why would He even allow that to happen, then?" Her frustration showed in the way she clutched her pencil in her fist.

"If He just made us all to love Him immediately, it wouldn't be a choice. It wouldn't mean as much. Love has to be freely given, not forced."

She stayed silent for a while, mulling that over.

"So our choices are to take His love or go to hell? Seems to me like He's stacked the deck, Paul. Love Me or else—not much of a choice, is it?"

Oh, Father, how lost Delilah is! Help me to show her the way into Thy arms. She's been hurt and sees things so differently.

"That's not the way to look at it. The truth of the matter is we've all sinned and fallen short of the glory of God, so we deserve death. God sent His Son to be the sacrifice so that if we choose to accept the magnitude of His love, we can live with Him forever and share His joy."

"How have you sinned?" She looked at him shrewdly. "You're a good man."

"Every time I think a mean thought about another. Every time I shirked a chore to come to this fishing hole when I was young. Anytime I said anything less than the honest truth. How we live day to day is filled with small choices. No one chooses the right thing every single time. The Lord doesn't call us to be perfect; He calls us to be the very best we can be. To look at ourselves and admit our faults and to actively try to be better."

"And if you make the wrong choice?"

"You repent, ask for forgiveness, and learn from the mistake."

"So even after you accept Christ, you still mess up and make the wrong choices, and you still go forward?"

"Exactly. Choosing God isn't a one-time decision. It's a decision we make every time we have a choice. And if we mess up, His grace continues to cover us. He promises to be with us always. God never turns His back on us—we're the ones who turn our backs on Him."

"It sounds like so much responsibility." She looked as though a heavy weight had settled on her shoulders.

"That's why God is there to carry us through. You have the assurance to know you never face anything alone. You just have to decide to choose His love and grace over your own independence."

She silently gathered up her supplies, and he followed her to the wagon. Neither of them said a word on the drive home. Paul prayed earnestly the entire way, knowing she battled her thoughts and doubts.

"I can't do it, Paul." She stood in the barn after taking care of Speck. "It is *my* choice, right? Please don't be too disappointed." Her amber eyes glowed with distress, pleading with him.

"I can't help being disappointed, Delilah." His voice sounded gruff even to his own ears. "I don't want to lose you."

"Listen to me." Her jaw was set. "If you're talking about after we die and all of that, I have to tell you that I've seen death claim a person I loved. Nothing is more final. They've gone and you can't follow them. There's nothing left of who they used to be." Her voice cracked, and he put his arms around her.

"It's not just that, Delilah, although that's very important to me." He took a deep breath and said what had to be said. "The Bible tells us we can't be unequally yoked."

"What does that mean?"

"A believer cannot wed a nonbeliever."

She pulled away from him as though his touch burned her.

"Delilah, please understand what I'm saying."

"Oh, I understand perfectly," she spat bitterly. "I'm not good enough for you the way I am, and your loving God who allows you any choice you please won't let you accept me." Tears sparkled in her golden eyes as she whirled and fled to her cabin. Even from the barn, he heard the door slam.

Chapter 16

With a heavy heart, Paul plodded to the kitchen. *Lord, why does it have to be this way? This is too hard.*

Miriam took one look at his face when he entered the kitchen and shooed him into the parlor and onto the sofa.

"What happened?"

He poured out the entire exchange, desperate for any advice she could give him. When he finished, she asked quietly, "Paul, you put a lot on the table today. Now you've got to give her enough time to take it all in."

"I didn't handle it very well, did I?" He buried his face in his hands.

"You'll have to trust that the Lord knows how best to reach her. You've been seeking His will and asked Him to speak through you. Only He knows what it'll take to break through that wall around her heart. He's been tapping."

Paul let loose a heavy sigh. "It hasn't worked. If you ask me, it's about time He gave it a good knock."

As much as Delilah tried to ignore it, the knocking wouldn't stop. It seemed as though Paul was determined to break down her door.

"I said go away, Paul!" She buried her face back in the pillow to muffle her crying.

"It's Miriam, you goose. Now open up this door so we can talk."

Grudgingly, Delilah got up, threw the bolt, and cracked the door open. After peering around to make sure Paul wasn't lurking anywhere nearby, she pulled her cousin inside and locked the door again before sinking back down on the bed.

"If you want to know what happened, you should talk to your brother-in-law." Delilah heard the bitterness spewing from her mouth but couldn't stop it. The pain poured straight from her heart.

"I already did." Miriam sat down beside her, put an arm around her shoulders, and tucked Delilah close.

"So he told you about being 'unequally yoked'?" Her voice sounded tiny and far away.

Miriam nodded. "Yes. I knew it would come down to this, though. Chance men don't consider marriage lightly." Her cousin tried to look at the bright side, but Delilah would have none of it.

"He's not thinking about marrying me—he's thinking about not marrying me!" She ended on a wail and cried into Miriam's shoulder.

When the sobs led into a case of distressed hiccups, Miriam spoke again. "You know very well that wasn't what I meant."

"But—*hic*—it's true—*hic*—and you know—*hic*—it!"

"Let me see, now. The man told you he doesn't want to lose you and is disturbed by the thought that he can't marry you. Sounds to me as though he cares for you. Deeply."

Delilah drew a shuddering breath. "I feel the same way about him; that's why it hurts."

"Just so long as you're clear on what he tried to tell you."

"Most of it. I'm just not ready to give my life to God yet," Delilah bemoaned.

"Let me ask you something." Miriam looked at her intently. "If Paul asked you, would you marry him?"

Delilah took a minute to really think about that. Could she trust him with her life? "Yes."

"But you know he's given his life to God, right?"

"Um-hm," she mumbled.

"So if you give Paul your hand, you're trusting it to God in a way, aren't you?"

"I never thought about it that way."

"Well, Paul is a man of the Lord. It's just as much a part of who he is as his brown hair. So at least some part of you already trusts God." Miriam patted her shoulder one more time and got to her feet. "I'm going to leave you to your thoughts. I already told Paul you'd be needing some time, so take as long as you need."

Miriam kissed Delilah's forehead, gave her one last hug, and toddled out of the room, hand resting fondly on her enlarged tummy.

Delilah did some quick calculations. It would be six weeks before Caleb came into the world. By then, Alisa would be pretty far into her pregnancy.

And where will I be?

"San Francisco?" Paul repeated dumbly, unwilling to believe what Reba told him. He ignored the racket of the guests around the barn to listen closely.

"That's right." The older woman smiled smugly. "I thought it might be good to mention it to you before I passed the message along to her. You're sweet on little Delilah, aren't you?" She took his silence for the affirmation she sought. "Have you told her yet?"

Paul grimaced, remembering the week before. He and Delilah had hardly spoken since then, and his nerves were stretched tighter than a rope around a bucking bull's neck. Still, he knew he had to respect the distance she kept. Until she spoke to him, he'd told himself to be content with sitting by her during supper and working himself into exhaustion on the ranch. It was the only way he could sleep these days.

"Botched it that bad, eh?" Reba winced. "Seems to me you'd best mend your fences before she deserts them altogether."

"Your friend and her husband are serious about setting her up in a studio in San Francisco?"

"That's right. They own a gallery back there and think they'd do well to feature Delilah's art. So are you going to go and clear up those muddy waters, or are you going to watch them wash under the bridge and off to San Francisco?"

"In My time." The refrain that had haunted him all week whispered in his ear once again.

But I've waited, Lord. I've tried to be patient! What if she doesn't speak to me before she goes? What if I just asked Reba not to tell her?

" 'Trust in the Lord with all thine heart, and lean not unto thine own understanding,' " Polly's tiny voice piped out happily a few yards away.

I get the message, Paul grudgingly conceded.

"Are these people decent folk, Reba? Can we trust them with one of our own?"

"As surely as I stand here today," Reba vowed.

"Then it's up to Delilah." He abruptly turned from Reba and headed for the barn, cutting through the throng of neighbors yacking about anything and everything.

"Psst!"

Delilah looked around to see where the whisper came from. Hezzy gestured wildly from behind the corner of the barn. Obie stuck out his arm, holding a letter clutched in a massive fist with a grin beaming from ear to ear.

Delilah set down the empty pitcher and made her way as inconspicuously as possible. It seemed as though the women had written back to their beaus, and judging from those scruffy smiles, the news was good.

"So they wrote back?" she whispered, respecting their obvious wish to keep their neighbors in the dark for now.

"Yep. Looky 'ere, Miz Delilah." Obie thrust the much-creased sheaf into her hands. Delilah smoothed it and read:

Dear Mike,

You do me great honor in asking me to be your bride. God rest her soul, your mother knew your devotion each day of her sickness until God called her home. In those days, I learned of your tender heart and strong hands. I wanted to help you out in that sad time, and since you left, I've prayed God would bless you and your brothers. Hearing you are well made my heart leap, and when I read on and saw you were seeking a bride, I knew then and there 'twas every dream I ever had coming true.

Yes. Yes, yes, a million times yes. I'll come to Californy and marry you. I'll work hard by your side, cook your meals, and bear your children.

I talked with Eunice and Lois. They're a-wanting to come along and marry up with your brothers, but their aunt is balking. She reared them from a young age, and she's been carrying on something fierce. My sister went calling on her. You know Lovejoy—she could reason a possum into a pie. It took some doing, but she managed.

You can tell Hezekiah and Obadiah that their intendeds will be coming, too.

None of the three of us has much to call her own, but we'll come with willing hearts and working hands. I'll be like Ruth in the Bible, going to a new place and getting married. I pray God will bless us as He blessed her and Boaz.

With high hopes and a happy heart,
Temperance Spencer

"Oh, that's wonderful!" Delilah smiled and hugged each brother in turn.

"Mike's grabbin' Reba so's we cain send the money on the stage tomorra," Obie gushed.

Hezzie hooked his thumbs on his suspenders and all but strutted. "Cain you believe we's gonna get us some brides?"

"I couldn't be happier for you," Delilah assured them both. "When do you think they'll get here?"

"Near as Mike cain reckon, they'll be here afore winter. We cain't hardly wait." Obie stopped talking as they heard footsteps.

Mike, with Reba in tow, came around the corner. He plunged his hands into his pockets and thrust a fistful of cash at her. "So you'll send it tomorra?"

"First thing," Reba promised. "Congratulations, boys." She patiently listened to a lengthy recital of the Trevor sisters' charms before turning to Delilah. "If you have a moment, we need to talk."

Paul saddled Speck, vaulted on, and took off. He didn't really aim for any place in particular, just so long as he wouldn't have to be polite to anyone for a while. He had some questions to ask the Almighty.

Dozens of thoughts drummed around in his head, making his temples throb before he realized he'd wound up at the fishing hole. Loosely hitching Speck to a nearby tree, Paul headed over to the very place he and Delilah had gone earlier that week.

He could scarcely believe that just days ago he'd sat in this very shady knoll with Delilah, enjoying the beauty all around him and answering her questions about God. It was then he'd driven her away from them both.

"Lord, if she goes, a part of me goes with her." Silence met his announcement, and his shoulders slumped in defeat.

"Why didst Thou bring her here only to take her away? Why did I think she loved Chance Ranch as much as I do?" He paused. *Why did I think she loved me?*

Chapter 17

Probably because Delilah does." Daniel's deep rumble came as a surprise to Paul.

"What are you doing here?"

"Don't know yet, but I figured you looked like you might do something stupid if nobody came after you."

"What are you blathering about?"

"Seems to me the last time you had your mind on that woman when you were riding, you broke your arm." Daniel plunked down on the grass beside him.

"I—" Paul's mouth snapped shut when he realized there was no denying the truth of his brother's assessment. He maintained a stubborn silence until curiosity got the better of him. "What do you mean, Delilah does?"

Daniel gave a heavy sigh. "Aside from maybe Miriam, have you ever seen a woman fix her mind so on helping out around here? She didn't know how to cook; she learned. She saw we didn't have a flower garden; she planted one. Polly and Ginny Mae yammer on about something or another she's done with 'em most every night before bed. And even I can see how much she likes this place just by the way she painted it." He made a broad, sweeping gesture.

"And that's what's got us into this mess in the first place," Paul grumbled, not certain whether Dan's estimation of Delilah made him feel better or worse.

"What makes you think she's leaving?"

"Reba's friends are offering to take Delilah back to San Francisco with them, set her up in a fancy studio, and sell her paintings in their gallery."

"Still doesn't mean she's leaving."

"I haven't given her a reason to stay."

"So give her one."

"I can't. She's not a believer, Dan." Paul watched as Dan shook his head. "You just don't understand."

Dan's head jerked up, and he spoke fiercely. "Now you listen and listen good, Paul Chance, because I know a lot more than you understand. A good woman is a gift from God, someone who completes you and gives you joy." His voice almost cracked as he continued. "When you find that, you've got to hold on to it with both hands before He takes it away again. You have to fight for her with everything you are, or you'll lose her. You haven't got what it takes to go through life wondering if there was anything else you could've done. You don't have a reason to keep on going." Paul knew Dan spoke of his daughters.

"You don't really believe all that, Dan."

"More than anything else," he swore fervently.

"Then prove it," Paul challenged. "If Delilah and I do get married, you'll be the one to walk her down the aisle. None of this not attending the wedding."

Emotions warred on Dan's face. "All right," he spat out gruffly before he got to his feet and stomped away, leaving Paul to his thoughts once more.

"When you find that, you've got to hold on to it with both hands before He takes it away again." Dan's words echoed in Paul's mind, resonating in his heart.

Lord, is she being taken away by Thee?

No response came.

Maybe I should listen to Dan and ask her to marry me. I've seen Thee stirring in her soul, and I know Thou wilt bring her to the fold.

Grim determination took hold of him. *She's my match, Lord! Thou knowest that! Why shouldn't I keep her for Thee?*

As soon as the thought crossed his mind, he knew the answer in his heart. *I wouldn't be keeping her for Thee. I'd be keeping her for myself.* Paul straightened his shoulders. *Still, we belong together as man and wife.*

"And two souls shall become one." The scripture Miriam had read at her wedding crossed his thoughts. He struggled to accept what his heart told him.

No. The Lord still holds my soul. I've already given it to Him. This way I'll just be bringing Delilah to Him, as well. Even as he reasoned his case, he knew the truth: A man and wife stood together as one in the eyes of God. If he married a nonbeliever, that could not be. He'd never find peace because he'd forever be torn between the Lord and his wife. That was no way to raise their children.

Lord, please let her stay. Help her to see Thy love and accept Thee so that I can take her as my bride. How can I choose between the two things most dear to me in the world?

Even as the prayer went up, Paul knew the awful truth. There had never been a choice.

Delilah opened her folio and put in the watercolors she'd worked on this last week. The sheer number of them showed how hard she'd tried to keep her mind off Paul and her disappointment over how he hadn't spoken to her once since that awful day.

All the better. She blinked back another onslaught of tears at the thought of leaving him behind her. *At least I can remember Chance Ranch.*

She shut the folio and began pulling her clothes from the wall pegs, leaving aside the traveling set she'd worn when she first arrived. Her heart clenched as she folded the forest green day dress Alisa had given her, then altered for her.

I will have a studio of my own, she reminded herself. *A home where I can work on my paintings in peace without feeling dependent on anyone else. It's just what I've always wanted. I should be happy.*

Then why aren't you? a tiny piece of her heart demanded as she held the jewelry box Miriam had given her for her birthday.

Because I hoped Paul would ask me to stay, her heart cried, *but he didn't say a word.*

She glanced out the window, spying the tender green shoots of the garden they'd planted together. She gathered her resolve. *From the start, I've said I couldn't stay here forever.*

"I am happy." She spoke aloud, shooing away her doubts.

"I'm glad to hear that." Miriam and Alisa came through the doorway.

Not certain what to say, Delilah shot them a smile before opening the drawer on her washstand.

"I can't believe you're leaving this afternoon! It seems like you just got here." Alisa pulled Delilah into a spontaneous hug.

"Here. We finished it last night." Miriam held out a cloak made of the soft wool they'd bought from Reba not so long ago.

"We couldn't let you go traveling without it, even though it'll be summer soon." Alisa folded it up and laid it in Delilah's satchel.

Touched by their thoughtfulness, Delilah fought a fresh onslaught of tears.

The women helped her finish packing, and Delilah picked up her satchel. Noticing how much heavier it was than when she'd arrived, she walked up to the waiting buckboard. She gave one last look at the homestead and realized the weight of that valise couldn't compete with the heaviness of her heart.

Paul numbly watched as everyone at Chance Ranch said their good-byes to Delilah. When she reached him, he took her hand in his, looked into her golden eyes one last time. "May God be with you, Delilah." His final words were a fervent prayer, one last plea for her to change her mind about everything. About God. About being his wife. About leaving for San Francisco.

"Good-bye, Paul." Her voice caught. When she drew a shaky breath and tugged her hand out of his grasp, he knew he was letting her go. . .possibly forever. He tried to swallow the lump in his throat but couldn't speak as she climbed onto the buckboard and drove off.

Lord, I chose Thee. Now what wilt Thou choose to do with each of us?

Six days later, Delilah let loose a sigh of relief as she unbuttoned her shoes and curled her toes for the first time all day. She stretched and smiled as Shortstack pounced on a tattered ball of yarn in the corner.

The Munroes had been as good as their word. Founders of the San Francisco Art Society a mere year before, they'd set her up in a clever little cottage and introduced her to the artisans of the city.

Today they'd unveiled her first display at their gallery, and she'd heard so much praise, her head felt as though it would burst. One thing was certain: She'd find no shortage of patrons here. As a matter of fact, she'd best get some sleep. Tomorrow she'd need to paint enough to replace the pictures sold today.

Shortstack curled up at her feet as Delilah snuggled into bed only to find her mind too active for sleep just yet. This had been happening ever since she left Chance Ranch. In the short span of time she'd been in San Francisco, she'd found herself so restless, she'd been working rather than sleeping. Pushing aside the covers and ignoring an indignant meow from Shortstack as she scrambled out from under the pile, Delilah padded across the room and began lighting lamps. She passed by the small round mirror on the washstand and caught a glance of dark purple shadows under her eyes.

Well, I may not be getting my beauty rest, but at least I haven't been idle.

She sank her toes into the large braided rug she'd made over the last week and ran her palm over the quilted coverlet she'd begun with Miriam and Alisa but finished alone. She made her way toward the window, wanting some fresh air. Deciding against opening it at night in a town still too strange for comfort, she fingered the curtains she'd stitched and hung, trying to make the cottage her home.

These would be so charming in my cabin back at Chance Ranch. I always wanted to decorate with a splash of color. I would have loved to hang some of my landscapes on the wall. I'd put one right over the foldaway desk. She closed her eyes and imagined how different the cabin would seem with paintings resting against the freshly whitewashed walls, her first quilt cushioning the bed, and the sprigged curtains fluttering in the warm summer breeze while Shortstack batted the edges. *And if I looked out the window, I'd see the garden in full bloom.*

She shook the thought away. She had a new life now—a home of her own and independent means. She purposely strode over to her desk and picked up her sketchbook.

Settling into a nearby chair, she began flipping through the pages, setting aside those she thought would make the best paintings. The various landscapes of Chance Ranch tugged at her heart. There was the homestead as it stood when she left, her garden beginning to blossom. Here she'd given her imagination free rein, depicting lavish blossoms amid a sea of green.

Sorrow engulfed her as she set that one aside. Putting up that portrait for sale would be like selling her dreams. *Maybe I can go back someday to visit Miriam and see Caleb.* Somehow that thought only made her more aware of how she'd be missing Caleb's birth.

What if something goes wrong, and I'm not there to help? Fear washed over her. *There's nothing I can do all the way out here.* She wanted to cry at the very thought of not being there for Miriam, who'd given her so much.

Paul always prayed. I could, too. For the first time, Delilah didn't push the thought away. What harm could come from it if she tried? At best, she'd gain God's blessings for her cousin and some comfort for herself. At worst, it wouldn't work and she'd feel just the same as she did now—helpless and alone.

She took a deep breath and plunged in. "Lord, I know I have no right to ask You for anything when I've denied You for so long. To be honest, I'm still not sure I can trust You, but I'm not asking this for myself. Please be with Miriam and Caleb while I can't. I'm not free to go to them."

The thought of Paul's stoic expression as she'd waved good-bye stung her deeply. How could she face him when he'd made it clear she hadn't made the choice he wanted her to?

I still can. Didn't I just pray? Doesn't that mean something? Plagued by her thoughts, Delilah pulled open her dresser. Surely if she began painting, she'd exhaust this restless energy. She reached into the drawer and saw her mother's Bible resting beside a folder of her very first sketches.

Maybe the answer won't come from my hands, Delilah realized. *There's no shame in admitting I might be wrong.* She picked up the Bible, her fingers sliding over the leather, worn smooth by her mother's hands.

Trembling, she clasped it to her, hugging it tight. She hadn't opened it since Mama died. Crawling back in bed, she laid it on the pillow beside her, letting it fall open.

" 'If we say that we have no sin, we deceive ourselves, and the truth is not in us,' " she read.

I never said I had no sin, Delilah protested, but her gaze stayed riveted to the page. The words seemed strangely familiar, and she remembered Paul quoting this passage the morning he'd broken his arm and taught her to gather eggs.

" 'If we confess our sins, he is faithful and just to forgive us our sins, and to cleanse us from all unrighteousness.' "

I haven't confessed them, she admitted. *But since I have sinned, even if I did repent, why would He be faithful and just to forgive me?*

Shortstack hopped onto the bed, reaching out a dainty paw to bat the frayed edge of the ribbon Mama used as a placeholder. Gently pushing the kitten away, Delilah flipped over to the bookmark and found a marked passage in John 3.

" 'For God so loved the world, that he gave his only begotten Son, that whosoever believeth in him should not perish, but have everlasting life.' "

I remember learning this when I was little. That's what was niggling in the back of my mind when Paul spoke about living forever! Excitement mounting, she kept reading.

" 'For God sent not his Son into the world to condemn the world; but that the world through him might be saved. He that believeth on him is not condemned: but he that believeth not is condemned already, because he hath not believed in the name of the only begotten Son of God.' "

That's me. This is what Paul was trying to tell me. Because I don't believe in God, I'm condemned. But I don't feel lost in despair because Mama died. She believed in this. And it's not too late for me to believe, too. But can I trust Him?

That thought brought her up cold, until she remembered what Miriam had pointed out. *"If you give Paul your hand, you're trusting it to God in a way."*

"I do trust Paul. I trust him because he's not like Papa." For the first time, she allowed herself to make the comparison. "He won't put an insubstantial dream above my feelings."

But Paul put God before my feelings. The realization took her breath away and made her head whirl. *And I trust Him enough to put Miriam and Caleb in His hands. When did God stop being some vague notion and an important part of my life?*

"When you let Me."

Tears trickled down Delilah's cheeks as she prayed long into the night, thanking God for His unfailing love and forgiveness and finally accepting her need of them.

Chapter 18

Paul corralled the last steer and walked Speck over to where Logan and Bryce rested on their mounts, deep in conversation.

"No question about it." Logan's somber pronouncement made Paul uneasy. "It has to be done."

"What has to be done?" The way the two of them jumped hardly offered any reassurance. "What're you two scheming now?"

"I'm calling a Chance vote, that's what." Logan's bravado wavered somewhat when he snuck a glance at Bryce for confirmation.

"About what?" Paul walked Speck a step closer, pleased that his younger brothers stood their ground, but irritated nonetheless.

"You'll find out along with Gideon, Titus, and Daniel. There're on their way over now." Bryce pointed to three men on horseback.

Paul shifted in the saddle, anxious to find out what was afoot and suddenly eager to get back to work.

"What're y'all lollygagging around for?" Daniel grumped as soon as they all stood within earshot.

"Logan and Bryce"—Paul jerked a thumb in their general direction—"are calling a Chance vote."

"About what?" Titus and Gideon seemed just as wary as Paul felt.

"Well," Logan said, straightening in the saddle, "no offense to Miriam and Alisa, who do their best around here, we know, but seems as though things around here are on the decline."

"Yep. We've gotten used to certain. . .comforts," Bryce interjected. "So basically, what we're saying is—"

"We want to eat good food again!" Logan abandoned any attempt to make their cause seem lofty.

"Miriam needs her rest." Gideon glowered at the upstarts. "She's due this month!"

"Aw, anyone can see she's 'bout ready to pop, Gideon," Bryce soothed. "We wasn't talkin' 'bout her."

"Well, Alisa hasn't been well, either," Titus groused.

"You don't get it," Logan grumbled. "We ain't complaining about your wives; we just have a solution. A way of making sure they're not overworked and we're not underfed."

"Oh, no, you don't," Paul barked as soon as he saw where this entire debacle was headed.

"Oh, yes, they do." Daniel's habitual scowl disappeared into a cheeky grin. "All in favor of bringing Delilah back?"

Only Speck backed up Paul's nay, and even that was more of an equine whinny than anything else.

"And we know how Miriam and Alisa would vote if they were here. Motion passed. Now I vote Paul goes to fetch her." Daniel leaned back, pleased as punch to see Paul outvoted once again. "That settles it. You're going."

Less than an hour later, Paul sat on the buckboard, driving toward Delilah. *Lord, I have to say I have my doubts about this. I'm not sure if I can bring her back and not aim to keep her. Please give me strength to do Thy will. Please watch over my love.*

As he passed through town, he pulled up in front of the mercantile. He clomped toward the back, his heavy footsteps suiting his mood.

"Hello there, Paul. Let me just grab my bag, and we'll get to Miriam straight away!" Reba bustled through the curtain before he could get a word out.

"Not yet, Reba!"

She poked her head out and peered at him. "No?"

"No. But Miriam sent this with me." He thrust a letter toward the older woman. "She said it might be her last chance to write her parents before the babe comes."

Reba clucked her tongue. "And to think you had me all riled. Couldn't it have waited until next Sunday?"

"Probably," Paul allowed, "but I was heading through anyway."

"Where you headed?"

"San Francisco."

A knowing glint shone in Reba's eyes, and Paul hastened to correct her. "Miriam and Alisa need the help, that's all."

"Sure it is." Reba swapped him a handful of peppermint sticks for the letter. "For your trip."

Paul chuckled as he left the store, certain she'd intentionally given him peppermint rather than black licorice because she thought there might still be a future for him and Delilah.

Lord, I hope she's right.

Delilah hummed happily, if a bit off-key, as she walked back to her studio from the Munroes' place.

The fledgling city bustled almost nonstop; from boots clicking on boardwalks to buildings being built, one could never escape the sounds. Since the establishment of the San Francisco Bar Association, businesses had sprung up seemingly overnight, relying on Joshua Norton's plan to bridge the bay between San Francisco and Oakland. As prosperous and energetic a place as this was, she would gladly trade it all to be sitting by the fishing hole at Chance Ranch.

Thank You, Lord! They still want my paintings even if I have to ship them from Chance Ranch. Now. . .

Her jaunty step slowed as she contemplated what she planned. *Please give me the courage to go back. I don't know if You will bring me and Paul together or not. If not, it'll break my heart.*

Fresh doubts flooded over her. *No, no, no! I am putting my faith in You, Lord! Even if I don't stay at Chance Ranch, the Munroes have been so kind as to assure me of a place here. Still, I do wish there were some way I could be sure I'm doing the right thing.*

She turned onto the walkway to her studio and halted when she saw someone peering into her window. Despite her instinct to leave immediately, something held her fast. Those broad, powerful shoulders, the brown hair curling beneath the brim of a well-worn hat—Delilah's heartbeat quickened.

"Paul?" He must have heard her hopeful whisper, because he froze, then turned to face her.

Oh my. Lord, I just asked for a sign, and there's no questioning this has to be one, but his eyes are guarded. Why is he here?

Sunlight framed Delilah, bathing her in gold and making her even more beautiful than he'd remembered. *Lord, she seems so serene, like she fits here. I see none of the sadness she bore when she left us. Is she finally happy, and I'm supposed to ask her to leave it all behind?*

He cleared his throat. "I need to talk with you for a minute."

"Come on in." Her warm smile sent tingles down his spine as he followed her into the charming structure. It resembled a cottage more than anything, but her easel stood by a large window next to a worktable.

With easy grace, she sank into an armchair by the small fireplace and gestured for him to do the same. She waited patiently for him to speak.

"I've come to bring you back to Chance Ranch." *Oh, well done, blurting it out like that. This was a mistake. Will she be disappointed I didn't come to fetch her as my bride? Even worse, will she be relieved?*

"I'll be ready to go in half an hour." He watched in amazement as she began tucking loose leaves of paper into her sketchbook and binding her folio. Dumbfounded, he walked over to explain. Didn't she want to know why? What if she misunderstood?

He held out a hand to stop her, only to have her push art supplies at him.

"Why don't you go put these in the wagon while I pack my satchel?" She disappeared behind a partition, and he heard the rasp of a drawer opening.

Lord, what do I do? Dumping her things onto one of the armchairs, he strode over behind the partition, only to be brought up cold. She'd dumped the contents of her drawer onto her bed. He gulped at the sight of delicate stockings and the corner of a white ruffled petticoat peeking out from under them.

Certain his ears were redder than ripe strawberries, he seized the only option left to him—retreat. He rushed back to the armchair, grabbed her art supplies, and didn't stop until he stood in the warm sunshine by the buckboard.

Delilah stifled a giggle at the look on Paul's face as he fairly ran out of her studio; then she shoved her unmentionables into the valise. Well, no use crying over spilt milk. The bigger question was why he was taking her back.

Lord, I'm trying so hard to trust in You and in Paul, but I'm going to burst if I don't find out soon whether he came because he missed me or something else. He doesn't seem worried like he'd be if anybody was hurt back at the ranch. Give me patience, Father!

She finished packing as quickly as possible, looked around one last time, and hefted her satchel to the doorway, where Paul took it.

"Come here." She picked up a squirming Shortstack, grown far bigger than she'd been on Delilah's birthday, and tucked her into a large basket. Shortstack gave an indignant meow before settling in. The cat gave a lurch to pop her head up through one of the basket flaps. When she seemed content just to see what was around her, Delilah couldn't bring herself to shut the basket again.

As they began leaving town, Paul cleared his throat. "Do you need to talk with anyone—make arrangements so everything's fine when you come back?"

Refusing to be discouraged by that statement, Delilah shook her head. "It's all been taken care of. I left a note on the table." Taking a deep breath, she looked him in the eye. "Will I be coming back?"

"That's up to you. For now, Miriam's pretty much in bed until the baby comes, and Alisa's green around the gills every day until the afternoon, but they're both too stubborn to admit they need help. We took a Chance vote, and I came to fetch you."

Another Chance vote, Delilah mused. *And to think, once I wondered if one of those famous votes would let me stay at Chance Ranch.*

"But that's not unusual. Neither of them is ailing other than that?" She had to make sure.

"Nope."

Now what? Is he going to stay quiet all the way home, Lord? Will he not say more than the bare minimum the whole time I'm at Chance Ranch? Give me strength and wisdom, Lord!

Chapter 19

"I'm so glad to hear that." Delilah debated whether or not to continue. "I've kept Miriam and Alisa in my prayers."

"We all have."

Delilah knew the instant her words sank in. Paul whipped his head around to face her and brought Speck to a dead halt with one jerk on the reins.

"What did you just say?" His intense gaze searched her face hungrily, and she smiled to see how desperate he was to hear her say the words.

"I've prayed for you all." Her heart sang as his face lit up with wonder.

"You've accepted Christ?" His voice was low and gruff. When she nodded, he gathered her in his arms and held on tight. "Then He's answered my prayers, too. What changed your mind?"

"I sat in San Francisco, completely independent, with a home of my own and new friends, but it wasn't what I'd thought it would be. I wasn't at Chance Ranch anymore, so I had to trust God to take care of the people I love. It was so much easier than I'd thought, once I made the decision. And since then, I've remembered all the things you've told me about God's love, and I can see it all around me."

"Whatever is good and lovely cometh from the Lord." He cupped her chin in his palm. "Now do you know why I think of God so much when we're together?"

"No," she confessed, "but it doesn't make me jealous."

"It never detracted from our time together. I think of Him when you're near me because, to me, you're the loveliest thing He ever made. I love you, Delilah." His voice deepened as he took her hand in his.

"I love you, too," she whispered, raising a hand to stroke his cheek.

"Delilah, will you do me the honor of becoming my wife before God and man?"

"Yes." As his lips met hers, a warm rush tingled from her lips to her toes. Delilah rested in the circle of his arms, feeling more cherished than she'd have ever thought possible. "Let's go home."

"The second I saw you two holding hands, I knew we'd done right by you, Brother." Daniel clapped a hand on Paul's shoulder.

"Now if that's not the sorriest excuse I've ever heard for your meddling, I don't know what is." Paul grinned to take the sting from his words. "Truth of the matter is, she'd just told Reba's friends she was coming back here, so don't get too cocky."

"Aw, I'm just ready for some of those flapjacks tomorrow. Now let's get to bed. The sooner we wake up, the sooner we'll be at the table."

"I'm all for that." Paul hung up his hat. "It'll bring us one day closer to the Sunday you walk Delilah to the altar."

Daniel's brows knit together as he scowled. "About that. . ."

"Oh, no, you don't. A man's word is his bond." Paul flopped onto the bed. "Besides, you should've seen Delilah's face when I told her you'd volunteered."

"Humph. Volunteered," Daniel grumbled but ventured one last question as he put out the light. "Made her happy?"

"You'd better believe it."

Delilah watched with satisfaction as everyone—including Alisa—polished their plates. *Lord, how light I feel due to Your grace. I sit here as a member of not one but two families. I belong at Chance Ranch, but You claim me as Your daughter. Thank You so much.*

She cleared the table and shooed Miriam back to bed, where Polly and Ginny Mae followed.

Alisa sank down on the bench. "It's so good to have you back. It feels as though you never left."

"Oh, I don't know about that." Delilah smiled and handed her a glass of cool water. "But I'm glad to be here."

"You know. . ." Alisa cocked her head to the side and scrutinized Delilah. "You're right. You've changed over the past weeks—you seem so much happier. Anyone can see the Lord shining through you now."

Delilah laid a towel over a bowl of bread dough and turned when Polly and Ginny Mae tumbled into the room.

"Auntie Miri-Em!" Polly gasped, pointing to the bedroom.

"What's wrong with Auntie Miriam?" Alisa hurried over.

"She had"—Ginny Mae lowered her voice to a confidential whisper—"an accident."

"I'll go help Miriam while the two of you keep an eye on Auntie Alisa, okay?" Delilah hurried off to find Miriam stripping covers off her bed.

"What's wrong?" Delilah hastened to her side.

"My water broke. The baby's coming." Miriam calmly finished stripping the bed and laid down freshly laundered but tattered old quilts. "Go and ring the dinner bell so Gideon'll know to fetch Reba."

Delilah raced back to the kitchen, clanged with all her might, told Alisa the news, and went back to help Miriam change into an old flannel nightgown and get in bed.

For the next hour, Alisa kept Polly and Ginny Mae busy while the Chance men milled around anxiously, each one steadfastly refusing to leave the house.

It was obvious the memory of Hannah weighed on their minds, and when Delilah hustled in to boil water, Alisa's worry was evident.

Delilah took her aside for a moment. "Listen, the contractions are pretty close together, but she's in good spirits, and Reba will be here any minute. Why don't you pray for Miriam and Caleb?"

"I have been. I want to be with her." Daniel overheard Alisa's request and broke away from the pacing herd of men. "Go ahead. I can take care of my little Pollywog and Ginny Mae." He bent down and started tickling his girls while Alisa followed Delilah back to Miriam's cabin.

"How are you doing?" Alisa sank down on the bed beside Miriam and held her sister-in-law's hand through another contraction.

"Pretty good." Miriam gave a wan but convincing smile, and Alisa relaxed visibly.

Reba sailed into the room and got down to business. After a few minutes, she eyed Miriam suspiciously. "How long have you been having contractions?"

Miriam waited to reply, gasping through another set before answering. "About three hours."

"You're one of those rare women who get through it in hardly any time at all." From that moment, there was no room for chitchat, and scarcely an hour later, Delilah handed Reba the twine and scissors to tie and sever the umbilical cord.

Delilah held a squirmy, slippery red baby and walked over to the basin of warm water to bathe the squalling infant. His little face screwed up as he wailed indignantly, and the only sounds able to rival his lusty lungs were the happy shouts of his papa and uncles as Alisa told them mother and son were just fine.

Delilah wrapped Caleb in a blanket and walked over to the bed, where an exhausted Miriam smiled beatifically and reached out to hold her son.

She nuzzled her cheek against the soft duck fluff covering Caleb's head as Gideon strode into the room, tears of happiness filling his eyes at the sight of his wife and boy.

"Praise God," he got out hoarsely as he put an arm around Miriam's shoulders.

Delilah couldn't have agreed more.

"You may not have heard the news yet," Gideon announced, beaming at the congregation. "But that's my son, Caleb, in my beautiful wife's arms, so next Sunday we're going to have a christening."

Whoops and cheers from the crowd drowned out anything more Gideon said as the men whistled and stomped their approval over the first boy born in Reliable. When things calmed down a bit, Gideon raised an arm and continued.

"And that's not all, folks. We have another special occasion that fine day. I'm pleased to announce that the marriage of my brother Paul to Delilah Chadwick will also be taking place."

A hush fell over the crowd before ominous rumblings began. Hats moved back and forth as men shook their heads. Paul stood up next to Gideon.

"Everyone's invited." It did no good. Paul looked out at the sea of faces and saw set jaws, menacing scowls, and knuckles cracking.

Elias Scudd jumped to his feet. "Oh, no, ya don't, Paul Chance." He jerked a thumb toward Delilah. "This un's spoken for."

Paul crossed his arms over his chest. "Yes, she is. By me."

"That ain't what he meant, and you know it!" Ross Dorsey yelled near the back rows.

"Why don't you explain it to me." Paul refused to lose his good humor. In all honesty, he couldn't blame the menfolk for being put out with him. "Who's spoken for her?"

In an instant, benches crashed to the ground as the men of Reliable jumped up to stand their ground. Every male on the premises let loose a resounding "Me!"

"She can only have one husband," Reba managed to choke out before she burst out laughing.

"We know!"

"Just so long as his last name ain't Chance," Rusty growled as the crowd rumbled agreement.

"We done told ya from the first that was the way it had to be," Elias Scudd shouted.

"Yeah!"

"Sure as shootin'!"

Ross Dorsey shook a fist. "You greedy gophers already got two fine wimmen to care for ya!"

"Leave somethin' for the rest of us!" Rusty roared as the men became more worked up by the minute.

"She's ain't a flapjack, fellas!" Obie, Hezzy, and Mike waded to the front. "Ya cain't go claimin' her like that."

"Sure we can!" someone shouted back.

"No, ya cain't. Ya hafta treat a woman proper. Now if Miz Delilah wants ta marry up with Paul here"—Hezzy clapped Paul's shoulder so hard his knees just about buckled—"you'll hafta git your own brides." Obie glowered from under bushy brows.

"Whatsa matter with you MacPhersons? None of y'all have a bride, neither!" Scudd glared right back.

"Sure we do." Mike stepped forward when Scudd scoffed at him.

"Yeah, right. How come nobody's seen 'em?" Rusty challenged.

"They'll be here afore winter." Hezzy rocked back on his heels.

Stunned, the men stayed silent for a heartbeat. Then someone offered a tentative, "How'd ya manage that?"

"Like I said, ya gotta court a fine woman, gentlemen. We wrote to 'em and asked 'em ta come down."

"Yee-haw! More women are on the way!" Everyone got riled up again at that realization.

"Now see here," Obie barked. "Temperance, Eunice, and Lois are taken. Don't you be thinkin' they's fair game."

Groans filled the air. "Aw, come on!"

Paul decided this had gone on long enough. "If you left sweethearts back home, I say you should write to them. Travel a bit—find the woman who makes you happy. But I've already found mine, and I don't want to hear another word about it."

The throng parted when Delilah swept past the overturned benches to stand beside Paul. "I know you're all fine men, and I'd be honored to marry any one of you."

Elias Scudd preened at that comment, while Ross Dorsey smoothed his sideburns.

"But you see. . ." She laced her fingers through Paul's. "I've given my heart to Paul Chance. I had hoped you'd all come to our wedding and share our happiness."

Everyone stayed silent for a stretch, the only sound the scuffling of boots in the dust as every man looked down, ashamed.

"Of course we will, Miz Delilah!" Rusty promised from the back.

Amid a flurry of "Of course we will's," Delilah stood up on her tiptoes to plant a soft kiss on Paul's cheek. Life had never been better.

Delilah peeked out from behind the barn door and felt her heart might burst from fullness. Paul stood at a makeshift altar, dressed in his Sunday best and looking like the most handsome man on earth. The benches fairly groaned as everyone in Reliable settled in.

Miriam cuddled Caleb in her arms while Gideon held her. Logan and Bryce sat near the end, holding a place for the girls. Titus began singing "Blest Be the Tie That Binds" as he and Alisa marched down the aisle of benches to take their respective positions of best man and matron of honor. Polly carried a basket and strewed petals from their garden as she passed, grabbing handfuls and dropping them in tiny clumps. Ginny Mae toddled after her, carting along a patient Shortstack in a stranglehold until they reached their bench and plopped down in front of Reba and Gus.

All of these people had come to Delilah's wedding because they cared for her. *Thank You, Lord. You have blessed me beyond my biggest hopes.*

"Ready?" Daniel offered her his arm and a rare smile as she gave her golden dress one last brush.

Delilah dimly realized that everyone got to their feet as she came into view, but she kept her gaze fixed on Paul and his smile, full of love and warm promise. She was a gambler's daughter and had sworn not to follow in her father's footsteps. But here she stood with everyone she loved, taking a Chance who would change her entire life. She'd come home at last.

A Letter to Our Readers

Dear Readers:

In order that we might better contribute to your reading enjoyment, we would appreciate your taking a few minutes to respond to the following questions. When completed, please return to the following: Fiction Editor, Barbour Publishing, Inc., P.O. Box 719, Uhrichsville, OH 44683.

1. Did you enjoy reading *California Chances*?
   ❑ Very much—I would like to see more books like this.
   ❑ Moderately—I would have enjoyed it more if ______________

____

____

2. What influenced your decision to purchase this book? (Check those that apply.)
   ❑ Cover ❑ Back cover copy ❑ Title ❑ Price
   ❑ Friends ❑ Publicity ❑ Other

3. Which story was your favorite?
   ❑ *One Chance in a Million* ❑ *Taking a Chance*
   ❑ *Second Chance*

4. Please check your age range:
   ❑ Under 18 ❑ 18–24 ❑ 25–34
   ❑ 35–45 ❑ 46–55 ❑ Over 55

5. How many hours per week do you read? ______________

Name ______________________________________

Occupation ______________________________________

Address ______________________________________

City ______________ State ______________ Zip ______________

E-mail ______________________________________